THE BALTIC PRIZE

JULIAN STOCKWIN

THE BALTIC PRIZE

HODDER

First published in Great Britain in 2017 by Hodder & Stoughton
An Hachette UK company

This paperback edition published in 2018

1

A CIP catalogue record for this title is available from the British Library

Paperback ISBN 978 1 473 64099 3

Typeset in Garamond MT by Palimpsest Book Production Limited, Falkirk, Stirlingshire

Printed and bound in Great Britain by Clays Ltd, St Ives plc

Hodder & Stoughton policy is to use papers that are natural, renewable
and recyclable products and made from wood grown in sustainable forests. The logging
and manufacturing processes are expected to conform to the environmental regulations
of the country of origin.

Hodder & Stoughton Ltd
Carmelite House
50 Victoria Embankment
London EC4Y 0DZ

www.hodder.co.uk

Admiral Sir James Saumarez
Guernseyman, fighting admiral, diplomat

in respect

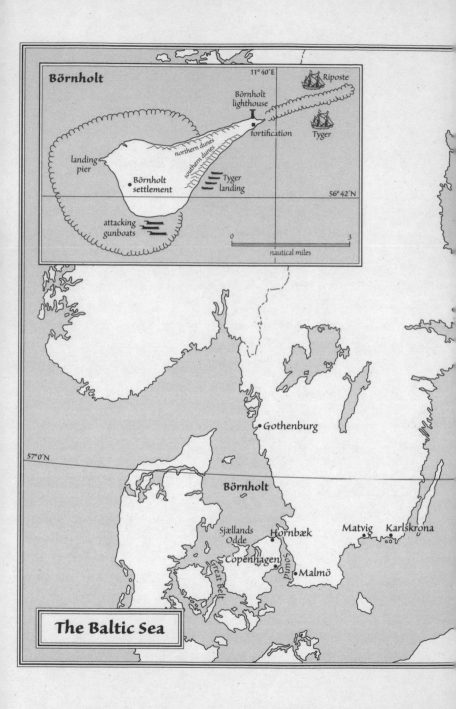

Börnholt

11°40´E

Riposte

Börnholt
lighthouse

fortification

Tyger

landing
pier

northern dunes

southern dunes

Tyger
landing

Börnholt
settlement

56°42´N

attacking
gunboats

0   3

nautical miles

57°0´N

Börnholt

Gothenburg

Sjællands
Odde

Hornbæk

Matvig   Karlskrona

Copenhagen

The Sound

Great Belt

Malmö

The Baltic Sea

Gulf of
Bothnia

20°0′E

23°50′E Saumarez, Battle of
Baltic Fleet Rågervik

59°0′N

Rågervik

Rågervik

Wreck of
Fenella

0   3
nautical miles

N
W   E
S

St. Petersburg

Kronstadt

Sveaborg Gulf of Finland

Rågervik

Reval
Rågervik

Stockholm

Helsingfors

24°58′00″E Sveaborg

Lonna
(Cronstedt
parlay island)

Archipelago
fleet

Sveaborg
fortress

hiding
place

60°08′24″N

King's
gate
ice crossing place

Baltic
Sea

0   5
nautical miles

Vallisaari
Island

0   200
nautical miles

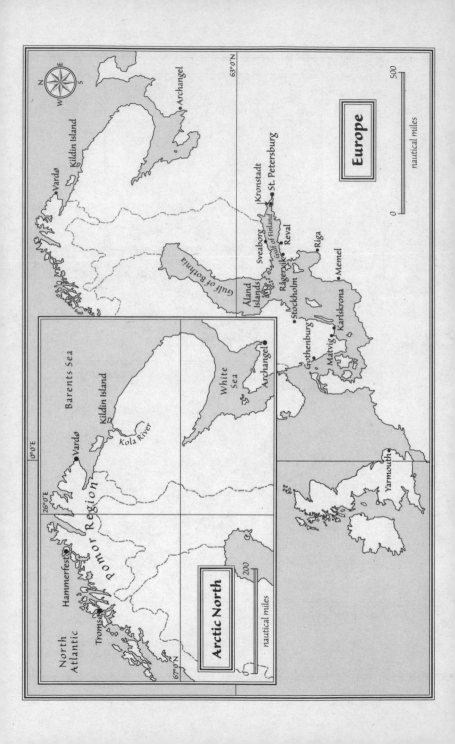

Europe

nautical miles

0   500

Archangel

Kildin Island

Vardø

Kronstadt

St. Petersburg

Sveaborg

Gulf of Finland

Reval

Åland Islands

Rågervik

Riga

Stockholm

Karlskrona

Memel

Gothenburg

Matvig

Arctic North

nautical miles

0   200

Barents Sea

Kildin Island

Vardø

Kola River

White Sea

Archangel

Pomor Region

Hammerfest

Tromsø

North Atlantic

Yarmouth

26°0'E

0°0'E

63°0'N

67°0'N

Dramatis Personae

indicates fictitious character

*Sir Thomas Kydd, captain of HMS *Tyger*, a.k.a. Tom Cutlass
*Nicholas Renzi, Earl of Farndon, friend and former confidential secretary

Tyger, ship's company
*Bowden, second lieutenant
*Bray, first lieutenant
*Brice, third lieutenant
*Clinton, captain, Royal Marines
*Darby, gunner
*Dillon, Kydd's confidential secretary
*Doud, quartermaster's mate
*Gilpin, midshipman
*Halgren, coxswain
*Harman, purser
*Herne, boatswain
*Joyce, sailing master

Martin, captain, *Implacable*
*Mason, captain, *Riposte*
Moore, lieutenant general, commander of the Northern Expedition
Mulgrave, first lord of the Admiralty
Nauckhoff, Swedish admiral
Oakley, secretary of the legation
Parker, captain, *Stately*
Perceval, British chancellor of the exchequer
*Perrot, boatswain of the Guildford Naval Academy
*Persephone, Kydd's wife
Portland, British prime minister
Puget, captain, *Goliath*
Rosen, governor of Gothenburg
Russell, admiral, commander of the North Sea Squadron
Saumarez, vice admiral, commander-in-chief of the Baltic Fleet
Saunders, captain, *Tribune*
*Strömsson, captain, *Krigare*
Swenson, Danish gunboat captain
Thornton, envoy to the Swedish king
Trampe, count, Danish governor of Iceland
Upton, captain, *Sybille*
Van Suchtelen, Russian commander
Willemoes, first lieutenant, *Prinds Christian Frederik*
Wood, lieutenant

Prologue

White's, London, spring 1808

'In fine, I really don't see how we can go on for much longer.'

The words cut through the drone of talk at the table like a knife. 'You may leave us,' one of the diners told the steward of the exclusive London club. The man bowed and retired, drawing the double doors of the private dining room firmly closed.

'Charles, you choose the most awkward times to make your opinions known.' Cuthbert Hertford, a portly man in blue and buff, drew appreciatively on his Havana and, with a droll glance at the speaker, added, 'Even if we'd no doubt be entertained to hear it.'

'I mean it, sir.'

The others paid wary attention to Charles Brougham, the elegantly dressed individual whose features held the ruthless austerity to be expected of the head of one of the oldest and largest trading firms on the floor of the London Stock Exchange.

'How so?'

'Do I need to spell it out? Here we have the Continental System, Boney's answer to Trafalgar. And it's working, God help us.' He lifted his port glass and peered into it as though it were a crystal ball. Bonaparte's sweeping declaration of a state of blockade against Great Britain had included savage penalty for any nation trading with her, and after his recent crushing successes on the Continent, few dared.

'Now the French have taken Lisbon we have to accept that the entire shore of Europe, from Cádiz to Königsberg is shut in our faces. Near all our natural market denied us – we can't import what we need and, worse, our undoubted leadership in manufacturing and industry is as dross if we can't place our goods in the marketplace.'

'We've suffered worse, dear fellow. The League of Armed Neutrality not so long ago? A direct threat to our freedom of the seas, and all it needed was for us to send in our glorious Admiral Nelson to knock heads together and they saw reason directly.'

'Hmmph. It seems to have escaped your notice that things are much different now. The old ways are not open to us and—'

'You said we can't go on, Charles,' a dry, intense individual interrupted. With a sharp, legal mind, John Newton was principal director in a sizeable canal enterprise and had every reason to fear these words.

'Too much has turned against us recently. Boney's system was a near dead letter while we could ship in and out of Denmark. A neutral, all our exports went into Husum or

Tonningen as a paper trade, for re-export under the Danish flag a few miles overland to the Continent at large. A sovereign highway into Europe as served us well.'

'And now we've laid waste to Copenhagen . . .'

'It's closed to us.'

'There's still one who defies Boney.'

'Sweden? Our ally, yes, but with a deranged autocrat on the throne and the country having no convenient border with the Continent, a lost cause, a liability. And besides which . . .' He paused significantly. 'Do I need to remind you? Russia has declared war on us and must now be accounted the enemy.'

A brutal, conservative and backward nation of unknown millions and with a large navy, it was about to turn the Baltic into a Russian lake.

'So the Baltic is lost to us. Why on earth can't you merchantry open up somewhere else?' Newton asked. 'The Spanish-American colonies spring to mind.'

'Let me answer that,' Richard Egremont, a precise and quiet man in curiously plain attire, intervened. 'I know I'm a guest here tonight, but pray give me leave perhaps to enlighten some.

'You are all captains of industry or bankers with concerns of your own. I am at a Treasury desk and see figures in the aggregate. And I'm grieved to say that, in my opinion, Charles is in no wise guilty of exaggeration. The situation is dire, gentlemen, and I cannot readily conceive how we might recover from it.'

'What is it that you see, Richard?'

'This Baltic trade is our tenderest point and he who severs it brings us to our knees, to nothing less than capitulation to Bonaparte's will, I fear.'

3

'Oh, come, sir, that is a trifle rich!'

'Nothing less, Cuthbert. Let me throw you a few figures. The navy demands twenty miles or some such extraordinary amount of rope to set a ship swimming and several times that for wear in its lifetime. Where does this rope hemp come from? *Ninety-five per centum* by poundage from the inner Baltic. The same can be said of spars, decking timber and so forth, and therefore before long we look to having our sure shield floating about quite helpless for lack of repair.'

He smiled thinly. 'And there's worse. Before the late unpleasantness with Denmark, do you know the value of goods carried by our near seven thousand ships a year going through the Sound?'

'A pretty penny, you'll be telling us, Richard.'

'You may believe it. If we take all other trade we conduct, wherever in the world, then our commerce with the Baltic is more than twice this entirely added together.'

'Good God – I'd no idea!'

'And a last figure, and one I ask you refrain from repeating lest it cause undue dismay.'

'Say away, I beg.'

'Very well. It is that after our lamentable harvest of the past year there is a shortage of grain in these islands in the calamitous amount of some twenty per centum. A fifth of our people therefore will have no bread and must starve, are we not to take steps? In the past it's been our practice to mount a grain convoy or two to obtain the deficiency from beyond our shores. But . . .'

'From the Baltic.'

'Just so. Prussian wheat and Russian corn. Both now denied us.'

'And time is running out.'

'Quite, Cuthbert. But my immediate concern is that the Baltic ice is, as we speak, giving way and a host of merchants find the season for sailing is now open to them. They must have answer – dare they sail into the pit?'

Chapter 1

The anchorage at the Great Nore

His Majesty's Frigate *Tyger* came to, her bower plunging down to take the ground at last. She carried two prisoners, Count Trampe, the Danish governor of Iceland, and Jørgen Jørgensen, its self-styled king, to be landed into the custody of Sheerness dockyard, and a new-wed lady to step ashore.

For Kydd the last few weeks had been dream-like, a procession of unforgettable scenes, from the Stygian dark landscape of Iceland pierced by the glitter of vast glaciers, the fumaroles, the blue lakes, the wheeling gyrfalcons – and the vows solemnly exchanged in a timber cathedral.

And now he and Persephone were one, man and wife; there was not a soul on the face of the good earth who was as happy as he.

'Sir?' Bowden, his second lieutenant, proffered a paper with a faint smile playing.

'Oh, yes, thank you.' Kydd dashed off a signature and,

too late, realised he hadn't stopped to check what he was signing. He collected himself: it would not do for the captain to be seen adrift in his intellects even if there were good reasons for it.

However, this was no doubt the fair copy of his brief report to be forwarded to Admiral Russell on blockade off the Dutch coast with the North Sea Squadron he'd left at Yarmouth. It told of the recent happenings in the north and the necessity to land the two main players in the drama to be dealt with by higher authorities in London. They had already been sent off, with his main report to the Admiralty, who would either detain him as a material witness or release him to resume his duties with the North Sea Squadron.

'Ah, Mr Bowden. A favour of you, if I may.'

'Sir?'

'Would you be so kind as to conduct Lady Kydd to the residence of her parents for me?'

'Of course, Sir Thomas. I would be honoured.'

With a stab of tenderness, Kydd knew that it was only the first of the many partings that sea service would demand of him but this, so soon after their marrying, would be harder than any. Feeling a twinge of guilt, he didn't envy her what she had to do. Not only had she to let her father and mother know that she had not disappeared and was very much alive but also that she was now wed to a man they detested.

They had lunch together before she left, a quiet occasion and charged with bitter-sweet feeling – and then it was time to part. Kydd saw her over the side, and as the boat shoved off into the grey sea for the distant shore his heart went out to the lonely figure carrying his hopes and love. She waved once and he responded self-consciously, watching until they were out of sight, then went below without a word.

The Admiralty's response, when it came, was neither of the possibilities he'd foreseen. He was not required in the matters of Jørgensen and Count Trampe but neither was he to re-join the squadron. Instead he was to hold his command in readiness for duties as yet not determined.

It was odd, a first-class frigate not snapped up for immediate employment, but he'd seen before how, in their mysterious way, the Admiralty had chosen to deploy a pawn on their chessboard to effect a grand strategic move that made perfect sense later – the tasking of *L'Aurore* so soon after Trafalgar came to mind. That had taken him to the Cape of Good Hope and conquest of an entire colony at the end of the world.

In a surge of delight he realised what it meant: not needed for a routine idleness and away from an admiral's eye, he was free to take leave with his bride – a telegraphed communication with Plymouth would have him notified within an hour or so of any orders.

Blank-faced, his first lieutenant, Bray, had accepted charge of the ship and, accompanied by Tysoe, Kydd was quickly on the road for the Lockwood mansion. By now Persephone would have broken her news but as a precaution he took rooms at a nearby inn and sent on a message.

Her reply was instant: 'Come!'

Kydd immediately set off. He had been to the Arctic regions but nothing was as frigid as the Lockwood drawing room where he was received.

'I'm obliged to remark it, sir, I find your conduct with my daughter impossible to forgive. You have—'

'Father, you promised . . .' Persephone said, with a look of warning.

Her arm was locked in Kydd's, and she was the picture of happiness. None but those of the hardest of hearts could have condemned her. After an awkward pause, it seemed the admiral was not to be numbered in their company and he gave a mumbled blessing on their union. At the dinner that followed he even found occasion to reprove his wife, telling her that the pair had chosen their path together and let that be an end to it.

The strained atmosphere slowly thawed and by the time Kydd had expressed his sincere admiration for the oil painting in pride of place above the mantelpiece, a remarkably accurate depiction of the sea battle of Camperdown, he and the admiral were in animated conversation discussing technical features with growing mutual appreciation and respect. Kydd was touched by Persephone's secret smile of relief.

It took more effort to win around Lady Lockwood, who sat mutely, her eyes obstinately averted. Only a suggestion of a reception in honour of their marriage brought forth any conversation.

Chapter 2

One more duty awaited. 'My love, I do believe that my dear parents would find it strange if I don't make introduction of my bride.'

'Of course, Thomas! I'm so anxious – what will they think of me?'

Kydd held back a grin but quickly sobered. This visit of all things would reveal to her just how humble were his origins, the true status of the family into which she'd married. She knew he'd been a pressed man and probably suspected he came from yeoman stock but, no doubt in deference to his feelings, had never pursued it further. Now she would discover the truth.

Evening was drawing in when the coach made the corner and began the hard pull up the busy Guildford high street.

Kydd let the sensations of a home-coming wash over him: the old baker's yard, the little alley to his dame school, the shops that crowded together, all smaller than he recalled but still there, quite the same, while he had changed so much.

Some he barely remembered: the apothecary shop with its dusty human bones, the pastry emporium, the rival perruquier now long transformed to a haberdashery, still others. He felt her hand on his, squeezing, then caught her look of loving understanding and, yet again, marvelled at his lot in life.

The horses toiled further, and just before the Romanesque plainness of the Tunsgate columns they slowed and took a wide swing into the medieval entrance of the Angel posting-house. Persephone was handed down and immediately went back to the high street where she looked around, admiring, and exclaimed, 'What a charming town.'

Kydd stood awkwardly by her. 'As this was my life for so long – but I can hardly remember it, truly.' Although he was in plain clothes, the innkeeper immediately recognised him. The best rooms in the Angel were his – and be damned to the bookings!

They sat companionably by the fire in the snug, cradling a negus, while a messenger was sent to ask if it would be at all inconvenient for him to call. His mother would fuss but at least she would have some warning. Both her children had left home: Cecilia to life as a countess, married to Kydd's closest friend, Nicholas Renzi, now Lord Farndon, and he to fame as a sea hero. How was she coping on her own with his blind father?

As they sat together, Kydd haltingly told Persephone of his youth in Guildford: making wigs in the shop that they'd presently walk past, being brutally taken up by the press-gang in Merrow – and when, as a young seaman, his father's failing sight had obliged him to give up the sea and return to wig-making, his soul-searing desolation cut short by Renzi's brilliant idea to start a school on naval lines . . .

The thoughts and memories rushed by, and then the breathless messenger came back, wide-eyed, relaying expressions of delight: Kydd's parents were expecting him home this very minute.

Arm in arm, Kydd and Persephone went up the little path by the red-brick Holy Trinity Church, making for the road now called School Lane. Above the school buildings the blue ensign flew proudly from a trim mast and single yard. The place looked in fine order, its neat front garden in fresh bloom, testament to his mother's delight in flowers, a white picket fence setting it off from the quadrangle beyond.

'Sir T, ahoy!' came a bellow. Jabez Perrott, the school's boatswain, stumped up on his wooden leg, with a grin that split his face in two. 'An' ye're castin' anchor for a space?'

'It's right good to see you again, Mr Perrott,' Kydd said, with feeling, shaking his hand, still with the calloused hardness of the deep-sea mariner. He turned to introduce Persephone. 'This is, um, Lady Kydd, my wife.' He was still not used to it. 'How goes the school?'

'Oragious, Sir T! We had, b' Michaelmas last, five lads as followed the sea, an' many more who's got their heart set on't.'

'Well done, sir!' Kydd said, in sincere admiration. 'I'll see you at colours tomorrow.

'Now, you'll pardon, I have to pay duty to my parents. Carry on, please.'

With Persephone on his arm and unsure what he'd find, Kydd knocked on the door.

It flew open and his mother stood there, beaming. She hugged and hugged him, murmuring endearments, a frail, diminished figure but still full of life. 'How do I see ye, son?' she managed, unable to take her eyes from his. 'Ye're well?'

'Very well, Ma,' Kydd said awkwardly, then brought

Persephone forward. 'Ma, I'd like you to meet Persephone, who must now be accounted my wife.'

His mother blinked, as if not understanding. Then her eyes widened as she took in Persephone's elegant appearance and hastily curtsied.

Concerned, Persephone raised her up and said gently, 'Thomas is now my husband, Mrs Kydd, who I do swear I will care for with my life.'

'Oh, well, yes, o' course,' she said, clearly flustered. 'Please t' come in, won't ye both?'

Kydd's father was in the parlour and, hearing them enter, rose creakily. 'How are ye, son?' he said, his eyes sightlessly searching for him.

'I'm well, Father, and I've brought my new wife, Persephone.'

Mr Kydd jerked up in surprise. 'Any family I knows?' he asked at length, as she came forward and took his hands in hers.

'No, Pa. I married her . . . I wed her in Iceland,' he said, with a chuckle, then thought better of it. 'Who comes from an old English family . . .'

'From Somerset,' Persephone put in softly.

It was all a bit much for the elderly couple and the evening meal passed in an awed hush. Kydd took his cue from Persephone, who brightly praised her first encounter with Guildford, remarking on the sights and mentioning as an aside how they had met in Plymouth and again in a foreign place, where they determined they could not be apart any longer.

'An' where will you live?' his mother asked hopefully.

'In Devonshire, where the air is bracing and healthy, and the victuals not to be scorned,' Kydd said firmly. 'And not so far by mail-coach, Ma.'

* * *

In the morning there was nothing for it but to muster at the main-mast, the boatswain fierce and unbending before the assembled pupils of the Guildford Naval Academy, standing in strict line, eyes agog to see the sea hero they had been told about so often.

Kydd was in uniform, albeit without his knightly ornaments, the quantities of gold lace of a post-captain quite sufficient for the occasion, and he stood next to the headmaster, Mr Partington, now a gowned and majestic dominie. His prim wife took her place behind him.

'Pipe!'

The ensign rose in reverent silence, the squeal of the boatswain's call piercing and clear above the muffled bustle of the town. To Kydd's ears it was so expressive of the sea's purity against the dross of land.

'Ship's comp'ny present 'n' correct. Sir!'

'Very well.' Kydd stepped forward to say his piece, but he was put off balance by the scores of innocent faces before him as they waited for words of courage and hope. In desperate times at sea he'd fiercely addressed his ship's company before battle but now he found he couldn't think what to say.

'A fine body of men,' came a fierce whisper behind him. He repeated the words and she went on to hiss, 'As fills you with confidence for England's future . . . only if they faithfully and diligently pay attention to their grammar and reckonings . . . that the good captain-headmaster is taking pains to teach them . . .'

The awed students were dismissed to their lessons and Kydd was escorted on a tour of the classrooms, where he bestowed compliments and earnest assurances that the subordinate clause was indeed a handy piece of knowledge to hoist inboard for use at sea.

He was touched by the little building at the back that had been made to resemble a frigate's mess-deck. There, industrious boys bent hitches and worked knots under the severe eye of Boatswain Perrott – and at the right and proper time took their victuals, like the tarry-breeked seamen they so wanted to be.

A civic reception was a grander occasion and, in full dress with sword and sash, Kydd spoke rousing words of confidence to the great and good of Guildford. He then accompanied the mayor out on to the town-hall balcony beneath the great clock to address the citizenry much as, long ago, after the battle of Camperdown, Admiral Onslow had invited Kydd up to join him as one who had made his victory possible.

It was unreal, a dream – he'd changed beyond all recognition since those days and needed time to take it all in.

Kydd took Persephone to see the old castle, the weathered grey stones just as massive and enduring as he remembered, then down to the River Wey, its gliding placidity reaching out to him in its gentle existence. They followed the tow-path, silent and companionable, letting the tranquillity work on them until it was time to return to his parents.

'We have to be off now, Ma,' Kydd said quietly, 'to see to our estate, to set up our home.'

'Yes, m' darling. I know ye'll be happy there, wi' your Persephone. Do come an' visit when ye can, son.'

Chapter 3

Duty done, and knowing that their time together would be brief, they posted down to Ivybridge. There, they took horse for Combe Tavy and the old manor they had chosen. As Kydd dismounted before the dilapidated Tudor building, he was dismayed to catch the sparkle of tears in Persephone's eyes. 'My love – what is it? We'll soon have the place squared away, all a-taunto, never fear.'

She clung to him, but when she turned to speak he saw she was radiantly smiling through her tears. 'Oh, Thomas, dear Thomas! I'm such a silly, do forgive me. It's just that I'm so happy.'

He kissed her tenderly.

The old couple caretaking were surprised to see them. 'We thought as you'd forgotten us, sir,' Appleby said, aggrieved. 'The manor needs a mite o' work, an' that's no error!'

'It does,' Kydd agreed. 'And we will make it so, for this is our home as we shall be moving into, just as soon as we may.'

Mrs Appleby clasped her hands in glee. 'How wonderful!'

she exclaimed. 'To see Knowle Manor have life in it once more!'

There was no time to lose. They made tour of the house, noting what had to be done, and by the time Tysoe arrived in a cart with their luggage they had enough to set priorities. That evening they sat down to a fine rabbit pie, Mrs Appleby wringing her hands at the sight of such a humble dish to set before them.

With imperturbable dignity Tysoe did the honours as butler, finding among the few remaining bottles in the cellar a very passable Margaux, and afterwards, replete, Persephone and Thomas Kydd sat in bare chairs by the fire and began to plan.

By his sturdy wardship of the manor, Appleby had earned his place as steward, and his wife was well suited to serve as cook. Lady Kydd would require a maid, of course, and there would be need of others, but these could wait while workmen attended to repairs and furbishing.

Kydd insisted that the land must remain wild for the time being – after all, the manor had first to be made fit for his lady. Furniture, hangings, fitments, stables, horses, a carriage, it was never-ending.

In the days that followed, from the chaos came forth order, and by the third day, after expeditions to Exeter and Plymouth, something like a degree of comfort and refinement was beginning to take form.

Then Persephone suggested they should take their first steps to enter in upon the acquaintance of their neighbours and tenants. 'My darling – you are Lord of the Manor, at an eminence in Combe Tavy, and must make yourself known.'

For Tom Kydd, one-time wig-maker of Guildford, it felt like a fairy tale. He was now Sir Thomas Kydd and of the landed gentry, come to take up his seigneury as local squire and magistrate: his land and his people. With Lady Kydd at his side, a village ox roast passed off in fine style. At first awed then delighted that a famed frigate captain, lately in the national news – and so handsome with his beautiful lady – had chosen to make his ancestral home among them, they flocked up to be noticed.

Kydd made acquaintance with them all: the red-faced, brawny blacksmith Tovey, the one-eyed innkeeper Jenkins, the white-haired and seamed old sheep farmer Davies, these with their being so firmly one with the land.

On the eighth day they had visitors.

'When we received your letter I had to sit down and cry,' Kydd's sister Cecilia confessed, after hugging them both. 'So romantic! To see you two together at last . . .' She dabbed her eyes. 'Do forgive us for the intrusion but we had to come – and we've brought some little things in the hope we can have a house-warming party.' She went to the door and beckoned. In came a succession of footmen bearing carefully wrapped delicacies, which found their place on the kitchen table.

It was a decisive moment. As the celebration warmed Kydd realised that a point in his life had been reached. This was no longer a dream, it was the reality. For the rest of his days this would be the centre of his existence, all else to be at a radius of so far from here, where his heart truly was.

Persephone had been adamant about his future, saying, 'My dear Thomas, I knew from the first time we met each other that you were of the sea, born to it and never to be parted from it. I accept this – if you gave it up you would be only half the man and that I could not bear. You shall go to your *Tyger* and have adventures without counting, then return to me. And I shall be content at that.'

In trust and confidence he would sail away over the horizon to who knew what lay ahead in the knowledge that he would come back to Persephone, their home and hearth together. It was incredible after all his years a-wandering, but it was true: he had put down roots.

Several days later a messenger from Plymouth Dock arrived with the expected summons, a terse one-line signal from his first lieutenant. 'Orders received on board.'

It was time.

The whispered promises, the touch of a hand, a look in the eyes – this was what untold numbers of naval wives had endured over the centuries as the price of Britannia keeping the seas as her own. He must now depart, and while he faced the perils and decisions of war, she would be left to hide her fears and live on for him.

'My darling, you go with my eternal love,' she breathed, distractedly adjusting his neckcloth. 'Promise to write.' In a shaky voice, she continued, 'I've packed more shirts, you're sure to need them, and your cravats and . . . and . . .' She bit her lip and turned to Tysoe. 'You'll look after him for me, won't you? Of course you will.' Her voice softened and she brought out a little package. 'This is for you.'

The man took it.

'Classical poetry. You didn't know, did you, Thomas, that Tysoe in his off-duty hours takes pleasure in a well-turned conceit, the shining phrase?'

Tears sprang: a last embrace and then into the carriage, a final wave and sight of the inexpressibly dear figure standing forlornly – and Kydd was on his way to war.

Chapter 4

The Cabinet Room, 10 Downing Street

'It's as bad as that,' confirmed Lord Bathurst, president of the Board of Trade. A heavy silence descended on the table.

'Can't we—'

'No!' Canning, the foreign minister, snapped. Perceval was chancellor of the Exchequer but, in his view, by no means possessed of a sound perspective on foreign affairs.

'I was only going to suggest,' he responded cattily, 'that, with these adversities before us, we revisit Fox's treating for peace. While we still hold a modicum of influence, not to say military force.'

Portland, the ailing prime minister at the centre of the table, looked up wearily and said weakly, 'Chancellor, we've been into this before and—'

Canning cut in impatiently, 'Bonaparte's sworn to extirpate these islands, all that stands between him and the world at his feet. Why should he talk peace now?'

'Surely the question should be, do we abandon the Baltic or no?'

Castlereagh's languid tone seemed to goad the ambitious Canning. 'Given the figures we've heard,' he retorted venomously, 'for those with any backbone at all, the question most certainly is, do we force the issue or roll over and die?'

'Oh? We'd no doubt be gratified to hear of your proposings . . .'

'Gentlemen, gentlemen,' Portland muttered, and broke into a wretched coughing.

Waiting respectfully for the fit to pass, Perceval asked, 'Are we not making too much of the hazards? I'm no naval sort of fellow, but it seems to me that the Baltic convoys have served us well in the past. Why don't we simply double the force of their escorts?'

'A perfectly rational suggestion, Chancellor.' It was Mulgrave, the first lord of the Admiralty. 'With but a single flaw.'

'Oh?'

'Your convoy is a capital system to defend against gunboats, privateers and even a cruiser. Here we have quite a different foe – the Russians. With a battle fleet in Kronstadt big enough to give pause even to a Nelson, what do you conceive the result to be should it fall in with a convoy? No escort we could mount could possibly contend with such a weight of metal. This is no solution.'

'We send 'em in anyway!' Canning's brutal riposte came immediately.

'What can you mean?'

'Safety in numbers. There's who knows how many thousands of merchants eager to chance their cargoes. Send 'em in like a shoal of fish – some must get through!'

'I choose not to hear that, Foreign Minister,' Mulgrave said cuttingly. 'And might I remark it, did we not at great cost to our honour lay waste to Copenhagen for the sole purpose of preserving our passage into the Baltic? Is this now to be accounted a nullity, a mistake?'

'Not so, and you, sir, should know it! By it, Denmark is left with no navy worth a spit and cannot bar our entry in any wise. It's what awaits us once inside – the Russians.'

'Then what, sir, is the answer?'

Canning paused for effect, then said, 'A mighty battle-fleet to enter the Baltic and stay there.'

'Are you seriously suggesting we create a great fleet out of thin air and—'

'If the Russians desire to contest our presence then we hand them a Trafalgar and all problems solved!'

Mulgrave sat back heavily. 'Sir, have you any conception of what you ask? To send a fleet of force into a sea where every shore is hostile, dominated by the enemy? How might we sustain it? The Mediterranean Fleet is supplied by a dozen friendly ports, fresh victuals to be found for the asking, water on friendly coasts. And Cádiz, hours sail only from the naval stores of Gibraltar, the beef of Tetuán. There's no recourse to anything like it in the Baltic.'

'Damn it, these are footling details. Get the ships in and worry about that kind of thing later.'

Castlereagh gave a lazy smile, then asked Canning innocently, 'For myself I'm more exercised over just what this large and expensive armada is expected to do. Float about in one part of the whole looking menacing – while in another the Russians savage our helpless merchantmen? Or scatter in all directions in their defence and thus be unable to face the enemy's might as one?'

'You have a better plan?' Canning hissed.

'I do.' Castlereagh became suddenly energised. 'We achieve our goals in quite another way. Show common cause with the only friend left to us, Sweden. In this way, while the southern shores of the Baltic are all in Bonaparte's hands, the entire northern region remains free. Besides which, one side of the Sound at least is thereby made secure, guaranteeing our passage in and out.'

'How is this common cause to be evidenced, pray?'

'We land a strong military force to take position directly opposite Copenhagen. This will have two purposes – to demonstrate our willingness to come to the aid of an ally, and the other, to stand athwart the likely route of the invasion army, now massing around Denmark.'

Canning glowered but said nothing.

'I have my reservations,' Mulgrave broke in. 'Any army on a foreign shore must have the navy at its back at all times. It means I must of necessity find a fleet for it in support, in just the same way as the alternative proposition. Where is the advantage?'

'And for me,' Bathurst said, concerned, 'we're talking here of an intervention in Europe by our own military, the first long-term engagement of its kind on the Continent, an entanglement that could prove disastrous if things turn out against us. We pay subsidies to other countries to carry the war to the enemy. Why not in this case?'

'We already do,' muttered Perceval, 'and in the sum of some hundreds of thousands a month, no less.'

Through the charged atmosphere came a feeble but determined voice. 'Gentlemen, I have heard you out,' the prime minister said. 'And I'm resolved on any action rather than see the Baltic lost to us.' He lapsed into silence, staring into nothing, as though in misgiving at what he was about to say.

'Then which of the two is that to be, my lord?' prompted Canning, leaning forward.

'It shall be . . . both.'

'Sir?' It was unusual to the point of incredulity that the wasting figure of Portland was taking a firm and positive grip.

'My lord Castlereagh, do set before me a military expedition of size, say some ten, fifteen thousand for the purpose adduced. Whom do you suppose we should place in command of our only army outside Great Britain save the West Indies? The Duke of York?'

'Ah, I could not conceive of a more superior commander, my lord, than General Moore, late of Shorncliffe.'

'Very well, let it be so. First Lord, a fleet to set before that of the Russians. One to command respect and dismay – I leave the numbers to you, bearing in mind that there is no funding in the Treasury for any undertaking on the scale of the creation of an entirely new standing fleet upon station.'

'Sir,' Mulgrave said, pained, 'I do well comprehend the reasons for parsimony in expenditure, but may I be allowed to point out that we have a resource to call upon in the sea service that is not to be reckoned in terms of ships and guns. It is respect. We shall bring out such a company as shall be honoured and feared by any and all. The fleet that enters the Baltic shall be led as flagship by the immortal Nelson's *Victory* and have numbered in it the most daring captains of our time. Keats of *Superb*, Codrington of *Orion*, Kydd of *Tyger* and—'

'Under whose flag?'

The first lord of the Admiralty pondered. 'For a command of such delicacy and with a seniority worthy of it, I cannot but put forward the name of Admiral Sir James Saumarez.

He of St Vincent, the Nile, Algeciras – his honours place him among the foremost commanders of the day and he retains my complete confidence.'

'I've never heard of him, but I let that pass,' muttered the prime minister. 'Know only that we have this day made shift to preserve the fortunes of this country and if any do fail us . . .'

Chapter 5

HMS Tyger, *at anchor, the Great Nore*

'A good leave, Sir Thomas?' Bray greeted Kydd.
'Yes, a good leave, Mr Bray, thank you. Now, you have something for me?'

Tyger was in immaculate trim, and his first lieutenant's assurance that they were stored and watered in expectation was what he'd hoped to hear. He was lucky with his uncompromising second in command.

They lost no time in going below to Kydd's cabin to open the orders.

Dillon looked up from his work and smiled winningly. 'A good leave, sir?'

'Yes, yes, a good leave. Carry on, if you please.'

The order pack was very slim – those concerning a foreign commission of adventure and far roaming were fat with injunctions, signal instructions, coded challenges and so forth.

Kydd broke the seal and on a single sheet all was made

clear. 'We are no longer with the North Sea Squadron, Mr Bray.'

'Sir?'

'We're to join a venture named the "Northern Expedition" assembling in Yarmouth, under the flag of Vice Admiral of the Blue Sir James Saumarez.'

Bray brightened. 'Damme, but this sounds more my ticket,' he growled happily. 'Swinging around an anchor for a couple of months and not a smell o' powder, it's not Christian.'

'Don't get too exercised, Mr Bray – it looks like it's going to be fleet work, under eye of a senior admiral.'

There was a knock at the cabin door and Bowden appeared. 'Oh, I didn't wish to disturb, sir.' He waited pointedly.

'Very well, come in and take your fill of the news,' Kydd said, with resignation and a weary smile.

'Thank you, sir. I trust you had a good leave?'

'Very fine, Mr Bowden, very fine. We're off to Yarmouth to join an expedition and—' He broke off at another knocking. 'Come.'

Brice entered, his expression guileless. 'Watch-on-deck mustered and correct, sir,' he said crisply. Then he added shyly, 'Did you have a good leave, sir?'

'Be damned to it!' Kydd spluttered. 'I've a mind to turn up the ship's company to tell 'em all at once that I had a thundering good leave, thank 'ee.'

The assembly date for the expedition was still three days away but Kydd was keen to know what was in the wind. 'We proceed in the morning, Mr Bray. Ship is under sailing orders.'

'Aye aye, sir!'

As his officers left the cabin, Kydd's thoughts turned to Saumarez. He'd first known him while he'd been commander of the humble *Teazer* brig-sloop. So long ago now, another life, but he'd never forgotten the courtesy and understanding Saumarez had shown him at a particularly difficult time . . . and the wounding disappointment he'd made known in what he'd assumed was an incident of Kydd's moral depravity.

Intelligent, a master of detail and with high expectations of his subordinates, Saumarez would be a fine but demanding commander-in-chief of whatever expedition this was.

The following day Yarmouth Roads were duly raised – and what a spectacle! It brought all *Tyger*'s crew up to marvel at the biggest assembly of naval might any had seen since Britain had stood alone before Trafalgar – and, glory be, wasn't that the grand old lady herself, HMS *Victory*, there at its centre?

'Their lordships mean some mischief on the enemy, I'm thinking,' breathed Bray, in admiration.

No less than a dozen battleships at anchor in fine array, their lines of guns a stern portent to any who might think to challenge the rule of the Royal Navy on the high seas.

'Isn't that Nelson's *Vanguard* – astern of *Implacable*?'

'It is,' Kydd confirmed. He would never forget witnessing Nelson's selfless order, from that dismasted ship-of-the-line heading for the rocks, to Captain Ball of *Alexander* to abandon him and preserve his own vessel – and the stout refusal to obey orders that had finally saved *Vanguard* and the great admiral for further service to their country.

Joyce, the sailing master, rubbed his chin. 'My eyes are on the barky yonder,' he said with feeling.

'*Orion*?'

'Aye. Just think on it – she took her first knocks at the First o' June, then St Vincent, an' then the Nile before she's there mauling Frenchies at Trafalgar. Seen her fair share of action, she has.'

Kydd recalled those fevered days. 'Did you know that Saumarez was her captain at the Nile? Took a bad wound but kept on. I wonder what he's thinking now.'

'You were there, Sir Thomas?'

'Yes, l'tenant only but saw much that night. There – *Goliath*. It was Foley who led us in, and it was he who had the almighty gall to sail inside their line of anchored ships, which saw us victorious that day.'

It was thrilling – and puzzling. Here was a constellation of names that had resounded down the years, battle-hardened veterans with the habit of victory. What audacious stroke was being contemplated that needed such a splendid band at its centre?

Chapter 6

'The last, Sir Thomas,' said Dillon, with a frown, bringing out the final piece of the morning's paperwork. 'And I ask pardon that I must trouble you with such a trifle.'

He handed it across. It was a short letter, painfully written in a child-like hand, dated that same day from HMS *Brunswick*, Yarmouth Roads, one of the 74-gun ships-of-the-line lying with the fleet.

Kydd glanced at the signature and rank. His eyebrows shot up in astonishment. A volunteer first class, addressing the captain of another ship? They were the lowest form of life, essentially apprentice midshipmen, performing menial tasks.

'As I know your views on young gentlemen in a ship-of-war,' Dillon added smoothly, 'yet I believe deserving of a form of reply.'

Kydd scanned it quickly. 'So the rascal wants to remove into *Tyger*. I'm not having it, of course.'

'We only have two midshipmen aboard, sir, and—'

'I've nothing to say against the beggars as who should stay,' Kydd rumbled, 'but a crack frigate is not the place to be learning your trade. Better a ship o' size where you're under eye when you make your mistakes.'

'Some would say the navy demands that all should share in the training up of its future officers.'

Kydd tossed the paper in with the others. 'That's as may be. We've a reefer in each watch, and that's enough for me.'

'Sir, you may have omitted to notice that the youngster comes recommended by a naval school and we may presume therefore he has his nauticals.'

There was a moment of dawning suspicion before Kydd snatched up the letter again and read more slowly. One Christopher Rowan was modestly offering to present a recommendation by his captain-headmaster, Mr B. Partington of the Guildford Naval Academy, in respect of any naval service to which he might see fit to apply. The Kydd School!

Tyger's captain glanced up suspiciously, but Dillon was absent-mindedly sorting the completed papers, seeming unaware of the Kydd family connection.

'Ah. Well, that could make a difference,' he harrumphed. The lad would have got a decent grounding in bends and hitches, knot-work and the sea lingo from the school, and even a solid foundation of the three Rs, more than some he'd known. The stout boatswain Perrott could be relied on not to suffer any charge of his to go out into a stern sea world without the requisites of a good moral compass and a fearless spirit.

He felt himself weakening. 'We've no room for another volunteer,' he said doubtfully.

'Sir, I rather thought you'd rate him midshipman. A spare of the breed while he learns?'

'Um, possibly.' It was quite within his power to do so, but

with one strict proviso. 'Only if he's put in his sea time. Regulations – three years afore I can rate him so.'

'And if he hasn't?'

'Then it's hard luck for him.' He leaned back with a sigh. 'Have the duty boat's crew go to *Brunswick* and bring the youngster here. I'll talk to him.'

Ship visiting while at anchor was a sailor's privilege and that a lowly volunteer was indulging would not be an obstacle.

Well within the hour, the mate-of-the-watch delivered Kydd's visitor.

'So. You've a mind to desert your ship, younker.'

The boy stood rigid, his eyes to the front, cap held before him. 'Sir, that's . . . Yes, sir.' He was slightly built, fair hair and hazel eyes, a delicacy of manner unusual in one of his age – and a presence that, for some reason, reached out to Kydd.

'How old are you?'

'Th-thirteen, sir.'

'And how long have you served at sea?'

Those eyes – something about . . .

'Two years. That is, nearly three.'

The powers-that-be wouldn't argue over a few months in these desperate times. 'All in *Brunswick*?'

'Sir.'

'And you want a more exciting time in a frigate?'

'Sir, it's . . . it's that I want to serve under you!' The eyes pleaded so pitifully with him, tearing at Kydd's detachment.

'Ah, this is a fighting frigate,' Kydd frowned, 'as may be expected to see a mort of action.'

'Yes, sir,' cried the youngster. 'I know! Mr Perrott told us what it's like, how you won all your hero battles against the foe and—'

'Belay all that,' Kydd snapped, at the same time embarrassed and touched.

Then it came to him: those eyes – they were Persephone's.

He fumbled for something to say. 'Um, why did you go to sea?'

'Oh, sir, it was that night after the Dutch battle when Admiral Onslow made his speech at our town hall and called you up to stand beside him as a hero too!'

'Then you joined the school.'

'I begged Papa to let me go, but he said as how the sea was not for proper gentlemen, so I asked him if he really thought Lord Nelson not a gentleman and he got cross with me.'

'But sent you.'

'He told me if I desired it so, he would send me, but only if I should promise that if it really was to be my profession I would be diligent and faithful to learn, and would apply myself to it with all my heart.'

'I see.'

'And then we heard of the battle of the Nile, that you were in it, and Bos'un Perrott cleared lower deck and told the whole school as how you'd gone from being a sailor boy all the way to a King's officer, and then when you came to the school and spoke to us all about duty and courage I – I wanted to be like you, sir!' he blurted.

Kydd melted. A feeling almost of fatherliness came over him, touching him to the core and surprising him with its intensity. In a warm rush he knew then that he wanted to grant the boy his wish – for reasons he was still coming to terms with.

It was quickly followed by guilt. What right had he to thrust this child before enemy guns, to fight aloft in a gale, go out on a hard-fought cutting-out expedition?

34

Equally swiftly came the reply: that the youngster had made choice of the sea, and if he did not take him, others would.

'Very well. I've a mind to speak to Captain Graves with a view to shifting your berth to *Tyger*. Not as a volunteer but rated midshipman. How would you like that?'

'S-sir, th-thank you! I won't let you down, sir, I'll—' the lad stammered, the hands on his cap working.

'Then so be it.' He allowed his expression to lower to a fierce glare. 'You'll be rated acting midshipman only. If at the end of the year you've shown yourself unworthy of my trust, then you'll suffer disrating and be put out of the ship. *Tyger* is at the first rank of the service and no place for the weak or indolent. Do you understand me?'

'Aye aye, s-sir.'

'But if you do measure up you'll have your warrant as midshipman as a full member of *Tyger*'s crew.'

The eyes were wide as the lad acknowledged.

'And while I think of it, I'd advise keeping mum about your service at the naval school. There'll be those who'd take it on the wrong tack as how you're now in this ship.'

'Sir.'

'We sail within days. Do hold yourself ready to step ashore and get yourself in rig for I won't have you aboard without you're togged out properly. That's a midshipman's chest, full uniform and dirk. Yes?'

'Sir!'

In a kinder tone, Kydd added, 'You'll probably need something to get those rascally tailors to work. Here, five guineas – no, seven. Against your pay, of course,' he said, in mock severity. 'Back to your ship now and await my word.'

Chapter 7

Tugging his bicorne tighter against the brisk wind, Kydd mounted the side-steps of *Victory* to the ornamented entry port, his boat-cloak billowing.

'A pleasure to have you aboard, Sir Thomas,' murmured Dumaresq, the flagship's captain. An awed midshipman took his cloak. 'The others are on the quarterdeck.'

For the first time since the tense days with Nelson in pursuit of the French, Kydd had come aboard the legendary ship to confer with the commander-in-chief. He hugged the memory to himself.

On the spacious quarterdeck, knots of officers conversed amiably, in the spring sunshine an impressive study in blue and gold. His heart lifted at the sight: these were his peers, his comrades-in-arms, his friends. Not the louche and raffish society he'd been so recently involved with – stand fast Prinker and a few others.

He looked around: there were none he knew. Then he spotted a tall, aristocratic figure in languid conversation with another. This was Byam Martin of *Fisgard*. In the earlier

Revolutionary war, as a junior lieutenant, Kydd had admired him from afar.

Attaching himself to the pair, Kydd heard that iron water tanks were being trialled and had been a success. In time the fleet would be fitted with them. This was interesting: no more massive water casks to fill and stow in tiers at the lowest level of the ship above the bilges, at risk of cracking and spoilage.

He introduced himself. 'Saw you in *Tamar* off Hispaniola in the last war with a string of privateers at your tail.'

'Ah, yes. I don't think we've met, sir,' Martin said distantly, offering a limp hand.

Kydd took it, noting the significant look exchanged with his companion, a sharp-featured captain with powder burns on one side of his face who didn't offer to introduce himself. Taken aback, he was saved from further embarrassment by the appearance of the flag-captain who announced that Admiral Saumarez looked forward to the pleasure of their company in his day cabin.

They sat about the deeply polished mahogany table in order of seniority at either side of a large central chair. Kydd found himself between Barrett of *Africa* 64 and the powder-burned captain, who it turned out was Mason, *Riposte* 32, a frigate.

Neither seemed inclined to conversation but very soon the unmistakable figure of Saumarez entered with two others. All stood until the commander-in-chief took his seat in the centre with the two who had accompanied him at either end of the table. Both were admirals – one was Keats, whom Kydd recognised as the commodore of the Great Belt Squadron the previous year, at Copenhagen, to which he'd been attached.

'Good afternoon to you all, gentlemen,' opened Saumarez, courteously. 'I hope I find you in good fettle for we have much to do in the near future.'

Kydd saw that of them all, apart from Saumarez, only the other admiral wore the star and sash of a knighthood. Not for the first time he regretted that, while honour dictated he should not spurn the decoration, it had the unintended effect of singling him out as one wanting to be seen as a cut above the rest.

'I wish to make introduction of Rear Admiral Sir Samuel Hood as my second-in-command and Rear Admiral Richard Keats, whose role will become clear later.'

He looked about the others. 'With captains of the calibre of Byam Martin, William Lukin, Peter Puget, Thomas Kydd and, in fact, all of you here seated, it gives me great confidence to face the task set before me by their lordships.

'Whatever you may have heard, we are not part of the Northern Expedition. That is a military force, as is a motion to come to the assistance of His Swedish Majesty in these troublous times.' He lifted a paper significantly. 'While we will assist in providing naval escort and other services to this endeavour, ours is a greater object. In fine, to make entry into the Baltic Sea and maintain a fleet there indefinitely for the security of our trade in those waters.'

A rustle of anticipation went around the table.

'This is constituted as the Baltic Fleet and its objects are many and varied. Its primary purpose is to keep the Sound open, whatever the cost. The second is to afford the Swedes whatever support we can in their disagreement with Russia. The third is to sever all communications the Danish may still have with their possessions in Norway.'

It was a large enough task for any squadron, implying a

division of force that could considerably weaken their main fleet.

'In addition there are other objectives. The Baltic supplies nearly all our naval stores by necessity. It comes as no surprise to know that the French have an equal reliance on this region. Therefore we shall deny it to them by any means. Added to which we are ordered to place a strict blockade on the southern Baltic that does counter both any enemy imports and exports whatsoever.'

There was quiet while the purpose of the mission was digested. Kydd found himself asking, 'It's to be expected the Russian fleet will dispute it, Sir James. Do you anticipate a major fleet action at all?'

Saumarez looked at him. 'It might so transpire, and in due course I shall be issuing my fighting instructions accordingly. I'm sanguine that we shall prevail, Sir Thomas.'

This sparked a lively interest in the younger officers – if there were to be a Trafalgar-class action against the Russian Kronstadt battle-fleet it would be a glorious opportunity for valour and distinction – and who knew what honours and promotion to follow? Saumarez had the most experience by far of them all in any sizeable engagement, his first as admiral as far back as 1801 – the spectacular and successful action at Algeciras. Whatever faced them ahead they had a commander well able to take them through to victory.

Details followed. Accession to a squadron was always a complicated business. 'Different ships, different long-splices,' sailors said to new hands aboard, and it was the same at higher levels. It had to be discovered to what degree of diligence weekly accounts should be rendered, how punctilious gun salutes should be, what pet enthusiasms were to be pandered to – gunnery, sail handling, station keeping.

Kydd had the advantage: he'd served under Saumarez in the Channel Islands and knew him to be strict but fair. There would be no futile squaring of yards at anchor or row-guards at island anchorages. Above all, he knew the admiral to be decent and honourable in all his dealings.

'I've heard tell that ice is well to be feared in the Baltic,' offered one of the captains.

'Quite,' Keats said, with feeling. 'I've had a hard winter in the Skagerrak looking into the Great Belt and do not desire to see any more. Be satisfied that, spring now upon us, the ice has retreated beyond Memel, and Reval stands ready to be released. I would not, however, account this our greatest weather foe . . .'

'Easterlies from the depths of Tartary, I'd wager,' prompted Barrett of *Africa*. 'Hard, biting cold and as like to kick up the devil of a short sea in those waters.'

It was gratifying to hear this professional talk about the table, and Kydd put forward the sprawl of tiny islands that seemed to infest every port offshore to the peril of night navigation, but was cut short by Keats. 'Not to be considered against the greatest menace of all.'

The table waited, curious to know of any worse.

'It is your sudden calm.'

'Sir?' Barrett enquired politely.

'Your quiet calm, stark calm, dead calm – any name you care to give it. In the Baltic they can fall without warning, leaving the best sailer adrift in a glassy sea for a damned long time. Should the gunboats hear of it they're out in a swarm, and even a frigate might find itself embarrassed by their attentions.'

There was more talk: the unreliability of charts and the need for survey of the trickier parts as had been done with the Great Belt, not to mention the prospects for watering when every southern shore was hostile.

No doubt there would be many more of these social gatherings: Kydd remembered Saumarez liked to keep a fine table and used his hospitality to be close to his captains. And later, what better forum to exchange experiences, wrinkles discovered and warnings of enemy activity? Apart from providing convoy escorts into the first part of the Baltic, the navy had not penetrated deeply, had never had a persisting presence within it. There would be much to discover and learn.

With the news that they would be under weigh for Gothenburg in three days, they gathered in the admiral's great cabin for dinner. It was a magnificent affair, the napery, silverware and crystal quite up to any Kydd had seen in London, table decorations a-plenty and, with the stirring atmosphere of the legendary ship, it promised to be a memorable occasion.

He was seated next to Puget, a lieutenant in the Vancouver expedition with the felicity of a sound named after him, now in command of *Goliath*, who showed interest in Kydd's explorations in Australia. He was an agreeable dining companion and Kydd nearly overlooked the young frigate captain on his other side, tongue-tied in the presence of a popular sea hero.

The dinner proceeded well, a talented hidden violinist adding to the mood – he must later offer Saumarez the services of Doud, *Tyger*'s gifted singer, Kydd thought.

'Wine with you, sir,' he proposed to Mason, who was sitting opposite and giving slavish ear to Graves of *Brunswick* on his right.

To his surprise he was ignored. Louder this time: 'I said, wine with you, Mr Mason.'

Graves broke off his description of a Leeward Islands

fever epidemic and glanced enquiringly at Mason, who grudgingly picked up his glass and half-heartedly saluted Kydd before returning to hear more of the fever.

At a loss, Kydd could only frown at the discourtesy, then brought to mind that Keats, seated not far to his left, had never once acknowledged his presence. Neither had Byam Martin, sitting next to him. Were they jealous of his successes at sea or was it that they had been put out to see one of their number hobnobbing in high society, cutting a dash above his station?

There was nothing he could do about this and he didn't intend to let it affect him. The real question was whether Saumarez took the same view; the admiral had been until now in the same station where he'd known him before, the tranquil Channel Islands that Kydd had left to enter the greater war and eventual fame.

He had his chance as the evening drew to a close and a small number of officers remained with a convivial brandy before taking boat for their ship.

'A fine evening, sir,' Kydd ventured, edging into Saumarez's view. The eyes regarded him steadily. 'Lady Saumarez is well, I trust? I have the most lively recollections of her kindness to me.'

'She is well, thank you,' Saumarez answered evenly.

The other officers drifted away, leaving them alone together.

'Then you'd oblige me, sir, should you convey my sincere regards and inform her that I am recently married, to a woman who commands all my love.'

Saumarez softened. 'I'm delighted to hear it. The marriage state is the richest blessing we might attain under Heaven and I'm persuaded is to be commended even to the most stiff-necked bachelor.'

This was the decency in the man responding – but it said nothing about his view of Kydd professionally.

'A hard field to plough, their lordships have presented you with, I fancy,' he dared.

Saumarez gave a polite smile. 'As we must strive to achieve, of course. All hands to the traces, as it were, in the common cause.' He paused significantly. 'Even the most ardent of our band must needs rein in his steed to stay with the labourers, I believe.'

So Kydd's reputation as a thrusting frigate captain had reached him. Was he seeing this as the last thing he needed in a delicate, complex theatre of operations? 'I understand, sir. You will have my wholehearted support in your mission.'

'Thank you, Sir Thomas,' Saumarez replied, with a slight bow of acknowledgement. 'We will meet again in Gothenburg.'

Chapter 8

Heart thudding, Christopher Rowan gazed up at the big frigate from the sternsheets of the cutter bringing him to be one with her company. *Tyger* – her lines were strong, uncompromising; this was a pugnacious fighter, which had achieved daring feats that had set the whole country talking.

They were close enough now that he could see figures moving about the decks, one smartly swinging into the main-mast shrouds, another sitting astride a fore-royal yard, hundreds of feet up, apparently working a splice.

He gulped. Could he ever think to match up as one of the crew under the famous Captain Kydd?

'Aye aye,' bawled back the bowman, in answer to the hail from the quarterdeck. It would be a long time, if ever, that this cry would be for him, signifying an officer in the boat demanding due respect to his rank.

He felt strange and awkward, almost as if he was in disguise, for it was only his second day in uniform, that of a warrant officer no less! It had been a miraculous transformation from the insignificance of a volunteer with no formal duties, apart from that of keeping out of the way of every single man aboard, to this, someone who could roar orders at any, short of the exalted beings who strode the quarterdeck.

Roar orders – he cringed at the thought. Would they laugh at him? Would Captain Kydd regret taking him aboard?

Closer still, and the majestic lines of the frigate took on the fullness of a living structure, details of scrollwork, gun-port lids and well-tended rigging all complementing the underlying sweep of sturdy timbers and wales fore and aft.

In a practised curve, the boat came alongside and hooked on at the main-chains. A bluff, unspeaking lieutenant had shared the journey out and Rowan sat rigid and unmoving as the officer rose to leave the boat. He wasn't about to make the cardinal blunder of getting out first: it was the inviolable custom for the senior to board last and leave first and he duly waited until he could mount the side-steps.

At the top he swung clumsily over the bulwark, his dirk scabbard catching in something as the drop to the deck was less than he'd anticipated after *Brunswick*. He straightened and looked around. No one seemed interested in his arrival but he knew his duty and marched smartly up to the officer-of-the-day.

'Midshipman Rowan reporting as ordered, sir,' he announced.

The officer, in comfortable blues and faded lace, looked at him with a faint curiosity. 'To join ship?'

'Aye, sir.'

'Well, well. They get younger every day. Get your chest and we'll find you a berth.'

Rowan hesitated.

'Out of the boat and on deck, here,' the officer said, as if to a simpleton.

Face burning, Rowan went to the side and looked down

into the boat. Heart in his mouth, he hailed down to the upturned faces, 'Er, send up my chest, there, you men.'

They looked at each other in astonishment.

'That is, this instant, you – you blaggards!' he shouted as loudly as he could.

It got attention, but not from the men. Watched by the frowning officer, one of those talking at the main-mast bitts detached himself and went over to him.

'Now, m'lad, we does things properly in *Tyger*,' he said kindly. The jolly-faced man must be the sailing master, for he wore their newly introduced uniform with the stand-up collar. 'We rigs a whip an' hoists our dunnage inboard in one, saves the men straining their backs, like.'

'Thank you, sir, I'll remember.'

'Miller, see to it, will ye?' he threw at an idle seaman.

A little later two men hefted his chest as though it was a feather-weight and, taking it down the main hatchway, they deposited it before the polished door in the centre of a sweep of panels that partitioned off the after end of the ship. *Brunswick* had a wardroom, but he knew enough that a frigate had a gunroom, which this would be and which he had no right to enter. The more humble compartment set out to one side would be his home – the midshipmen's berth.

It was panelled only to half-height, with drawn curtains for the rest and another serving for a door. He could hear the murmur of conversation within. Tucking his brand-new cocked hat under his arm he took courage and went to the curtain 'door' but then found himself at a loss – how did you knock? He compromised by tapping hesitantly on an upright.

The voices stopped.

'Come!' The voice was manly and commanding. Rowan pulled the curtain aside and stepped in.

There were just two sitting at the table, a splay of cards in front of them.

'Good God! A ghost – an apparition!' cried an older midshipman of about sixteen, goggling at him in mock horror.

'Um, my name's Rowan and I've come to join *Tyger*,' he stammered.

'It speaks! Ye gods and little fishes, it speaks!'

'Can I put my chest here?'

'Why?'

Unable to think of a reply he didn't move, feeling foolish.

'Come on in, then, apparition,' the older said, with a sudden grin. 'Sit y'self down and tell us all about it.'

The compartment was all of twenty feet in length, mostly occupied with a long table and lit by a single guttering lamp. Homely implements were hung on the bulkheads and a colourful but grimy print took pride of place at the forward end.

Self-consciously Rowan came forward but there were no chairs.

'We use our chests to park our arses.' There was no hostility in the tone but no warmth either.

He dragged in his sea-chest, aware of their gaze on him. Once seated, he looked up to meet their eyes.

'I'm Daniel.' It was the other, younger, midshipman. 'Daniel Teague, that's Tilly to you. And this is Neb Gilpin. Where are you from?'

It wasn't his home town they were asking after. '*Brunswick*, 74, Captain Graves.'

'My, you've done well to be quit o' the old hooker into a crack frigate.' Gilpin looked genuinely puzzled. 'As our sainted captain swears he can't abide snotty-nosed reefers aboard his ship, how did you swing it, whatever-your-name-is-again?'

'I . . . I wrote him a letter.'

Gilpin's face hardened. 'Don't flam me, fish-scut! You got family or what?'

'No, no – that's how it happened, honest!'

'I don't believe you, but we'll leave it for now.'

'It's as I said, er, Neb – and my name is Christopher.'

'Kit Rowan? It'll do. Methinks we need to drink to it.' He fished around under the table and came up with an anonymous brown bottle. Three chipped china mugs were found and coarse red wine gurgled out into them.

'*Tyger*, as never a finer frigate swam.'

'*Tyger!*'

Rowan had never drunk wine before: his father was abstemious and disapproving. It nearly made him gag.

'Another!'

'Thank you, no. I have to report to the captain and—'

'Not aboard till sundown. We're a hard-drinking crew in the middie's berth, aren't we, Dan? So drink up. Now, who's family?'

'Oh, my father's a well-respected articled clerk with Hanson and Hanson and—'

'That'll do. Mine's something in stock-jobbing. Never could work out what he did for his cobbs but it pays him well. Dan's folks are—'

'My father has the living of Bicknoller, which is in Somerset.'

Gilpin was about to retort when the curtain was yanked aside and a gleeful messenger poked his head in. 'New mid. Desired to report t' the cap'n right now! An' he's in a right taking he's to wait upon your leisure!'

Stricken, Rowan got to his feet and raced for the upper deck and aft to the august and fearful quarters of his captain. In the confines of the lower deck he hadn't heard the boatswain's call piping him aboard for, unlike *Brunswick*, there were no guns and therefore no open gun-ports. Of all the disasters possible to start his time in *Tyger*!

Breathlessly he entered the coach and announced himself to the marine sentry, who half opened the door to the great cabin and blared, 'Midshipman Rowan, sir.'

Inside a muffled voice called something and the sentry closed the door and grunted, 'Busy. Will see yez shortly.' Without expression, he resumed his vigil.

The waiting was hard to take and Rowan tried to occupy himself coming up with an alibi. Then he remembered Perrott's gruff words. 'In the navy you can have y'r reasons but never an excuse. Tell it like it was, an' take it like a man.'

It steadied him, and when the time came, he marched in, cocked hat under his arm, and stood rigid before Captain Sir Thomas Kydd. 'Reporting aboard, sir!' he blurted.

'Oh, yes. Sorry to keep you waiting,' Kydd said mildly, giving something to what was presumably his secretary. So much for the messenger's dire prophecy — he'd made sport of him.

'Um, yes, sir.'

Kydd looked him over politely. 'A fine showing, Mr Rowan. We're to sea very soon, however, and I'd suggest a seaman's trousers more the thing than breeches. Have you found your berth?'

'Sir.'

'Then we must see about your duties. You shall be under Mr Bowden for divisions and he will be responsible to me for your instruction. Make yourself known and he'll take care of the details.'

'Aye aye, sir.'

'Good. You didn't say where you come from?'

'Chilworth, sir, which is near—'

'Yes, where they make the gunpowder as gives us our bite and roar. Well, Mr Rowan, you'll be very much occupied so I won't delay you further. Good luck, apply yourself diligently, and we'll both be satisfied. Off you go, now.'

In a gust of relief, Rowan made his way back to his berth. But it was now a different place: at the far end of the table in the unnatural quietness sat a master's mate, who was writing at his journal, while the two midshipmen sat opposite doing the same – Teague industriously scrawling, but Gilpin leaning back, glassy-eyed and sucking the end of his quill.

The master's mate looked up sharply, then laid down his pen. 'Ah, Johnny Raw now aboard,' he said lazily. 'I'm David Maynard – Mr Maynard to you. And I'm to welcome you to the *Tyger* Cockpitonians. You've made acquaintance with . . .?'

'I have, sir.'

'None o' that, fellow. Only when I get my step to l'tenant, which has to be soon. Now, tell us about yourself, curly-top.'

All his personal details were laid bare: that he was not of noble ancestry, apparently an asset, and that he came from the same part of the country as Kydd was accounted his good luck. As advised, he kept his time at the Kydd School to himself.

'You'll do. I see Mr Gilpin has yet to finish his journal so I call on young Tilly here to take you on a grand tour of our noble barky – and if you can't tell me where everything is a-low by the first dog, you'll do it again in the last.'

'Yes, Mr Maynard.'

'And square away your chest and ditty bag first. Mr Bowden has the deck – you can see him after eight bells.'

The tour was thorough but, in a way, an easing of anxiety: all rated ships were largely the same. *Tyger*, as a frigate, lacked a poop-deck and had only one line of guns instead of two but, apart from small things, he could find his way about just as easily as he'd learned so painfully in *Brunswick*.

More useful was the information he was absorbing about her company.

Captain Kydd was as fierce and demanding as any crack frigate commander and all that he'd heard about his audacious exploits was true. And, if Tilly were to be believed, even in this unpromising fleet situation their captain could be relied on to snatch an adventure or two.

The frightening first lieutenant thankfully found midshipmen beneath his notice and the other two lieutenants were good sorts, but strict.

Maynard was a square-sailing cove, who didn't stand for young gentlemen to disturb his quiet, but Gilpin would bear watching. Older, confident, his seamanship had brought praise even from the well-seasoned boatswain but his navigation was an ill-tempered trial. For the rest, he would find out in due course.

As foretold, in two days the fleet put to sea.

On the quarterdeck in his new uniform and dirk, Rowan was thrilled to the core as Kydd rapped orders that had them weighing anchor, men leaping to the shrouds and doing incomprehensible things that would be his study from now on.

Standing erect, and under every eye, he witnessed *Tyger* taking station seaward on watch and guard while the great fleet assembled in two lines, the commander-in-chief's flagship, the famed *Victory*, in the van. If only his father could take in the scene now! The majesty and consequence of a ship-of-war putting to sea, the colours, salutes, the deadly purpose of prows cleaving the seas on their way to claim their rightful supremacy – it was electrifying, magnificent.

Chapter 9

Vinga Sands anchorage, western Sweden

The Baltic Fleet made an uneventful crossing to Gothenburg in grey, sullen seas before casting anchor, ten miles to seaward of the port but safely clear of the maze of offshore islands and in easy reach of the open sea.

The Northern Expedition was on its way, and would arrive in a few days, but here was a powerful fleet, token for all to see that Britain took her obligations to an ally most seriously.

A response from the shore was quick in coming, and Kydd found himself stepping on to Swedish soil in full regalia for a reception by the governor, joining three admirals and a cluster of senior captains in carriages to be whisked through the broad streets to the residence.

He was quite a different creature from the one he'd been just a few years ago. Then, awed, he had floundered in fashionable and influential society. Now he was at ease at the highest levels. He couldn't help noticing that he was the only frigate captain, in company with but half of the ship-of-the-line commanders. So Saumarez had seen fit to include him in the select band who would represent their country on this diplomatic occasion. Or was it on account of his splendid star and sash?

In the hushed murmuring of the gathering, it dawned on him that, while he may have been flaunted for the occasion, perhaps in fact he was being covertly appraised by Saumarez or his flag-captain. This was nothing like a social occasion or even a political gathering – he could sense the edge to the easy talk, noted the unblinking eyes and calculated gestures of politeness, the languid and polished phrases.

It was a skill just as much as reading the wind to trim the sails – and was essential to develop, if he was to become anything more than a warrior captain. To be trusted with a delicate situation, to be left on his own to make diplomatic decisions, have his reports and assessments valued, these were the crucial accomplishments required of an officer of flag rank.

He felt a thrill of what might be. It would be years yet but if he was under eye there was more than a fleeting chance he could achieve the ultimate felicity if he had the right competencies.

Kydd saw Saumarez speaking genially with a be-sashed Swede. He would be looking now to forge the very links, military and diplomatic, that would set in motion the strategics of his immense tasking. If he was anxious or distracted he didn't show it.

Keats was in polite conversation with a whiskered gentleman of advanced years, amid much amiable bowing and a modicum of guarded merriment, while Hood was in careful talk with two Swedish naval officers. What wouldn't he give to overhear what passed! Others were doing their duty, some wearing expressions so controlled as to appear blank, others with countenances more to be seen on the quarterdeck with an enemy in the offing.

An affable and distinguished Swede with a broad blue sash across his chest, accompanied by an unsmiling military officer, looked at him with mock concern. 'I say, young fellow, you haven't touched your champagne. Is it not to your liking?'

'On the contrary, sir,' Kydd replied courteously, impressed by his command of English. 'Sir Thomas Kydd, captain of *Tyger* 38.' He was acknowledged by a short bow with a click of the heels, Continental fashion. 'I was in admiration for your paintings. Are they of your royal family?' Kydd continued.

'They are. His Majesty Gustav IV Adolf stands in the centre, his family about him.' He smiled benignly. 'Axel Rosen, governor of Gothenburg. This is Colonel Lagerhjelm.'

Kydd sipped at his champagne. 'A fine entertainment, sir. And I'm looking forward to making closer acquaintance with your country in the near future.'

This prompted a sharp glance, which left him at a loss to interpret, so he continued warmly, 'As the alliance of our two nations is newly signed, that is. Should we not be friends?'

Rosen gave a faint smile. 'Sir, we may be allies but not necessarily friends. Do enjoy yourself tonight, Sir Kydd.'

He moved on, leaving Kydd to untangle what had just taken place.

There was little time for thought, however. The swirl of guests was thickening and he was claimed by two youthful naval officers, who asked if he was indeed the same Kydd who had taken on three frigates off the Prussian coast. Now wary, he answered briefly and factually and, despite ill-disguised prodding, refused to make criticism of the Prussian showing before Tilsit, leaving them disappointed.

Just what had Rosen meant? He determined to find out more of how the wind blew in this part of the world.

Hood seemed headed in his direction, accompanied by a tall, acidulous-looking individual with impressive diplomatic decorations. He paused. 'Sir Thomas Kydd, sir, a fighting seaman and ornament to our profession. Kydd, this is Sir Edward Thornton, our envoy to His Swedish Majesty, new returned from Stockholm to welcome our Northern Expedition.'

'A pleasure to make your acquaintance, Sir Edward,' Kydd responded, unsure how an envoy figured in the watch and station bill of an embassy. Above or below an ambassador?

'Likewise, Sir Thomas. Your exploits are known even in these far parts and I honour you for them.' The tone, however, was chill.

On impulse he asked, 'Sir, I'd be glad of a steer in the matter of what Mr Rosen said to me.'

Thornton stiffened.

'He said, "We may be allies but not necessarily friends", and I'm curious to know what it means.'

'Sir! You should be well advised to refrain from touching on matters above your competence,' he said, in a low, hard voice. 'Affairs are not necessarily what they seem, and are at a most delicate stand. Do confine your pleasantries to the weather or some such trifle.'

'Sir. Allow that I've had my share of confidences at court and similar,' Kydd bit off. 'If I'm in shoal waters here, it's for want of a pilot. Do tell what I must appreciate, if you will.'

There was a reluctant glimmer of a smile. 'You're not to

know, of course. However, I'll be open with you. The Swedish king stands alone in his defiance but is confounded in his intellects in a court packed with Francophiles. His military have set their face against us and are untrustworthy, and I've news that the Russians have just fallen upon Swedish Finland and are even now advancing at a pace.'

'So your King Gustav needs all the friends he can find. Why did Rosen say we're not?'

'Rosen you can trust. He's intelligent and, as governor of a great seaport, is not dazzled by Bonaparte's victories on land. He knows the true winner in a long war is going to be the one who rules the open seas, not the bounded land. He's a friend to England whom we'd do well to hear, and what he's telling you is that Sweden as a whole is seething in factions and cannot be relied upon. And he's right – I've a task worthy of Tantalus himself to find a path to put together a working alliance in this enterprise.'

'Then I do wish you well of it, sir,' Kydd said sincerely.

Chapter 10

He'd been aboard *Tyger* for just a few days but she had taken him to her and he had responded willingly. The serene lift and heave of her deck, measured and regular, was at one with the rise and fall of his mother's breast as she had held him as an infant, the sturdy enfolding bulkheads and decks now a comfort and refuge from the harsh world without. He knew it was romantic nonsense, but Christopher Rowan felt without question that *Tyger* was bearing him on, taking him to adventures and perils that would, in the end, make him a man.

She was graceful and handsome – the sweet curves of the deck-line, the lofty spars wreathed in an intricate tracery of rigging against the sails, taut and bellying, that urged her on in a forceful swash of bow-waves. There was something artistic in the tints and colours that gave her character – the black spars with their white tips against yellow masts, the scarlet inner bulwarks, against which rested gleaming black guns on their red and green carriages, the rosin bright-work, and everywhere the scrubbed purity of the decks.

He tried not to be noticed as he watched her company go about their shipboard routines, for these were not the pressed men of *Brunswick* – Captain Kydd would never have need of such. Instead these were a higher breed, all volunteers into the most famous frigate of the age. Hard, capable and the picture of deep-sea sailormen, they were the fighting core of *Tyger* and looked the part. They moved lithely, their motions sure and confident, no petty officers spluttering in frustration as officers blared at them: these men were aboard *Tyger* because they wanted to share in her honour and acclaim, and he quailed again at the impossible vision of taking charge of them.

It had to be faced, though. He would soon be expected to do just that, for there could be no passengers in a first-rank frigate, and if he failed . . .

His eyes caught activity further forward by the starboard side. Gilpin was taking charge of a party of seamen to leeward. They were preparing to pull on a rope, some kind of sail trimming. He was standing back, hands on his hips, looking up, gauging times. As each fell due he barked the order and the men flung themselves into it, hauling low and hard. It was impressive: the young man's voice had broken and there was a crack of authority in it that had them sweating at their work.

The seamen completed the task to his satisfaction and, dismissing them, he sauntered back to the watch group near the helm and reported languidly. Although he was only a couple of years older than Rowan, there was a gulf of experience and knowledge between them that Rowan couldn't hope to bridge.

The *ting-ting* of the ship's bell brought him back to earth. It was time for the young gentlemen's instruction.

This was in the coach, part of the outer captain's quarters where the master's mates would correct charts, the ship's clerk do his bookkeeping and the first lieutenant spread out his watch and station workings.

At this appointed hour all were elsewhere while the midshipmen took their daily instruction. Teague was there ready and Gilpin eventually arrived, his look of boredom barely concealed.

'You're all leagues astern of station in the article of navigation,' Lieutenant Bowden pronounced dismissively. 'You'll take inboard what the master gives you today or it's double tides into the dog-watches. Clear?'

The sailing master bustled in with books and papers, his brow furrowed. 'Celestial navigation.'

There was a groan from Gilpin.

Ignoring him, the master continued, 'I want to see y'r workings for Canopus, should we observe him at this time, and at this hour-angle and declination thus. Height of eye twenty-three feet. Now, first, what's y'r apparent altitude? Mr Gilpin?'

Holding his breath in fascination, Rowan heard the two stumble through the process, the patient master reminding, reproving and encouraging – but it meant not the tiniest thing to him.

'Use your almanac, Mr Gilpin! It's all there. And ye've forgotten y'r refraction correction again. That's to say, pi divided by a hundred and eighty as multiplied by y'r apparent altitude, the tan whereof . . .'

While it droned on, Rowan snatched a quick look in a well-thumbed volume: *Nories Nautical Tables*. It seemed to consist of nothing more than a dense thicket of numbers in endless tables. Applying the sun's total correction to the observed altitude of a limb of the sun? Meridional parts and haversines? The augmentation of the moon's semi-diameter – what did it *mean*?

Mr Perrott's robust art of the arithmetic was not up to this, and Mr Partington's mathematics had all been Greek triangles. The more he plucked at the pages the worse it got until he guiltily slid it away. He didn't know where to start and it was plain he was expected to catch up to the others. How could he do it?

Eventually the master got around to him. 'Why, Mr Rowan, is it? We've been neglecting ye. Now, these gennelmen should know their reckonings and we need to have ye up with them. An' I've the very medicine right here. Hamilton Moore, bless him, *The New Practical Navigator*, which contains all y' need to know. Take it, an' for the first, learn out all y'r definitions.'

Rowan gingerly carried the book to the corner of the coach. It was old – over forty years, according to the title page – but lovingly cared for. The ancient typeface, with its *f* for *s*, was not an obstacle, for many of the navy school's texts were of a past age, but what made him hesitate were the assumptions.

He knew as well as any fool what a mile was, but apparently they used a different mile at sea. *The New Practical Navigator* explained: 'If AB is an arc of the meridian which contains O and subtends an angle of 1 minute at K, the length of AB is the length of a nautical mile at O.' Did this mean a ship sailed a different distance, depending on where it was?

In despair, he discovered that if he wanted to take the shortest distance between two ports separated by an ocean, it was no use simply finding a ruler and drawing a straight line on the chart. Bizarrely, a looping great circle was more to be desired.

It was noisy and distracting, the exciting things happening on deck evident by occasional cries and rushing feet, but he'd promised his father he'd diligently apply himself in the calling he had chosen.

'Mr Joyce,' he asked the sailing master, in a small voice, 'would you lend me this book that I can go away and read it quietly?'

'O' course, m' lad. Look after it well. I wants it back, mind!'

Chapter 11

S ome days later, the Northern Expedition arrived at Flemish Roads, the inner anchorage, close by the city for disembarkation. Scores of ships; men, horses, guns. Stores to keep an army of ten thousand fed and watered for the voyage, and with munitions and spares sufficient for a long campaign. And aboard, soldiers looking longingly at the shore: even the one week they'd been cooped up in the cramped and reeking decks of the troop-ships had left them with a compelling need to set foot on the good earth.

But first their commander, Lieutenant General Sir John Moore, had to pay a courtesy visit to the Swedes and make due arrangement for their reception.

Within the hour a boat put out and in its sternsheets against the grey sea could be seen the scarlet and gold of a high military officer. At the quayside a small group awaited him; these were not Swedish for he'd been asked first to attend a private meeting with the British envoy in the house of the consul.

* * *

Thornton stood by the fireplace in the spacious room with tall windows looking out over the flat, sprawling city. The bare masts of the expedition ships just offshore in a huddle gave point to what they were about to discuss.

'General Moore.'

At the door was a slightly built man in dress regimentals. He had soft brown hair, a well-rounded face and seemed startlingly young to be a general, but as he advanced to meet him, Thornton noted the lines of determination and rigid bearing of a dedicated career soldier.

'Sir Edward? You wished to see me.' The voice was controlled. This was the handsome creature who had lately stolen Lady Hester Stanhope from the ardent clutches of none other than the foreign minister, Canning.

'Thank you, Sir John, I did. You're about to make acquaintance with the Swedes, our allies. I rather thought I might be able to assist you in your dealings with them.'

'I'm quite capable of settling my own arrangements, and any consideration of military deployments need not concern you, sir.'

It was said without rancour, a flat and impersonal statement.

'Sir, my capacity as envoy to His Swedish Majesty has allowed me insights into the condition of this country that—'

'Quite. And if they are of military interest, my aide would be pleased to take notes at a later time, thank you. I have interpreters attached and you will not be troubled in the petty details of the disembarkation.'

'There are significant problems of a political nature attaching to this expedition,' Thornton said carefully, 'that do considerably impinge on your mission, sir.'

'Sir Edward. I'm a soldier. My objectives do not include

diplomatic niceties at the cost of operational effectiveness. Do grant that I can be relied upon to stand by my orders from Horse Guards while you are free to fulfil yours from the Foreign Office.'

Thornton winced. The thought of this no doubt brave but single-minded general blundering into the rickety patchwork of delicate understandings that was all he'd been able to achieve in the way of an alliance was dismaying. But he'd caught one thing that might be important. Moore had his orders from Horse Guards, the highest echelon of military command, in just the same way as Saumarez had his from the highest naval body, the Admiralty. 'Indeed, Sir John. As they will be the expression of the will of the government we both serve,' he said smoothly. 'Might I be made privy to them?' As the ranking diplomat he had every right to ask it.

'Certainly,' Moore said crisply. 'The first, as leader of the Northern Expedition, I'm to secure communications to the Baltic, by which is understood to mean that my army shall be placed in such manner that the enemy will not be suffered to violate Swedish territory. Deployment to the province of Scania directly opposite Denmark has been mentioned in this regard.'

'I see.'

'The second is to establish and defend a base of operations for our military and naval forces. Marstrand, where I understand our fleet foregathers, would seem acceptable.'

'Go on.'

'And to render such assistance to the King of Sweden as should most discomfort his enemies, wheresoever they be found. This, sir, is the essence of my orders. Now, I have much to accomplish – disembarking my men into a shore barracks and putting in train their provisioning and supply, to make local currency conversion of the pay chest and—'

'General. Your orders are plain and well meant, but they will not do. They will certainly not do in the circumstances.'

'Sir! Dare you question my orders? If so, I can only—' Moore responded, clearly outraged.

'I must, for they are impossible to carry out.'

'Sir, what do you mean by that, exactly?' Moore said dangerously.

'What if I tell you that King Gustav's prime ambition is that of detaching Norway from the Danish Crown to add to his?'

'That cannot possibly be of any concern to me, sir.'

'It is, for you will find your first task will be to join with his forces in a grand invasion of Sjælland, the island of Denmark whereon the capital, Copenhagen, lies.'

Moore fell back in disbelief. 'No! This is preposterous – your sources are a mockery, they—'

'Sir, this I heard from the lips of the King himself. Do you then question me as to its veracity?' He brought to mind the morning just days ago in Stockholm, the cunning leer as Gustav had disclosed to him his grand plan for the restoration of Sweden to the table of great nations, the hunted look as reasonable objections had been raised and the sudden storm of vilification and accusation that had ensued.

It was an unhappy fact of these times that, in stark contrast to Great Britain, all of the Continental powers had autocratic monarchs who knew no check to their rule. Few used it well. Some, like the Queen of Portugal and the King of Denmark, were irretrievably insane while others were as out of touch with the real world as they were with their subjects. It made diplomacy a nightmare of unreason, and a graveyard of ambition to any high-minded minister.

Gustav was a particular difficulty. Lacking both foresight and patience, his judgement of men ludicrous, his decisions were so often wildly askew, so grotesque, that he'd been suspected of madness and attempts made to dethrone him.

Yet Gustav was implacably, mystically opposed to Bonaparte, holding that he was none other than the Beast of Revelation, who would not rest until he'd drowned Europe in an apocalyptic blood-bath. This had not stopped him demanding outrageous sums in subsidy before taking the field against the French.

The temptation was to abandon him and let Fate take its course, but Sweden was the one and only ally left to Britain. The alliance must stand – and succeed, for the alternative was unthinkable. He had therefore done all he could to bring it about and—

'Sjælland? Have you any conception of what we'd face if we made assault?' Moore threw at him.

Thornton had, but let it pass.

'Thirty thousand and more under Bernadotte – and I'm expected to make landing with my ten thousand and a handful of Swedish conscripts? It's not to be countenanced, sir!'

'Just so, General. But I do advise—'

'And with the Russians devouring Finland as we speak! I was led to believe that my task was in the securing of the entrances to the Baltic, releasing Swedish resources to fly to the frontier in its defence. Any talk of Norway or Sjælland is madness, sir!'

Thornton smothered a sigh. 'I can only remind you of your orders – to render such assistance to the King of Sweden as should most discomfort the enemy. If the King in his wisdom decrees Norway to be the field of honour, then should you not—'

'Damn it all to blazes! I will not be a party to this absurdity.'

'So you will defy your own orders, General?'

Chapter 12

The air was bracing and invigorating, in keeping with Kydd's mood that the quarterdeck of *Tyger* was a most fitting place to find oneself, the gift of Heaven and their lordships who had seen fit to place him there and, extraordinarily, even pay him for the privilege.

The anchorage – called 'Wingo' by British sailors – was an unkempt scatter of low, bare islands, some with straggling bushes and, like so many naval anchorages, without any special interest. Much more to catch the eye was the Baltic Fleet, a stirring martial sight with its near two dozen men-o'-war at single anchor, pennants a-flutter and ensigns floating above lines of guns that were the instruments of Britain's domination of the seas.

It was, besides, to the men aboard each ship, the source of anything that would happen to them in the near future. Eyes were perpetually a-weather for any sign of excitement: the sudden snapping of signals from the flagship or the hasty putting-off of boats to fan out with urgent fleet orders.

* * *

'Mr Rowan.' The boatswain stood suddenly across his path, his arms folded.

Tyger's new midshipman stopped warily. 'Mr Herne?'

This was the hard-featured but quietly spoken senior hand answering to the first lieutenant himself and in charge of the seamen for every manoeuvre of the ship and the maintenance of the miles of rigging. He was one of the standing officers, who would see captains come and go, and experience all her voyages and battles until the ship finally went to her rest.

His calm eyes regarded Rowan gravely. 'I don't recollect as I've ever seen ye aloft, Mr Rowan. Ain't natural, a midshipman not skylarkin' in the tops. You'd oblige me b' giving me a hail from yon main-top.'

It was unfair! He'd been aboard only days and they expected him to make the fearful climb up there? It was the haunt of topmen, prime seamen, who were the cream of any ship's company.

'I I don't think as—'

The boatswain simply pointed up, his face implacable.

When Rowan hesitated, Herne called across a seaman. 'Leckie! Mr Rowan here wants ye to show him the way to the main-top. If y' please . . .'

The man was mature, the hair touched by grey, but he had an open, uncomplicated appearance – and the barrel chest and powerful arms of a deep-sea mariner. 'Aye aye, Mr Herne,' he replied, swiftly sizing Rowan up. 'Ah, there's but one way t' do it,' he confided, 'an' that's the right way.'

Satisfied, the boatswain moved on, leaving them to it.

'We mounts the shroud hand over hand but first we leaves the deck – this way.'

With a practised leap he caught the forward-most shroud

well up and, in the same movement, drew his legs up to the bulwarks and hauled himself upright, swinging to a rest on the outer side of the shrouds. 'See?' He made room for Rowan.

It took three tries before Rowan caught on to the need to perform all motions simultaneously but then he stood breathlessly next to Herne, clutching the shroud tightly. His courage ebbed as he looked down: twenty feet or more below was the cold grey depth of the Baltic.

'Y' sees how we has the shrouds set up, an' it's important y' has a good notion of what it's about, else you'll be in wi' the fishes an' all.' He looked at Rowan as if in doubt of his taking the point.

'Now these thick lines going up are y'r shrouds.' He patted familiarly the inches-thick tar-black ropes soaring skyward.

'And right across 'em we puts the ratlines, as we'll use to get up.' This rope was much thinner and was secured to the shrouds to form a ladder.

'Now, what I want ye to remember always is that when we goes up any kind o' sea-ladder, never grab hold on the one that's going across, always the one going up 'n' down. If y' ratline let's go on ye, it's a backward flip an' into the oggin, right?'

Rowan nodded but his gaze had transferred up to the narrowing step-ladder that led to the underside of the main-top. 'R-right, I'm ready,' he said nervously.

'You first, Mr Rowan,' Leckie said firmly. 'As I'm here t' catch ye.'

Rowan took a deep breath, felt for the next step and hung there, indecisive.

'Easy, really,' Leckie said conversationally. 'Jus' take it one at a time, y'r right leg, left arm, other leg, right arm – that way ye has always three out o' four pins safe. Have a try, lad.'

It made sense and, miraculously, he was climbing the ratlines. In a laborious rhythm, true, but he was on his way up.

Conscious of Leckie beneath him, he neared the fighting top, much bigger than it looked from on deck. He glanced down curiously – and froze. Strangely distorted by height, the deck below was transformed into a faraway place quite different from the blustery upper realm he was in now, but at the same time thrilling in its sensation of thrusting speed and liveliness. He'd never really been prey to a fear of heights and began revelling in the sensation of cutting free from the common and pedestrian lower world.

'On y' goes, mate,' Leckie urged. 'In through that big hole.'

In the shadow of the jutting fighting top he was close to the big driving sail, a vast expanse of taut canvas, the reef points pattering busily, the down-draught like an airy water-fall. He reached the underside of the top and in the last few feet of the ratlines was able to pop his head through and surprise a seaman at work on one of the dozens of lines soaring up further.

Hauling himself up he managed to stand freely on the railed platform, gingerly steadying himself with a line from aloft.

He'd made it! Exhilarated, he took in the grand sights – great sails straining at the tackles that held them, the widening traces of the white of the wake in continual formation, the sea stretching out in a boundless expanse of blue to a horizon many times more distant.

He became aware of movement and, on the weather side of the top, Gilpin's face popped into view. Not for him the convenient opening next to the mast – he'd gone around the edge of the top and heaved himself up and over to join him. Gilpin affected not to see him, striking a noble pose against the wind.

Leckie eased himself in through the opening and let Rowan take his fill of the scene, then said, 'Well done, nipper. We'll get back now. Same way as ye came, face into the ladder.'

'Aye, but up through the lubber's hole?' Gilpin said lazily, his smug confidence spoiling Rowan's exhilaration. 'Marks you out as a Johnny Raw every time.'

Without a word Leckie casually reached up – and launched himself into space.

In one breath-taking move he transferred his weight to his hands gripping a stay, swinging his legs up to cross around it, and in an effortless show slid hand over hand to the deck far below.

The gunner looked up in surprise.

'Er, Mr Bowden said as I'm to make your acquaintance, Mr Darby.'

'You the new reefer?' The voice was a guarded rumble.

'Rowan, sir.'

The forward magazine was eerily lit by outside lamps in glass-panelled sconces that shone a dusky light inside. Darby was at a folding desk, writing up his muster accounts, and close by was the bulk of a seaman Rowan had seen from a distance, catching his attention by his almost feral presence. Oddly, the man wore a knotted red bandanna on his head, piratical fashion, instead of the shapeless Monmouth cap sailors usually favoured.

'So you've made m' acquaintance. That all?'

Stacked in array against the four sides of the magazine

were countless grey serge cartridges, each as big as a figgy duff for a whole mess, a frightful menace of pent-up wrath. Behind them could be glimpsed the dully gleaming copper walls, floors and deckhead of the flame-proof lining.

'Er, I was hoping you'd tell me something of your guns, Mr Darby,' Rowan asked, as respectfully as he could.

'Ha! As if I've time f'r that!' He glowered, not inclined to put down his pencil. Then, relenting, he muttered to the seaman, 'You do it, Toby. Take 'im topsides an' clue 'im in on our barkers, would you, mate?'

The man was sewing cartridges with deft, strong pulls; he put down his work. 'Out!' he commanded Rowan, who scuttled away hastily. 'Up!' He pointed, his glittering dark eyes unreadable.

Obediently Rowan clattered up the steps to the orlop and, without prompting, aft to the main hatchway, then up to the seamen's berth deck.

'No guns here, cuffin,' the seaman said gruffly.

Rowan hurried up the steps to the upper deck, into the grateful sunlight of the waist where a row of guns stretched away on each side, secured by their sea lashings.

The big seaman crossed to the nearest and lightly caressed it, turning to him. 'Stirk, gunner's mate,' he grated. 'Let me interdooce ye to my babies. This'n is your eighteen-pounder. It's the biggest we got an' it's had its fair share of smitin' the enemy.'

'Um, how does it work, Mr Stirk?'

'Why, we puts in powder an' shot, an' fires it off with a gun-lock, is all.' There was hostility now: was it because he was so young to be asking or simply that the man resented being taken away from his work to answer footling questions?

'I mean, how do your gunners get it to load and fire?' He

had some idea – in *Brunswick* his station for quarters was as a powder monkey for the upper deck twelve-pounders but in exercises he'd been more concerned with racing back and forth to the magazine fast enough to satisfy the quarter-gunner. Never had they got around to actually firing live.

Stirk regarded him closely, then launched into a proper explanation, pointing out the staves and worms, quoins and breeching, apron and side-tackles. At the young midshipman's evident interest he warmed and told of the skills of the good gun-captain, the relentless drill that could, by increasing the rate of fire, be the same as having half as many guns again in the fight.

Rowan was suddenly consumed with a need to see the gleaming black iron beasts in raging thunder and asked eagerly, 'Will we be firing an exercise soon, do you think, Mr Stirk?'

'Not while we're with the fleet, younker. They're like to shy in fright as to what we're a-firing at. Don't worry on it – Cap'n Kydd is a right hard horse when it comes t' gun practice.'

They went to the quarterdeck and inspected the nine-pounders there, and to the stubby thirty-two-pounder carronades on each side, with their slides and brutal cup-shaped muzzles.

As they went forward to see a swivel gun Rowan tried to make conversation. 'I'm so lucky to be in *Tyger*,' he said sincerely, 'Captain Kydd being so famous. Do you think that?'

'He's famous f'r what he did, not f'r who he is,' Stirk replied seriously. 'A natural-born seaman as ever I seen, an' a noggin as can fathom what's best in the worst gale o' wind. I'd follow the bugger anywhere, I own I would.'

'Have you known him long?'

Stirk stopped and looked out over the tumbling seas for a long time. 'Aye,' he said in a strangely soft voice. 'And I knows 'im more'n most, I reckon.'

Chapter 13

Kydd towelled down after Tysoe's swift and efficient shave under the skylight, absent-mindedly rubbing his chin. 'I know it's the regular-done thing in other barkies and I've a mind to do it myself.'

'And what's that, Sir Thomas?' Tysoe answered, from the washplace.

'Breakfast,' he answered briefly. It was his practice at sea to invite the off-going officer-of-the-watch to the meal and hear the events of the night and how *Tyger* had behaved herself during the dark hours.

'I'm going to have the mids to breakfast, too – one at a time, o' course. Find out a bit more about 'em.' And today he'd invite the youngest, Rowan.

'Sir Thomas?' came the child-like voice at the door.

'Come in, Mr Rowan. Take a chair. Mr Brice will be along presently.'

The midshipman eased himself in cautiously and took

his place at the table, his eyes dropping in the presence of his captain.

'Coffee? Or is it to be tea?' Kydd offered.

The youngster had been on board only a short time but it seemed he was finding his feet in the rush and tumble of a first-rank man-o'-war, and had even entered the third dimension, aloft.

'Are you on course in your learning, Mr Rowan? A lot to hoist in, and not so much time, I'm persuaded.'

'I am, Sir Thomas,' the lad answered, in a small voice.

'Oh? Then what has Mr Bowden for you this forenoon?'

'Bends 'n' hitches with Able Seaman Leckie, sir.'

'Good. Pay attention to Leckie, he's a taut hand.' Kydd helped himself to the toast and marmalade. 'Are you getting along with the other boys?' It came out too quickly – these were 'young gentlemen', even if they were the same age as mere schoolboys.

'Yes, sir.'

In another prick of regret Kydd reminded himself that if Rowan was being bullied he, as captain, would never hear of it.

His third lieutenant arrived, shaking out his oilskins in the coach. The rain squalls of early morning were a trial for the watch-on-deck at this latitude.

'Good morning to you, Mr Brice,' Kydd said, after the man appeared. 'A good watch?'

Brice sat quickly, his red-rimmed eyes token of the hours of concentration as the ship had plunged on into the blackness where other ships of the fleet also sailed with all the danger of an unexpected encounter ending in a disastrous collision.

'Nothing to worry of, sir,' came the cautious reply, with a curious glance at the awed midshipman.

'Mr Brice,' Kydd said significantly, looking at Rowan out of the corner of his eye. 'Tell me, what do you say is the chief concern of a good officer-of-the-watch?'

'In course, sir. The four Ls.'

'And what are those, pray?' He knew very well – Kydd's first acquaintance with them had been in the Caribbean as a young seaman with the quiet sailing master Jowett, whose octant even now was in his cabin.

'Why, sir, these I take to be lead, latitude, log and longitude. These are before me at all times.'

'Just so,' Kydd said solemnly, trying not to sound sanctimonious. 'And speaking of latitudes, when may we see you at the noon sight, Mr Rowan?'

The head dropped again. 'Sir, I . . . I'm finding it a bit hard. To understand the words in the definitions, I mean.' He looked up in mute pleading.

'Oh, er, yes, and it's a cruel beat to wind'd for those without the lingo.' On impulse, he added, 'I had a good teacher as showed me the main strands first, before the hard words. When you're finished with Leckie, come down and I'll give you a starter on 'em.'

Damn it, but those *were* Persephone's eyes – and their effect was continuing to awaken deep feelings.

Chapter 14

Tyger met the day as always with a brisk holystoning of the pristine decks, followed by a stout burgoo breakfast, then turned to for a forenoon watch of exercise at the guns. But this day turned out differently.

A pinnace appeared, heading purposefully for them. A single officer was in the sternsheets and when the boat had hooked on he came in over the bulwarks, punctiliously doffing his hat and reporting to Kydd. 'Sir Thomas? Lieutenant Cartwright and I'm bid by Admiral Saumarez to desire you to prepare for sea this hour.'

'My orders?'

'Ah, these are being readied and will be dispatched to you shortly.'

This was irregular but not unusual for a frigate and, with a quickening of his pulse, Kydd recognised the preliminaries to some swift dash to adventure.

The officer had a pleasant manner and showed no pressing inclination to leave so, finding a quiet corner of the quarterdeck,

Kydd asked him casually, 'You know what's in the wind, then?'

'Well, it's all a bit curious,' Cartwright drawled. 'Not to say a puzzler.'

'What is?' Kydd said, hiding his impatience.

'Sir Thomas, you were at Copenhagen for the recent complications?'

'I was.'

'When the Danish Navy ceased to exist, everything that swam was carried off to England, leaving nary a thing under sail to the Danes down to their last admiral's barge.'

'Yes, I saw it.'

'Then, sir, I'm desolated to have to tell you that the job was botched.'

'What the devil do you mean?'

'You quite overlooked a powerful 74 skulking in Kristiansand harbour in Norway.'

So, would it be a cutting-out expedition against a ship-of-the-line? A bloody affair, if that was the case, but why all the haste?

'You said a puzzler?'

'I did, Sir Thomas. A fine ship – *Prinds Christian Frederik*, commanded by one Carl Jessen, a veteran of the Caribbean against us there. And her premier, this is none other than Peter Willemoes, a hero of theirs at the first Copenhagen, facing Nelson himself.'

'Damn it, sir, what is this to me?'

'She's sailed.'

'What the devil . . .?'

'We've intelligence from the Swedes that she's been sighted leaving harbour and heading south with all speed.'

'This way?'

'Safely to seaward around our fleet. And directly towards the Sound.'

'Then why haven't our own sail-o'-the-line put to sea after the rascal?'

'General Moore is in some sort of a tizz with the Swedes and won't disembark his troops. Admiral Saumarez declares he can't spare any of his ships of size until the expedition is established ashore, so . . .'

'Are you telling me that a single frigate is being ordered to—'

'No, Sir Thomas.' The lieutenant straightened, realising that Kydd was not to be baited further. 'There are two 64s joining as reinforcement, *Stately* and *Nassau*. They're being dispatched south after them. You're to accompany, flag in *Stately*, Captain Parker.'

'And this is your puzzler?'

'No, sir. I'm rather thinking it passing strange that the Danes are risking their only precious battleship to do what seems only to be a descent on our trade shipping into the Baltic.'

'Rather than tying up the fleet in watching it. Yes, an odd thing, I'll grant. Well, Lieutenant, you'll be wanting to get back?'

It was all around the ship in a trice.

In the midshipmen's berth a wide-eyed Rowan heard Teague give voice to his fears. 'Neb, what's it like? I mean, when you sights the enemy and—'

Gilpin leaned back and regarded them disdainfully. 'Listen close, Tilly – and you, Kit. I'm older, I've smelt powder so I knows the griff. Like when we chased a whole convoy with only a pawky sloop lying off, rare do's that.' He rubbed his chin in reminiscence. 'It's when you sees 'em lifting over the horizon, guns run out an' all, and coming at you like a dog after a rat that you knows in your gut it might not turn out well.'

'What do you do then, Neb?' Teague whispered.

'Why, there's only one thing you can do.'

'What's that?'

Gilpin snapped forward with a harsh glare. 'Your duty! Stand afore the enemy, take the worst they can do – and ask for more!'

White-faced, Rowan ventured, 'Then you're not . . . scared, as who should say?'

'Scared?' he said scornfully. 'What word's that, then?' Gilpin continued, 'And when you sees Tom Cutlass on the quarter-deck, cool as you please, you worry more you'll fail him as anything the Frogs can do. When you've been in battle as much as me, you'll understand.'

Rowan heard the words with unease. Gilpin was much older and must have sailed with *Tyger* into countless battles. Would he himself be able to stand up in the face of an evil enemy like that? He hadn't even heard a gun go off, let alone been in any fighting. What if the enemy came right up and made to board them? 'Repel boarders!' He'd seen it at the theatre but in real life . . . With his little dirk against a towering French officer who'd singled him out and . . .

He gulped and tried to smother the hot images.

Chapter 15

Tyger lay at short-stay in readiness and her orders were passed up by a dispatch cutter within the hour.

It was much as Cartwright had said. A single objective: to seek, find, burn and destroy that Dane. But it implied that *Tyger* would be sent off in a fast dash south to interpose herself between the 74 and the haven of the Copenhagen defences until the slower 64s could come up and join battle.

This was a chilling prospect. No frigate could contemplate taking on a ship-of-the-line except in extreme circumstances. With double the guns, and these considerably larger in bore, it would rapidly turn into a scene of carnage unless aid came quickly. How long should he suffer, throwing himself back and forth across the bows of the battleship, waiting for the slow 64s to come up?

It had been done: Pellew in the frigate *Indefatigable* in the legendary action that had seen the destruction of the 74 *Droits de l'Homme* in Audierne Bay in a gale – but he'd had *Amazon* with him. And Kydd had no illusions about the

83

tenacity of the Danish, or their motivation after the humiliation of Copenhagen.

They got under way without delay; the rendezvous was given for the south-west and *Tyger* stretched out nobly to her fate, whatever that was to be.

Kydd hadn't yet briefed his officers but into his consciousness stole a new consideration. He'd long ago come to terms with the imperatives of combat: the primacy of cold rationality over hot blood-lust, the iron control over fear and the ruthless suppression of instincts of survival. Now for the first time there was an additional factor in the equation, one that threatened to overturn those tried and true responses.

As battle was joined she would be there with him. She, whom he adored more than life itself and who, he knew, bore him such love in return. When the time came, would he flinch from giving the orders to lay alongside the adversary, to fling himself at the foe with no thought for himself? Or with an enemy at the point of his sword, would her image rise before him, causing a fatal hesitation, a faltering?

There was no way to foretell. Only in the crucible of battle would he discover it.

In the late afternoon, well into the Kattegat, the main passage between Denmark and Sweden before it narrowed into the Sound, a cry from the masthead announced a successful rendezvous.

The two 64s were an odd pair: *Nassau* had been Danish, captured at the first battle of Copenhagen, her lines stumpier to take the Baltic seas more kindly. Although rated as a 64 she mounted only fifty guns under the British flag. *Stately* was old and slow, built as far back as the American war, a troopship, hurriedly fitted out as a man-o'-war for this Northern Expedition.

These to take on a 74? This was going to be a serious business, mused Kydd, as *Tyger* slipped into position to leeward of *Stately*, her neat motions so contrasting with the ponderous heave of the other.

He raised his speaking trumpet to the figures on her quarterdeck and hailed. 'Joining in obedience to orders, sir. What are your instructions?'

A thin voice came back faintly against the swash of the seas as they lay hove to together. 'It is imperative this vessel is found and put down. All else is inferior to this objective. Do you understand me?'

'I do, sir.'

'I have *Lynx* sloop in addition. I will keep her with me as I enter the Sound in search. You will not enter. Instead you shall cruise with *Falcon* sloop to the northward of Sjælland and into the Great Belt. In the event you come upon the *Prinds* you will dispatch *Falcon* to alert me, taking all measures necessary to delay and hamper her movements until I arrive. Clear?'

'Yes, sir.'

So Parker was taking the more direct route into the Sound, presumably in the expectation he would converge on the battleship somewhere off Copenhagen. This meant *Tyger* would not be faced with a wild fight to bar the big 74 from entering.

But there was an even chance that the canny Danish captain would take advantage of his local knowledge to go by the longer route, out of sight via the Great Belt, and if that happened in those confined waters, *Tyger* would be in a perilous position.

Now, her yards braced around, *Stately* got under way without further ado.

Damn this General Moore, Kydd cursed. But for his peacocking they'd have with them at least another pair of first-rank men-o'-war and frigates to match. As it was, there would be a close-fought and bloody action where there should have been a clean and overwhelming crushing.

Tyger paid off to leeward and took up on a broader tack for the Sjælland coast in the gathering dusk, preparing for the coming encounter.

Chapter 16

Night drew in. It was calm and tranquil but, with the moonless dark, few conditions were worse in approaching a low sea-coast at night. Sailors took a brisk wind as welcome, for a line of startling white breakers was fair warning of a nearby shoreline and the same winds were useful in hauling off quickly. Now there was nothing but clamping gloom and from the deck all that could be seen was an impenetrable blackness with an occasional white wave lop flicking into existence and disappearing as quickly.

'Shorten sail, sir?' queried the first lieutenant.

'No need, Mr Bray. Ease to starboard a point and we'll crack on.'

That brought frowns of apprehension but few dared object and, under full sail, *Tyger* sped on into the night on a direct course for the Danish shore.

'Sir, I really—'

'Keep on, if you please.'

Kydd knew there was really no danger, and before midnight, first one, then several points of light glimmered into existence, spreading miles up and down the coast, an unmissable show.

Bowden caught on first. 'Ah. Of course – the Bight, I should have smoked it!

'Where all the merchant vessels go to anchor who mean to take passage through the Sound but must remain for a fair wind. It's not foul for the south so they must be waiting for our Baltic Fleet to take 'em through.'

Even in the dim light of the binnacle Kydd could catch the man's admiring look and he smiled to himself. 'Yes, Mr Bowden, and I shall have intelligence from them.' The scattered points of light came from the cabins and stern windows of anchored ships and Kydd could take his pick.

Bowden was boarding officer and returned in a short time. 'They've been here these four days and have seen no ship-of-the-line of any kind.'

Kydd nodded his thanks. It only meant that the 74 had not passed this way, not proof that it had taken the other route into the Sound. The search must go on.

It would be much more difficult now. They had reached the north coast of Sjælland as per orders. From here on they must turn west to edge along the coastline, knowing that at any time – around the next point or deep into a bay – they could be flushing out a dangerous opponent and be forced into a critical decision.

There was no point in continuing in the darkness: he was in position, and could make the sweep along the forty-odd miles to the entrance of the Great Belt in a morning; to overlook the menace they were all seeking was out of the question.

At first light they secured for sea and, with the brig-sloop *Falcon* dutifully taking post astern, they slipped away from the scores of huddled merchant ships to begin their search.

Lookouts in the tops and crosstrees scanned ahead and to the low, smooth coastline, splotched with the dark green of vegetation and an occasional settlement or windmill.

Quite soon the sandy hillock of Gilbjerg Head came into view, the chart importantly noting that, as the northernmost point of Sjælland, it marked the boundary between the Sound and the outer Kattegat. It was the first substantial land with height sufficient to hide a large man-o'-war on the other side. If the 74 was beyond it, guns would be in play in a very short time.

Kydd couldn't take the risk. 'To quarters, Mr Bray.'

Steadily, with practised movements, *Tyger* cleared for action.

The ship quietened as they neared the cliffs, with the light breeze fair on the beam and every man at his station. Kydd paced slowly, Dillon at his side, notebook in hand, a study of indifference.

'Sir, purely out of interest, if the beast be lying in wait beyond, what will be your motions?' he enquired.

'Should he be at anchor, I shall lie off while *Falcon* brings up our big brothers, in course.'

'And if at liberty to sail?'

'Why, then . . .' This would be the moment when life and death hung in the balance, depending on his decisions in the face of the enemy. Kydd paused, then continued strongly, 'If the enemy is a-sail, we shall do all we can to delay or disable him.' By manoeuvre, stratagem and cold-blooded courage in closing with a battleship.

They swept around the point but beyond it was only the sandy shoreline, falling away to the south-west in an unbroken line. Nowhere the shocking sight of a ship-of-the-line.

'Sir, stand down from quarters?' Bray asked. Balked of

action he looked crestfallen. Custom dictated that after a famous battle a first lieutenant stood to get his own ship.

'No, we've a deal of searching still to do – the brute could be anywhere. Do stand down the men at the guns for now.' In his bones Kydd had the uncanny feeling that in a short time there would be a reckoning.

The shoreline was featureless, low and sandy for miles, but the chart showed a large inland stretch of water not so far ahead, marked as Isefjord. The hydrographicals with Keats the previous year had not had time to survey it but at six or seven miles across inside, if there were depth of water, it was an obvious haven for the big ship.

Well before noon they were up with the mile or so gap in the endless tedium of vegetation-topped dunes and were looking into Isefjord. Kydd's heart sank – it was a broad stretch of inland water that extended way beyond any sighting from the masthead. The Dane could be anywhere within.

Should he send *Falcon* in? How long would it take to cover the area? If they flushed it out, was this any place to clash in battle with such an adversary? The questions hammered at him.

Then he had it. If this same entrance did not have depth of water enough for a ship-of-the-line, without any doubt it could not be anywhere inside.

'State o' tide, Mr Joyce.'

'Not t' worry of in these parts, sir.' Therefore no allowance needed for high or low water.

'Mr Brice, Mr Bowden. Take a good man with a hand lead and I'll have soundings out from each side to midway as soon as you may.'

The boats put off and stroked strongly inshore on their

mission and sensibly began work with the lead where the water deepened towards the middle of the entrance.

The two warships hove to were attracting attention, however. There was a small hamlet on one side with a prominent church and windmill, and on the foreshore figures were gathering.

'Ha! They's sore puzzled what we're doing,' chuckled the master.

It would be a dismaying sight – out of the blue two enemy warships appear to launch boats, then engage in menacing and baffling activity close to their homes.

The boats were back quickly, reporting no depths beyond three fathoms – so *Prinds* could not be anywhere in Isefjord.

The last stretch of coast before the turn south into the Great Belt was going to be the worst.

The island of Sjælland came to an end in a slender finger of land hooking around in a wicked finality at the notorious Sjællands rcf. In a series of invisible rock ledges and treacherous sand shoals it extended more than five miles out into the open waters of the Kattegat – and the Danes had removed the light at its tip.

To keep in with the shore in search would be hazardous in the extreme, but Kydd spotted that the charts revealed just one little fishing harbour of note, Havnebyen, in its entire length, and thus no hiding place would be possible until the swing down into the Great Belt, so *Tyger* was free to give the reef a wide berth.

In the early afternoon, with men still at quarters, the helm went over and, with a gentle northerly breeze, they entered the Great Belt proper.

This was well surveyed by now, and it wasn't the first time *Tyger* had been through. But the detailed charting only served to throw up the uncountable number of islands and headlands, any one of which could be concealing the 74.

Kydd took stock. The big ship was presumably on its way to the other end of the Sound, then to the south part of Sweden, where at the choke-point of shipping entering the Baltic it would set about the slaughter of the trading fleet. It was consequently not interested in hiding or delaying its arrival there, so if *Tyger* did not overhaul it in the Belt, he could be certain it had made passage to the open sea and would then be a concern for the 64s.

He ordered course to be set for mid-channel and the frigate drove on under full sail, alert for the sudden cry of discovery at any moment. On each side islets and shoals sprawled, their names alien and incomprehensible, Gniben, Samsoe, Vollerup, some with a scattering of red houses and a small, austere church. One or two fishing boats dared the inshore waters but in the main it was a passing series of endless low islands in an ominous placid grey-blue sea.

By mid-afternoon they were approaching the middle section of the Great Belt and still no sign of the battleship. A long, sinuous peninsula lay across their path and *Tyger* eased to starboard to round it – and directly ahead, at less than a mile distant, a full-rigged ship was under comfortable sail.

In an instant Kydd had his glass up – but this was no 74. In a surge of relief he realised he was looking at *Sybille*, one of Keats's frigates of the previous year, part of the squadron patrolling the Belt, evidently still on station.

That would be Jonas Upton in command, older than Kydd

but junior to him on the captain's list. He gave orders that had *Tyger* heave to, secure from quarters and a signal made requiring Upton to report on board.

'Sir Thomas, I hadn't heard you're back with us,' he began, seemingly put out by Kydd's abrupt summons.

Kydd lost no time in setting out the situation. 'So you haven't sighted a Danish 74.'

'I didn't know such still existed.'

With relief, Kydd accepted that, with *Tyger* coming from the north, *Sybille* the south, between them they would have seen *Prinds* if it'd been in the Belt. They hadn't and therefore it must have gone the other way.

There would be no desperate delaying action.

Night was not far off but there was no great haste that demanded he hazarded his ship in the maze of skerries and sandbars about Sjælland reef in the darkness.

'I shall anchor until morning, Jonas. I should be glad of your company at dinner.'

The man looked mollified. 'If I should be so bold, Sir Thomas – this is the southern end of my patrol and marks the northern point of *Tribune*'s.' Hesitating, he went on, 'Sir, we're accustomed to . . .'

'Then we shall be a threesome. At seven?' Kydd would not be the one to set aside the comfortable practice of these frigate captains chained to the monotony of patrol and finding ways to deal with it. And with *Tribune*'s Saunders junior by a year as well he could afford to be magnanimous.

Tribune appeared later, under lazy topsails, effortlessly taking advantage of the swift currents to make progress and no doubt startled to see two frigates at anchor.

The captains were piped aboard, the men cheerfully at

their grog below. In the great cabin Tysoe saw to the table silver and the officers' wine, and a hearty evening promised.

The two had been on station since the ice had retreated, their continuing task, as with the other three around the island, preventing, by their very presence, any communication or reinforcement of Sjælland. In their lonely vigil they'd had no recent word of developments and were grateful to hear of them along with any news Kydd could tell them about England and home.

Not long into the first remove the conviviality was abruptly cut short.

Muffled cries from on deck stilled their conversation and froze the motion of their glasses. Their eyes met in apprehension.

An indistinct order roared out. Running feet were followed by the clatter of steps on the after hatchway and a breathless figure appeared at the cabin door. 'Respects from Mr Brice an' the Dansker's sighted above the point!'

With an appalling crash of crockery all three shot to their feet and bolted for the upper deck.

In the gathering dusk above the Røsnæs peninsula they saw the unquestionable top-hamper of a ship-of-the-line slowly moving along and about to appear in full view before them.

They were caught in the worst possible situation: they could either man the guns or win the anchor, not both – and well before either, the 74 would be on them.

As if mesmerised they saw the big ship pass beyond the wooded tip of the point and burst into sight, a chilling menace in the last of the light.

Rowan was at his place by the deserted helm as part of the watch-on-deck at relaxed readiness. In one moment the seamen were idly dismissing the Dane as a shab, frightened of a single frigate, and the next it was there before their eyes, soon to fall on them with death and destruction . . . a terrifying reality, which he must now face like a man. His heart thudded painfully.

'To quarters, Mr Bray,' Kydd blurted.

From *Sibylle* and *Tribune* came an answering thunder of drums, the two stranded captains shouting maniacally for their boats.

It was the Danish 74 right enough, and the question now was, how would the destruction begin?

The answer was not what Kydd expected.

Trimming sails, the battleship put over its helm and came into the wind, hanging there as if considering its next move.

And then an utter surprise. Squarely across the mid-point of the channel *Prinds* struck sail and anchored.

Open-mouthed in astonishment, Upton gasped, 'He's moon-struck! Why doesn't he go at us before—'

In a gust of relief, Kydd answered him. 'Not so, Jonas. Can't you see? He doesn't care for a fight in the darkness among these shoals and reefs. He'll wait for daybreak because he knows we won't run.'

For the moment it was a stalemate. There would be no night action in these treacherous waters, and a cutting-out expedition against an alerted battleship was an absurd notion. *Falcon* had already been sent flying off with the news. What more could they do?

'So, gentlemen. We'll stand down from quarters and wait for the morning. I see no reason why we shouldn't finish our dinner.'

The meal resumed, the enemy – no less than a full-sized ship-of-the-line – anchored peacefully over in the shadows beyond the point, manned by sailors who were sworn to destroy them, no doubt sitting down to dinner in much the same way.

Down on the mess-deck of *Tyger*, there would be similar thoughts but expressed more pithily, and as well some would be weighing their chances against such odds.

As the cloth was drawn Upton, with an appreciative sip at Kydd's fine brandy, murmured, 'Should be interesting times come daybreak.'

'Will he wait for full light before he makes his move, do you think?' Saunders wondered, idly twiddling his glass.

'It's what happens when he does that's my curiosity,' Upton said, with a sideways glance at Kydd. 'Three on one, should be a stout milling match, b' God.'

Kydd came back, 'I'd not take it as a holiday, any number of frigates facing a sail-o'-the-line. Why do you think we're kept out of the line in a general engagement? If they get in a single broadside from those great guns it'll finish us.'

Upton put down his glass and glowered. 'The three of us? One raking by turns while the others are entertaining with manoeuvres or some such. That's what'll give us our famous victory!'

Saunders gave a twisted smile. 'No signals, we just go at him – like Nelson.'

The talk went on, bold and aggressive.

Kydd needed to take the air. Excusing himself, he reached the upper deck with its anonymity in the darkness and cool night breeze. He was senior – all decisions were his and his alone. In the morning men would go to their deaths because of them. His fellow captains were obviously mystified as to why he hadn't been more bloodthirsty or loud in an urging to battle. Was he becoming soft now that he was married?

He gazed out at the larger blackness in the night, knowing that as first light began to steal in, he had to be ready with a plan and orders.

An image came to him of Persephone, that unbearably tender special look that was for him alone, but extraordinarily, in the same moment, came resolution.

If he wavered, for any reason stepping back from the field of trial, as daughter of an admiral she would think less of him, be disillusioned, disappointed in him as the man she had thought him. He would have failed her and therefore be undeserving of her.

She expected him to do his duty – and that was what he would do.

In a wash of relief he saw that he could continue his dedication to the sea service and make decisions that were based solely on the martial elements before him. The only difference now was that after the fires of combat he would be cherishing the vision of returning to her, head held high, the conquering hero.

If the fortunes of war dictated otherwise, so be it. That had always been the warrior's lot and always would be, and that, too, she would understand.

He drew a deep breath. Whatever he decided, she was giving him the strength and will to see it through.

Almost immediately his mind began to work. The presenting problem: there was no possible end but piecemeal destruction if they took on a ship-of-the-line in these restricted waters. Should they refuse battle, retreat? In England it would be seen by the public as cowardly, given they outnumbered the enemy three to one. This was not an argument: men's lives were more important. Only the objective was sacred.

A glimmering of something started to coalesce, triggered by his mulling over what Jessen would likely do next. And that depended on what the Dane's objectives were. A veteran captain, widely experienced, he would be reaching for his own higher purpose.

What were his orders? If these included the preservation of the Danes' only major warship whatever the provocation – a reasonable assumption – they were in no danger. But if that was so, why had he anchored? The only possible reason would be to open hostilities at daybreak.

Just why had the big ship been sent at such hazard in the first place?

The bigger picture: the Swedish as the only British ally. If they were knocked out of the war there would be incalculable consequences, but if this were to be brought about, it had to be before the Baltic Fleet of Saumarez came on the scene. Yes! Something was most certainly afoot for the Danes to risk this, their most valuable asset.

Was it coincidence that *Prinds* was taking the Great Belt route rather than the more direct Sound? But, if so, it would know it had to deal with the frigates on watch so why . . . That was it! His head cleared. He knew the purpose now – and it threw everything into a different perspective.

Keats's frigates were there for a very good and effective reason: to stop the movement of troops and munitions to the main island of Sjælland, which until now they'd handsomely achieved. But if Bernadotte could flood the island with his army, they would then be looking directly across at Sweden's flat coastline no more than ten miles distant. Victory would be theirs in an hour's sail.

Prinds had been sent on a mission – not to disrupt trade but with the far higher aim of luring the frigates away while the tide of war quickly crossed from Fyn to Sjælland.

Kydd knew in his bones he was right. And now the stakes had immeasurably increased: well before any of the Baltic Fleet could arrive to intervene, it would all be over. Only he could stop it happening.

He returned to the great cabin. 'Well, gentlemen, what do you think of my brandy?' He chuckled, resuming his chair.

They looked at him, bewildered.

'As I wish you to raise your glass to our success of tomorrow.' Kydd leaned back expansively. 'I've made my dispositions, and I will brook no argument.'

He waited until they had given a troubled acknowledgement.

'My orders are simple, and they are this: that tomorrow you will both return to your usual patrol. That is all.'

There was an incredulous gasp, and both broke into loud protestation. Kydd held up his hands. 'No, this will not do. I'm issuing written orders to that effect, which you will disobey at your peril.'

'We're entitled to an explanation, I believe,' came Upton's surly response.

His seniority was junior to Kydd's by months only – and probably he had the notion that Kydd wanted the battle all to himself. This was a flattering perception of his powers but he would tell them the full story.

He outlined his reasoning: that it would need a bait as potent as a ship-of-the-line to draw away all the frigates and the Danes had provided it.

'Sir, have you any proof of this plan o' theirs? I say we've sighted a Danish sail-o'-the-line and it's our bounden duty to settle with him before he gets in among our trade.'

'I have proof,' Kydd said mildly.

'Being?'

'At dawn you will see *Prinds* win its anchor – and then it'll sail north, back into the Kattegat.'

Chapter 17

In the cold pre-dawn dark Kydd stood watching as preparations were made for unmooring and fighting. The men worked silently, their movements concentrated and deliberate. He knew the signs and could tell that they realised what was being asked of them but there was no hanging back. For himself there was an additional tension: was he right in his assumption?

By imperceptible degrees a tentative light stole over the scene, the distant dark bulk of the battleship taking on clarity, colour. It was definitely making ready for sea.

Kydd sniffed the wind. A gentle north-easterly. Fine for a quick passage south – but chancy for any return north and too light for his liking. If he'd guessed correctly Captain Jessen's intent would be to lure the three frigates north and out into the open water of the Kattegat – but only one would follow: *Tyger* must trail the menace closely to see where it was headed and, if necessary, bring it to a delaying action.

While their anchor was hove in, he fixed his gaze on the Danish ship with a fierce intensity. Before it could trip its hook, sails and rigging had to be braced around to catch the wind in the right manner to take up its intended course – smoothly to lay over and away. This would be a give-away of that direction.

Prinds and the British frigates were tide-rode, facing south, stemming the strong current. If Jessen was going on to bring them to battle he need do no more than set sail and advance. But if Kydd was right, it would be sail aft that was spread to swing the ship around the pinioning anchor until facing the other way before headsails were thrown out to bring the vessel evenly on to the starboard tack, close-hauled and away.

And there it was! The big driver aft was hoisted and hauled to the wind, the mizzen topsail loosed with seaman-like skill and stay-sails soared up.

He was right! Kydd saw the big ship swing and, at just the right moment, her anchor emerge in a swash of white. She paid off to larboard and, under topsails, made off to the north and the Kattegat.

In exactly the same sequence Kydd brought *Tyger* around and, less than a mile behind, she followed, *Sybille* and *Tribune* returning to resume their patrol.

The breeze was frustratingly light but *Prinds* seemed in no hurry, gliding through the glittering waters of the morning, with her distinctive swallow-tailed *orlogsflag* proudly at the main and her rows of gun-ports with the black muzzles of her guns visible, token of her battle readiness. If she was disappointed that she was luring only one frigate away there was no sign of it.

The Rosnæs peninsula to starboard, the Stavnsfjord to larboard, the hours passed.

Now with Sejerø abeam they were only a dozen miles

from the open water, and once sea-room was reached, Jessen would turn on his pursuer. Probably his original plan was to take on all three frigates where space to wheel and charge was vital.

The wicked hooked tongue of Sjælland Odde was way over to starboard, its hidden reef extending underwater for miles. Kydd had ordered the chart to be brought up with a table, and as he followed their track, it told of a maze of sub-sea horrors from which the prudent mariner was advised to lay well off.

But *Prinds*, with its local knowledge, was confidently making more to larboard and Kydd had no other option than to do likewise. Yet if this course was followed for long—

With preternaturally tuned senses, he caught a very slight judder through the timbers of the deck and moments later the bow fell off course with a cry of alarm from the helmsman. Kydd raced to the side as the ship slowed, dreading what he'd see – and there was the fearful sight of clouds of particles boiling up from a sand-bank.

This was the very worst: to run aground in the presence of an enemy. Heart pounding, he roared orders to clew up the sails to take the strain off the masts.

There was no clue how the bank was oriented as the calm seas left no distinguishing ripples but one thing was sure – if the 74 caught sight of their predicament their future would be brutal and short.

'Mr Joyce – into the jolly boat with a leadline. Tell me how she lies.'

White-faced, the master started to sound along the length of the ship to build a picture of their plight.

But then ahead Kydd saw *Prinds* had altered its perspective, the three masts opening up as it wore about – their situation had been seen!

It could only be the end for *Tyger,* lying helpless: the bigger ship would choose an approach that avoided her guns and enabled it to destroy the frigate with a pitiless raking down her length.

Joyce knew what was looming but he kept up his steady bellow of depths and soon it became clear to Kydd that while *Tyger* was gripped all along her larboard side, there were soundings enough to starboard.

'Mr Bray! All hands to cast off all guns to larboard and move 'em to the other side. Now!'

Each eighteen-pounder, with its truck and gear, some two tons of weight, would create a heel to starboard and, even if it were by inches, it would free the ship for forward movement. It was their only chance – but it would leave them helpless.

With a roar the boatswain leaped into action, bullying gun-crews and a growing crowd of seamen, sweating and fighting with the iron beasts in the fearsome toil of shifting the guns one after the other across the deck.

Prinds was wearing ship around the wind, a slower but surer means to stay about, and a measure of Jessen's confidence. The end was now certain.

By eye Kydd could see the course he was taking to bring destruction to *Tyger.* With the wind large it seemed it was to be bow to bow until point-blank range, in the perfect confidence that at that angle *Tyger* could not fire a single gun in her defence. At the last minute the 74 would yaw and open with her full broadside, leaving a shattered, smoking hulk running with the blood of her crew.

Kydd sensed Persephone with him. A steady warmth of

presence, of understanding, even as he faced his fate in the knowledge that he had done all he could in obedience to his loyalty to Crown and country.

Then he felt a movement, a sudden canting to starboard. Was it . . .?

Prinds kept on, its heading precise and deadly, as he'd expect from one of Jessen's experience.

A definite shifting – and then a relieved wallow. They were free – but it was too late. Nothing they could do now would change the onrushing charge of the big ship. He braced himself for the onslaught, mind freezing in anticipation of the killing blast – but incredibly, wonderfully, it didn't happen.

The 74 was yawing, turning, but there was no obliterating broadside, the ship continued until it was right around, close-hauled and heading northward again.

It didn't have any meaning.

An incredulous shout came from forward. In the distance, two ships were cautiously finding their way around the far extremity of Sjælland Reef and, Heaven be praised, they were quite unmistakably *Stately* and *Nassau*, sought out and summoned by the faithful *Falcon*.

The Danish 74, it seemed, was not going to waste its broadside on *Tyger* with greater prizes in the picture, and it steadied on a closing course for the 64s.

'Get those guns back in place!' Kydd roared. This was an action between battleships, but there had to be a part they could play, even if it wasn't immediately plain.

Under way again, he followed in the wake of the 74, ready for any move.

It came well before the Dane closed with its two adversaries.

With the distant British ships wary of the shoals and beyond the last of the reef, *Prinds* executed a smart turn to starboard, tacking about and insanely making straight for the hidden rocks and shoals of Sjælland Reef.

In a leap of insight, Kydd saw why: Jessen didn't want to tangle with the 64s – even if he were only damaged in the encounter it would put paid to his vital mission. Instead he seemed to know a safe channel through the middle of the reef, which would allow him to make for the shelter of the guns of Fortress Kronborg, back along this north coast, there to wait until the British gave up and left.

Kydd saw that *Tyger* now had her purpose. He would shadow the 74 closely, keeping to the shoreward of it.

This would have two vital results: the Dane must keep clear of *Tyger*'s guns for fear of a chance crippling hit, and this would force her to seaward towards the 64s. On the other hand, its very presence inshore would give confidence to *Stately* and her consort that there was depth enough to manoeuvre and grapple.

It would take seamanship of the highest order for he must go into the reef with *Prinds* without charts or knowledge of the deadly ground.

He had one priceless advantage: once in the brig-sloop *Teazer* he'd served in the Channel Islands, probably the worst rock-and-reef-strewn sea area of them all, made more terrible by the greatest tides found anywhere. He knew the sea-lore he'd gained in those waters was what was needed now and he would damn well take his ship through.

'We follow him,' he snapped at the group at the conn.

'But, sir—'

There was only one practical way he could do it. Throwing aside his coat and hat, he swung into the fore-shrouds and mounted steadily. In the fore-top he took in the scene. The square sails were all behind him, only the soaring head-sails in front end on, giving a fine view of the sea ahead.

With a seaman in either shroud below, in sight of both him and the wheel, he was ready.

A mile or so ahead *Prinds* was making for a particular location – he could tell by its slight alterations of course as the wheel was aligned more finely. Taking out his pocket glass he concentrated on the sea surface either side of it.

The wind was fluky but had picked up a little and now there was sufficient liveliness to show lines of darker wave hollows and therefore the betraying trend of the currents beneath. He widened his view: there was a definite curving conformity to her larboard where seas were crowding through an unseen cleft, and on the other side there was a suspiciously glassy-smooth expanse, which told of an extensive ridging of the sub-sea rocks.

Light winds made progress trying, hours of sailing passing uneventfully. No doubt Jessen wouldn't mind; if it came on to night, all the better for him to escape in the darkness – except that *Tyger* would be at his heels.

Warily, the 64s kept well clear, Parker probably wondering at the foolish stubbornness that had *Tyger* plunging after the 74 into such danger.

Tyger reached the reef. The lengthening shadows of evening made it even clearer: the gyres where invisible sea-bottom hollows lay not so far below, the fan-shaped rush of waters over a rock, the line of confusion above a sub-sea cliff – and, as well, the regular advance of waves on a broad front, which told of deep water.

Kydd's crisp arm signals were relayed to the wheel and, with increasing confidence, the frigate won through and into the sweeping bay of Sjællands Odde beyond, with, less than a mile ahead, *Prinds* standing for the far headland and escape.

Kydd returned to the deck in the knowledge that very soon he would be forced into another decision: whether or not to throw his ship at the 74 in a desperate attempt to delay its retreat.

But by this the 64s had been spared the need of rounding Sjælland Reef and, with the winds now on their quarter, made good speed compared to *Prinds* hard by the wind, and began converging. It was a race – not between ships, but to join action before darkness gave the bigger ship the chance to get away.

Yard by yard the ships plunged on, *Tyger* slowly closing on the stern of the ship-of-the-line to be in position for the final act – when the big ships would be locked together in the striving of mortal combat.

In that hour the fortunes of war turned decisively against the cool and intelligent Jessen. The light winds chose that moment to falter and die, then picked up again, but now veered more to the east, heading *Prinds*. There was now no possibility the unhandy ship-of-the-line could weather the headland on this board.

Kydd could only admire the swift decision that had *Prinds* wheeling about on the other tack, clawing directly out to sea to make the necessary offing – and into the path of the oncoming 64s. At the last possible minute he fell back on his old tack for the headland, but things had now changed.

The wind was dropping to little more than a whisper and the big 74 slowed to a crawl. *Tyger* was close enough that even when darkness fell the faster frigate could stay with him and, fatally for the Dane, could indicate to Parker his location at any time. Darkness could not save him now.

As the day ended and a dusky twilight gave way to gathering darkness Kydd saw how the battle would develop. *Stately* and *Nassau* began to diverge as they approached *Prinds*, now pinned against the shoreline. It was obvious Parker was aiming to take the 74 on both sides, a simple smashing match between line-of-battle ships, and this would be no place for a frigate.

Darkness lay over the scene like a cloak and Kydd had a vital part to play.

'We'll have a blue light both fore and aft. Lay us off her quarter and stay there.'

Two lights. Parker would know what it meant: the higher aft, the lower forward would be a direct pointer at *Prinds*. If the distance between foreshortened, it meant that the 74 was changing course or putting about and he would be warned accordingly.

The dark bulk of *Prinds* showed ahead but by now out to sea Parker's invisible ships would be making for *Tyger*'s lights. It would be galling for Jessen – would he lose patience and turn on the betraying frigate?

They were running along the low shoreline almost invisible in the gloom. The charts gave good bottom this side of the reef, and Kydd could rely on keeping in just a couple of cables offshore to enable him to see the stolid blackness of the land against the gleam of the sea. And if ever—

A livid gun-flash lit the sky and a sullen boom rolled across the water. A ranging shot – the two sides were in contact.

More, and these from different sides. Parker had his disposition, thanks to Kydd's initiative.

'Stand down the lights!' he bawled, their duty done.

The firing quickly became furious, the stabbing flash of guns illuminating the sea and the ships in a fiendish glare, with a rolling bass thunder that could be felt in the stomach.

It grew rapidly savage, prolonged, details of the combat now and then hidden in swelling clouds of red-hued gun-smoke.

Mr Midshipman Rowan, a messenger by the side of the first lieutenant, was transfixed for long moments. Guns! These were not only the first great guns he'd heard in his life but he was in the middle of a real battle, one which could sway either way. *Tyger* was remaining silent in the outer darkness and he could hear clearly the sounds of the furious contest. To his surprise, the guns didn't give a colossal *bang* but much more a heavy *blam*, which was felt as much as heard.

In the dark, leaping gun-flash illuminated the ships in stark silhouette, roils of smoke hiding detail, and on its underside redly reflected the firing, while the combat arena was a calm black sea that mirrored the savagery above, a grand and fearful sight.

But locked in a merciless duel the knot of ships were unknowingly in a current drift to the shore. As if in a nightmare Kydd saw an end to the battle – all three helpless wrecks on the strand.

'Quickly, damn you – as before, but rig red lights!'

He could make out the shore but, blinded by gun-flash, the others couldn't – yet they would see his flaring marks at the limits of depth.

The lights spluttered to life. *Tyger* came to precisely the point where she was between the raging fight and the shore, where she lay, a warning to all.

For an hour, more, the ships hammered into each other in the night, the stink of the gun-smoke raw on the night air.

It was impossible to tell which way the battle was going. From reflected glare Kydd saw that all had their masts still but the fury of the contest would without doubt cause ruin and destruction in spars and rigging.

The Danish 74 was fighting for its life, serving both sides of guns, but the 64s needed only to serve one side, that facing the Dane. Would this make up for their lesser weight of metal?

It was a hard-fought, cruel contest and, as at Trafalgar, Kydd knew there was nothing a lone frigate could do to intervene.

At about nine the fire slackened and died to an eerie silence.

If the 64s had been crippled or were retreating, this left *Tyger* trapped against the shore to become the sole attention of a vengeful ship-of-the-line, or was it that Jessen had struck after a fearful mauling?

There was only one way to find out.

Tyger ghosted seaward, the terrible silence broken only by the occasional thumps of floating wreckage shouldered aside and the plash of her bow-wave.

Quite suddenly the massive bulk of a ship-of-the-line loomed out of the blackness. Lanthorns were being hung in the rigging to illuminate the deck, and as they drew nearer Kydd could hear alien cries and shouts, and the heart-tearing shrieks of wounded under the surgeon's saw. In the dim light the ragged upper rigging was visible, all torn sails and trailing rope but nowhere was a flag or ensign to be seen.

By its size it had to be *Prinds*.

Beyond was the dark shadow of another vessel lying off. It had a pair of command lanthorns in its fighting tops – it was *Stately*.

Aboard, they, too, were raising lights, and he could hear

the sounds of hurried repair above the muffled shrieks of the wounded. There was similar destruction: lines in the water, yards askew, the same shot-torn sails.

As *Tyger* came abeam she was hailed. 'The Dane has struck. Prepare to make boarding to prevent loss of the prize on the shore.'

'Aye aye, sir.'

'Er, and do send a boat, old fellow. Ours are all shot to pieces and I mean to take possession.'

Kydd turned to his first lieutenant. 'Mr Bray, away all boats with the carpenter, his mates and as many good men as you can spare. We've a prize to secure.'

'Aye aye, sir. First division o' larbowlines, muster in the waist,' he bellowed.

Appalled, Kydd saw young Rowan hurry to join them. 'What's that, Mr Bray? Send back the boy this instant!'

'He's a larbowline, sir!' Bray's indignant bawl came back.

'Send him back!'

Kydd had too many times seen the aftermath of a close-quarters action: it was no place for a stripling.

He caught Rowan's look of disappointment, but he wasn't about to expose the child to the sight of decks running with blood and worse.

His barge was quickly in the water and pulled briskly to *Stately*, Kydd aboard to act as Parker's second.

Parker lowered himself heavily into the boat by the dim, flickering light of the lanthorns, his uniform stained grey and rent open in one place.

'A hot night of it, sir,' Kydd opened, as they stroked to the motionless hulk of the now vanquished ship-of-the-line.

'Aye, it was.' He did not seem inclined to discuss it so Kydd refrained from conversation.

At the top of the side-steps of the 74 there was a lanthorn and a small group of men, who pulled back as they came aboard. A dull-eyed but dignified officer stepped forward. '*Kaptajn* Carl Jessen. I find I must yield the vessel I have the honour to command to you, sir.'

'Captain Parker, His Majesty's Ship *Stately*. The gallant defence of your ship does the greatest honour to your flag, sir.'

'Even as it came at grievous cost,' Jessen said, in a low voice, gesturing at a still figure lying by the main-mast covered with the Danish ensign. 'Løjtnant Willemoes, who may be known to you from his valour before Nelson in a previous age.'

'Indeed. Shall you . . .?'

Jessen slowly unbuckled his sword and offered it to Parker. After the barest hesitation he passed it on to Kydd.

'Thank you, sir. And the keys to the magazine?'

It was a mean act – in his place Kydd would have returned the sword. Cynically he reflected that Parker would know the action had not been one that the public would take up by reason of the odds in two against one, however hard-fought, and he was claiming what glory he could.

Tyger's boats came alongside and her seamen boarded, many awed and subdued by the carnage and destruction, others hurrying to the more obvious ruination.

'I shall send report, sir,' rumbled Bray, who was clearly seeing it as his business to take the matter in hand.

Kydd left him to it, now drained and exhausted by events. After seeing the prisoners on their way out of the 74, he returned to *Tyger*.

He dozed off in his armchair, still dressed, without touching

Tysoe's ministering whisky, but was wakened a short time later.

'Mr Bray's respects, and says as how he can't save the ship.'

Shaking his head to clear it, Kydd got to his feet. 'Coming,' he croaked.

Bray met him at the side.

'Rudder stock took a hit so we've no steering. Means we can't spread sail and I fear boats in tow wouldn't make much way in this.' The night breeze was blowing broadside on to the damaged hulk, its obvious fate now to be driven ashore.

'Then anchor.'

The bluff lieutenant gave a twisted smile. 'Danskers cut the cables before they took their leave.'

Even in his tiredness Kydd could see that there was nothing more to be done. The ship was no longer a threat and that was the chief concern. 'You've done your best. She'll go aground but it's two hours to daylight. We'll see what we can do then.'

A cold grey dawn revealed a shattered wreck aground on the foreshore, not far from a hamlet, while the two 64s were anchored offshore and under repair. It took little time to survey the remains and realise that nothing short of a massive salvage effort could free the vessel.

Parker took the news petulantly. 'Can't see why you couldn't think of something to stop the beggar driving ashore.'

'A lee shore, no steering?' Kydd couldn't help himself. His men had laboured for no result, but all Parker could see was a prize going to waste.

'That's as may be. You know what to do,' he snapped peevishly.

In the early light, villagers had seen the huge bulk of the ship in the shallows and a small crowd gathered when the gunner's party arrived in boats. They climbed aboard and disappeared below for a time, then hastened back to the boats and put off.

A little later the first wisps of smoke rose, increasing until the flames became visible, catching the tarred rigging, flaring up and spreading fast. Within an hour the battleship was ablaze, a crackling inferno.

The crowd held back from the appalling sight and in another hour the inevitable happened.

In a cataclysmic eruption *Prinds* exploded, wreckage tumbling and pattering from the sky, leaving a blackened and smoking length of ribbed timber where once the last of Denmark's proud battle-fleet had found its rest.

Chapter 18

The residence of Axel Rosen

'My dear Thornton,' enthused the governor of Gothenburg genially, 'and you've brought a soldier friend. Do make yourself comfortable, gentlemen. *Akvavit?*'

Thornton took a seat. So his good friend Rosen was being entrusted with the agreements for the first disposition.

Moore sat stiffly, cradling his drink.

'King Gustav IV Adolf asks me to extend fraternal greetings to his new allies on his behalf and enjoins me to do all in my power to facilitate matters,' continued Rosen.

'We are honoured and flattered by the attentions of His Swedish Majesty and wish only to advance our common cause in the most advantageous manner,' Thornton replied.

'Very good. Then it is only a matter of the military priorities.' He looked directly at Moore. 'General, we should not lose time in preparations. It is planned that Sjælland is conquered and garrisoned within—'

'I will not do it, sir!' Moore spluttered. 'It's impossible –

and, God forbid, even if we do prevail, how shall we garrison the entire territory? Thirty, forty thousand at the least in permanent cantonment. And not to mention supply, pay. Sir, it's nonsense!'

Thornton waited for the storm to pass.

Rosen said smoothly, 'If this is your military judgement, General, it will grieve the King to hear of your . . . uneasiness to assist him but there is an alternative. The unpleasantness in Finland has to be countered, you'll agree. The King has a plan to this end – to make quick conquest and occupation of Norway while the Danes are unable to defend it, before turning to the east, now with all his forces to command in the task of ejecting the Russians.'

With an effort at control, Moore bowed his head jerkily and said woodenly, 'As my judgement of before. The scheme is . . . the plan is not possible in any wise.'

Raising an eyebrow, Rosen continued pleasantly, 'My dear General, you have been in my country bare hours and you are dismissing our strategic initiatives outright. I shall withdraw for a space to allow your esteemed envoy to apprise you of the more . . . conspicuous elements involved. One hour?'

After the governor had left, closing the doors after him, Thornton rounded on Moore. 'Sir John, I do counsel—'

'That I should concur with this madness? I will not, sir!'

Thornton bit his lip. He knew the type: dedicated, loyal to a fault and absolutely committed to the goal to hand. But confrontation was going to achieve nothing. 'Very well, I do concede your point. We will seek agreement that your troops will not be expected to do service in either Sjælland or Norway.'

Moore visibly collected himself. 'Quite. I should consider

deploying in Scania opposite Copenhagen or any other within reason and the scope of my orders. Time presses, sir.'

'Then we shall speak more generally of the nature of your military assistance.'

Rosen returned, smiling with effortless urbanity.

Thornton told him, 'Axel, we have spoken, and General Moore quite sees the urgency of the situation and offers to take up immediate station in Scania to release your army there for Finland.'

'Your offer is generous and appreciated, General,' Rosen said, with a civil bow. 'I can see how we may together advance the cause of His Swedish Majesty and the greater war against the tyrant.'

'Then I shall give orders for my troops to disembark when I have details of their barracks or other accommodation.'

'Excellent. Then that leaves only the small details to conclude.'

'Oh? What are these, then, Axel?' A stab of premonition shot through Thornton.

'Merely the clarifying of the chain of command once the general and his men are on Swedish soil. My king is quite willing to take chief command of all forces in Swedish territory, and your military under this fine soldier.'

Moore stiffened. 'That is impossible, sir.'

'Oh, why so?'

'My orders do not allow of it. I am instructed and commanded by my own sovereign, King George, sir, and I cannot be made subject to two masters. Pray bear this to your king with my regrets.'

Rosen looked at him steadily for a space, then answered equably, 'I shall do this, sir.'

'Then I should like to land my men after their fatiguing voyage. What are your arrangements, sir?'

'Ah. I do not think that advisable at this time, General.'

'Not to disembark my men? What can you possibly mean, sir?'

'You must know, General, that the sudden appearance of tens of thousands in our midst to provision would place a grave strain on our local supply. It would drive up prices for staples beyond the people's enduring to the hazard of public order. I cannot risk this, sir.'

'Until conditions for the alliance are, er, further advanced, is your signifying,' Thornton said evenly.

'Quite.'

'Then we needs must take our leave to consider our position, sir. Good day to you.'

In the consul's residence Thornton stood in a bitter mood, avoiding Moore's eye.

It was absurd, irrational. Rosen was clearly under orders and they came from Stockholm. While Gustav needed every soldier and military resource he could lay hands on he was playing foolish games to get his way. This was bad enough but in Moore he had a blinkered military type who couldn't see past his orders. Not like Admiral Saumarez, who was diplomacy itself in the handling of the Swedes. If only Moore could have been more agreeable, accommodating in his ways.

'General, I cannot easily see where we can go from here, and—'

'I can,' Moore said abruptly.

'Yes?'

'My men cannot be expected to endure incarceration for much longer in those execrable hulks the Transport Board provides. So, if I'm not permitted to land, I shall return with them to England.'

'No!' Horrified, Thornton knew that the alliance could not possibly stand after such an insult. The unstable Gustav could do anything in spite – conceivably even take against the British and change sides with incalculable consequences. He thought feverishly. 'No – there's another way.' Only one course offered even the glimmer of hope.

'Sir?'

'General, you and I will take ship immediately for Stockholm and seek audience with King Gustav himself!'

Chapter 19

The admiral's day cabin, HMS Victory

From below the broad sweep of stern windows, a hubbub of voices rose, some in angry shouts, unseemly in a man-o'-war, let alone a flagship.

Saumarez winced and laid down his quill with a sigh. 'Flags, do go and find out what all that fuss is about, there's a good fellow.'

The lieutenant was back in a short while. 'Sir, it's a deputation.'

The admiral's head jerked up. 'What! A mutiny, d' you say?'

'Not as who would think it, sir. These are a parcel of ship's masters, desiring they should lay before you a pressing matter and the officer-of-the-watch will not do.'

Saumarez frowned. 'If they think to—'

'I fancy it's to do with their detention in Gothenburg when they had hopes of an early start to the season.'

'An insolence, of course, but I quite see their anxiety.

Desire the flag-captain to attend and I'll see a dozen of the more presentable.'

'Aye aye, sir.'

Awed by their surroundings, but clearly determined, they were shown seats around the same dark mahogany table that had seen councils-of-war since Keppel and the old French royalist wars. Weather-beaten, obstinate and in plain sea rig they were nevertheless the men who by that same stubbornness were defying the elements, the malice of the enemy and economic adversities to carry Britain through these dire times.

'Gentlemen. What is it that you wish to discuss with me?' opened Saumarez.

'When are we going to up hook an' into the Baltic? I've a freighting as is costing me guineas a day and—'

The younger man was cut short by one older, more mature.

'Cap'n Purley, *Pride of Lothian*. Admiral, we heard o' your troubles with the gen'ral as won't land his soldiers. Now, we sailed from England t' be assured of your protection and interest as we enters the Baltic and now we find you can't stay by us. It's bad luck as sees a whole fleet o' the King's navy brought to a stand by the army as won't give 'em leave to sail. But our—'

'Captain, this is no business of yours! There is an expedition afoot that bids fair to relieve you and your kind from concern that the Swedes will turn against us. Allow that I'm aware of your eagerness to be started but this delay is unavoidable, I regret.'

'I wonder if y' does, sir,' Purley said meaningfully. 'There's them among us has cargo spoilin' in the hold, others hold short-call bills as will see 'em embarrassed should they not discharge main quick, and all has crew tuckin' away victuals an' the ship idle. We can't keep like this'n for much longer. Sir.'

'You're asking me to send my fleet into the Baltic immediately. Mr Purley, this I cannot do while I must remain available to guard the army as it lands.'

'Then we has no choice, Admiral.'

'Pray be clearer, Mr Purley.'

'I means that we has to go in, whether you likes it or no. The neutrals are at sea, they're stealing our market, and we can't wait. We sails now just as we did in the older times.'

Saumarez looked pained. 'Captain, please be reasonable. I ask you to consider the situation. Things are changed, and for the worse with the Russians now at war against us. None of us knows what it's like in there. You may be set upon by enemy forces of unknown enormity lying in wait for you, there may be—'

'As will be our risk!'

'The risk, sir, is to your owner, who will not look kindly on your spurning a guaranteed protection for the sake of a little more time.'

It sank in, but another voice intervened, hard and confident: 'Hold there, Admiral. There's one thing you've laid in your lee as you can't get by.'

'And who the devil are you, sir?'

'Abraham Scoresby, supercargo in *Success of Bristol.*' A man of years, with a face of hewn granite.

'What's your meaning, sir?'

'Your orders, as well we knows, for that's why we're here.'

'Your point?'

'Just this. The top one of all – that y' hoists your flag over all these battlers for the purpose of securin' the Baltic for England's trade. We're the trade – secure it for us!'

Saumarez held his temper and began reasonably, 'Mr Scoresby, as I've mentioned before, my hands are tied. I cannot divide my fleet and—'

'Then this is t' tell you that we're sailin' on the tide. Into your Baltic. If we gets nobbled then ye've failed your orders. And our yardarm's clear as we've begged f'r protecting an' you've seen fit not to listen to us.'

'You're determined on this course.'

'We are, Admiral.'

Saumarez and his flag-captain exchanged glances.

Scoresby waited patiently.

'Very well. If you are bent on this foolish action . . .'

'We are.'

'Then this is what I'll do. The sail-of-the-line will remain together as my battle-fleet. All unrated vessels – cutters, sloops, gun-brigs and the like – these will be turned over to trade protection. That is all I can do.'

'A squiddy cutter to think to preserve a bunch o' ships with cargo worth twenty times y'r own flagship?'

'It's all I can do. I'm sorry.'

Scoresby looked at the others in scornful disbelief but one by one they rose and left the cabin, the last in an undignified scramble for the upper deck.

Saumarez, tight-faced, got out of his chair. 'They don't know it, but their griefs are mine. Be damned to that strutting redcoat Moore!'

Before evening had fallen, by ones and twos the first of England's Baltic trade fleet put to sea, course south – to Elsinore and the Sound.

Chapter 20

Copenhagen dockyard, shortly after the 1807 bombardment

The two friends picked their way through the bleak emptiness, only a shattered cask, cast-aside debris and untidy fakes of worn rope left to show of a great navy. They paced slowly past the vacant docks where only a short time before there had been rows of battleships and frigates with names remembered from the Swedish wars when Denmark had shown how it was to be a great power.

Now nothing. Just the last sullen smoking from the ruins of Copenhagen, their capital city, bombarded to surrender by the British in order to seize that same fleet.

With a swelling anger in his heart Kommandørkaptajn Krieger trudged past the empty storehouses, the silent workshops, the emptiness and desolation. What was in Denmark's future now? What was in his own?

'I wish to hell that I'd done it, Johannes, orders be damned,' muttered Kommandør Steen Bille beside him, kicking at a broken bucket.

As commander of the fleet, Bille had been thwarted in torching it to prevent it falling into the hands of the all-conquering British. The ineffective military commander, Peymann, now on court-martial for his life, had forbidden it. Instead, the city had been silent witness to the humiliating scene of their entire navy being towed away in procession, storehouses ransacked, everything that floated confiscated.

They walked on, wrapped in bitter thoughts.

'What now, old friend?' Krieger muttered bleakly. 'Officers without a navy, sailors without a ship, like to be cast up on the beach.'

The thick-set, hard-jawed Bille didn't reply for a moment, then said quietly, 'Johannes, it's not what becomes of us, but what of the *Helstat*, our honour? Are the Danes to be cast out from history?'

Krieger choked back a reply, and Bille continued, 'Not all is adverse, my friend. Our fleet is no more, true, but the English have gone, too – they didn't treat us as a conquered nation and left us still a sovereign people.'

'Who are now weak and unprotected, damn their blood!'

'We're at war with them but that doesn't mean we are friends now of the French. Crown Prince Frederick holds the line in Holstein only to deter the French from "protecting" us. We're still free to set our own destiny.'

'Steen, that is well, but what sticks in my throat is leaving the bastards to crow over their victory. Denmark is down but not finished.'

'So what do you want to do to 'em? Throw stones?' Bille said, then seeing the desolation on Krieger's face, clapped a hand on his shoulder. 'You're in the right of it, Johannes. Denmark is down but, if I've anything to do with it, she's not out.'

They came to an end of the dockyard and took a boat across the water to Nyhavn for the taverns and bustling humanity to be found there, by unspoken agreement wanting to get away from the derelict sadness of Holmen.

'Where are they all?' Krieger said in astonishment, seeing the deserted tables and stillness.

A pot-boy told them, 'They's all gone off to Vor Frue Kirke to hear Schack Bissen give 'em heart.' He was a fiery poet, known for his nationalism, but how could this be possible? The old cathedral had been spectacularly brought down in a consuming blaze during the bombardment.

Soon, at the ruin, they saw that the tumbled rubble and melted copper had been dragged away and in a roughly levelled area a swelling crowd – hundreds, a thousand or more, stood together in the stink of ash and charred timbers in shared despair.

There was a simple lectern where the altar had been. A tall, bearded man in severe black was holding forth, the crowd still and respectful.

The two edged in. Not in uniform, no particular notice was taken of them, and quickly within earshot they listened to the powerful oration. Of the long history of their Nordic forefathers, who had suffered before them but had gone on to voyage far and conquer. Who had taken heart from calamity, had risen above affliction and placed their traditional ways before all. And never should it be forgotten, in this time of self-doubt and humiliation, Denmark could hold to its heart that those same men had once seized a crown – the Crown of England itself!

It was stirring, moving, and gave perspective and meaning to what was happening to them.

'Holger Danske may be a myth,' Bissen intoned, invoking the hulking Viking celebrated by medieval Danish minstrels, 'but in his very existence he carries the torch of liberty and courage for all Danes! Let us take strength from the past as we cross into our future and—'

'Strike back!' roared a red-faced man at the front of the crowd. 'Show the English how we value our honour!'

Another shouted, 'Or lie down and die!'

Bissen listened sorrowfully, then held up his hand. 'Your true-hearted feelings do you credit, friends. But it is our fate that while the English were on our soil the army was far away and our navy was trapped in harbour. Now it is no more. They are a sea race and the largest army can do nothing to touch them.'

'So we give up, crawl back to our homes?'

This was met by a frustrated roar.

Bissen waited for it to subside. 'This is a time for enduring, for holding to our breasts that we have done what we could while the violators of our land were wreaking their worst. But now we must accept that there's nothing more we can do to confront them – nothing!'

His words provoked a tide of dissatisfaction and resentment.

Bille stiffened and bellowed, 'Hold!'

Heads turned and the commotion died. He pushed through to the speaker and hailed up as if to the main-top in a storm. 'This is not so! There is a way to strike out and recapture our honour.'

Bissen's eyes narrowed. 'And who are you to state this, sir?'

'Does it matter? I tell you now that there's a way to take just revenge. The British – they have a weak spot, a vulnerability.'

'Oh? Pray enlighten us, sir.'

'Their Baltic trade! All of our misery comes from their desperate necessity to keep open their last artery of trade to Europe. If we fall on this with all the force we can muster, it will be sweet vengeance indeed.'

'Sir, I'm a poet, no military man, and I can see no possible way we can do this. I beg you will accept our galling condition without repine until the Good Lord sees fit to visit peace upon us once more.'

'I say again, there is a way. And I will tell you. In all our time of affliction under the bombardment there was one body of men who took the fight directly to the enemy. I had the honour to command those men – the valiant seamen who manned mere gunboats to face a great fleet and who did so much to wring honour from defeat. These will be the instruments of revenge we shall wield!'

'Boldly said, sir. But I do not think I'm mistaken when I say that all our gunboats were taken from us, none left. How then will your men – gallant as well they may be – how can they inflict anything of consequence upon the enemy without the means to do so?'

There were scattered titters and frowns but Bille gave a grim smile. 'We build 'em. Start now, and by the time the ice goes in spring, we will have a great fleet of the same gunboats that brought ruin and death to the English before. And we will use these to sow terror and dismay among their merchantmen, which will cause them to flee rather than dare the Sound.'

'Build them? His Majesty will never countenance the expenditure. The navy is finished, gone. Why throw good money after it?'

'Hr Bissen,' Bille roared, 'you underestimate the heart of the Danish people, who long for retribution.'

He moved up to join Bissen and addressed the crowd:

'Fellow Danes! I stand before you to make supplication. The honour of Denmark is in your hands – I'm no orator or rouser of people but this day I offer you a course of action as will keep the flame of Danish valour alive! I ask you humbly to contribute your means in a public subscription as will see those gunboats built. When that is done, leave it to me and I will crew them with brave sons of Denmark who will take them into the very heart of the enemy!'

An outcry of fervent cheering swept over the crowd: here was a positive action that any might join and know they were doing their part for Danish honour. It went on and on until, with a pitying smile, Bissen held up his hands for quiet.

'A gallant and spirited gesture – with but one fatal flaw.'

'Sir?'

'With all the will in the world, it cannot be done. We might throw in our skillings but what of that when Danzig deal and Prussian fir are denied us? We're at war with England. They will not let it pass and without timber we cannot build our gunboats.'

A baffled hush fell but a strident voice could be heard from the back. 'My house is to be repaired. I'd gladly sleep in the fields and know the timber's going to a better cause!'

Another bellowed an offer, and more came until the meeting broke down into bedlam. That Copenhagen's devastation must wait was nothing compared to the surging spirit that had come over them all at the realisation that they were no longer helpless.

They would have their gunboats.

Krieger knew just where to go in the deserted Holmen: the drawing office where the plans of all Denmark's ships had been stored from the glory years past.

A curious doorman watched as he drew out those of the celebrated Swedish naval architect, af Chapman. These were the basis for the Danish gunboat force that Krieger had taken into action against the English not so long before.

Stout and clean-lined, they were, weight for weight the most powerful naval vessels ever designed. Their lethal effectiveness was in their gun: not a small-bore cannon but a single great gun of a calibre only ever seen in a ship-of-the-line. In a flotilla together, these would have the formidable fire-power of a battleship.

And they were designed for Baltic service: no hardy sea-keeping qualities that the English favoured but more the deadly speed that forty oars could give, the impetuous united rush on an unsuspecting prey from behind any one of the myriad islands of the archipelago.

While Bille saw to the organising of the public subscription he would study the plans carefully.

The gifted Chapman had a multitude of designs, large and small, but mostly for the sole purpose of defence. The fleet that defended Stockholm had been famously successful but that was not what Krieger wanted. Not defence – attack! A form of swift, well-armed galley that could be readily deployed and which would find haven and hiding in the many little ports around Denmark's coast. A host of tiny assailants that in sum would cut the artery of trade and let the life-blood of England spill uselessly into the sea.

Chapter 21

The following spring, Hornbæk harbour, north Sjælland

After a hard winter of frigid easterlies it was glorious to feel the warmth of sunshine on the skin, then to see the ice retreat, break up into floes and vanish. Deeper into the Baltic the ancient ports were still locked in by ice, not yet ready for the flood of trade of the new season, but it would not be long.

Krieger looked about the little harbour in satisfaction. Here was a sheltered haven, two moles enclosing a natural indentation in the sandy coast, the five-fathom line a comfortable mile or more distant, keeping any sizeable English marauder well out of gunshot.

And being readied alongside was a fine pair of gunboats, both *kanonchalups* – *Svane* and *Ænder*.

They were full-blooded aggressors. Sleek and low, with a monster twenty-four-pounder long gun mounted on slides over the fore-deck and a nine-pounder on the stern-quarters, they were designed such that the whole boat was aimed with rapid manoeuvring at the oars, doing away with the elaborate tackling of larger ships.

Two-masted with a simple lugger rig, they could, if necessary, run out a bowsprit and jib and, with a try-sail aft, make good speed even in the lightest of winds. But it was the great number of double-banked oars that brought a deadly advantage: to be able to proceed directly into the wind. And in a calm, while a sailing-ship was dead in the water a gunboat could run rings round it.

It came at a price: to man the gunboat at least seventy men were needed on the oars and to serve the guns, and living conditions on any protracted passage would be nothing less than squalid. Krieger knew that this was not a limitation, however, as the boats would be, like here at Hornbæk, stationed locally, ready to dart out, snap up prey and return.

'Peder – are you done with your primping?' he threw at the officer in *Svane*. 'I heard the English merchant jacks have grown restless and are off through the Sound on their own.'

What the big British fleet was doing in Gothenburg was anyone's guess. Most probably it was something to do with the Swedish alliance, which, rumour had it, involved an invasion of Norway at Gustav IV Adolf's goading – or was it intended to confront the Russians? Either way it was not troubling them, remaining at anchor and not convoying trade through the Sound.

'I'll have no slip-ups in front of the *forbandet* English,' Bruun retorted. The right side of his face was still livid with gunpowder burns where his *kanonchalup*, *Stubbekøbing*, had exploded during the frenzied, reckless fighting before the bombardment.

Swenson, the captain of *Ænder*, growled happily, 'As every

round shot is polished, the pikes will split a fly and we've men enough to make her dance!'

'Well and good,' Krieger conceded, hiding his pride. 'You'll get your chance soon enough – and then we'll see if you remember your tactics.'

This was going to be the first trial of gunboats in the open sea instead of harbour defence and much was riding on how things went.

Hornbæk was well placed: on the north coast of Sjælland at the mouth of the passage south where all shipping must funnel into the Sound. It had a sturdy church spire that served to keep lookout over the two or three miles to its centre, and the fishing town could well feed and house another hundred men.

They hadn't long to wait. In the early afternoon came a clanging of the church bell – a sighting!

Merchantmen – typical Baltic traders, three brigs, about four hundred tons or so. In blithe trust that, with Kronborg well away into the Sound, they had nothing to worry about, they were under full sail four miles offshore.

The breeze for this time of the year was balmy and slight. Conditions were ideal.

'Take 'em out!' roared Krieger.

The signal gun thudded and men streamed from houses and workshops to converge on the harbour, finding their oars in the boat-house and manning the row-thwarts of the two gunboats.

'Room for a passenger, Peder?' Krieger shouted and, without waiting for a reply, boarded *Svane*'s broad afterdeck. There was no way he was going to miss the party.

They swept out of the mole and, ignoring the north-westerly, headed directly for their victims.

At first there was no change in their aspect: against the coast the oar-powered gunboats would appear anything but threatening and they pressed on across their front.

As they drew nearer, their intent was discovered and the scattered ships came together protectively in a loose gaggle.

The oarsmen stretched out like heroes. The rhythmic rise and splash had urgency in every stroke.

A mile away – it was time to close the proceedings.

Svane diverged to the right and the gun lashings were thrown off. Gunners swarmed over the weapon and the gun-captain indicated readiness.

'Peder?'

A grim-faced Bruun took the tiller and aligned the craft, a gunner crouched ready. At the right time Bruun roared, 'Oars!' and with blades out of the water in respect for the expected recoil he chopped down his hand.

With a monstrous concussion the twenty-four-pounder fired and somewhere before the bow of the leading ship the plume of a shot-strike rose majestically.

For a space nothing happened. Then, as one, the three brigs slewed about to run downwind.

Swanson in *Æider* knew what to do and his gun slammed out to raise a series of gigantic skipping splashes on the other side.

Krieger gave a satisfied smile. On the decks of those merchantmen there would be something like panic. Even the slowest-witted would realise it was as prizes that the gunboats wanted them, why they were aiming off – but they would know too that this was war, and if they did not yield, it was the duty of the gunboats to pound them to splinters with their giant guns.

One by one they struck sail and lay to, awaiting the gunboats to board.

But Krieger's smile faded as they approached the workaday merchant vessels. This was no great victory: these were no more than common sailors following the sea and should not be expected to go up against such odds. Just how much duty did they owe their ship and its owners? They might take on privateers but there was no future in defying these ship-smashing naval guns.

They boarded a merchantman each, the sullen seamen on deck with their few belongings in sea-bags, one ship's master shaking his head in disbelief. 'To be captured is a hard thing, but by a pair o' row-boats is a right humiliation.'

While they were taking possession of the first two, the third took advantage of their distraction and hastily made off but Krieger was well satisfied with his haul. Not only the value of the ship and its cargo but the insurance pay-out in London would hurt the English. A good day's work.

It was easy – too much so? It did not take long to bring in the two prizes and they were ready to turn around and go back on the prowl. How long could it last before word got about? Better to spread the mischief: Gilleleje, along the coast further, would do.

They seized two independents who thought to take the alternative Great Belt route to the south – but several others got away. They needed more gunboats.

Chapter 22

In Copenhagen, Krieger's little navy was the toast of the town and there was no difficulty with an increase in numbers. He had ambitions to go further – much further.

'I'm going to do it, Steen,' he said to Bille. 'Else we stand to be known as a mosquito fleet only. I want to make 'em bleed!'

Together they plotted their great stroke on the charts. Off Copenhagen's harbour was the desolate four-mile-long island of Saltholm, with its surrounding shallows, and a bare three miles further across was the coast of Sweden, Malmö. Between these two must pass any who entered the Baltic but did not wish to risk the perils and the greater distance of the Great Belt.

What Krieger was planning was nothing less than a massed gunboat assault on a convoy, a slaughter of the lot.

The English had now begun gathering the impatient merchantmen in loose convoys, but these were escorted by ships of the Royal Navy – at the moment small ones, true, but he had a grudging respect for their valour and professionalism and knew what he was up against.

In Nyholm there now lay a satisfying twenty-five gunboats, a firepower not far off that of a broadside from a battleship, but conditions had to be just right before he sprang his trap. The crucial requirement was for the wind to drop right down so the escorts could not race to the rescue of their flock, while under oars they would be taking their pick of their victims. At the same time there had to be enough to waft the convoy to its doom.

He had to be patient. Quite a number of independents could be seen against the far shore but he was waiting for larger prey.

On the eighth day a fast galley brought warning from Taarbæk in the north that a great convoy was on its way: seventy merchantmen, a huge prize. But it was guarded by four naval vessels, even if they were only gun-brigs.

They came on slowly and it wasn't until after midday that the close press of sail appeared in view. They would be very aware that any threats would come from the hostile shore of Denmark to their right, not the rumpled placidity of the Swedish shore to their left. As a result the four gun-brigs took station along the outer right, their ensigns limply flapping in playful zephyrs, faced with the near impossible task of protecting all seventy sail spread out over a mile of sea.

This was Krieger's chance: in unhurried fashion twenty-one gunboats assembled inside Saltholm island, their low presence undetectable over the scrubby flatness. He watched and waited. The light north-westerly meant that when he signalled their appearance it had to be such that a retreat back into the Sound against the wind in the confined waters was out of the question.

The hours ticked by. Then the fickle breeze faltered and

died, leaving sails listlessly flapping and the convoy drifting helplessly.

The timing was perfect.

'Advance by division – let's help ourselves, *kammeraten*!'

With elated shouts the men bent to their oars and the gunboats surged forward towards the mass of sail, spreading out to give a field of fire to each.

It was an exhilarating charge but almost immediately Krieger saw that things were not going to be easy. Between them and the convoy were all four gun-brigs with just enough way on in the whispering breeze to slew around to bring their broadsides to bear. They wouldn't open fire until they got closer for, like most lesser warships in the Royal Navy, their armament was in carronades, heavy in metal but inaccurate at range – close in, on the other hand, they could obliterate any oared craft.

To get at the convoy they had to break through these but they showed no sign of shrinking from what faced them.

There was really only one course: they had to put down the escort.

Warily a dozen gunboats closed in a semi-circle on the nearest drifting gun-brig. Out of range of the brig's guns first one gunboat, then a second opened up with their great guns on its beam. The sullen concussion of their discharge thundered and rolled over the calm seas, one after another.

In a hopeless defiance the brig returned fire, the crack and thump so pitifully less, gun-smoke in the still air hanging in great smothering clouds between them.

The shots told: in the first minute the gun-brig's main top-mast toppled, bringing down a tangle of canvas and rigging that smothered the mainsail. Another hit sent wreckage leaping up from her fore-deck, but still the fierce resistance continued.

On the ship's quarters several smaller gunboats began taking position closer to, at an angle that prevented the brig's guns bearing on them. Like hounds baying at a cornered stag, they added to the fire-storm.

The captain was going to sacrifice himself for his charges and for this Krieger could only honour him – and put an end to it.

'Take her in, Peder,' he grunted.

Straight in – for the battered stern-quarters.

The firing died away as their killing lunge began. Another two gunboats got under way and made for the bow, and as they prepared to board by storming, seamen appeared at the deck rail with pikes and cutlasses, determined to repel boarders in a last heroic stand.

'Oars – hold water, Peder,' Krieger murmured, and as the gunboat slowed he hailed up to the brig's deck through cupped hands.

'The British captain, ahoy!'

A figure detached itself from the defenders. 'Aye – L'tenant Wood.'

'Sir, I've seventy men in this craft and two more lie off your bow with the same. You've done all that honour demands and I ask that you yield to me.'

There was no reply and Krieger thought he'd not been heard, then the voice hailed back, 'As I'd spare my men a useless blood-letting, so be it.'

From the deck of the defeated vessel he saw what the courageous man had achieved.

Overcoming his ship had taken a quarter of Krieger's force and with another three to batter down there were not so many on hand to do the work of seizing the convoy. Quick thinking by someone had the convoy turned about and, in a slightly stronger breeze, it was straining to make for the safety of Malmö. There was not going to be a wholesale slaughter.

At the same time he saw with rising satisfaction that half a dozen, maybe even a score, of trading vessels had been taken and each was now under the Dannebrog flag, but with the time bought by this sacrifice the remainder were being shepherded into Malmö and out of reach.

As the prisoners were led over the side into captivity he couldn't help but reflect that, if all convoys were to be escorted by such, a stiff fight lay ahead.

Chapter 23

Copenhagen inner harbour

'They're not going to take this for much longer,' Bille said, watching the prizes warped alongside safely. 'That's a fair pile of gold we've taken from them. Their merchants will be howling in England, I'd wager.'

Krieger smiled wolfishly. They were standing on the dockside in Nyholm. Where before it had been a deserted wasteland, now it was alive with gunboat activity. 'We've only just begun, Steen. Whatever they try, we'll be ready for 'em.' Even a great trading nation like England couldn't take this punishment for ever.

Tonight there would be a famous party in Holmen – in these hard times successes of any kind were rare but this day his sea warriors had brought their people a victory.

'So you'll be happy to hear I've just had word that there's another convoy on its way and even bigger this time. Are your men up to it?'

* * *

The next morning the gunboats assembled once more. Again, conditions were all that could be asked for – early-summer light breezes already beginning to drop, a sure sign of a calm to come.

'I want this lot to be massacred,' Krieger growled. 'A full effort.'

At twelve the citadel signal tower threw out the flags that told of the enemy in sight.

They waited, oars across the boat, the gentle murmur of wavelets and the screech of seabirds on Saltholm the only sounds.

It was taking some time for the mass of sail to reach the Flintrannan, the narrowest part of the Sound, but when it did, Krieger gave the signal and the gunboats thrust forward into the open.

In an instant the whole picture changed.

It was indeed a juicy convoy but before it on the Danish side loomed the bulk and menace of a ship-of-the-line! Krieger recognised it – *Africa*, which he'd heard had been with Nelson at Trafalgar, a veteran of the war at sea.

The English had made their move. Now they were guarding their convoys with the unanswerable threat of a battleship.

'The party's over,' Bruun said darkly, as the onrush of gunboats slowed at the sight. This ship carried guns just as powerful as theirs and could be counted upon to be a steadier platform. There would be no standing off and pounding with this monster.

But Krieger's eyes gleamed. 'Not so, Peder,' he hissed, his eyes fixed on the big ship. 'No, this changes things our way, by God!'

Astonished, Bruun tried to make out what he was saying.

'All boats,' Krieger roared, beckoning furiously. 'Close with me!' He stood erect, his gaze still on the barely moving sail-of-the-line, waiting until he had his captains all within hail. '*Brødre til søs*,' he roared at last. 'Today we go on to make history!'

'How?' whispered Bruun.

'I change your orders as of this moment.' He paused significantly. 'They are now . . . to leave the convoy untouched! Do *not* go against it!'

He surveyed the gunboat's crew. Weather-hardened men looked puzzled but trustfully up at him, in shapeless hats and with the good open faces of honest Danes. His heart swelled.

'Instead I give you honour and glory enough to take to your grandchildren for years to come. This day our contemptible little gunboats will seize and take a battleship!'

Gasps of surprise changed to cheering as he went on, 'We wait until we have a total calm – then we move in on the helpless beggar in a combined horde. Løjtnant Swenson, return to Nyholm with my orders – that every damned thing that floats is to be manned and join us out here.'

He filled his lungs and bellowed, '*Gud og den retfærdige sag!*' God and the righteous cause!

If they could prevail against a Royal Navy ship-of-the-line their fame would resound down the ages for ever. It would give untold heart to the nation, and the moral value was worth far more than the convoy, which, seeing the gunboat threat, was taking its chance to slip away from the ponderous sail-of-the-line.

At about two in the afternoon the fluky winds failed entirely and *Africa* became motionless in the water, every sail hanging limp, gun-ports open along her length in two lines but with the guns impotent, unable to train.

'Advance!' cried Krieger.

The gunboats got under way, each slipping into its pre-arranged position well out on the quarter and bow of the massive ship.

The first gun-fire was from *Africa* – a shocking salvo from the quarterdeck of at least nine-pounders, sending solid shot skittering and plunging among the crowded gunboats. Their positioning preserved them against a twenty-four-pounder broadside but not this – they could not close to point-blank range in the face of it and must lay off to inflict their punishment.

One by one the mass of gunboats opened up, their big guns thundering out in heavy slams of sound. The stretch of water and the ship became hidden by immense roiling clouds of gun-smoke. Only the upper sails and rigging of *Africa* showed above it – but this was all that was needed. Krieger had decided earlier that if he was going to take the battleship they would aim for the rigging to cripple the vessel, partly to prevent it turning on them if the wind got up, but more that in the end he didn't want to make prize of a wreck. The smaller-bored *kanonjolle* could be relied on to batter at the hull.

Pulse racing, he goaded his men on, knowing that the breathy air could return as a breeze without warning.

The minutes turned into an hour – of deafening cannonade, the muscle-burn of serving hot guns, the crash and splinter of shot from *Africa* as she drifted round with the current, giving a chance for a gun or two to bear on a Danish foe.

Still the ship-of-the-line fought back. A lull in the gun-fire revealed her bowsprit trailing in the water, her sails torn and pierced, but her ensign still defiantly aloft. The mauling went on.

With a crash and screams one of the gunboats took a direct hit, the round shot smashing and splintering the fragile hull to lethal skewers, impaling and lacerating human flesh. In another direction floating oars, some splintered, were witness to a further savage counter-blow.

The pounding went on, a wounded beast surrounded by cruel tormentors who bayed for its blood. Another hour passed, the sun sinking to its lair. The shattered ruin must surely yield soon!

The powder smoke lifted a little and, with a clear target, the firing redoubled, but, heart sinking, Krieger sensed something. There was the barest stirring of the air. He felt its coolness and knew what he'd feared was coming to pass.

The evening land breeze was making itself felt. In a short while the stricken monster would be able to pick up steerage way, to react and turn its cruel broadsides on them with vindictive savagery. It was time to pull out.

Before the drooping sails could catch the wind Krieger signalled the withdrawal.

It had been a near thing: given only a little longer it might have ended differently, but he could go back with the glory that his gallant band of tiny boats had taken on the greatest antagonist the enemy could throw against them.

Chapter 24

Stockholm

Moore paced along behind, grim-faced and silent as the little group made their way up to a waiting carriage.

'Really, sir, this is not to be borne!' puffed Franklin Oakley, secretary of the British legation. 'You come back here without any kind of warning and expect us to beg His Swedish Majesty to grant you immediate audience on a mere military matter?'

'I do, sir, touching as it does on the very core of the alliance that exists between us, which is now most surely in peril,' Thornton replied.

'Then I shall endeavour to—'

'Sir. Should you fail to bring about a meeting within twenty-four hours I shall be obliged to take extraordinary measures. Do you understand me?'

Unexpectedly, Oakley gave a smile. 'Perfectly. You know Gustav Adolf, however. And I tell you now, he's more . . . difficult than ever. All will depend on how well or no he breakfasted when I petition.'

Thornton had dismal expectations of the encounter to come. He was well aware that this king, believing himself the last great Vasa, had extreme views of his importance, which were not in any way affected by reality. An autocrat of another age, he loathed radicals and revolution, holding that Napoleon Bonaparte was the Antichrist and the Beast of Revelation and raging at any who questioned his opinions.

His father mortally wounded in a coup attempt, he was nevertheless a calamitous judge of men and allowed himself to be surrounded and advised by French-leaning opportunists who, with the Uppsala radicals, were wreaking diplomatic sabotage on all Thornton's efforts.

Quarters were hastily prepared for them in the legation, but before they had settled an equerry arrived, advising that Gustav IV Adolf would grant audience that very hour – or not at all.

'So, Thornton, you've brought me a curiosity?' King Gustav IV Adolf was slight, his long face and slicked-back hair at odds with his imperious gestures.

'Your Majesty, this is Lieutenant General Sir John Moore, military commander of the Northern Expedition.'

'Yes, as I've heard.' There was a fleeting, almost comical expression of distaste.

'Who wishes as a matter of some urgency to conclude his arrangements to—'

'To make descent on Denmark. Yes, I can understand this.'

Moore breathed deeply. 'Sir, this is not to be considered. I do not—'

'General, King Gustav is more accustomed to be addressed as "Your Majesty",' Thornton said reprovingly.

'Your Majesty,' Moore hissed, 'my government's instructions may not be put aside so easily. They do not include any provision for the landing of my forces on a foreign shore, especially that of Sjælland, which is too well defended to contemplate invading.'

'If you will not join me in carrying the war to the enemy – as in an alliance I should surely expect – then I will act alone in the matter.'

'How will you move on a territory defended by at least twenty-five thousand? On their own ground? Without—'

'Have a care, General,' Gustav spat. 'This is Sweden, I am its king, and I've eighteen thousand fine men here in Stockholm alone. I shall have my way, sir!'

'Sir – Your Majesty. Do you not think them better employed in facing the Russians in Finland? They press you sorely. You must secure your flanks before—'

'General. If I asked for troops then it is to make war against my enemies, not to have them sit on their hands, waiting. Those who think only of defence are useless to me. Give me those of stout heart and nothing is impossible.'

Moore's jaw clamped shut and he glared defiantly back.

Thornton intervened smoothly: 'I rather think the general means he wishes to act more aggressively, given his wish to strike at the Russians in Finland. I dare to remind you, Your Majesty, that they are our enemies as well.'

'Know that I'm quite capable of defending my kingdom, Thornton. This is a strategical matter, touching as it does on the sovereignty of my realm. I might be trusted to see to the best interests of the same, don't you think?'

'Just so, sire.'

'Then if he is desirous of a more active employment we

should be discussing the Norwegian plan.' He turned to an aide. 'Tibell, bring in the Norway maps — I want to open the eyes of my stiff-necked English friend to my grand strategy.'

Chapter 25

In the legation as the evening lamps were being lit, Moore paced backwards and forwards in a rage of frustration. 'It's madness! I won't do it! The man's demented if he believes half of what he says.'

'Yes, yes,' Thornton said wearily from the depths of an armchair. 'But as always I remind you that Sweden is our last remaining ally and should the alliance fall . . .'

'You don't understand what you're asking. I'm entrusted with England's only military expedition of size and you want me to sacrifice it at the whim of a lunatic?'

'He may be . . . demanding, but there's more to this than military honour. Sir, I ask you to remember again your highest order: to do all in your power to safeguard the Baltic trade, against which all else is posturing.'

Moore stopped abruptly. 'This, then, is your view of my situation, sir?'

'Essentially, yes.'

'Then, sir, I must retire to consider my position.' He turned on his heel and marched out of the room.

He was back in less than an hour.

'You have reflected on the higher principles?' Thornton asked evenly.

Moore was considerably calmer, composed. 'I have. And in the absence of greater authority have made my dispositions in the light of what I've heard.'

'May I know what these are?'

'Since there is no reasoning with a mad king, and at the same time you seem to have no knowledge of the military implications, I have taken steps.'

'General?' Thornton asked warily.

'I have this hour sent off a letter to King Gustav. In it I have informed him that my orders do not allow me to engage in military activities of the kind he proposes. Nor is it to be suffered that I place myself or any of my force under his command. Therefore there is no point in my continuing the inhuman confinement of my troops aboard ship and I will be quit of his realm.'

Appalled, Thornton could not think of a reply and Moore went on, in satisfaction, 'So tomorrow, Thornton, we take ship for Gothenburg and thence back home, where I trust my men will be better valued. Good night.'

At a little before midnight Moore was wakened by a sharp tap on his door. 'Who the devil is it at this hour?' he roared.

'Someone to see you, General,' replied the major-domo, in an unnaturally controlled voice.

Ill-tempered, Moore threw on a dressing gown. 'Come!'

An extravagantly dressed older man with a piercing gaze bowed politely and declared something in Swedish, waiting patiently for the major-domo to translate.

'Sir, this is Fältherre d'Ahrenheim, adjutant general of

Sweden. He desires to inform you that His Majesty forbids you to leave Stockholm without his express permission. You are to remain here until the matter under consideration is resolved.'

'God damn it, but he's no right to detain me against my wishes!'

'Sir, you are not a member of the British *corps diplomatique* in this kingdom and are therefore subject to the King's wishes.'

Thornton hurried in, tousle-haired and with a set face. 'Fältherre, should you carry out this act you will be seen to have made arrest of a most high-ranking British officer on a government mission and I cannot answer to the consequences if His Britannic Majesty's ministers hear of it.'

'The general remains in Stockholm.'

'And if he does not?'

A meaningful look conveyed the answer.

Thornton remained with the ashen-faced Moore after they'd left.

'You're now under house arrest, you know that?'

'Yes, but it does settle one question.'

'Oh?'

'The man is most definitely deranged and I was right to take action as I did.'

Thornton looked away in despair. The Northern Expedition was now in ruins, whatever lay in the future. And it was all the doing of this stubborn and unbending soldier. 'I must consider this carefully,' he muttered, and took his leave.

Chapter 26

The next day Thornton was received promptly by King Gustav.

'A good morning to you,' the King said breezily. 'Sleep well?'

'Tolerably so, lying as uneasily as I did.'

'Was I so hard on your man?'

There was only one card he could play. 'It was rather my concern for Your Majesty that bore upon me.'

Gustav IV Adolf cocked his head. 'How so?'

'Should my government hear of this misunderstanding I'm fearful it could – possibly – impair the delivery of your next subsidy.'

'What? Are you . . .? How dare you threaten me, sir? This is monstrous – if you seek to coerce me by such blatant means you'll live to regret it. Do you hear me, sir?'

A monthly and a yearly subsidy was paid to the Swedes because, with the Continent cut off to their trade by reason of the alliance with England, they were in economic difficulties. Thornton had been reluctant to raise the subject, knowing how sensitive it was. But by doing so now his hope was that it would allow himself to be later mollified by the concession of releasing Moore.

The King ranted and raved, the small, ornate throne room echoing with his shouts. That the King of England would ever think to abandon his Nordic brother was a scandal, and who did he think Gustav IV Adolf was that he needed the bribe of silver to stand by his sworn objective to bring down the Antichrist? Much better would it have been in the first place to send a more respectful and intelligent general as emissary and commander.

Wearily, Thornton heard him out and returned to Moore. 'I've tried. The Good Lord above is witness that I've tried.'

'Then try again, sir! It's not to be endured that I must be kept in idleness here while the world burns!'

The Northern Expedition was finished, but in the vital question of the Baltic trade, an even higher element now weighed in.

If by some means he could get Moore back to Gothenburg and on his way home, Admiral Saumarez and his fleet would then be released to set sail at last into the Baltic to confront the Russians and safeguard the crucial trade. It took precedence well before hopeless manoeuvrings about military assistance.

The King had to be accounted at the least irrational, and the sooner it was done the better. The alliance? It might just survive: Gustav needed friends just as much as Britain did.

The next morning the legation's open carriage was seen calling at the door.

Oakley climbed in and Moore, with much ostentation, accepted his place next to him for a healthful drive to take the air. Sentries watched impassively – the two were in full view and Moore's scarlet coat was easily recognisable.

What they didn't see was the cursing figure crouched in the well of the vehicle suffering the indignity of boots resting on him.

The carriage clattered off, its high-stepping horses snorting and restless. It made a circuit of the outer perimeter, at the far point stopping to allow Moore to step down and admire the view before it swept on and finally returned to the door. The two occupants briskly descended and disappeared inside.

Once out of sight the under-secretary of the legation took off his red tunic and handed it over, task complete.

A gardener dropped a sack next to the figure hidden in the long grass. 'Quickly, sir – this way!'

Moore rolled down the bank, threw on a dark cloak from the sack over his red coat and was led away. Thornton was waiting for him in a closed carriage – it had worked.

'Neatly done, sir,' Moore conceded. 'And now?'

'You're free to proceed to Gothenburg – overland as will not be expected. Once there, you'll present Admiral Saumarez with my dispatch, and I can promise you he'll be heartily thankful for it. Goodbye and farewell, General.'

Chapter 27

Copenhagen

There was news from the north. A lone frigate was heading south towards them, making good speed in the steady northerly. It didn't affect them for they had no business confronting such a predator – it was probably a probing patrol into the Baltic and would pass by quickly. They were safe where they were.

'What's to do at the Trekroner?' wondered Krieger, as signal flags were emphasised with a gun sounding from the island fortress.

'Enemy in sight, sir,' the signal boatswain said importantly.

'The frigate? How in Hades can he see it?' The Swedish shore and usual channel were a good ten miles or more distant.

It wasn't long before the matter was resolved. The frigate was indeed alone, but in an act that was the product either of an ignorant fool or an exceptional seaman it was shaping course for the Danish coast instead, plainly planning to take the inner channel within a mile of the harbour fortifications of Prøvestenen.

Her captain was apparently brazenly seizing the opportunity of looking into Copenhagen harbour on his way past, and out of range, there was nothing anybody could do about it.

The hard part was ahead, however. The treacherous Middle Ground sandbanks off the harbour entrance had to be passed with every buoy and sea-mark removed, and then the half-mile passage inside Saltholm island and the Danish shoreline, the Drogden, had to be found and followed exactly – a frigate aground in these waters would have only a very short time to live.

By now there was no question: her captain was a masterly seaman. Holding course and ignoring the random shots thrown at him, he carried on and, at the stump of the Nordre Røse light, put over the helm the point or two to starboard, which had the handsome vessel on a direct course for the open sea.

Krieger acknowledged the feat with a twisted smile. A pity the winds were with him: if they turned foul or dropped it would be another story.

He turned back to his work.

Within hours a breathless rider brought his horse to a crashing halt – and in minutes his message was in Krieger's hands.

'Be damned! And I won't pass this up for any man.'

Bille put down his pen and regarded him with amused resignation. 'And what shall you be adventuring this time, Johannes?'

Krieger was already on his feet. 'From the watch at Dragør – that saucy frigate's now in Køge bay and becalmed, by

God!' His expression tightened. 'Steen, I'm going to finish what we started with *Africa* – a fine frigate is like to be taken this day if I'm to be judge of it.'

He leaned out of the door and hailed the sentry. 'Pass the word – alarm, all boats! And I mean all, damn it!'

Chapter 28

Aboard HMS Tyger

'I mislike this breeze,' the sailing master muttered, to no one in particular. 'Reminds me o' that time off Tangier in *Patroclus* frigate when we lost all way, an' this swarm of—'

Kydd cut him off quickly. 'You're saying as there's a flat calm coming on, Mr Joyce?'

'Aye, sir. I'm sanguine as how we've got the last o' the airs now. With the barometer as it is, we'll get naught till the dog-watches.' Kydd recalled Keats warning that calms in the Baltic were sudden, local and more to be feared than any storm.

Bray looked up at the sagging canvas with a thunderous glare. 'This stretches my patience more'n a man can stand. A frigate just ain't the animal to send into waters like these.'

With the fleet still at a stand at Gothenburg, *Tyger* had been sent to patrol the southern end of the Sound and had encountered nothing but light winds and unfamiliar currents all the way.

'In course this is weather for gunboats,' Brice agreed unhappily. 'And isn't that their bolt-hole we passed by up the coast?'

'If they're not afraid to mill with a sail-o'-the-line they'll not stop at a frigate, I'm bound to say,' Bray boomed. 'And what can we do about it? Not a damned thing,' he added darkly.

Kydd felt a chill clutch his heart. The business with *Africa* had been a near thing, many killed – even her captain had not survived – and only the fortunate return of a light wind had saved them. A smaller victim such as *Tyger* had even less chance. The canny Danish had found a way to strike back and they were making the most of their formidable weapon.

In the next few hours . . . He had to do something! It was the age-old pact of the sea: he was the captain with power over every man – but in return they looked to him for a true steer because they would be carried along by his decisions whatever they were.

They hadn't sighted a sail lately – did this mean the gunboats had not been told of their plight? Sooner or later they'd be discovered and their fate sealed.

The talking tailed off but there were nervous glances in his direction. Kydd was left by himself, the elemental lonely figure of command faced with an intolerable circumstance and with none to share the burden. If a ship-of-the-line had been nearly overcome, how could he be expected to prevail?

Tyger ghosted along in the last of the dying wind – should he use it to head out to sea where it might be stronger, or go inshore in this wide bay perhaps to catch an offshore breeze before they were finally reduced to complete immobility, dead in the water?

Or . . .?

'Clear away both bowers for mooring!' he barked.

They goggled at him as though he'd lost his senses. Anchoring? With both anchors as if a gale was about to break on them?

'This instant!' he lashed at them.

The starboard bower had cable bent on as usual at sea but it needed sweat and labour to bring up cable from the tiers to the other.

'Sir, may I know—'

'As I desire to do a running moor, Mr Bray,' Kydd answered him sharply. 'A simple enough exercise, I believe.'

The boatswain hurried over as if to be certain he'd heard aright but left as quickly, and the fore-deck became alive with activity.

The frigate glided ahead slowly; there was little enough time before they would be losing all way through the water.

'Both bowers cleared for mooring,' reported Bray, expressionless.

Kydd looked over the side. Two, three knots – it was going to be a near thing.

He was searching for the current. The general trend for the Baltic was opposite to the Mediterranean – a continuous outward flow instead of the constant inward thrust at Gibraltar that had so often balked Nelson.

Here in the bay a counter-current could be expected and it was essential for his plan to find it. He gazed over the glittering, pond-like sea and there it was, the barest shadowing of ripples, oriented parallel with the shore a half-mile or so away.

He sniffed the tiny wind – he could do it!

'Stand by, forrard!' he roared. The anchor would be at the cathead, now lowering to brush the surface of the sea. All was in the timing.

'Bring her round.' *Tyger* answered her helm languidly until aligned to cross the current at right-angles. 'Let go, larboard!'

The big anchor fell. The sea-bed was not far below, silt and sand.

A running moor needed sea-room but he had plenty of it. First one anchor would be let go while way was on the ship, the cable paid out to its greatest extent and then, only then, the other would go down, leaving the ship with two widely separated moorings.

Tyger slowed with the last of the airs and obediently swung under the greater influence of the current to face into it, her anchors neatly in place, out on either bow.

'Pass the springs, if you please.'

A line would be seized halfway down the cable and led back to the ship – but in through a side gun-port well aft, one to each side.

'They's coming!' came an excited call. 'The buggers are on to us!'

Everyone's head snapped up and took in the frightful sight of an endless stream of gunboats appearing around the rocky point at the end of the bay and heading directly for them.

Under oars and scorning the lifeless airs, they massed together – dozens of evil craft, the gleaming black of their single big gun visible on their fore-decks. At some signal they separated into two divisions, which stretched out to take their deadly positions off *Tyger*'s unprotected quarters.

Kydd watched, his arms folded, waiting. On both sides guns were manned, gun-captains waiting too, their guns unable to bear, no target in their sights.

Bunched together out of sight of *Tyger*'s guns, the gunboats manoeuvred for the kill, and when they were in position,

Kydd acted. 'Larboard broadside, heave in starboard,' he said quietly.

The fall of the spring was taken to the aft capstan and the haul began, foot by foot – the line, secured at an angle to the anchor cable, tautened and thrummed through the gun-port. The ship was heaved bodily to that side, rotating around her anchors forward and thereby presenting her broadside at the gunboats where they had been expecting her weak and gun-less stern-quarters.

Kydd didn't hesitate. 'Fire!'

Every gun opened up together in a furious rage of sound and rolling gun-smoke. To Rowan it was like a physical blow in the face – the stupendous, mind-numbing blast of their great guns in anger for the first time.

When it cleared he could see the devastating effect. Shattered boats, oars, bodies in the water – and all those who could pulling frantically for the opposite quarter.

Hauling hard, the other spring was brought in – and the starboard broadside ended the fight.

With an inert and helpless ship suddenly brought to life to deal out death and vengeance, it was too much for the gunboats. As one they fled back to where they'd come from, leaving the sorry remains of two of their number behind.

Chapter 29

Tyger's recall came by dispatch cutter, whose captain wasted no time confiding, 'Gen'ral Moore's gone off in a huff. Won't play at war with the Swedes, and now His Nibs can sail when he likes.'

It was welcome news, and Kydd was on his quarterdeck when the frigate raised Gothenburg and the fleet. Sharp eyes noted *Victory* and the others with sail bent on the yards – at long last the fleet was on the move.

Kydd had his orders and there was no need to report so he lay to, bringing aboard last-minute stores and ready to take position when it was time.

The longed-for signal came down smartly in the flagship.

Then, in accordance with the order of sailing, the fleet formed up in line ahead for nearly a mile of unchallengeable puissance, the legendary *Victory* in the van, leading the grand progression that was England's Baltic Fleet off into the unknown. Gathering astern was an uncountable number of merchant ships at last on their way, and ranging ahead were the frigates.

It was to be the Great Belt route to the Baltic, no flaunting off Copenhagen but the pointed insertion of the battle-fleet between its island and the mainland a far more potent demonstration of effortless superiority in the subjection of Denmark to the will of England.

The airs were light and erratic and it took patience and skill to conn the fleet through the eighty-mile passage to the open sea, but with the sight of the steep white cliffs at the tip of Langeland, Saumarez and his great fleet entered the Baltic. Course was shaped to larboard to thrust deeper into the sea. As the distant blue-grey of the lands to starboard slipped by, Kydd reflected that this entire coastline from end to end was in Bonaparte's hands – it was chilling testimony to how the war had so turned against them that now only Sweden remained a friend.

As a scouting frigate, *Tyger* soon left the fleet astern, reaching out into the seas ahead, her station the south Swedish coast, which they would reach the next day.

It was Kydd's customary first-night-at-sea-on-a-mission dinner and his great cabin was suitably dressed. Tysoe had laid out the green and gold china service that Persephone had insisted Kydd must have and, with the silver he'd acquired as a result of successful actions over the years, he could boast a very respectable table.

Above the cabin door was the framed needlework by an unknown hand – 'Tyger, tyger, burning bright!' – and along the varnished panels were other adornments that Kydd's wife had lovingly chosen for him: miniatures of wild creatures, calm and stately scenes of country life, wistful and charming rustic moments.

And, most precious of all, a self-portrait done at his insistence. It had been executed in haste, yet the strong, bold daubs without the customary delicate finishing gave such vitality to the piece that he could feel her presence radiating out to him, the warmth of a smile that was for him alone. It found its place in the centre over the line of the stern windows, above where Kydd sat now, host of the evening.

'Come now, gentlemen, we're to show our respect to the cook with this feast!'

It was a welcome chance to make the most of fresh shore-side produce while they could. It would be a challenge from now on for Saumarez to victual his fleet, given the hostile lands on all sides and the far distance to the victualling yards of England.

The dishes were taken appreciatively, and when the loyal toast had been given, the brandy made its appearance.

Kydd allowed the low murmur of conversation to wash over him, a little subdued under the realisation that they were essentially alone as they penetrated deep into a hostile sea in a headlong rush into the unknown. The Baltic might well turn into the next ferocious crucible of contending powers, Britain fighting for her life against the colossal forces that Russia with France could bring to bear – and they would be in the forefront.

Kydd's gaze roamed over the table. The hard, ruthless and efficient first lieutenant Bray; the patient intelligence of Bowden, who'd been with him since those far-off days of his first command; the unsmiling and prematurely matured Brice, whose conquering of his own demons had led to Iceland and Persephone.

And the others: the genial and utterly competent sailing master, Joyce, the brave and modest Royal Marine captain, Clinton, the careful but shrewish purser, Harman. And, of course, his confidential secretary, Dillon, whom he'd trust with his life and who had become, of all aboard, the closest to him.

In the glow from the brandy his thoughts were drawn to the mess-decks where shipmates of old had their being. Without doubt they were spinning yarns and entertaining each other with tales of the seven seas – and keeping the world at bay as old shellbacks always did.

Toby Stirk, messmate with him since Kydd had been a pressed man in the old *Duke William*, who'd quickly come to believe that Kydd would go far and now trusted him as a captain he would follow into the gates of Hell itself.

Ned Doud and his inseparable friend Pinto, both of whom he'd shipped with before the mast and shared adventures with, and who had taken to following him as well.

Then there was Halgren, his big Swedish captain's coxswain – how did he now feel, Sweden invisibly out there in the darkness? And—

'Gentlemen, your attention, please!' The talk fell off immediately at Bray's forceful growl.

This was irregular – they were all guests at Kydd's table and Bray had no entitlement to demand speaking rights.

'I'm not one for words,' he began, triggering smothered smiles all about him, 'but now seems right to say m' piece.'

Having the table's rapt attention he got to his feet and faced Kydd. 'Sir, it's been a while since we faced the three frigates not so very far astern from here. We all threw in our coin t' get something for the ship as will help us remember that day, 'cept the scurvy crew that did it were well adrift in their timings, but now I has it. Sir, on behalf o' *Tyger* frigate, we ask you'll look after this'n for the noble barky.'

He was handed a bulky package, which was passed on to

Kydd, who had to beg a seaman's knife to cut the string, his own long put away.

It was a punch bowl, not the usual chaste silver but of well-turned plain china, which was perfect for the purpose. In rousing colours and trimmed with a gold base it had a remarkably accurate and detailed depiction of the engagement on one side and on the other a pleasing vignette of what could only be himself, splendidly poised, training a telescope on the enemy, standing on the quarterdeck by the helm and under an unduly large and billowing flag.

'Why, this is beautiful,' Kydd said, admiring it from all angles. 'The gold rope trim is hawser-laid, I see, none of your lubberly cables. And here, finished with right true Carrick bends as will stand any sea and still give good service, the ends seized as will prevent capsizing.'

Everyone in the cabin nodded, the metaphor most pleasing.

'I'll certainly take good care of it, gentlemen, and it will come out for every visitor who needs to be told of *Tyger*'s valour.' He was sincerely touched, for this was not only a gesture to himself but an expression of their common bond with *Tyger*.

'On behalf of the said lady, I do accept this distinguished ornament in perpetuity.' The traditions of the service held that the trophies of a ship that went out of service would be stored respectfully, then passed on to the next with the same name. 'Thank you indeed – all of you!'

Chapter 30

The morning saw them passing Bornholm to starboard, on course for the patrol line later that day at the fleet rendezvous, which would be off Karlskrona, the main Swedish naval port.

Kydd had been in the Baltic before but that had been in the southern part, off Prussia and the ancient Hansa towns. This was the north, colder, more sparsely settled and with the islands bare and patched with scrubby vegetation rather than forested, a bleakness that was distinctive and solitary.

A little after eleven the topsails of the fleet were sighted and shortly all the ships sailed on together until they reached the lee of one of the many offshore islands where their anchors tumbled down into the ice-grey waters.

Talk on *Tyger*'s quarterdeck became animated. Would the fleet be kept as a whole and flaunted off Kronstadt to tempt the Russians out or would it be sent piecemeal to the various parts of the Baltic that needed a presence?

Saumarez wasted no time in summoning his captains,

and Kydd joined the others in *Victory*, keen to know how the commander-in-chief was going to employ his fleet.

As evening was falling he returned with a satchel of orders, notes and instructions. 'Mr Dillon – my cabin, instanter!' he ordered, as soon as he was inboard.

The table was brought out to full size and the satchel contents slapped down. 'We've to hoist these in before we sleep, Edward. It's a fleet we're joining, and this one's set fair to be the hardest-worked of any I know.'

Dillon groaned at the sight. Each of the orders and instructions had to be entered into the right place, ship's standing orders amended and everyone from the gunner to the purser apprised of their duties. Charts and sailing directions to the master; signal codes to Brice as signal lieutenant; victualling demand forms to the purser; returns expected from the boat-swain – it was endless.

'I'd take it right kindly in you should you give me an offing,' Dillon said, his sea lingo not up with his erudition in foreign languages.

Kydd agreed as it would allow time to take a glass before they began. 'Very well. In first, he's to let Admiral Keats take care of the Great Belt as he's always done, the Danes showing so valiant with their gunboats. This is his prime attention, keeping the gates o' the Baltic open.'

'What about the Swedes?'

'I'm coming to that. His orders tell him to give assistance, but they're aggrieved with how it's to be done. So Admiral Saumarez is playing cautious. We're not going into Karlskrona dockyard. He'll keep the seas until there's a firm arrangement as sees both sides happy. And that's exercising him more than any.'

'Why so?'

'If he can't touch at any port, how can he victual? We're leaving the soft tommy for hard tack in a week, and where will be found all the beef and pork fifteen thousand men must have daily?'

'You say "he". Does this mean . . .?'

'It does. The fleet stays together in these waters so as to make itself useful, whether it's a mort of trouble in the Sound or from deeper into the Baltic. On the other hand almost all frigates are on detached service. Two in the south Baltic to clap a stopper on any of Boney's trade wanting to get out, put down privateers and such vermin, two to rove off Norway and the Skaw and two in the upper Baltic to keep an eye on the Russkies.'

'Ah. Then we . . .?'

'Not any of these, Edward, dear fellow. Ours is another course entirely.'

'Attending on the fleet.'

'God forbid. No, we brought it on ourselves – it's outside the Baltic, far away. None other than our old friend Archangel.'

'The Arctic north!'

'Yes. Having been there before, *Tyger* is seen as best suited to go again. This time we go in war array against the enemy. A short cruise only but they'll know we've come visiting, I believe.'

In the morning he broke the news to his officers, who were impatiently waiting for word: that Saumarez thought it proper to investigate the ports of the north and gain intelligence on the Russian military, that they were not amassing a battle-fleet there and that the Dutch had not joined them in an unholy alliance.

Tyger was the obvious choice for the task and so important was it deemed that reinforcements had been requested from England to accompany them.

The rendezvous for the little squadron, Captain Sir Thomas Kydd in command, was to be the west Swedish port of Marstrand, one week hence. There was no time to lose and, stores complete, *Tyger* sailed.

Chapter 31

As winter quarters for the British fleet, Marstrand was well placed. Ice-free, only fifteen miles north of Gothenburg, it was sheltered on all sides and ashore offered a fleet-worthy establishment of storehouses and repair sheds, even a tavern or two. On the bare slopes above it was the stern round tower of the Carlstens fortress.

The day they arrived, however, it was less than a welcoming sight for a steady drizzle drifted across in ragged curtains. Kydd watched as the anchorage opened up, keen to know what his reinforcements amounted to as sent by a reluctant Admiralty. But all he could see was a single brig-sloop, not unlike *Teazer* of old, and a gun-brig of lowly size tucked close in to the shore.

Noting their British colours, *Tyger* cast anchor near them, but unaware of their pennant numbers Kydd simply hoisted 'all captains'.

The gun-brig was first away, her little cutter making wet but determined progress toward *Tyger*.

Kydd waited at the side. An officer came over the bulwarks

and advanced to greet him. 'L'tenant Garland, captain of *Snipe* gun-brig,' he blurted breathlessly. 'Reporting as ordered.'

Absurdly young, his look of sincere admiration was almost comical in one so damp.

'Captain Sir Thomas Kydd, *Tyger* frigate,' Kydd responded, doffing his hat in reply to the youngster's removing his. 'And if you'll attend on me in my cabin.'

He was taken below while Kydd waited for the brig-sloop's pinnace to reach the side. The ship looked familiar but he couldn't place it: one of the many of her kind that were doing every task that came their way along the seaboard of Britain, this one distinctly old-fashioned with her bluff bow and sharply curved, ornamented beakhead, not often seen in today's plain wartime craft.

There were bumps alongside as the pinnace hooked on, and shortly after, the worn cocked hat of a commander appeared, then the man himself, in a dripping boat-cloak, who punctiliously faced aft and uncovered before doing the same for Kydd.

It was Bazely. His friend since the days when Kydd had been a young commander of a brig-sloop.

'Why, who would have thought it so?' Kydd said with delight. 'M' dear fellow! Step aboard and you're right welcome.' The sloop was, of course, *Fenella*, from those far-off days on the coast of Cornwall.

Bazely merely gave a short bow and remained mute.

'Come to join the sport, hey?'

'Reportin' as ordered,' he said woodenly.

Kydd was taken aback at the attitude but the last time he'd seen Bazely was during some of the wilder excesses he'd descended to while on leave in London. Among other things, he had been seen in public with the disreputable Prince of

Wales and his circle. Kydd had since left that behind, but he recalled Bazely's bitter words when they had parted that Kydd had forsaken the sea for high society. Surely Bazely didn't still hold it against him – didn't he know that the high seas were where *Tyger*'s captain's heart lay?

'Let's get below out of this cursed weather,' Kydd offered and led the way below.

Tysoe had a hot negus ready for them and Kydd, taking one armchair, gestured to Bazely to take the other, Garland contenting himself with a straight-back chair.

'Well, gentlemen, we've some excitement ahead, I believe.'

Bazely regarded him levelly, saying nothing, cradling his drink.

Kydd was annoyed by his attitude: now was the time to be open and forward. He needed to have a measure of his captains, their experience, their views on the mission, their dedication to the team. For all their long acquaintance, he'd never known Bazely as a fighting captain, and had little knowledge of his seamanship skills.

He deliberately turned to Garland. 'We're for the north, the high north. Have you service there, perhaps?'

The young officer coloured. '*Snipe* is my first command, Sir Thomas. I've only service on the east coast. I'm sorry, sir . . .' He trailed off.

'No matter, and you, sir?' he said evenly, looking at Bazely.

'None.' Still the wooden tone.

'I see. Then you'll both have to be guided by me. *Tyger* has been this way before and knows the ropes.'

'Sir. These Arctic waters, shall we be expected to fight at all?'

'I do not say it's impossible, Mr Garland.'

'It's just, well, to think to fall on the enemy while in conditions that . . .' He was pink with embarrassment.

Kydd sympathised. The young man had probably seen no real fighting. His little gun-brig was a small enough craft to challenge the high north – and his imagination was no doubt seething with frightful images of ice mountains and polar bears. 'It's not so hard a place in season. Why, there were quantities of merchant jacks from Hull and similar that used to make the voyage to Archangel every year without inconvenience.'

He looked deliberately at Bazely. 'Do you have any concerns at all, Commander?'

'Many.'

'So?'

'How am I to rig m' men against the weather, without I've any slops of the right sort t' give 'em?'

'This is a fleet yard. You'll have my note to draw what's necessary before we sail. Anything else?'

'Victuals. If we're on a cruise t' the north, *Fenella* don't have the endurance, let alone *Snipe* here.'

'You'll be on *Tyger*'s books while we're away – and that's my complication, not yours. More?'

Was it that Bazely, still only a commander after all these years, resented Kydd's rise, having to take his orders?

'Yes. What in Hades are we about in these latitudes?'

Kydd drew in his breath. Should he demand respect, the occasional 'sir', the formalities of rank? In the kind of mission Kydd was anticipating, men's lives would be at hazard and a sulky subordinate was the last thing he needed.

'Intelligence, looking into Archangel to see if the Russians or any are intending mischief. And on the way I've a mind to stir up both them and the Norwegians, who I'll remind you are the enemy in these parts.'

It seemed to satisfy but Garland stirred uncomfortably. 'Should we not be rather reporting to Admiral Saumarez, Sir Thomas? We've little enough force together, I'm persuaded.'

He shrank under Kydd's look, but then Bazely took it up. 'He's right. If it's intelligence we're after, that's what we're there for, aren't we, for God's sake?'

Kydd bit off his retort and answered shortly, 'Understand that there's higher matters involved here, as make it damn near imperative. Our course is set and I will not have argument.'

He'd arrived at some far-sighted conclusions that he was confident were the right ones. He'd been to the high north before and knew its remoteness, a frozen territory far removed from the usual ebb and flow of the civilised regions. It was untouched by the great war that was raging, age-old practices still observed, people following the same time-worn rhythms of life in their isolation. Now he was returning: to lands that were enemy but defenceless. If he came down on them with fire and thunder it would be carrying the war directly to Britain's foes for a remarkably small outlay of naval force.

And the result would be that in fear all trade would cease. To defend the long coastline, troops and ships would have to be diverted to the dread conditions of the north, all at great expense to the enemy, and loss of those numbers to the battlefield in England's ally Sweden's war.

He didn't really expect any war-fleets in Archangel. How would the Russians have got ships there, given there was only the one route, out of the Baltic, through Saumarez's fleet and around the entire swell of Sweden, Norway and then the Barents Sea? No, as last time his would be the biggest ship on the coast. *Tyger* would do her duty and visit but he'd be surprised if there was anything at all to report.

Bazely folded his arms coldly.

'So. Stores complete, we sail two days hence.'

'Orders?' Bazely was pointedly requesting written orders covering eventualities such as falling in with the enemy, rendezvous in stress of weather and the like. Kydd nodded an agreement: he'd get them, even if Dillon would be working long nights again.

There was desultory discussion over charts, pilots, watering and other matters, but each officer found reasons not to accept an invitation to dinner.

As they stood to go, Kydd said quietly, 'Ah, Commander Bazely, a word with you before you leave?'

After Garland had closed the door behind him, Kydd opened, 'Edmund, I'm at a loss to account for your bearing towards me. I'd reckoned you a friend. Are you offended in some way?'

Bazely's eyes glowed but he did not respond.

'Is it something you've heard, a false—'

'I've nothing to add t' what I said when we last parted.'

'About my exchanging the sea for the high life ashore? If that's all it is, then I can tell you—'

'Anything more . . . sir?'

It wounded Kydd. There were few enough friends left from his younger days and Bazely's usual colourful banter had always brought a smile. Now they were working professionally together for the first time and it had to be like this.

'No, I won't detain you any further,' Kydd replied, saddened that his good fortune and rise in society had triggered resentment and surliness unworthy of the man he'd known.

Chapter 32

Leaving the Atlantic facing Norway to the British squadrons already on the coast, Kydd's plan was to go to work beyond Tromsø and the Arctic Circle to the far north before the descent into the Barents Sea.

Sailing into a freshening north-westerly, *Snipe* was making the running. Kydd was gratified to see that the young lieutenant clearly knew his ship: with lee gunwales nearly awash, the little brig was bucketing along in fine style.

As they thrashed northwards the cold was bitter and insinuating, felt in every wind-blast, rain flurry and dash of spray. Kydd spared a thought for the others in his little convoy. The Tygers knew what to expect, but in *Fenella* and *Snipe* men would be entering the first stage of misery when work on deck would leave them numb in body and mind, and without a galley fire in these harsh seas, they were denied the solace of hot victuals.

They would be paying little attention to the marvel of the midnight sun, the sharp spicules of driven ice crystals on the air, the green-white monstrous surging of the polar seas. Kydd had had the foresight to send senior hands from *Tyger* across before they left to give homely advice to the seamen of the pair, and purser Harman had obliged in the matter of recommendation for stores and clothing. If this had been followed they had the best chance against the elements, and once they'd rounded North Cape the battering from the north-west would ease.

Seventy-five degrees north latitude reached, it was safe to bear away around the top of Norway.

It had been a kinder passage than the one *Tyger* had done before, the stark plunging cliffs of North Cape appearing out of a mild haze over to starboard on time as expected. Now to put his plan into train.

The sailing master had conscientiously recorded their movements before and he was better prepared with reliable charts and notations, so Kydd confidently stood on until the coast began to trend south-easterly. And he found what he was looking for: a fjord deeply incised into the iron-black coast with a sharply twisting entrance that gave excellent shelter. The wind was cut off, as if by a knife, as they rounded the entrance and glided in to anchor off the massive scree-slope of one of the encircling mountains.

Here he would stay for several days while the smaller ships recovered – and at the same time take the opportunity to assess the situation.

The high north prospect was as frightful as he remembered: the majesty of snow-streaked peaks, the peculiar intensity of the smell of brine, the infinite desolate dark crags, the immense clouds of sea-birds. And the silence.

From first *Snipe*, then *Fenella* wisps of smoke rose out of the galley and the three ships lay to their rest.

* * *

But soon it was time to put out into the Barents Sea.

'*Sail hoooo!*' The cry came almost immediately they met the open water – a galley-built barque, low in the water and strange in looks, with its up-rearing bow, faired-in stern and brightly coloured hull.

'A gun,' Kydd ordered. A forward six-pounder cracked out and sent a ball across its bow. The effect was instant: its sails flogged about in panic until they were brought in and the vessel came to an untidy stop. There was no flag that he could see, and that meant an examination.

'Away my barge, and I'm to board myself. Mr Dillon, Halgren – you're coming with me.' He needed Halgren's Swedish and Dillon's Russian.

Veteran of countless boardings as a lieutenant, Kydd knew what he was after and it would be a rare bird to escape him with contraband on board, but it was information he needed more.

'Sir, says he's *Zemlya* out o' Vardø, bound f'r Hammerfest,' Halgren said at length. 'An' claims he's a Pomor and has a licence.'

The master was a long-faced individual with the largest beard Kydd had ever seen. His crew, bunched behind him, were shabby, frightened, and watched with dark, alien eyes.

'Ask him what flag.'

'Says again as how he's a Pomor, no flag.'

'What the devil—'

'They're sea gypsies,' Dillon explained. 'Half Russian, half Norwegian or neither. They've been fishing and trading in the north since the time of the Vikings.'

'No papers, then?'

A grubby parchment was produced, in Cyrillic characters and totally incomprehensible to Kydd. Dillon took it and pronounced that it was a licence to trade granted by the *Kem* of Solovetsky, which was in Russia.

'Doesn't mean he's Russian – only that he's squaring yards with them,' Kydd said. 'What's his cargo?'

In response the main-hatch was opened. The hold was tightly stowed with sacks of grain.

The Pomor master was clearly anxious. A powerful frigate of a foreign but distant empire comes from nowhere into their hard but untroubled world, firing guns. What did it all mean? 'No treasure, only corn, and does this offend the English sea-captain?'

Kydd grimaced. 'Ask the beggar whether he's seen other men-o'-war in these waters.'

'Says he's only a humble Pomor trading on the coast and—'

'Never mind. Tell him we're letting him go.'

This was no enemy to be wiped from the seas, still less to be made prize.

He returned to *Tyger* in an irritable mood. 'Signal "proceed",' he snapped.

The word would now get out that an English squadron was in the offing but that was all to the good for what he had in mind.

No sooner had they rounded the stern headland of another fjord than two more sail were sighted. One put about and disappeared behind an island but the other stood on.

'Take us beyond the island,' Kydd grunted to the master. A bad conscience was as good an indicator as any of prize-worthiness.

The ship, a little larger but much the same in build, saw the frigate cut across its path and decided to give up.

Kydd boarded with Halgren and Dillon once more and found a similar situation – the ship in corn and headed the same way.

He ordered the hatch opened. As before, a tightly packed cargo of grain sacks.

'They take corn west and dried fish east while the weather holds,' Dillon translated.

At this rate— Kydd paused. Why was the first ship nowhere near her marks and this, equally loaded, low in the water? He glanced into the closely stowed hold. What if . . .?

'I want five hands to rummage this hold!'

With the sullen crew and nervous master watching, they hoisted out layers of grain sacks – and then, open to the daylight, there was the true cargo. Tubs of tallow, chaldrons of pitch, resinous tar, linseed, wax, iron, furs. All exports of a blockaded Russia, contraband, on their way to the wider world.

'And his papers?' Kydd asked, but knew it was too much to expect a manifest, charter party or port clearances, none of the usual maritime commercial evidence that could condemn the ship as prize. And who could say for a certainty that these were Russian goods?

In the usual run of things, the vessel would be judged good prize after a Vice Admiralty court hearing, but they were in the inconceivably remote north. The correct way was for the vessel to be carried into an examination port by a prize crew, but the nearest would be Leith, a thousand stormy miles away. And the value of the cargo was in no way compensation – it was of far more worth to Russia, whose revenue depended on getting its exports out.

Kydd considered his options. Destroy the ship? That would make him judge and executioner in one, and his sense of fair play rebelled at this – and in any case, was this what his little squadron should be doing? Taking the inoffensive ships of the wandering Pomors? It was highly improbable that the

Russians would send any forces so far into the wild north to protect them so it had to be accepted that his main objective was not being gained.

In any case, when word got out, all would skulk in port until he'd wearied and left.

He focused on the larger picture. The Russians were getting past the blockade. They were deriving war-paying income from this and it had to be stopped. Not only that but the harmless grain for fish exchange was keeping Denmark's vassal Norway fed while its fish went to the Russian war effort.

Should he return now with his report to Saumarez, proposing a standing force on the coast? After all, apart from the Baltic, this was the only access Russia had with the rest of the world, and if it were severed it would cause incalculable harm to their cause.

'Where's he from?'

'Vardø, as was the other. This is their main port.'

Back in *Tyger* he had the master produce his charts. 'Vardø – where's that?'

It took a little while but they found it: in Finnmark, a Norwegian port and therefore fair game. It was tucked away in one of the fjords not so far distant.

Kydd looked closely. Well sheltered, apparently in the lee of a mountain chain – and on an island.

His eyes gleamed. It was all very possible.

He summoned Bazely and Garland, who sat warily to hear his plan.

Kydd outlined what he'd learned, principally that the ancient Pomor trade was now smuggling contraband and had to be stopped.

'I've heard o' this crew and they're naught but fisher-folk and beggars scraping a living,' Bazely grated. 'Why do we have to go against 'em, poor bastards?'

Kydd held his temper. 'Because they're aiding the enemy. And we've a chance of striking at the heart of the whole business.' He smiled grimly. 'By going instead against the merchants as give them their cargoes.'

'I don't understand, Sir Thomas,' Garland said, wide-eyed.

'He means, knock at their door an' demand they kindly stop.'

'Commander Bazely!' Kydd flared. 'Be damned to your distemper! I'll have you pay respect due my person or it'll go further, I promise!' An adverse report to the commander-in-chief would put his sea career in jeopardy, something Kydd was reluctant to do. He kept his gaze fixed on the man until his eyes dropped.

'This is my plan. Vardø is well sheltered by a pair of overlapping offshore islands. I've no doubt the Pomors choose the inshore route to the town but we shall stand in between these islands to give us our surprise. Once in, we shall see what opposes us. If there's a fortress of size or anything larger than a frigate we shall withdraw. If not, I shall stay hove to in order to assess the situation with a view to the most effective motion we can contrive, which I will hail across to you both.'

Garland looked as if he wanted to speak.

'You have objection?' Kydd asked coldly.

'Oh, no, sir! It's just that, well, we're sure to come across quantities of these Pomor craft, all capital prizes. Do you think—'

'No, I don't. We haven't the prize crews.' He relented, aware that any talk of prize-money to a needy lieutenant with a ship to care about was decidedly attractive. 'I regret it, but we have a wider war to take notice of, Mr Garland.'

'So we take, burn, sink and destroy the beggars . . . sir.'

'You heard me, Commander – I said we'd lie off while I decide the manner of our engagement.' He paused. 'Depending on circumstances we may require to send in a landing party. Royal Marines and seamen from *Tyger* and *Fenella* and, if necessary, a further division of seamen. Prepare these for deploying at any time after we appear off the town. I shall expect all action to be broken off and a complete retiring before dusk. Inform your men of this, and that consequently any left ashore will stay there. Signals and other instructions will be ready in the morning. Any more questions?'

There were none, and after they had returned to their ships, Kydd was left alone with his doubts. Just what could a frigate, a sea cruiser, do against a town? Even if in company with a sloop and gun-brig. He'd never heard of such an action since the age of Vernon and the Spanish Main, and this was completely different.

What if there was opposition? Any determined repulse might well end with him damaged and unable to proceed on to his larger mission. Should he give up tamely and sail away to the contempt of all?

No – he was making what he believed would be an active and significant strike against the enemy.

In extended formation the three ships raised the outer islands of Vardø at dawn, cleaving the polar seas on their way to war. For the sailors, in their thick clothing against the biting chill, this was a strange and disturbing sensation. The islands were bare, bleak and with not a single tree anywhere, simply naked rock with blotches of green in crannies and clefts.

'Quarters, sir?' asked Bray, his face suspicious and tense.

'In a little while, perhaps. Keep 'em below decks for now, out of the cold.'

He could see Bray was uncharacteristically on edge, distracted, but he'd joined *Tyger* after their previous Arctic voyage and these conditions would be new to him, the sights harsh and alien. A proud man, he wouldn't ask questions.

'Form order of sailing,' Kydd grunted, as they passed between the islands. The flags shot up, fluttering loudly in the frigid breeze.

'And now you may go to quarters,' he added.

Snipe shook out more sail to take the lead with *Fenella*, *Tyger* staying prudently astern – he would be warned soon enough if there was any menace within.

The two smaller ships disappeared through the passage but did not return. *Tyger* held her course and, after clearing the rust-red bluffs at the end of the island, the whole prospect of the port of Vardø opened up.

Kydd took it in: the town was in the centre of the bay, more than a quarter-mile of huddled wooden buildings, once brightly coloured but now faded and drab. The waterfront had its cargo-working gear to one end, three vessels alongside it, more offshore waiting and, behind, a row of warehouses. Nowhere was there a man-o'-war and the gentle slopes did not bear any sort of fortification.

As instructed, the two brigs separated and went to either end of the settlement, then put about and beat in towards each other, their blue ensigns streaming out for all to see.

Kydd paced on his quarterdeck. Vardø was there before him – helpless, vulnerable. A wind flurry bit into his bones and in that moment he felt melancholy at what war was demanding. He caught himself and brought to mind why they were there.

Then he heard a distant thud and saw a rapidly disappearing puff of smoke from the ridge above. They'd finally woken up – his blood quickened and he looked for others.

Another – this time from the opposite end of the ridge. He couldn't see where the ball had gone; the two brigs, well inshore, had held their fire and were apparently untouched.

Minutes passed. Then the first opened up again, a flat *blam* against the wind. He saw the shot strike in the sea well out from the two brigs, and far wide of *Tyger*. Another shot from the second gun, its ball nowhere to be seen. Kydd shook his head in disbelief. Just two cannon to defend a town!

Snipe and *Fenella* were converging on *Tyger* for orders.

By the time Bazely rounded to under their lee Kydd had a plan.

'*Fenella*, ahoy! You are to take aboard my landing party, and with your own will land them at the wharf under Captain Clinton.' Bazely would have the sense to cover one half of the party landing with the other half.

'They are to set afire the warehouses and godowns under the protection of your battery. Once ablaze you will then re-embark them and retire. Understood?'

There was a short space before Bazely replied, in a flat monotone, 'What if the town goes up in flames, too? Set ashore a rescue crew or—'

'Do your duty, sir, is all you're asked!'

'The Pomor ships? They'll make a fine blaze.'

'Leave 'em alone. Carry on!'

It obviously surprised Bazely but Kydd had his reasons. The Pomors were not the target: the merchants were. If they

189

howled at their losses, demanding protection, Kydd's objective would be served without the need of further destruction.

The marines and seamen mustered, Captain Clinton with his men in fine array, the seamen, loose-limbed and restless, a midshipman in charge— Kydd looked again. 'Mr Clinton, stand down that midshipman immediately, sir! He's to report to me, this instant.'

Rowan reluctantly left the group and hurried up, sheathing his dirk and removing his ridiculously large cocked hat.

'Mr Rowan, what do you think you're at?' Kydd blazed. 'This is a dangerous landing in the face of the enemy, no place for one so young, sir.'

The midshipman did not reply, a stubborn look conveying all.

'Well?'

'It's my duty, sir,' he said flatly.

Kydd's face tightened: it was most unlikely that he'd been placed in charge without special pleading. 'Mr Rowan, you're confined in *Tyger* until I give word, else – understood?'

The boats pushed off, and Kydd quickly had his pocket telescope up to see progress. An anxious scan reassured him that no soldiery was massing to contest the landing, only figures running, boats putting off, general disorder. The red coats of Clinton's marines were visible as they landed briskly and took position to establish a perimeter before the seamen came in.

The first flicker of flame came from a barred window of the furthest warehouse to the left. His trust in his Royal Marines captain was not misplaced: this was upwind and the blaze would be carried down to the rest.

It didn't take long – soon the conflagration leaped and devoured, advancing down the row unstoppably.

Before dark the entire party had returned aboard. 'A fine stroke, sir,' Bray rumbled, as they watched the eager flames. 'Looks like it'll spread, if we're lucky.'

Kydd did not feel proud of his work, especially when it became obvious that the fire had taken hold in several of the nearer buildings. The entire town was of timber, not a stone edifice in sight, and there would be real fear and panic setting in by now.

It was time to go.

The little squadron reached the open sea and shaped course south-east towards the Barents Sea and Russia.

Kydd retired to his cabin.

'A word with you, Sir Thomas?' Dillon asked from the door.

'O' course, old fellow. What is it?'

Dillon sat carefully in an armchair and steepled his fingers, choosing his words. 'Sir. I pray you won't take amiss what I say.'

'Good heavens, Ned. Whatever's on your mind?'

'A small matter. Sir, it's said in certain quarters that . . . that you're favouring one of the midshipmen. Protecting him, making his path smooth.'

It gave Kydd a jolt. 'You mean Rowan.'

'Just so, sir.'

'Do you think I am? He's only a child.'

'Sir, this may be so but he's a warrant officer and has to learn how to be one.'

'I can't let him rush in, waving a sword and—'

'It's not in his best interest, you standing between him and what he has to do.'

Chapter 33

A day later, and without any change in the hard, bleak coastline slipping past, they arrived at their destination. As if on cue a spiteful squall came from nowhere filling the air with whirling snow particles, sharp and icy, cutting visibility to yards.

Kydd rapped out orders that had sail taken in and a minute gun begin its monotonous bark to keep the little fleet together. The misery continued for three hours until it lifted as quickly as it had come, revealing a measureless immensity of heaving grey sea under a dismal lead-hued sky.

Morale was suffering. Kydd knew what was needed – some real action against an armed and dangerous enemy, with something to show for it at the end.

It came rather sooner than he'd hoped.

A large island loomed ahead. *Tyger* led the way past its ten miles or so of louring crags that ended abruptly in vertical bluffs with a flat footing at its base curving around out of sight.

Beyond was the blue-grey bulk of the coast of Russia,

nearer than Kydd cared for after the recent squall, and he gave orders that took them further out to sea.

Brice, the officer-of-the-watch, had his telescope trained astern at the island. 'I'd swear . . . Yes, it is.' He straightened and handed the glass to Kydd. 'Sir, if you'd take a sighting to inshore of the flat area . . .'

Kydd focused the big telescope carefully. 'Masts. And of a size.'

But for their lofty height they would have been concealed by the footing. 'Signal to both "investigate line-of-bearing sou'-west b' west",' he threw at Maynard at the flag locker.

Tyger made to heave to as the pair wore around to beat back to the island.

Their sail disappeared as they rounded the footing and into some kind of bay beyond.

Before they could return, the sudden muffled thunder of heavy guns erupted from inside the bay.

'Down helm – take us back!' Kydd roared. If a battle-fleet was moored there the two scouts were in serious difficulties.

Tyger came round slowly as men raced to quarters.

The guns continued – and Kydd agonised: they must be pounded to wrecks by now.

At the turn of the bay, *Tyger* swept around. There was no battle-fleet at anchor but dozens of ships, some full-sized ocean-going merchantmen, huddled together in a sheltered cove. And on the slopes directly over the anchorage a fort was firing furiously at the fleeing brigs.

Snipe's topmast was a tumbled ruin where it must have taken a shot strike but *Fenella* had gamely passed a tow under fire and was making slow progress seaward. They were saved only by the hopeless inaccuracy of the fort's gunners, probably army-trained artillerymen unused to distances over sea.

The three vessels made for the open sea. Kydd, however, had no intention of letting it rest. The big merchantmen were worth going for alone – they would be bound for the larger world and from them wealth uncountable would flow back to Russia and its war.

By the time the horizon was innocent of land he had a plan and summoned his captains. 'I see you've swayed up a jury topmast already,' he complimented Garland. 'Well done.

And my respects to Commander Bazely for his timely tow.' There was no response.

'It's my intent to make assault against the shipping,' he said, without preliminaries. He looked deliberately at Bazely as he spoke but there was no change in expression. 'They think we've been driven off and are no doubt celebrating.'

'It's madness,' Bazely broke in. 'Close in, with that great fort, they'll knock us t' flinders before we've even set about the merchantmen. Sir.'

Kydd gave an icy smile. 'Do allow me to finish before you make judgement, Commander.'

He spread out a roughly sketched chart of the end of the island. 'The island's name is Kildin. It's near uninhabited but its purpose is to guard the entrance to the Kola river, well used by the Norwegians and others. The fort is to watch over their safe anchorage.' He paused and added, 'Tonight after dark we will take the fort by storm. Afterwards we'll attend to the merchantmen at our leisure.'

Garland looked unhappy and shot a quick glance at Bazely.

Kydd continued, 'We have the advantage of surprise and, more than that, we will be landing here, the opposite side of the island and less than two miles behind them.'

'The whole coast is cliffs! We can't scale 'em in the dark, for God's sake!' Bazely retorted.

Kydd thinned his lips and spoke very carefully, as if to a child: 'There is a cleft, a gully in the scarp. We mount up there to the top and deploy.'

Years ago, as captain of *Teazer*, a brig-sloop the same size as *Fenella*, he'd done exactly that in Guernsey, having topmen with tackles haul up a swivel gun with which he'd successfully stood off an army. He saw no reason why it couldn't work here, even though it had been only an exercise that time.

'I've never heard o' such a business. What if y'r gully is blocked or similar?'

'If the gully is impassable the entire action is called off.'

'This is—'

'Your part is safe enough, Mr Bazely, at dusk to sail about again and make motions against the ships as though cutting them out. The fort will fire away and, being blinded at night by the gun-flash, you have little to fear.'

Bazely coloured and bit off his retort.

'A blue rocket from me signifies success with the fort, at which you are to land and join with us. A red rocket means a failure and you are to withdraw immediately.'

'And I, Sir Thomas?' Garland asked.

'To sail about discharging your guns at random to confuse the Russkies still more.'

There were no further questions. The landing party would be Clinton's marines, with a division of seamen from *Tyger*, and as the brigs would not be involved ashore they'd no need of details.

Kydd's squadron stood out to sea, for all any on land knew, in full retreat. At the appointed time the course was reversed and as dusk drew in the island loomed ahead.

The brigs separated and headed for the inner anchorage.

Timing was critical: there was a low, near-full moon to the north but it would be gone in two hours. If they were not in position by then it would be futile going on, but as well a fearsome thing to return back down the scarp. Kydd remembered how long it had taken in Guernsey to scale the cliffs – and that had been in daytime.

He had a picked band to go in but they couldn't produce miracles. Bray had demanded command but Kydd decided to take charge – if this risky venture was not working out he could abandon the assault at that point rather than carry on obeying orders with vain heroics.

Tyger lay to under backed topsails as her boats went into the water. Kydd would be in his barge with the men detailed for special tasks, Clinton in the launch with his marines, and the seamen in the cutters.

On impulse Kydd called down the deck, 'Mr Rowan. With me – messenger.'

The lad raced up, his face a picture.

Guilt stabbed at Kydd. What if . . .? 'Stay by me at all times,' he warned sternly. 'You're my runner and I must have you near in case I've an order to send.'

'Aye aye, sir!' There was no mistaking the eagerness and excitement. 'Shall I have a cutlass, sir?'

'Runners don't have such. It slows 'em down.' The one thing the child would not be doing would be going hand to hand in a desperate fight.

They set off without delay, heading into the preternaturally ghostly shore, the slop and plash of the oars loud in the air.

The gully was easy to find, the open cleft a stark shadow with a tiny shell beach below. The boats crunched into it and the men tumbled ashore, their equipment and muskets piled in readiness while they assembled.

The moon cast enough light but it was at a low angle and threw long, dense shadows. That didn't deter the topmen: with their coiled lines over their shoulders their duty was to get up the dismaying tumble of rocks in the cleft.

Standing tense, the others waited for word while Kydd reminded himself that if there was no way up he could call the whole thing off without loss — at this stage at least.

One part of him half hoped that this would the case as he glanced at Rowan beside him, importantly doing his duty and seemingly unconcerned of what lay ahead.

After an eternity a low voice carried down. They were halfway up and had found a path.

Kydd went forward, grabbed the guide-rope and began to haul himself up, the seamen and marines following. An alien chill and spectral shades made it fearful going. In the utter stillness every sound was magnified as they clambered and slithered up in the shadows.

Pressing on, the line of men followed until unexpectedly the escarpment fell away, and they were on an uneven plateau bare of grass or scrub, undulating down to the south in the fading luminosity. They came together in order. Kydd took out his compass for a bearing and pointed the way. The enterprise was on.

Clinton's scouts moved out and the rest followed in a line. It was hard going over loose stones and sandy gravel; there were curses in the anonymous darkness, and as the moon lowered below the line of cliff-top, their progress slowed in the inky blackness.

As far as Kydd knew, their objective could not be more than a mile or so ahead, but reading a map in the dark was out of the question. They could move on only in trust that a single compass bearing would bring them to the right point.

And then – in obedience to orders – the night split apart.

Alarmingly close ahead heavy guns opened up, livid flashes leaping skywards as gun after gun crashed out into the blackness to deter the impudent British raid on the ships in their charge. The fort must be over the ridge, obligingly giving them confirmation of their position and positive direction. The little party hurried forwards.

Kydd's plan was that all attention would be elsewhere but it was a perilously close margin between coming within sight and making the actual assault. He goaded his men on as they stumbled and fell on the stony ground.

At last the rear of the fort came into full view in all its squat menace. It was as he'd seen from the bay: lengthy, to give maximum breadth to mount the cannon, and with quarters at the back. And, praise be, the height of the walls was a mere fifteen feet or so, nothing for agile topmen, and near the centre, large swinging doors gave entry and exit. No mighty fortress.

Kydd saw that Rowan looked petrified and thrilled at the same time. The gun-flash played on his young face as he peered ahead, spellbound.

But this was no time to be distracted and *Tyger*'s captain forced concentration on the task in hand.

Lying full length while the bellowing of the guns continued, he took reports. Brice – his topmen with their grapnels ready to go. Clinton – every man at arms, waiting for the word. Stirk – gunner's mate with the fearsome task of hunting down the magazine when the doors were opened in time to prevent a suicidal detonation.

Kydd didn't hesitate. 'Go!' he hissed.

The topmen raced across the open space, unchallenged.

It was the critical moment: Kydd rose, then loped towards the walls, expecting at any moment a line of muskets to appear but there was only the continued hidden crash and roar of the great guns.

Nearer, he could make out figures atop the wall – still no opposition!

The rest of the charge bunched at the big doors, completely vulnerable from above and then, from inside, scattered shots. Pistols? Sounds of scraping and thumping were heard at one door and then it swung wide.

Kydd flung himself inside, his sword out, ready for the sudden rush of defenders – but by the light of several stands of lanterns in the inside square he could see that, apart from a few running figures, it was deserted. His mind scrabbled for an explanation.

'Clear the guns!' he bellowed, gesturing with his sword along the embrasured fortification. His men sprinted for the stone steps at each side while Clinton coolly had his marines kneel in careful aim, picking off the gunners, who milled helplessly without orders.

Kydd realised why there was no real opposition: his distraction in the bay had worked better than he'd dared hope. The fort commander had sent his troops down to the wharves to confront what he'd assumed to be a landing, fatally overlooking the possibility of a simultaneous land assault from behind.

Rowan was close behind him, dirk out, uncertain, tense.

'Stay by the gate,' Kydd snapped urgently at him, then turned to Stirk. 'You take that side, I'll take this.'

Without a word, the big man turned and, with two others, left quickly on his deadly quest.

The magazine would have an entry port and steps down, but at which side of the fort? They had no time to think – he had to cover this part.

With Halgren his only companion, Kydd ran over to the base of the other side's steps.

He reached a door – it was open, and led into a room. Further in there was a sudden wisp of flame, its tawny light growing and dancing. Kydd burst in and saw a Russian officer bent over, dropping torn papers on to a candle in the middle of the floor.

The officer looked up in naked fury. Yanking out his sword he threw himself at Kydd, who met his charge with a hasty parry, the loud clash and hiss of steel the only sound. They swayed together. The man smelt rank, beast-like, and his livid moustached face was inches from Kydd's.

In a convulsive heave Kydd pushed him away, but his quick lunge was savagely knocked aside. Kydd hastily swept his sword up for a return slash and their blades met with a slithery *kraaang,* the power of the blow visceral and merciless.

Another wild swing came, which Kydd met with difficulty, its ferocious malignity suggesting it was coming from the fort commander whom he'd so publicly humiliated by defeat. *Where was Halgren?*

They pulled apart, panting, circling warily. The wildly flickering candlelight cast devilish shadows and he noticed the man's waving blade – a curved Asian weapon, almost a scimitar and heavy with it.

In a sudden onrush, the man was crowding, slashing, the confined space making any swordplay crude and brutish.

Kydd stumbled on some loose object and the man's teeth showed in savage triumph as he swept up his blade for a crushing blow to the head but Kydd's sword was up in time and it was met in a clash of steel on steel of shocking violence. *Where the Hell was Halgren?*

With a frantic twist to the side he was out from under, but too late to turn his blade. He smashed forward with the hilt of his sword into the man's face and heard a crunch. With a muffled cry the officer reeled back, clutching at his bloody head. Kydd did not waste his chance and his deadly thrust caught the man squarely in the chest, sending him to his knees with a look of horror before he slumped forward, dead.

Gasping and heaving, Kydd turned and stumbled out to see Halgren picking himself up, two bodies at his feet.

At the same time a seaman raced towards him. 'Mr Stirk's respects an' he's found an' made safe the magazine.'

The guns were now silent, abandoned by their crews.

It was a victory.

His eyes sought out Rowan, still faithfully at the gate as ordered. 'Find Mr Maynard,' he panted, 'and tell him it's a blue rocket this time.' Trembling with shock, Kydd sheathed his weapon and leaned against a wall to steady himself. It had been a near thing.

An image pushed itself to the front of his mind – Persephone, his dear and true love. Did he have the right to make her a widow?

The answer came with the question. He would always do his duty, as she would know he must. If it ended against him, it was as much his fate as a happy return to her.

And with it came another answer. That once the fight was on he need not fear the fatal weakening of her presence – from the nervous uncertainty before a contest through to the chaos and madness of a pitched battle there was no time for tender thinking, even if he wished it, and he could go on in confidence that he would never let himself or his men down in that way.

The present returned. 'Get those guns manned – they'll be coming back!'

When the first wave of soldiers topped the rise, they were met with the brutish thunder of heavy shot that sent them fleeing frantically in all directions.

Stirk came up, his face rueful. 'Ain't no way we're able to blow th' fort, sir. There's nary a pinch o' powder left to us.'

A parsimonious Russian bureaucracy had no doubt seen to it that this northerly outpost would receive no more than a nominal share of gunpowder. Kydd's crowning scene, the explosive end of the Russian fort, could not now take place.

But there was another thing they could do.

'All hands not guarding prisoners, to the guns. I want 'em capsized over the walls.' He added, 'And when they're down, get the prisoners to haul them to the cliff edge and tumble 'em off. Understood?'

At the deserted waterfront Bazely and a couple of dozen of his men waited for orders. 'What's to do with these all?' he asked, his sweeping gesture taking in the many ships now lying helpless before them. The tone was offhand.

To Kydd, again, there was no question of prize-taking. And a good two-thirds of the huddled throng were Pomors.

'Take all the three-masters and destroy by burning. Leave the rest.'

Chapter 34

Before the streaky pale dawn broke, Kydd had the squadron at sea on the last part of its mission – gathering intelligence on the Arctic town of Archangel, the only port left to the Russians until they broke out of Kronstadt, the dockyard at St Petersburg, and confronted Saumarez. If there were any moves against England by the Russians joining with the Dutch and French, Archangel was where it would be.

The mission needed careful planning. Following the coast trending south-eastwards through the Barents Sea, they would reach the fabled inland White Sea, the gateway into the heart of Muscovy. With an entry-width of not much more than twenty miles, it was beyond belief that, being at war and with the ice having retreated, the Russians weren't patrolling it, possibly with some of their large frigates. Should he take on a hard action all for the sake of what could be discovered within?

From past experience Kydd knew that Archangel was set well within a maze of flat marshes and endless muddy delta riverines. The last time he'd had a pilot with him – could he make it through with the countryside up in arms against him? It was a daunting prospect but it was the main mission of his cruise north and he had to find some way of discovering the truth.

The snow-streaked prominence of the end of the Kola peninsula loomed; they were now turning south and entering the White Sea.

It had been timed for early morning. There were two sail abroad; by their size they were Pomors, unlikely to contest his presence. Apart from them, the seas were empty and, in tight formation, the squadron forged south, keyed up for the first encounter.

By degrees the water took on a definite discolouring, a drab vegetable wash, the tell-tale sign of the great Dvina river issuing out from the immense land mass of Asia, on whose banks Archangel lay. They were now well within the White Sea in its south-east part, with vast uncharted regions to the west and south. Still no patrolling frigate or worse.

It was only a few hours' sail from the wide Mud'yugsky anchorage where *Tyger* had rested before. Men-o'-war could very likely be there.

Kydd sniffed the wind: the same steady nor'-wester – fair for arriving, foul for leaving. The next hours would be a tense time. The sea and landscape were exactly as he recalled, dreary, lifeless, repellent . . . and quiet.

The anchorage emerged ahead, a mass of ships all facing into the current from the Dvina. *Tyger* cruised past them, no colours aloft. Kydd examined the vessels closely. The dozens at anchor all had bare spars. No sail bent on, no movement to sea expected. And not one anything remotely like a warship.

Curious faces appeared on their decks but there was no panic-stricken rush to flee, just a careless lassitude.

He put about and stood out a mile before the squadron hove to. Should they sail away, satisfied that there were no threats here in the north? Or, as his orders read, 'Look into Archangel' for enemy activity?

Bazely and Garland boarded promptly and he took them below.

'So, no sign of the enemy. You've not been in these parts, I have. *Tyger* has too deep a draught to attempt the passage to Archangel up the delta. If *Tyger* can't reach Archangel then neither can the Russians.'

The gift of intelligence that he'd be bringing back was the priceless information that there could be no ship of consequence in these regions, for to go further in the Barents Sea they would meet the great barrier of Novaya Zemlya and the pack ice, no place for any naval squadron.

'I believe we've evidence enough there's no threat to us here.'

Bazely said nothing, his gaze expressionless.

'If you wish it, Sir Thomas,' Garland said keenly, 'I'd make attempt to—'

'Thank you, no.'

'The mission is over?' There was the barest hint of sarcasm in Bazely's tone.

'Not immediately. I've something in mind as will tell 'em we've come calling.'

'Which'll be . . .?

'No bombarding of Archangel, if that's what you desire. Instead a much more damaging stroke.'

It would be against the White Sea Company, which hunted

whales from Archangel even to the remoteness of Spitsbergen. He remembered the operation that had had the whalers putting to sea from Archangel with empty vats in which they'd concealed furs, but now they'd be back to their old calling. And that meant, on return, landing the vats of whale-oil at the receiving depot, Severodvinsk, where deep-draught vessels could safely load.

They set sail, the depot just an hour or so down the coast to the southernmost mouth of the Dvina.

It was a scene of desolation: a waste of frost-pale marsh-land extending across the entire horizon, unrelieved but for a sprawling huddle of wooden buildings next to a long, low wharf.

Kydd went ashore with the landing parties; he wanted to make sure the job was done properly.

As scores of workers fled their advance he led them straight to the warehouses where the vats were stored.

'Up-end 'em, then let the gunner's crew do their work,' Kydd ordered the seamen, then stood back as they moved in.

As they tackled the huge vats one by one, a fortune in whale-oil was spilled, cascading in honey-coloured streams into the sandy soil. The empty copper vats were then set upon by the gunner's party with hammer and spikes, effectively rendering them impossible of repair.

The fishy stench was all but unendurable and Kydd left them to it, finding a fringing sandy beach to stretch his legs. The land midges were out in clouds, the sliding muddy Dvina nearby, with its floating detritus of decayed branches and sod-clumps listlessly issuing out into the sea. It would be good to be quit of the place.

Unexpectedly a figure fell into step with him. It was Bazely, who stared ahead as if in thought, then turned to Kydd. 'I confess I've misjudged you, Sir T.'

Kydd stopped and smiled with relief. 'How so, old fellow?'

Bazely paused, then pronounced, 'Because I was wrong. You're much worse than I ever reckoned on.'

Kydd felt a dull heat rising, as Bazely continued, 'You were hell-bent on making y'r number with the nobs at court because you've got ambition.'

'What makes you—'

'Don't deny it. You've got so much ambition it stinks! Whenever there's a chance o' making glory you're into it, gives no mind to who's to pay for it. You're after your flag! Some poor buggers are going to be passed over as yellow admirals so you can hoist y'r bunting is what I can see.'

'You're out o' soundings, Bazely!'

'Why else all this roaring ashore, throwin' everything into a fright when all you're asked to do is get intelligence, which we got today in an hour?'

'If you don't know why, then it's not for me to explain it to you, Commander,' Kydd said tightly.

'All you're doin' now is puttin' in time before you gets y'r battleship. No more th' simple sailor you, Sir T, only the company of that scurvy crew o' politicians an' dandies will do. Well, this is to say you're welcome to 'em. Good day to ye.' He strode off without a glance back.

Kydd fought down anger, then came to a sad realisation. This was not jealousy or a mere accusation of ambition – every naval officer had ambition, and some had been blessed with good fortune, like himself. No, Bazely wouldn't have risked his standing by antagonising his superior unless there was a more compelling reason.

He'd been reaching out for the companion and step-ashore shipmate he'd known, and all he saw was a bird that had flown so high it was now out of reach.

There was absolutely nothing Kydd could say which could alter that. Bazely, in his way, was saying goodbye to his friend.

Chapter 35

They had made good landfall – *Tyger* was squarely astride the line of rendezvous off Karlskrona – but there was no fleet. Not a ship in sight.

The day was dull, metallic, the seas an unbroken expanse to the horizon, the winds fitful.

'They're off to settle the Russkies,' Bray said darkly.

Why else would Saumarez and his battle-fleet be absent from his carefully chosen strategic base among these islands?

To make certain, Kydd sent *Snipe* and *Fenella* on opposite courses along the rendezvous line; both were back before dark with no news. The age-old worry of a detached commander came back to haunt Kydd: should he go off in search of the fleet or stay where he was and wait for them?

He spent the night hours polishing his report. Whether the fleet had seen battle or no, the commander-in-chief would need his account of the Arctic regions of the enemy. There was nothing to say about a famous action, but he was satisfied with his initiatives to distract the Russians – there'd be consternation in Moscow when they discovered their entire northern flank exposed, and Saumarez would be grateful therefore at the breathing space this would give him as the Russians regrouped.

The morning broke with no grand line of sail lifting above the horizon.

The fleet could be in any direction – defending Stockholm to the north, standing before the Russian fleet to the east or meeting some threat from the southern Baltic. The only reasonable course was to stay on station and trust the commander-in-chief would remember them.

In the early afternoon *Snipe* came at a clip out of the west, leading a cutter, which brailed up in their lee.

'Admiral Saumarez sends his compliments and desires you do join him at Matvig,' came the hail.

'What's that?' Kydd blared back.

'The Baltic Fleet's new base. Follow in my wake.'

It was less than fifty miles to the west in the middle of the great bay of Hanö, with two approaches entering either side of a scatter of offshore islands and a broad harbour within. And with the priceless ability to relay warning of the advance of any hostile presence from island to island in minutes.

Victory was anchored in the heart of the fleet, her commander-in-chief's flag prominent. Kydd lost no time in putting off and making his number.

Saumarez rose and greeted Kydd cordially, sitting him immediately and taking a seat opposite. 'You'll have news for me of the high north, Sir Thomas,' he said.

Kydd detected an air of distraction but this was hardly surprising given the burden the man carried. The flag-lieutenant took his leave and Kydd loosened. 'I have, sir.

There are no signs of any kind that lead me to suppose the enemy has a presence of significance there.'

'I'm pleased and relieved to hear it.'

'And Archangel cannot have any ships of force at hand. This I can assure you, sir. The north is quite without menace.'

The lines on the admiral's face eased fractionally. 'One less anxiety for me in these fevered hours. You've done well, sir.'

'Thank you, Sir James. I should mention further that on passage I took the liberty of entertaining the enemy ashore, such that he is now to be distracted by fear for his unprotected north. I trust this will cause him to divert resources to its defence at the cost of those facing our friends.'

Saumarez stiffened. 'Am I to understand you took it on yourself to make descent on Russian sovereign territory? To attack the Tsar's realm?' he asked sharply.

Kydd quickly detailed the actions, at a loss to account for the suddenly hostile attitude. 'As they are the enemy, sir,' he concluded defensively.

The admiral got slowly to his feet and went to the broad sweep of the stern windows where he stood facing out for a long moment. He turned back wearily and took his chair, his face now lined with worry. 'It's not your fault,' he muttered, looking away. 'I should have seen it.'

'Sir?'

'Sir Thomas. You are deservedly a renowned and much-applauded officer. And from your position you believe it your bounden duty to take the war to the enemy.'

'I do, sir.'

'To seek out and destroy and so forth.'

'Sir James,' Kydd said resentfully, 'do you feel I've failed in my professional obligations to you in some way?'

'As you see it, no. As I must, it has been . . . unfortunate.'

'May I be told why this is so?'

'Very well. I will be candid, as your conduct is essentially blameless and correct.' He collected his thoughts and went on: 'The very qualities that make you an outstanding breed of officer are those very same that are an embarrassment to me at this time.'

'I do not understand you, sir.'

'The character of dash, initiative, daring. These are the qualities of a first-class frigate captain. Yet they are not what is wanted on this station. I shall be plain-spoken, as is your right to hear, and tell it from my side as commander-in-chief.

'Your reasoning for your actions is not to be faulted. Yet it does not take into account the larger picture, which I must tell you is delicate in the extreme.' He paused. 'What do you know of Russia?'

'A backward peoples ruled by a tyrannous tsar, who happens to possess the largest war-fleet that faces England at this time.'

'This is true, very true. Should I then fall on it with all my force and settle the matter once and for all?'

'That would seem logical, sir.'

'Then what of my orders, the principal one of which is the security and continuance of the Baltic trade?'

'As it is so preserved.'

'What if the fortunes of war favour the enemy, that my fleet is scattered? In a moment we are undone, the Russians are upon us as a wolf in the fold. All is lost. Better I stay my hand that the enemy are in doubt as to my motions.'

'I see, sir.'

'Now, conceive of what you may have brought about by your actions. The Tsar is a proud man, stubborn and imperious.

212

He hears of your assault on the soil of Russia, an insufferable insult. How do you say he will react?'

'To take troops and guns from before the Swedes and—'

'No, sir, he will not. He knows that we have no interest of our own in the north and, in any case, it would be foolish to invade or garrison it. There would be no point therefore in the transfer of valuable troops. Instead he will take other action as will restore his dignity before the world. He will be obliged to suffer his fleet to sally from Kronstadt and thus bring about the very thing we least desire.'

Kydd kept silent. This was not how he'd anticipated his reception.

'Not only that, but the Tsar, recently humbled at Tilsit, has his people to think on. A wretched crew, but their merchantry may well be turned against us by your destruction. These, sir, are the very ones we wish to take our goods and now they'll be driven into the hands of the French.'

'I – I'm truly sorry for what I've caused you, Sir James.' It was the only thing he could say in the circumstances.

'Don't concern yourself so. On balance, I rather think it may not occur thus. Tsar Alexander has much to occupy him with his incursion into Finland, which requires all his resources. And, as I said so lately, it were my fault to send so enterprising an officer into this situation and not expect him to act naturally.'

'It was only from my desire to aid our Swedish ally, sir.'

'And laudable for all that. Yet even there our condition is . . . intricate.'

'Sir?'

'Are you not curious that we are in this remote anchorage, in no way reliant on the support of this ally? When we could be safely within the bastions of Karlskrona? It is because of . . . of circumstances that demand I remain independent of action.'

'If you could explain further, sir,' Kydd prompted, picking up on the hesitation.

Saumarez gave a small smile. 'I shall do better than that. You shall discover it for yourself.'

'Sir?'

'After a series of reverses in Finland the Swedes are asking for naval assistance. I shall reply when I have greater intelligence of their capability – or lack of it. To this end I've been asked by the Swedish Admiralty to release an officer of rank to advise them. This same should be neither a junior officer they will not respect, nor a senior whose rank will flatter them for their importance. In fine, Sir Thomas, you are providentially on hand to render me this service.'

Chapter 36

Kydd had been assured the assignment would be for no more than a couple of weeks, and in his absence *Tyger* would be attached to the fleet for local duties.

He had much to think on as the aviso cutter slashed through grey seas eastwards to Karlskrona, the home port of Sweden's navy. Saumarez had taken his initiatives as a sincerely intended strike against the enemy, but he'd made no secret of his view that he was little more than a spirited frigate captain with scant idea of the larger picture.

And there was every reason to take this assignment as a means of cooling Kydd's ardour: in his instructions Saumarez had been at pains to point out that Kydd was not empowered to make promises or commitment of any kind, merely to give advice on current tactics of the Royal Navy, its capabilities insofar as that applied to the Baltic Fleet, and any suggestions of an operational nature that he might feel from time to time would be acceptable.

On the other hand, he was to see this as an opportunity to take the measure of the Swedes, their strengths and weaknesses, with a view to a future combining of fleets in the face of the Russian threat. All would depend on the openness of the Swedish, and on how successful he was in getting along with them.

At the same time there were many questions to which Kydd needed answers. Just what had happened behind the scenes with the Swedes that had General Moore abandon the Northern Expedition? Why was Saumarez taking pains to distance himself in his naval dealings with them? If Russia was the common enemy why were they not doing everything in their power to come together against the foe?

He remembered the reception in Gothenburg when the governor had let slip that while they were allies they were not necessarily friends – and Envoy Thornton's reaction at Kydd's question to him. Would he find what was behind it all?

They raised the outer islands that so effectively guarded Karlskrona. No commander of a square-rigged vessel of size would dare risk entering this offshore maze – the confined waters between made tacking and wearing against an unfavourable wind out of the question.

It was impressive: countless vessels of all classes moored in neat rows, larger vessels in the outer reaches of the five-mile-wide harbour. Kydd realised that numbers and types would be known to Saumarez and took in the prospect of a major Baltic naval port.

The cutter knew where to go, and before long Kydd was stepping up to the quay before the stern naval headquarters, the large blue and yellow-crossed ensign of Sweden floating free.

He was met by a neat, slight officer who stepped forward

and saluted. 'Welcome to Karlskrona,' he said crisply, his English nearly flawless. 'Örlogskapten Jens Strömsson, at your service. Sir Kydd, I believe?'

'It is, er, Commander.' They shook hands formally and Strömsson threw some words at waiting seamen, who took charge of Kydd's small baggage.

'My ship is the frigate *Krigare* and you are to be my guest.'

Processing quickly, they reached the end of the quay and a waiting four-oared boat. They were taken out to where a vessel lay moored, smaller even than his old command, the brig-sloop *Teazer*.

Strömsson saw Kydd's surprise and said, 'A frigate, yes, but modest and trim as will be at home among our islands.'

First impressions were good: clean, taut and well fettled, the little warship looked the part.

'How many guns?' Kydd asked.

'Four twelve-pounders and sixteen three-pounders.' Kydd kept a blank face. A puny enough fit for a sloop, let alone a frigate.

They were piped aboard and Kydd was taken to the great cabin immediately, even before being introduced to the two officers in the side party.

'My cabin is yours, sir,' Strömsson said, with an expansive gesture. Kydd knew better than to refuse his sacrifice and bowed in acknowledgement.

'We will take a drink together while we talk.' A light golden liquid in small glasses was proffered; Kydd recognised the caraway fragrance of *akvavit* but this was quite different from the Danish liquor.

'*Skål!*'

Putting down his glass, he saw that Strömsson was regarding him intently, as though making up his mind about something.

'Sir Kydd, or do I call you . . .?'

'If you allow me to call you Jens, then it's Thomas, my friend.'

'Thank you, Thomas,' he said, raising his glass with the hint of a smile. 'We will be friends, then.'

'Yes.' The intelligence in his features was matched by wariness but Kydd warmed to him.

'Do you mind if I speak directly?'

'As you will.'

'Your orders, Thomas. They must tell you to discover what you may about our navy, but more than anything whether we can, or will, fight next to you against the Russians.'

Cautiously Kydd agreed.

'I will tell you now of my orders. And they are to deny you this.'

'I see.'

'No, you cannot. We are a proud and great sea nation – in the century just past we ruled the Baltic as our own. And at Svensksund in 'ninety we scourged the Russians to a famous defeat. Why not now? And if you have a powerful fleet and we join with you, we'll be the inferior and therefore the subordinate one. My king will never countenance this.'

'Jens, it was your Admiralty that asked for me.'

'Yes, they did. That I and others may learn what they can of the navy of Nelson that will help us in our encounters with the Russians.'

'Why do you tell me this, Jens?'

'Those are my orders, which I have told you, and now I say they are foolish and disastrous. I will disobey them.'

Kydd blinked in astonishment. Strömsson went on, 'We're in common cause against Bonaparte and the Tsar both. Or that is what the world believes.'

'Are you not?'

'No, sir. We are too riven with strife and disagreements, too many divisions, factions. You should be aware that the King is surrounded by French followers, the worst of these includes foreign minister Ehrenheim, his own private secretary Baron von Lagerbjelke and many others. They see this Bonaparte win his every battle on land and their admiring knows no limit. They will not rest until they have an aligning.'

'Will they succeed, Jens?'

'The King is still on his throne and keeps all power in his hands. There are plots, conspiracies, betrayals — but none dare raise a hand against a Vasa.'

'You are still loyal.'

'To Sweden, and therefore her king. But . . .'

'Yes?' Kydd prompted.

'The King is not, as who should say, a warrior. His military decisions are sometimes . . . rash. His understanding of the world some would say is childish, others deluded.'

'And you, Jens?'

'I . . . I fear that he is as they say. An example — without declaring war, the Tsar has sent his armies into Finland to seize it from us. King Gustav's response? To send his army in the opposite direction to take Norway from the Danes!'

'Ah.'

'And worse. By insisting on personal command, he's lost the handsome offer of a British expedition to help defend his kingdom. Now he stands fair to losing the assistance of your Baltic Fleet in facing the Russians at sea.'

So this was what was happening at Matvig. Saumarez was keeping the eccentric king at arm's length, what he'd termed 'retaining his independence of action'.

'How goes it in Finland?

'Not so good. We lost our great frontier fortress of Svartholm within days and the Cossacks have ridden overland to defeat our best generals and take all of the south.'

Kydd brought to mind the chart of the Baltic with one finger pointing east, the Gulf of Finland, which ended in St Petersburg, and the other pointing north, the Gulf of Bothnia, which separated Finland from Sweden.

'They can't threaten Sweden itself. They need to cross the Gulf.'

'Oh, it won't come to that. We've lost the southern lands but they can't go on – the fortress of Sveaborg is still safely under our flag and lies in their rear.'

'Sveaborg?'

'Our most mighty and impregnable stronghold. It lies on an island and contains dockyards, stores and, above all, the *skärgårdsflottan*, our archipelago fleet of a hundred ships of many kinds and all designed for Baltic warfare.'

'Then what is your main worry? Military, that is.'

'I have been open with you, Thomas, as I must be. This is to give you fair understanding of our position when you go back to speak with your admiral. And I have to say to you now, our army morale has been gravely sapped by these events, as has the navy's. It means, sir, that not all officers are reliable. Their spirit is troubled, their allegiance uncertain.'

'Why do you tell me all this?'

'The stakes are very high. If we cannot best the Russians at sea, they are free to go on to invade Sweden. If we can, then they cannot support their armies and must fall back, and Sweden is saved. All depends on this.'

'And your forces are not enough to settle the matter.'

'On their own, no.'

'I can promise nothing.'

'I understand that.'

Kydd felt unreality creeping in. Here, in the cabin of a foreign man-o'-war, he was hearing near-treasonous disclosures from one who desperately wanted to ally with them against the common foe.

Then he understood: if in the future there was a joining of arms, and the British uncovered this state of affairs for themselves, there could be no more trust – the alliance would be a dead letter. On the other hand, if they were aware of it beforehand, then any agreement of combining would be with eyes open, no undue expectations, and therefore could be relied on.

'Then I believe we understand each other, Jens,' he said, with a broad smile. 'What shall we do now?'

The relief was evident and Strömsson eased. 'Thank you, my friend, for your comprehending of my position. There's much I would ask you but it can wait. We sail this afternoon for Sveaborg and on the way we will talk of sailoring and Nelson.'

Chapter 37

They were soon at sea before a brisk westerly.

Kydd saw the ship was manned well but that spirit and mood were lacking. At manoeuvres, instead of energetic and purposeful team-work, there were sullen shouts of command and reluctant hauling – how would this translate to a close-in fighting situation?

The two other officers were of quite a different stamp from Strömsson: older, suspicious and surly, so unlike the confident professionals of the Royal Navy. At dinner Kydd tried to engage them in talk about themselves, the war, the future. It was hard going. And at his customary evening turn about the decks before he retired for sleep, he heard a stream of snarled pessimism and hostility from the officer-of-the-watch.

Strömsson tried to make up for them. An educated and observant man, he was a good conversational partner and Kydd's respect for him grew.

'In my father's day we ruled the Baltic – the northern and southern shore both, all paid respect to our flag. Now we're held in contempt. I fear for our destiny, my friend.'

Kydd tried to change the subject. 'What's our task today, Jens, you cracking on at such a pace?'

'Dispatches. We call at Stockholm for the King's dispatches to Finland — to Sveaborg therefore. It's been a hard winter this year, there's still much ice. You've seen some?'

'I have — Spitsbergen, and I won't bother explaining why we were there.'

'Ah — well, we've nothing to stand before that, but in the higher Baltic in some years it's very reluctant to melt in the spring. We'll probably meet some on the way.'

Strömsson returned from Stockholm in a bleak mood and had *Krigare* back at sea and beating east without delay.

'The news is not good. The Russians are pushing further into Finland and our generals are letting them. In confidence, my friend, these dispatches for Sveaborg are from the King, true, but in their character are not what they need to hear. Defeatist — to hold the fortress to the last man and so forth. They need instead strong and encouraging words that stiffen and inspire, not this.'

'They'll hold, of course.'

'They will. We call it the "Gibraltar of the North" for its might and strength. And we have a matchless advantage — the fortress is commanded by none other than Admiral Cronstedt.'

'Oh?' Kydd said politely.

'As you island English will not know,' he said, with a smile, 'this is the man who won for Sweden the greatest naval battle in the history of the Baltic, Svenskund, against the Russians. He's no stranger to facing them on the field of battle. And within the shelter of Sveaborg lies our entire archipelago fleet. I have no fears for its survival, Thomas.'

The next day the weather grew noticeably chillier. Kydd recognised the keen, almost metallic tang that lay on the air: it was from wind that had recently passed over wide areas of ice. He shuddered.

Reducing sail they laid course to the north. Within a few hours Kydd saw the tell-tale luminous white glimmer in the low horizon ahead. Ice.

They raised the first outer islands – dark contrasting crags set about with fringing white, the sea around them now an ice-mush, floes disintegrating into yet smaller floating fragments. And, above the whole, a wreathing frost-smoke.

With a practised eye, Strömsson nodded. 'We'll not make Sveaborg in this.'

It was clear that, further in, every island was joined to the next, set in an unbroken flat expanse of ice extending as far as the eye could see.

Crisp orders had *Krigare* altering to starboard, making for one of the anonymous islets that sprawled across their bows. Kydd wondered how charts could be used when every sea-mark was the same – a hump of snow pierced by occasional streaks of dark rock.

'Vallisaari. We use it when iced-in.'

A boat was lowered and prepared, Strömsson's dispatches in their satchel placed carefully aboard. 'Do come, Thomas. You must meet Admiral Cronstedt if only to tell your grandchildren.'

The boat set out, the monotonous bump of ice against the bow increasingly continuous as they headed in to a small pier.

'Lazy fellows.' Strömsson snorted as they approached.

'No welcome?'

'They should have spotted us coming in. I'll rouse 'em out of their cosy quarters.'

They disembarked and headed for a scatter of farmhouse-like buildings. There were lights but no one seemed to be about.

Embarrassed, Strömsson went to the back where there was a small stable block spread with straw. He shouted once but there was no reply, merely three curious horses' heads appearing at their stall. 'Damn the blaggards!' he ground. 'We'll have to take horse by ourselves to cross the ice to the fortress.'

He saw Kydd's expression. 'Don't worry, it's quite safe.'

Impatiently he strode to a stall. 'I've dispatches that can't wait. Here, I'll ride this one, you take that chestnut.'

Saddled up, they took a flanking trail around the island.

It was yet another new experience for Kydd, crossing solid ice on horseback. As they rounded a point he was reassured by the number of black silhouettes on the whiteness between them and the blunt squareness of the white-streaked fortification. Some of the figures were huddled together; others walked; a few were on horses.

Strömsson carefully negotiated the irregularities at the edge and then on to the smoothness of the solid ice, the hoof-strikes sounding uncannily wooden and hollow. Kydd gingerly caught up and Strömsson broke into a smart canter, ice-chips flying up in every direction.

They passed one huddled group, then another.

From behind them came a cry of surprise. Strömsson's head whipped round to see. 'They're greencoats – Russians!' he yelled at Kydd, his face distorted with horror. Then he squinted ahead, as if in disbelief that the Swedish flag lazily floating atop the walls was still there.

'Ride! Ride for your life!' he screamed, crouching over his horse's neck and thrashing the beast unmercifully. It lunged forward in a frantic gallop and the two raced together over the gleaming ice in an insane frenzy.

Kydd could just hear the soft popping of musket fire above the thunder of hoofs but dared not look away. The grey-blotched, white-streaked walls were much closer now, but barring their way a group of musketeers were kneeling and bringing their pieces on aim.

Strömsson swerved giddily and drove straight at them. One or two puffs of gun-smoke appeared and they broke, unnerved, scattering. The two horses shot through and on to the ornamental gate. Soldiers appeared along the line of the battlements, spreading out along the walls – would they realise they were friends under pursuit and open the gate?

Nearer still Kydd saw that the gate had a flight of steps before it, surely impossible for a galloping horse – but Strömsson didn't slacken speed. At the last moment he brutally wrenched the reins to one side and his horse, caught by surprise, skidded sideways and fell sliding to its haunches before fetching up in a tangle of hoofs and tackle in the verge of snow-covered grass before the steps.

Kydd instinctively did the same and threw himself bodily aside. His snorting mount did likewise, launching his rider into the snow-drift. Then he felt himself tugged to his feet and dragged forward, the buzz and *spanggg* of bullets all about them. At last the gate opened and they stumbled through.

'Rare sport, Jens!' Kydd managed, but the officer was barking questions at a sergeant.

He turned back, his expression grave. 'Sveaborg . . . is under siege.' He caught his breath and continued, 'These last weeks. Helsingfors has fallen and we are surrounded.'

'Do you think—'

'No. We'd never make it back to the ship. Here we must remain until things become clearer. I have to go to the commandant, now. Stay with me, please, and do not stray, I beg.'

Horses were brought and, with a strong escort, they set off. On the way Kydd took in a vast fortification built on a complex of four main islands, walls and casemates bearing hundreds of guns, countless buildings skilfully laid out – and swarming with troops. There was no castle or stronghold so immense in England that he could bring to mind.

They dismounted at the imposing severity of the headquarters and entered. Kydd was left in an anteroom, a pair of sentries pointedly on guard at the only door, while Strömsson strode into an inner office.

After a short while he came out. 'Admiral Cronstedt desires you attend on him at once,' he announced, his face unreadable.

Kydd followed and bowed elegantly at the stern, upright figure seated behind a massive desk. Two others were standing close.

Crisp words in Swedish were exchanged and Cronstedt bowed slightly, his manner reserved and rigid. 'You're here for a purpose,' he said in a hard voice, his English heavily accented but understandable.

'Sir, it is not by my wish that—'

'I know how you came, Sir Kydd, don't trouble me with that. If I find you are here as a spy, then know we have a short way with such.'

Strömsson intervened in Swedish and Cronstedt relaxed fractionally. 'Very well. You are in the custody of Örlogskapten Strömsson, who is known to me.' He regarded Kydd with something like contempt and continued, 'We are under siege at this time and I cannot be held responsible for anything that may happen to you.' The admiral had a high, bulbous forehead and narrow mouth, almost ascetic in appearance. 'You will share rations and quarters. Any behaviour inconsistent with the status of guest will result in your instant imprisoning. You understand me?'

'I do, sir, and thank you for your courtesy to a stranger,' Kydd answered, with a bow. The two officers behind him glowered as Kydd followed Strömsson out.

Chapter 38

Strömsson returned to their small room at the end of the officers' quarters after spending some time with the adjutant. 'I don't like it,' he told Kydd.

'The siege?'

'Cronstedt. I knew him before, but this is not the same man.' He pulled himself together. 'I'll show you Sveaborg and you'll be happier for it, my friend.'

They strolled around the broad roads that connected the buildings. It was a spacious complex, the storehouses substantial and the defences extensive and in depth.

From a high place Kydd was shown the key points. To the north, not more than a couple of miles distant, was the city of Helsingfors, Helsinki in the native tongue, which covered the low hills for a considerable breadth on either side. Beyond it lay Finland in its shroud of snow.

Kydd made out the Russian siege-lines, at a respectful distance but seeming scattered, insubstantial. A few mounted patrols passed on their eternal round but, apart from them, little was happening. It was odd, jarring, and worried him. 'Jens, this is a siege and where are their guns?'

All sieges that he'd heard of involved an assault led by heavy pounding with a siege-train, massive guns that could batter down the thickest walls and defences. Here there were none, merely an uncomfortable silence on both sides. Surely the Russians could not be trying to starve them out when in a month or two the ice would have melted and supplies could be brought by sea.

'I don't know. This is troubling, a vexing mystery. Why is there not much fighting?'

They walked along slowly, passing scores of the great guns of the fortress – unmanned and laid into the middle distance, all deserted of crews. Then elaborate cantonments with soldiers at their ease, no marching columns or drill parades. Kydd counted the rows of barracks. There must be of the order of five to ten thousand men or more – if the Russians chose to attack frontally they would be butchered, if only by weight of numbers.

They topped a rise and, in the enclosed space where the four islands met, saw the archipelago fleet, iced-in but all of the hundred ships that Strömsson had spoken of, in neat, close-packed rows, secured bow and stern and covered with canvas, ready to throw off their confining and sail when the ice retreated.

'Your fleet, Jens. A brave sight, if I may say.'

Strömsson smiled for the first time that day. 'I cannot disagree with that, Thomas. But did you know that all is in the command of a general? The fleet belongs to the army and each ship has its colonel and ensigns, sergeant and privates. They count themselves the elite while I languish in the regular navy, which keeps itself at sea for the larger reckoning.'

There were docks and workshops, churches and schools – an extraordinarily impressive military presence. It was inconceivable that such could ever be overcome, a fortress impregnable in the full sense of the word.

In the roadway there were even women and children going about their daily lives with complete unconcern, probably those who'd fled Helsingfors to seek refuge in the looming citadel.

Strömsson touched Kydd's arm. 'Look, I have to find out what's going on. Stay in our quarters and I shall be back soon.'

Kydd was anxious to know their chances of getting out – to be detained away from his ship was always the hardest thing for a captain. A cartel with the Russians, a form of exchange? He flopped on his small bed and waited with as much patience as he could muster.

After what seemed an interminably long time, Strömsson returned with a grim face. 'One mystery solved, another in its place. The guns – this is because there is a truce in effect. Cronstedt has been treating with the Russian commander, van Suchtelen. They agree that if we do not fire on Helsingfors, where many of their officers' wives still live, they will not fire on us.'

'The mystery?'

'I cannot understand Cronstedt. Why is he talking to them? Where are his daring sallies to drive them off with his numbers?'

Kydd bit his lip. 'Jens. I will be frank with you. It is of the greatest importance that I get back to my commander-in-chief – and my ship. Soon.'

'I understand you, Thomas, and sympathise – but I tell you, there is something rotten at the bottom of things here and I mean to discover it before we trust anyone.'

'What do you mean?'

'The officers. I hear them talk. These are not the same as the ones in Stockholm. They're melancholy and heartsick at the way the war is going. It can only be the commanding officer who is to blame for this and that is my hero, Admiral Cronstedt, who is surely able to take charge and inspire this great redoubt.'

'So?'

'So I have been listening and what I hear is either vile rumour or a terrible condemning of one whom I believed my hero.'

'Tell me, Jens.'

'You should know that after Svenskund our king Gustav IV Adolf took envy of the popularity of Olof Cronstedt. He sent him away from Stockholm to take command of this eastern fortress and it's said that Cronstedt's never forgiven him, an admiral made to command a land fort, however important. He's been here since and has been brooding on the injustice.'

'As I can understand. But this doesn't—'

'There are those who say he's every reason to turn his back on the King, to make things easy for the Russians, to get his own back. I'm not one of those who believe this, but there are hard questions that must be answered. The biggest is that Sveaborg is the key to Finland. And I say that if it falls our province of Finland must fall with it – half Sweden is lost for ever. Would the patriot of Svenskund do this to his native land to satisfy a common grudge?'

'Surely not!'

'Then there are the factions. He has an army adviser, one Colonel Jägerhorn, whom you saw with him. He's of the peace-with-Bonaparte view. He's ambitious and unscrupulous and wants only for Cronstedt to fail. He fills his ear with every excuse why the army cannot stand and shamefully repeats every cheap rumour, but Cronstedt listens to him.'

'This is nothing but hearsay,' Kydd said. 'All he has to do is hold out for a month or two more – this great bastion with its mighty defences just can't fall.'

'Yes, Thomas, but there is one explanation some talk of that touches on all and satisfies in every particular.'

Something in his voice made Kydd hesitate. 'What's that, Jens?'

'That Cronstedt plans to yield up Sveaborg – for personal gain. He made parley with van Suchtelen after just a day or two of peppering with light field guns. He outnumbers the greencoats two to one but still he asked for a truce. Under the white flag he went to Lonna island to talk. Alone. No one knows what was said but a truce took effect immediately and has held since. Why did it? Because he told them that for a great sum in gold he will bring about a capitulation but, first, they must bring up reinforcements to make it appear good. The Russians like this, for a sum of gold is as nothing compared to the great cost of a long siege – and then they have all Finland fall into their lap.'

'Your greatest sea hero, seen to sell his country into ruin? I can't believe that!' Kydd was scandalised.

'He buries the gold on Lonna and then no one knows.'

Kydd stared at him. 'And you're saying that this means there's an agreement not to fight?'

'I do. Why give over a fortification that's damaged and filled with corpses?'

'No! He couldn't yield it up without his officers rebel and overthrow him,' Kydd said, floundering for reason.

'If he's in league with the peace faction . . .'

'He couldn't!'

'He's going out to parley again soon. If I'm right he'll go on his own and come back with every ground why he can't take the war to the Russians.'

If Strömsson was right, it was a dire prospect. Trapped and helpless, Kydd would be handed over to captivity or worse.

'We have to get away. We can't—'

'They're bringing up Cossacks to throw around Sveaborg. We'd never get through patrols of those brutes. No, my friend, we have to come up with something very soon.'

It was a simple, desperate plan. If there was any indication that the fortress was to capitulate, they would conceal themselves in the clock tower above the church and wait it out until after the surrender, then try to blend in with the Helsingfors refugees being returned to the city. To that end they would stock it with food and water for a few days.

Chapter 39

A party of Swedes gathered below the church. At the sound of a trumpet a lieutenant lifted up a plain white flag. Others fell in behind, and the small band set off across the ice to the low hummock that was Lonna island. A tight cluster of Russians waited on its foreshore.

Well clear, the Swedes came to a halt. A single figure rode to the receiving assembly. They moved away together into the centre of the island, no more than a hundred yards across, and disappeared from sight into a small, well-guarded building.

Atop the outworks, Kydd and Strömsson watched in silence.

In a little over an hour the lone horseman joined his comrades again and they silently retraced their course. Without stopping to speak to the waiting crowd, they disappeared into the headquarters.

'I don't like it,' muttered Strömsson, turning away. 'No noise, no display.'

They had not long to wait. A summons went out: all officers to gather in the great hall immediately.

In their billet Strömsson buckled on his sword. 'Wait here for me. I'll be back directly with any news.'

Strömsson stepped out the short distance to the headquarters and found a place in the packed hall.

The hubbub died away as Cronstedt came out to stand at a lectern. 'Your attention please. I have the gravest news, which I fear will cause much despondency, but I feel it my duty to inform you first.'

He looked over his officers with an expression of supreme regret. 'Stockholm has fallen. The Russian commander has given me these shocking tidings in confidence, together with his assurance that a powerful army is at this moment but days away and therefore a conclusion to this dismal war cannot be far distant.'

In a shocked silence, he went on, 'In view of this, General van Suchtelen has been kind enough to offer me generous terms . . . for the unconditional surrender of Sveaborg.'

The hall erupted into pandemonium, officers shouting and arguing, stamping out their rage and despair.

Cronstedt stood quietly. At length he held up his hands for calm. 'We have endured long and nobly. If we—'

There was a ragged shout from the body of officers. 'To tamely surrender in the face of a few barbarian Russians is not the Swedish way and never has been! We fight on, and with a whole heart. Be damned to this talk of a cowardly submission!'

A bedlam of argument followed and the big room rocked with noise. Grim-faced, Colonel Jägerhorn marched up to stand with the commandant.

Cronstedt waited with a pained expression, then continued, 'I've no need to point out that there are women and children from Helsingfors in great number within these walls, seeking safety. It is only humanitarian to spare them the cruelty of a bloody storming, and taking into consideration our present shortage of powder, I can see no alternative other than to accept these terms while we're able. Therefore – reluctantly – I've hereby agreed to the laying down of arms three days hence.'

'No! Never! Fight on while there's any true-hearted Swedes as will stand with us!'

Cronstedt nodded to Jägerhorn. A column of soldiers trotted into the room, their muskets tipped with bayonets. The officers broke in confusion, stumbling and fighting their way in a mad flight for the doors. Strömsson flung himself after them.

In their quarters Kydd sat appalled at the sudden uproar.

Strömsson burst in. 'Get your gear,' he panted. 'We go to our bolt-hole. It's over, we're to surrender!'

In the riot and anarchy no one noticed their rush to the sanctuary and when they were securely inside they quickly barred the entrance hatch.

'You were right, Jens. Dammit, you were right!' Kydd swore.

Strömsson said nothing, his expression stony. 'He lies, of course.'

'Cronstedt?'

'No, the Russian. There's no possible way they'd get across the Gulf to threaten Stockholm, let alone past our archipelago fleet there.'

'Then?'

'Bluff. The same with his big army on its way. And Cronstedt is going along with it.'

'Does he believe it?'

'I don't know – but I've heard the gunpowder magazine has been under strict guard these last weeks. Whether to prevent the people knowing how little remains or a move to stop powder being supplied to the guns, who knows?'

'Whatever, it's a hard place we're in.'

'I know it, Thomas. Now it's more than ever crucial you're returned to your admiral, else Sweden will never be trusted again and must abandon all hope of any sort of working alliance to save her.'

'So what do we do?' Kydd muttered, looking around at the dusty, littered room that was their quarters.

'Cards?' suggested Strömsson, with a wry grin, producing a pack.

Three days later, through a louvred opening in the tower, Kydd watched as the Russian forces approached over the ice, a long, snaking column of dark-green-coated troops flanked by fur-capped Cossacks on horseback. And through an opening on the opposite side, Strömsson followed what was happening at the Great Courtyard, which was on the highest point of the next island and where the ceremony was about to take place.

Neither spoke as they witnessed the proceedings: the distant tinny sounds of a military band, the endless tramping feet, the harsh commands. And the Swedish colours beginning its slow and despairing descent at the courtyard flagstaff and the brisk, jerking rise of the double-headed eagle of Russia in its place.

For the rest of the day there was confusion and dull noise, with multitudes of people moving in slow, sullen streams, pulling carts and barrows piled high, milling about in no particular direction. Smart squads of Russians marched here and there and listless Swedes without arms shuffled towards their barracks.

The night was eerily quiet, and in the morning the exodus began. Led by the exiled Swedish troops, a procession of people poured out over the ice towards Helsingfors, a mile or so distant.

'I'm not clear what's to be our plan when there's only Russkies here,' Strömsson whispered.

'At night. We wait until they're into their cups with celebration and then—'

A loud, ragged *crrummp* sounded nearby, cutting him off.

He stopped in surprise. 'What the . . .'

Hearing an even louder *whooomf*, he crossed to the other opening and gazed out. From the direction of the dockyard a vast column of smoke and sparks roiled up, shot through with livid flames and growing larger by the minute.

'It's – it's the sacrifice of a hero!' Strömsson breathed, transfixed.

'What do you mean?'

'Some man of immense courage has set torch and powder to the archipelago fleet. At the cost of his life he's denied it to the Russians.'

Kydd shook his head in admiration.

Strömsson became suddenly energised and pointed below. 'See them!'

On all sides there was general panic, figures running aimlessly to and fro, and then, as if in some kind of realisation, they were rushing on to the ice and heading for the foreshore.

'They're fearful the magazine will blow up,' he said, then declared firmly, 'And we're to join them.'

Snatching up his bundle, Kydd hastily followed Strömsson

down the ladder and out on to the slushy square before the church.

'This way!'

They raced down the short distance to the main quay, unrecognisable in their great-coats, and joined the panicking rush spreading out across the glistening expanse.

Slumping forward, driven by fear, they kept a prudent distance from the Russian escorts, who were helpless to stem the onrush, and then they were through.

Slackening pace they kept with the streaming multitudes, panting and witless, like the others, until they reached the Helsingfors shore. As though still in thrall to terrible events, they fled along the streets and away.

'Where are we going, Jens?' puffed Kydd.

'To my uncle's *dacha*,' Strömsson replied breathlessly. 'I regret, up on the hills.'

No one was resident in winter. Guiltily they broke in through the rear and settled exhausted on the shrouded furniture.

'Now, my friend, how are we going to get you back?'

Chapter 40

'A most intriguing and, may I say, entertaining account, Sir Thomas,' Saumarez said drily, raising his eyebrows. 'Where is the örlogskapten now, pray?'

'In close audience with King Gustav, I shouldn't wonder, sir,' Kydd replied, with a grim chuckle.

After a bruising overland haul together to the western shore of Finland, then a thrash in a fishing boat across the icy waters of the Gulf of Bothnia to Stockholm, he was probably the first officer to give detail and substance to the dreadful rumour of the fall of Sveaborg. How it would have been received by the stubborn and eccentric king was another matter.

'Then I'll have you give full particulars to my flag-lieutenant while I ponder what you've just told me.'

'I'd think it a grievous blow, sir.'

'Quite. And perfectly unaccountable in such a martial race. How we're to respond is the question, of course.'

'Finland lost to them.'

'I was more thinking of the higher Baltic lost to us. Sveaborg just twenty leagues opposite Reval, the Russian main fleet in Kronstadt not two days distant – I fear they will now be emboldened beyond our means to stop them.'

'Advance our base to block their ambitions?'

Saumarez frowned. 'Thank you, Sir Thomas, but you may safely leave such matters to me.'

'Sir.'

'Besides which there is the higher call on my services.'

'Sir?'

'That which is always to the fore, the greater cause I'm charged with.'

'The Baltic trade.'

'Quite so – which I'm grieved to say, even with our presence, stands in disarray and confusion. As one of my frigate captains, it's as well you're acquainted with it.'

He sat heavily, unconsciously wiping his brow. 'I will be brief. The prime cause is that of privateers. The entire western end of the Baltic is infested with the vermin. To their number must now be added the Danes, who not only crew foreign vessels but have the gall to plant privateer nests in the lesser islands.'

'What of our escorts?'

'That is not where the difficulty lies. We have enough to see off any attempt on our convoys. This is not in question. But consider this – we safely conduct merchant vessels in great numbers all the way from England. What happens to them then? They leave our protection bound in every direction for the port of their destination and thus fall prey to waiting scavengers.'

'To the ruination of our commerce.'

'The Baltic Fleet has secured passage in and out of the Baltic but cannot provide for them to finish their voyage.

Our only defence is for English cargoes to be landed in a neutral port and taken up again under a neutral flag for onward delivery. At this time there are now precious few neutrals, and even fewer who wish to take the chance under penalty of defying Bonaparte's blockade. So does this mean we must fall back on subterfuge, contemptible smuggling and false papers?'

Kydd knew Saumarez to hold his moral principles dear: he would be affronted at being involved in deception and trickery. There must be another way. 'Make escort to the port itself?'

'Sir Thomas, your suggestion is well meant but quite without merit. The main trading ports lie in sovereign lands, it is true, but these are all either French-occupied or under Bonaparte's subjection by other means. The appearance of a British man-o'-war off their ports will be understood by all as an act of hostility upon the territorial rights of the nation concerned and the tyrant will make much of it. No, this is a vexing and frustrating problem – that you will be faced with at source.'

'Myself, sir?'

'Indeed. Much as I'd desire to grant you rest after your ordeal I cannot. The situation now is too grave – I'm sending every vessel I can spare, especially frigates, to the southern Baltic, with a view to hunting down these vile privateers. This is now your prime duty, sir.'

Chapter 41

The next morning *Tyger* slipped from her moorings without fuss. Saumarez had forbidden the use of valuable powder in vain salutes so there was just the smart exchange of signals followed by a business-like stretching to windward.

Kydd's orders were terse and to the point: privateers and deterrence. The southern Baltic held the ancient medieval lands that England had traded with for centuries but now ships were being preyed upon mercilessly. Could he make a difference?

He had lesser craft assigned to him: brigs, cutters, sloops, gun-brigs. A frigate would never fear a corsair but these smaller vessels would find it a hard fight if they came upon one alone. And with the numbers that were swarming about in the south this was more than likely.

Kydd was no stranger to privateers – he'd once captained one himself, and knew their habits. And he could see how this coast would be prime hunting for them. If he was to be effective it would have to be by cunning, not force, and Saumarez would be expecting results.

There was a quick knock at the cabin door. 'Sir?' Dillon's head popped around. 'Some few matters, shouldn't take long.'

'Not now, old fellow. Have something I must do.'

Nestled in his waistcoat, next to his heart, was the very first letter he'd received from his wife.

'Then later. Good day, sir.'

It had been waiting in *Victory*, in the regular mail run from England. He'd only seen her writing a few times and there on the outside, in her rounded, flowing script, was his name. He'd opened it the first instant he could after seeing the commander-in-chief, and under the half-deck by the deserted wheel of the great ship he'd devoured it.

Now he drew the letter out slowly, savouring the thought of reading it once more.

My darling Thomas!

What a thrill to know that these marks I'm scribbling on this paper will in only a short time be in your own dear hands and then I'm talking to you! This sheet that I kiss because it will be held by you – my darling, how I miss you. And there I go, blubbering like a girl, and I promised you I'd be brave. I'm not good at letters, please forgive my poor words, but each and every one I vow carries my love and feeling for you.

Mr Appleby has finished repairing the stable and I'm to make trial of a delightful bay I saw at the fair. He's naughty and has spirit and I believe will do most excellently on the moors . . .

Kydd smiled, recalling the time when Persephone had invited him and Cecilia to go riding on Dartmoor, their stolen kiss as she'd come to his aid after he'd fallen from his horse. That all seemed so long ago, now.

As he read on about her latest painting, he could picture

Persephone at her easel in the room they'd chosen for a studio.

I made it a great-sized one. I couldn't help it, for you'll agree Iceland's prospects are stupendous and sublime and I'm so nervous at what you'll think . . .

The writing became more controlled, smaller.

We hear that the Tsar is threatening to invade Finland. I've looked it up in the atlas and it's so close to the Baltic! Do take care, my sweetling. I know you must do your duty yet I can't help but worry about what happens when your British fleet meets those Russian brutes. Know always, my darling, that I'm with you wherever you are.

He found a sheet of paper and prepared to write his very first letter to his beloved wife.

How to begin? What things would interest her? There was so much he had yet to discover about her . . .

My very dearest Persephone

No! Did he have more than one Persephone? Start again!

HMS Tyger, *Bornholm bearing ENE five leagues, wind fair, north-westerly.*
Dear Persephone

He chewed his quill. It was one thing being a captain of a man-o'-war and quite another to be husband to a beautiful woman.

I hope you are well. We had a little excitement when the last Danish sail-of-the-line thought to dispute the Great Belt with us. We put them down in a night action. I went ashore in Gothenburg and met the governor.

Really, not much had happened after that, and would she want to know the dull details of daily life aboard a frigate in hostile waters? Perhaps the Archangel venture.

We sailed north to Archangel in the White Sea, which is athwart the Barents Sea, and clear to northwards of the Arctic Circle but I can reassure you my dearest it is well to the south of the polar ice-pack. Tyger *did several noble deeds . . .*

It was hard to think of anything else and he ended the letter with some observations on the singular weather patterns to be encountered in the Baltic, closing with his undying love.

Chapter 42

The low grey coastline of the southern shore rose and firmed. It was time to begin.

Kydd had in all five supporting vessels, *Bruiser*, which was an elderly sloop, *Lapwing*, *Stoat* and *Larch* cutters, with a local-built gun-brig, *Vistula*.

He'd asked for *Fenella* but it seemed that Commander Bazely was indisposed at this time and unable to comply. It hurt when he heard this but he wasn't going to insist on it, or demand he join at a later time, and had to be satisfied with *Bruiser* and her cautious captain, Eliot. The cutters were small but handy and commanded by competent-looking lieutenants that he'd soon get to know more about, while the gun-brig was in the charge of an acting lieutenant, newly promoted from a master's mate and said to be from humble origins.

The cutters had been acquired from the Leith station and therefore were used to convoy operations and the all-important contraband searches of the North Sea. *Bruiser* had seen long service in the Channel and, like his old *Teazer*, would be no stranger to privateers.

It was not long before they were intercepted by *Diomede*, the frigate they were relieving. The two ships lay off each other and exchanged gossip, the burden of which was that things were bad, if not worse, than Saumarez knew. The Prussian ports were now being obliged to take French *douaniers*, officials to 'advise' port authorities on how to treat cargoes in accordance with Bonaparte's Continental System, but whose barely concealed job was to ensure that any taint of a British connection was rewarded by instant confiscation of ship and cargo.

Past the Niemen river it was no different. This was Russian territory and all the old medieval ports that England had been trading with for centuries – Memel, Riga, Reval – were now in the grip of the Tsar and his agents. It was a strange and fearful situation the merchant-ship captains were now finding themselves in, with Napoleon's decrees only months old and everywhere beginning to bite.

The privateers were making a rich haul, taking every opportunity to converge on the helpless merchant ships once they'd left the protection of convoys. It was going to be a hard fight.

Kydd saw the worn frigate sail away with mixed feelings. He was now on his own to do as he wished, but the stakes were getting higher.

He had no need to call a council-of-war with the captains of his little convoy. They knew their duty: the sighting, stopping and boarding of every sail, setting the wits of the boarding officer against the cunning of the merchant captains with the incentive of making prize of those in transgression.

He kept *Vistula* and *Lapwing* with him; *Stoat* and *Larch* were dispatched in the opposite direction with *Bruiser*. From now on their task would be to criss-cross off the ports, their presence a deterrent, but there were hundreds of ships to deal with so it would be a long job.

Kydd sent the little *Vistula* close inshore, her local appearance less likely to alarm, while *Tyger* kept her distance offshore, *Lapwing* well out on her beam.

The sweep began.

Within the hour sail was sighted, heading in to the coast. The comfortable, grey-weathered sail of a merchant brig, as usual flying no colours.

Kydd swung *Tyger* towards, and the ship hove to without being told, waiting patiently.

'I'll take this one,' he grunted to Brice, who, as third lieutenant, would normally expect this task, but Kydd wanted to get a first-hand feel for the kind of tricks current in this part of the world.

The boat put off the short distance to the vessel, which lay to, the picture of innocence. Without comment Kydd hauled himself aboard over the bulwarks and snatched a glance about the ship. Plain, utilitarian, with the master standing blank-faced by the main-mast.

'Good morning, Captain,' Kydd said, noting the battens on the main-hatch were loose. Ready for discharging or evidence of breaking bulk to stow an illicit cargo?

'Aye. *Success o' Peterhead*, Joscelyn, master.'

'Won't detain you more than we have to, Mr Joscelyn.'

'Well, here's m' papers, Admiral,' he said, as he handed Kydd a small bundle.

'Thank you,' Kydd acknowledged. He had no intention of being chivvied into a cursory examination. 'Your cabin?'

He laid them out, his experienced eye taking in the last port cleared, Hull, the bill of lading and other passage documents. Headed for Königsberg in iron goods and the crew-list showing no surprises.

'Which convoy did you take?' Kydd asked, knowing if he could not answer he'd catch him out instantly.

'Second o' the month, which is Cap'n Williams, *Steadfast* in escort command,' the man replied instantly.

'The thirty-eight with an odd patched fore-topsail?'

'No, sir – he's only a twenty-four and looks bonny an' trim.'

It was enough. With a last shuffle of the papers, Kydd looked up with a grin. 'Won't be detaining you longer, Mr Joscelyn. Best o' luck shoreside.'

He was one of the hundreds of humble British ships making possible the war with their stream of revenue, at the cost of so many lost to the enemy and weather. After coming this far, the old captain had now to navigate the rocks and shoals of paperwork in the knowledge that his ship and cargo would be forfeit if he made a single error of sin or omission.

The old masters, however, knew all the tricks, and if any could get through, they would.

Kydd let Brice go to the next. At a little before noon he returned with his report. 'Leith, in sea-coal. Prussian mate, short-handed and hoping to pick up some crew in Memel.'

Brice had been in these parts long enough to know the snares and blinds but a collier could not be disguised as anything else. Kydd nodded as he finished his report; the next time he'd make sure Bowden had his turn.

As dusk began closing in they sighted their first privateer.

Startlingly pale in the fading light, the sails of two inter-locked ships showed against the darker mass of the coast-line. There could be only one reason for the embrace and *Tyger* hauled around to run down on them, *Lapwing*, further out to sea, following.

Cool and deliberate, the predator brought its men back aboard and poled off, taking the wind immediately in a curving flight away. A topsail schooner, it sheeted in hard, its course clearly for the distant coast and no doubt one of the many small harbours scattered along it. It was sailing at least two points closer to the wind than *Tyger* so there was little point in a chase while the cutter-rigged *Lapwing* was coming up from miles astern.

This was likely to be the pattern for the foreseeable future – a privateer lurking offshore to take merchantmen bound for a given port and, if trouble eventuated, a quick dash back to the safety of the coast, all of which was friendly and available to it.

Over supper the previous evening Kydd had come up with a plan and was determined to try it out.

A little before eleven in the morning, the mist cleared, revealing a merchant brig under as much sail as she could show being overhauled by what was possibly the same schooner as before.

As soon as *Tyger* was spotted, the privateer broke off the chase and hauled its wind for the land – where *Lapwing* cruised. Cut off from its escape it put about quickly but by this time *Tyger* had the bit between her teeth and converged on the fleeing craft in a storm of cheering. Caught between the man-o'-war's guns of the cutter and the unanswerable menace of a frigate it gave up without a fight.

In a generous gesture Kydd allowed the young lieutenant of *Lapwing* to take possession and, with *Vistula*, sailed on to see if the trick could be repeated. But after wearisome hours it became clear it was too much to expect that they would reliably come upon a privateer in the very act of falling on a victim. It needed more thought.

Three days passed of quiet cruising, doubled lookouts, stopping and examining every sail that came into sight, outward bound or making landfall on Libau, Riga, Memel and other ports.

It was vital work, but after a week and only one privateer put down, it was tedious and unrewarding for a top fighting frigate. The main problem for Kydd was that any marauder in the business of capture for profit would instantly turn tail at the sight of a frigate and the chances were slim that he could bring many more to account on his own.

By tying up his assets in a co-operative sweep, he was bringing down the search focus to a few miles and depriving the larger picture of the services of the two smaller ships. In all his previous experience, the war against privateers had been always in the background, a necessary but incidental task. On this station it was different – it was the chief and foremost burden of his cruise – but in the face of this great threat to the Baltic trade he was achieving little.

Well into the second week, there was an additional and unwelcome element.

They spotted a deep-laden merchantman, its course unusually to the north-west. On sighting *Tyger*, it put over its helm in a hopeless attempt to flee.

'Bad conscience,' murmured Bowden, going below to get his boarding officer's kit.

A single shot athwart the vessel's bows was enough to bring it to.

As Bowden was carried across in the launch, five marines with him, the usual speculation broke out aboard *Tyger*.

'A Dansker in grain. Stands t' reason, headed nor'-west for the islands where they's a mortal need for same.'

'Loaded like that? A Prussian, in iron ore and off to Lübeck.'

Brice waited and, with a superior smile, added his contribution: 'She's Barrow-built and, with those crossed mizzen braces, country-manned. No colours but you can be sure she's a true Briton by her topsides, bright-sided and tar-black both. Only an owner as cares for his ships lays out coin for this.'

'Then deep-laden, why was she on a course out of the Bight?' Kydd asked.

Bray was in no doubt. 'British she may be, but we've just boarded an' recaptured a Frenchy prize! Accounts for her sheering off when she sees us and why she's away to the nor'-west, being carried off as prize.'

With some interest they awaited Bowden's return: if a recaptured prize, they stood to make a respectable amount in salvage.

The second lieutenant arrived back, accompanied by a slight-built man in a long coat and old-fashioned tricorne.

'Ah, Mr Wynn, master of the *Bristol Trader*, sir. I believe you'd want to hear what he has to say.'

So Brice had been right. This was nothing but a common Baltic trader with, no doubt, an elaborate excuse for his behaviour. Kydd took him down to his cabin and courteously sat him down.

'M' apologies I didn't strike sail when I first clapped peepers on ye,' the master began. 'As I got good reason for it.'

'What's that, then?'

'You're full-rigged, a frigate.'

'I am.'

'Just the same as the monster who's taken t' cruisin' about off Riga after our kind. That's why I runs.'

Kydd looked directly at him. 'A privateer?'

'The same. Excepting he's a beast o' size, one we can't hope to beat. Your reg'lar run o' the scum, why, you might have a chance with. This 'un is ship-rigged like you, carries men an' provisions for a long cruise so he can range out as far as he chooses.'

'Size, you said.'

'Aye. Six, seven hundred ton, sixteen long guns – and fast. Glory be, fast!'

'Mr Wynn, how do you know all this without you're taken yourself?'

'It's what's said among the captains. Three captured this month – one got clean away t' tell the tale and it's this. In the offing, a league or two distant, he looks like one o' yourn. Throws out a signal, confuses us, like. Then comes up and hails, we has to heave to. In a trice he's alongside, swarms aboard and it's all over for us.'

A privateer masquerading as one of the Saumarez fleet was bad enough, but this was destroying trust and confidence in the very merchant shipping the navy needed to win over. A double-edged stroke by the enemy and damned effective at that.

'You were on a nor'-westerly course when we raised you. Not to Matvig or . . .?'

'Aye. You're not to know, but it's a right dangerous place now, Königsberg and the others on this side of the Baltic. These *douaniers*, they've got Boney at their backs when they talk t' the port agents. Makes 'em slap the law on all who even smell of an English cargo or such. And that's a grievous thing – with a bit o' paper they confiscates ship an' cargo both for tradin' false. This means as it's gettin' too tough a thing to try to land a cargo. Like most now, I'm not even goin' to try after what I heard, an' I'm turned about and bound for Rostock, Lübeck, whatever, where they're not so fond o' the tyrant.'

'Papers showing you're cleared for this port?'

'For a rub o' silver it'll fadge.'

Or cynical betrayal for reward. From bad to worse: but first to deal with the rogue privateer.

'Thank you, Mr Wynn. I'll see you on your way.'

Kydd returned to his cabin, slumped into a chair and gave himself over to deep thought.

From the description, the privateer was probably something like a corvette, which some called a 'petty-frigate', larger than a British ship-sloop but smaller than a full-rated frigate. Whether it was a true privateer in the business of predation or a French national ship, manned by the navy, couldn't be known. What was plain was that it had to be found and dealt with – soon.

Item. It was reputedly fast, conceivably speedier than the foul-weather hero *Tyger*, whose performance in light airs was something less than sylph-like. Therefore merely sighting the creature was no guarantee of success.

Item. Combing the seas with *Lapwing* and *Vistula* in extended order was out of the question: either of them taking on a corvette was courting destruction, but if not, then it was a search of thousands of square miles by a single ship.

Item. *Bruiser* and her supporters were at an unknown distance and direction and could not be expected to join in the hunt, and the frigate further along on station somewhere off Reval would need something more tangible to entice her to join him.

Conclusion: there was nothing left but the hope of a chance meeting in conditions that suited *Tyger*. The odds on that? Near vanishing.

For something to throw into the conversation that night at the accustomed Friday gunroom invitation dinner, he put it to the table.

Bray's determination to convoy right up to the port itself was blown out of the water by Bowden, who pointed out that to convoy any ship was only announcing to the world that this ship had a cargo so valuable to the British that they needed to protect it. Any defence of the master that he was innocently conveying neutral goods would be laughed out of court.

Asked to better it, Bowden's scheme was to plot the prize-takings to get an understanding of the movements and practices of their opponent and lie in wait. Brice was the one who sorrowfully pointed out that, by definition, those who'd been taken were not in a position to report back the necessary positions.

The quietly spoken sailing master broke his silence to offer one possibility that had the fighting officers looking thoughtful. 'We'll never find him in these waters as are his own. Instead we lets him come to us.'

'How?'

'We sails a juicy-looking merchantman as bait with a parcel o' seamen and marines hidden aboard. They'll wait until he's alongside, then rise an' storm the devil.'

'Hmm. I like it,' Bray said, rubbing his chin. 'Except what if he's a fly one, and lies off the minute we stands and pounds us to a ruin? I'd rather *Tyger* was there t' share the glory.'

'Can't have her near. She'll tip the beggar off,' Kydd said, and ruminated. 'But it's a good idea and worth our thinking.'

'Grapnels.'

'Mr Darby?'

'I said, grapnels.' The grey-haired gunner was not one to volunteer words unnecessarily and the cabin stopped talking respectfully to listen.

'He likes t' come alongside to finish it. Our men aren't there as boarders. Instead they heaves grapnels over his bulwarks to hold him fast. Behind these are Royals wi' muskets, whose job it is to pick off any who dares touch the grapnels.'

'To what end?' Bowden wanted to know.

'This is *Tyger*. She's hull-down to wind'd, no sail higher than her courses so can't be seen. She's waiting for a rocket. If she comes quick, like, our men only has to keep 'em from the grapnels while she comes up on us.'

'Ha! You're a caution to us all, Mr Gunner.' Bray chuckled. 'The way we did it in King Richard's time with bows an' arrows!'

'Hold hard, Mr Bray,' Kydd said seriously. 'This could work out – while he can't cast off the grapnels he dares not let go with his long guns for fear of setting both ablaze. And we reducing to courses – our main-yard at about sixty feet puts us below the horizon at less than ten miles. Double this for their lookouts' height-of-eye and we've got ourselves upwind of the rascal, ready to loose all sail and be down on him in an hour or so while he's held to a check. Yes?'

'It'll be hot work,' mused Clinton, the captain of marines. 'Say five grapnels, three pieces covering each, reloaders, replacements – but a workable plan, with an assist from sailors.'

'We can do it!' burst out Bray. 'By God, but it's possible!'

Kydd let the table erupt into a happy buzz before intervening with a settler. 'I grant it's thinkable, even probable – but there's a detail that scuppers the whole.'

'Sir?'

'Your bait. I know a gallows deal more about merchant jacks than you gentlemen, and there's a score of reasons why a master of a fat merchantman wouldn't offer himself up as bait. Here's some. One, you're at the least obliging him to a delay as will be an embarrassment to his freighting and other arrangements. Two, his owners would offer him over to Davey Jones if he risked his ship and cargo so, and he would know it. Three, and here's the worst: he'd be stepping well outside the clauses of his insurance. If there's a bad turn which sees the barky taken, then we'd be liable to pay up, and I mean we – the Navy Board won't in any wise cover an action not approved by them. So?'

The let-down was hard to take, snatching away the only prospect of going active in this privateer war.

With the days that followed came news of other seizures by privateers. And twice a naval intervention ended with the sharp-lined corvette effortlessly making its escape.

On one boarding of a British merchantman Bowden broached the idea with its master but was laughed at to his face.

The fifth day brought an even worse outcome. They came upon their quarry – but it slipped away before their eyes.

A lookout watching downwind saw two sail together and unmoving. He hailed the deck and *Tyger*, under a press of sail, went in pursuit. Even before a mile was passed the corvette had recovered its men and was away in a slather of foam, an impossible chase.

In his cabin, some time later, Kydd found himself listening to a white-faced young man. 'It were a mistake. My pa should never have done it, God rest his soul.'

A brave but doomed attempt to prevent the boarding had cost the life of the master, the man's father.

'I'm truly sorry to hear it, Mr Gower,' Kydd said softly. In a tradition of centuries the ship was family-owned, the father having stakes in it, this eldest son the first mate.

'How's the vessel? Can we bear a hand?'

'No. It's only blood they won,' Gower said dully. 'Ship's left alone.'

'Then we'll have to be on our way. Again, my sympathy on your loss and—'

Gower abruptly raised his head. 'Sir, you'll oblige me on one thing.'

'Oh?'

'Do you hunt down the bastard and hang him from y'r fore-yard!' he burst out.

Taken aback, Kydd was about to reply when a sudden thought struck. 'I can and will – if I get the right kind of help . . .'

It took moments only to tell of the plan.

'Be damned, and I'm in it!' Gower spluttered. 'Cargo's iron-goods as won't go rotten, consignee is m' uncle, insurance don't have t' know. We're to do it, I think.'

An impromptu council-of-war was brief and decisive. If the merchant jacks were going to risk it, the King's men would surely do their part.

A likely ground was found: the broad sea approaches to

Danzig, sixty miles to the west and the probable next move for the privateer disturbed from his profitable ranging off Königsberg.

Hope of Maryport was not designed for war – but her stout sides were topped with high bulwarks to keep her decks from being swept by seas when rolling deep-laden. These and the raised hatchways would make fine parapets. What was to be done when the fateful lunge took place was rehearsed well: her crew would flee panic-stricken down to the fo'c'sle, leaving the concealed marines and naval seamen to do their work.

Tyger would take station below the horizon, her pin-prick bare masts near invisible in the light haze at the edge of the skyline, keeping track while upwind.

It all depended on the enemy now – if he was as rapacious as he seemed, he would strike, and soon.

Slow and cumbersome, *Hope*, with concealed drag sails, sailed back and forth over a forty-mile track, the image of an enticing prey. The red coats of marines were covered with oilskins as they lay on the deck, as many others finding hiding places below.

On the third day there was a response. Far to leeward the three upper sails of a full-rigged ship appeared above the horizon, keeping pace with them, like a wolf padding close to a frightened quarry.

Hope bore away nervously, her motions noted and followed. In a deliberately slow performance she put about to go back. The distant ship did likewise, no doubt encouraged by the laggardly show as proof of a small crew.

Keeping well down, *Tyger*'s seamen slithered to the opposite side. Theirs was now a waiting game.

Then their pursuer's helm went over and, hard by the wind,

it closed on the frightened merchantman, which sheeted in and tried to run from the menace – but the bait had been taken. It slewed about to a parallel course and, to the relief of the helpless victim, English colours broke out. They ran together as the other closed the gap between them to hailing distance.

Just as Kydd would have done, a voice blared out from her quarterdeck. 'HMS *Valiant*, and I mean to examine you. Heave to, I'm coming alongside!'

Obediently *Hope* backed her main and the vessels slowed together.

Tucked in below the main hatch coaming, the sailmaker was leisurely mending a sail. Out of sight, on the other side of a chain of lashed barrels on deck and below the bulwarks, seamen waited, tense and fingering their weapons. And at the helm there was no common sailor – it was Bray in seaman's rig with every detail under his eye.

There was a bump and a lurch as the two vessels touched. On the corvette a dozen men leaped to their feet with a hoarse yell and vaulted across, landing with a shout, bright steel in their hands.

'On 'em, Tygers!' Bray bellowed happily, and threw himself at the nearest.

There was a frenzy of action: boarders fighting for their lives as a flood of men boiled up from below with terrible shrieks, some with muskets, others clutching grapnels and, ignoring the vicious fray, behind them the red coats of marines taking up position.

The grapnels sailed out and thudded down.

Too late the corvette's commander realised what had happened. Desperate to free himself from the scourging attacker, he screamed orders for the grapnels to be thrown off – but the first few to try were mercilessly brought down. The rest cowered.

In minutes it was over. The grapnels that had last been hurled at a Russian fort were now being firmly belayed, locking the vessels together.

Muskets came into play, but against disciplined Royal Marines, they were of no use – trained for the battlefield, the redcoats methodically fired as targets appeared and swept the field.

There was no attempt at storming the big privateer. There was no need to: when *Tyger*'s sails were loosed and she sailed vengefully down from the eye of the wind, the sight was too much and a white flag was hastily flown.

Chapter 43

Kydd woke. There was no reason to at this time, the silent hours some little way after one or two in the morning, the motion of the ship in the slight swell a pleasing heave, the muted sounds of the night comforting, calming.

Reassured he lay back in his cot, watching the black shadows on the deck-head chase each other to and fro, a wan moonlight entering from the single gun-port, reflected by the sea. *Tyger* had had a rare success for a frigate on what amounted to a blockade, putting an end to the worst of the privateers plaguing the coast.

But he became aware of dissatisfaction, restlessness. The privateers were a menace, but what were they compared to the consequences of the iron grip Bonaparte was clamping on the ports, one by one? His strategy was a war winner that was succeeding by slowly strangling Britain's Baltic trade, its only gateway to the continent. Unless Britain could find a counter-move the future was dire.

Kydd turned and worried at the problem anew, a Damocles sword hanging over England. Yet again the same answer. They were doing their duty in *Tyger*, ceaselessly ploughing the seas to deter by their very presence – but he was quite powerless against matters that had removed themselves to the land. No cutting-out expedition, no daring landing or assault on a fort would have any effect on what amounted to nothing more than adverse Customs and revenue practices.

The mood stayed with him, robbing him of the usual pleasure of a new dawn, the light stealing over the seascape dispelling the gloom of the night into the promise of day.

Later that morning Dillon came to see him, a German newspaper in his hands. It had been given to him by one of the Prussians outward bound; merchant intelligence in such publications gave a good idea of conditions in the ports and interior.

'I see your *Amelie* has been made subject to a confiscation order,' he said.

Dillon's language skills had proved invaluable in keeping track of events in Bonaparte's empire that could have local effect. Now Kydd learned that the amiable and elderly master of the barque lately visited by *Tyger* had lost his argument with the Königsberg *douaniers*.

'Poor fellow,' Kydd muttered. 'Do sit down, Edward, and let's talk.'

Dillon pulled up an armchair.

'These confiscations.'

'A hard thing to bear.'

'Yes, but I can't help noticing some are getting through, landing cargo, putting out again. How are they doing it?'

'Quite. If there's a way, all should know of it, but I doubt that your regular run of merchant master wants to be free with his methods.'

'Aye, there's the rub. The beggars won't pull together. I do wish we knew, as we can tell 'em all.'

Dillon got to his feet and paced about the cabin. 'This might sound singular, if not odd in its particulars, but I've an idea. You may well scorn, but if it's successful we'll be able to find out.'

Kydd looked up doubtfully. 'Fire away, old fellow.'

'Well, it's this. You see before you an American gentleman of unimpeachable neutrality desirous of making landfall in these parts in order to visit his mother, sadly taken sick. He can't get passage on a packet, so ships in a merchant vessel as a passenger. He's there accordingly when the port authorities come aboard and may witness the entire procedure for himself.'

'Madness!'

'Why so? The *douaniers* are concerned only in the ship and cargo, not the affairs of a single harmless passenger. The Prussians will be more engaged in matters of Customs and revenue and be similarly indifferent. And both will not be particularly ready to upset the United States, you'll agree.'

'You haven't a passport.'

'It seems it was regrettably stolen, but I have a number of letters of introduction, which, as you know, are the usual means by which gentlemen identify themselves.'

'Which you will create.'

'As confidential secretary to Lord Farndon, I've a slight acquaintance with same.'

'And your obliging ship?'

'Your choice of one that is successful in the art. I'm placed aboard after a fat fee passes, and as I'm entirely ignorant and uninterested in anything in the line of cargo handling and ships, there will be no objection raised, I think.'

'A pretty plot, Edward. And quite out of the question. I'm not allowing it, and that you may take as final.'

Chapter 44

'An American, I told you,' Kydd said uncomfortably.

The master of *Dobre Miasto* regarded him steadily. 'So?'

'My orders are to carry him close to Königsberg and, where we may not, find a passage for him into the port.'

'In my ship.'

'If you will.'

'I don't take passengers.'

'An inconvenience, sir, I'll agree, but your helpful attitude I'm sure will be noticed by the boarding officer charged with examining for contraband.'

'I see. He keeps mumchance about coming from a British ship?' the master growled aggressively. 'I mean, he allows he's been nowhere near anything that smells English.'

'He will understand, I'm sure.'

Delivered to the merchant ship, Dillon was dressed for the part. Spectacled, he wore a shabby clerical black round-brimmed hat and affected an apologetic air, tripping over the boat's thwarts and ending in a tangle of feet among the amused crew.

He presented himself to the master. 'I do admire to be in your fine bark, sir,' he burbled. 'So fine, so fine.'

'Just stay out of my way, Mr Yankee.'

'I will, sir! I will.'

In hours the coast firmed ahead. A land with a king and people but conquered and under the heel of the French. Dillon shivered – with excitement or trepidation he couldn't tell but it helped that he'd been there before, although under very different circumstances, and knew what to expect.

On deck seamen coiled lines and prepared for docking.

As if absorbed, he stood on the diminutive after-deck, watching, as the squat fortress of Pillau passed before the final approach to the ancient Prussian city.

'The French are here, I believe?' he essayed at the hard-eyed master.

'The bastards are.'

Dillon shuddered. 'I don't reckon on them folks,' he said, with feeling.

'You won't see much of 'em if you do just as I says. All they wants is to choke off English trade, both ways, and they makes sure the local crew do it for 'em.'

A pilot cutter came into view, at the masthead a red and white pennant. The pilot came on board, gruff and broad. With him were two officials and an armed guard. Without a word the master went below with them.

'Oh dear,' Dillon said to the mate, who had taken over the conn. 'I'm so worried! Supposing there's trouble with the papers and—'

'There won't be,' the mate said tightly.

In a remarkably short time the master and the officials reappeared, blank-faced, and stood by the wheel as the ship drew abreast of the wharf and took in sail. Lines were flung out and *Dobre* hauled in to lay alongside.

With a rumble of wooden wheels, the brow went out, the officials stepped ashore, and the ship readied for discharging.

Dillon had minutes only. He hurried down the companionway aft into the saloon – and still there, on the table, not yet put away, he spied the pack of documents that were the ship's papers. Having worked with Kydd, he was by now a fair judge of the quality and significance of such – what Admiralty clerks termed 'fair' or 'colourable' for true or false papers – and these simply looked and felt too good. Neat, pristine sheets beautifully printed and filled in, they showing no sign of the wear of weeks at sea and different ports.

Hurriedly, he leafed through them and noted their comprehensiveness: a Prussian flag vessel, here was the basic bill of lading and manifest but with it were an unusual bonded voyage oath of compliance and a debenture certificate for drawback goods signed by the consul in Le Havre. A bottomry bond entered at Hamburg and the ship's registry, a clutch of affirmations and certificates – there were the equipage and other documents required by the French. It looked so faultless and—

The door was thrown open. 'What are you doing with those?' snapped the master, snatching the papers up.

'Oh, er, I've never seen anythin' so complicated in all ma life,' Dillon said, with a laugh. 'Saw 'em here and thought t' take a peek. Are these your ship's records, sir?'

'None of your business. Now you go ashore, voyage is over, right?'

'Right.'

'Don't forget what I told you to say.'

'I won't!' Dillon said fervently, and left.

On deck he fussed with his baggage by the brow while taking the opportunity to look about him. The main hatch was off but searchers were going into the hold equipped with hooks and gauges. These would be the rummaging crew and it looked as if they were in earnest. So the papers were not preventing a full examination.

Down on the wharf, five bored sentries in the blue and grey of Prussia lined a loose passage to a dockside office where the crew were being examined, and he was directed to join them. This was a far more rigorous business than any taking place in England but he knew what they were after. Evidence. Anything that could show that *Dobre Miasto* was in contravention of the five articles of Bonaparte's Milan Decree of several months ago: that the vessel had in some way had contact with Great Britain, however small. According to the articles, it could be as instantly condemning as an innocent entry in the log-book or as trivial as a label on goods in the hold that was written in English. If this was found, the ship was deemed 'de-nationalised' and therefore liable for immediate confiscation by the port authorities.

He was seeing at first-hand the lengths Bonaparte was prepared to go to in enforcing it.

Reluctantly he went over the brow and down to join the gaggle of men outside the office. 'What's to do, friend?' he asked one, a gangly youth, who shook his head in incomprehension.

He repeated it in deliberately poor Low German.

'They asks us questions. Hope to trap us.'

'What sort of questions?'

'If we sailed from Rostock, how many lighthouse can you see from the sea? What's your favourite tavern there? If we answer wrong they know we didn't sail from there.'

'I see.'

'Fools! Our master, he signs crew from there, they know all this,' he added scornfully.

'A smart fellow.'

'You has to be, these days. And have long pockets.'

'For bribes.'

The youth frowned and looked around distrustfully. 'You offer to the wrong one, it's finish for you,' he said darkly.

'The Prussians don't like the French,' Dillon pursued. 'How do they feel about making their law work?'

'They hate the French,' spat the youth. 'And the law means we don't get the fancy goods from England the ladies want.'

'Then if—'

'Herr Dillon?' An officious Prussian held a paper and was demanding attention.

'Dillon? I guess that's me,' he said in English, and stepped forward.

'Come!'

He followed the bulky figure into the last office, where the man sat at the desk, puffing with exertion.

'Passenger?' The passenger list was in front of the man, and as Dillon was the only entry, he could only agree.

'Papers?'

Dillon took out his carefully prepared letters of introduction and passed them across.

The man's face hardened. 'What's this?'

'Why, they're my letters of—'

'Passport?'

'It was stolen. Some jackanapes in Bergen who—'

'Passport?'

Dillon's heart contracted. To be taken up just when he . . . Then he realised what was going on. The fat Prussian's features were as hard and unforgiving as before but in a tell-tale gesture his hand was out. 'Oh, yes, I may have mislaid it.' He fumbled in his waistcoat pocket and came out with a few thaler, which he absent-mindedly laid out before him. There was no change in the unblinking expression. More joined them – it was fourteen thaler to the Köln mark, he remembered and rounded it up, looked at the man enquiringly.

There was no change of expression as the Prussian slid the coins across and put them away. Then a fractional easing and a jerking of the thumb over his shoulder – Dillon was through.

Chapter 45

'A wet trip back,' Kydd sympathised, helping Dillon out of his damp oilskins. The night was as black as pitch and, with the driving rain, it would not have been pleasant for the lurking boat's crew either.

'And was it worthwhile?' he asked down in his cabin, as Tysoe brought in a steaming toddy.

'Yes,' Dillon said. 'I know how it's done.' He buried his face in the tankard and inhaled deeply.

'Well?'

'The whole business is controlled and overseen by the French, who make a thorough-going job of it. But a very risky yet effective chousing by my captain, I'm forced to admit.'

'Bribery?'

'False papers. When I left, it was with Boney's minions crawling all over the vessel, trying in vain to find any evidence as will see the barky confiscated in open court. They couldn't. The papers were pure white as driven snow so, whatever their suspicions, they had to let 'em go.'

'Or if they didn't, they'd start an international hullabaloo. Those papers must be good.'

'They are. I saw them for a space and they're a work of art. They're not worn, well-used or other pretending. They don't need to be. A court-of-law is just interested in what's said on 'em.'

'That the cargo-book agrees with the manifest.'

'I was thinking more, for instance, that the port clearance from Reval, say, is signed off by the right name, one known to be in post. If they get that wrong, there's all the evidence they need that the declaration is colourable.'

'A devil of a risk. I wonder who's forging the papers.'

'It would have to be local or they wouldn't know who's in post where.'

'Well, some get through using false papers. What can we do with that?'

'Give them all false papers?' Dillon said, with a sheepish grin.

Kydd chuckled, then stopped short. 'At times, Edward . . .' His mind pictured the scene. Ports up and down the Baltic with ships carrying English goods ready to be landed in the heart of Napoleon's Continental empire. Others leaving with holds full of crucial exports of grain and hemp bound for Britain. The Baltic open for trade once again. 'It could work . . .'

Then reality surged in. Dillon's example of the wrong name would be all that was needed to condemn a ship out of hand. He'd seen a Prussian ship's papers – they'd be well aware of names and other petty details and be sharing these with each other. A British ship with false papers would not have this advantage and could be caught out immediately.

Nevertheless, what if . . . they could share as well?

274

At the moment the Prussians seemed to have it all to themselves. Cargoes would follow those who could show they could deliver. It would get about as to whom that might be, and they could then charge what they liked for the service. But the merchantry would not like this. Who stood to benefit most if the freighting market was open to all? The same business-folk. Then persuade them to assist!

He looked up in satisfaction to see Dillon regarding him oddly. 'You've a plan, yes? Storming ashore and setting all Boney's finest to their heels, and—'

'I have, old fellow. But a different idea, not so glory-bound.'

'Sir?'

'In every port not so long ago we had a consul to look after our interests. Local chap, knows all the nobs and those in the commercial line. Have you ever wondered what happened to them since the French took power? I wager they'd be there still, playing the market even if under a purser's name.'

Dillon blinked in incomprehension. 'I can't see how—'

'There we have it! He's on the spot and knows just the same particulars that the Prussians have for that port. If he tells us what he knows, we can forge our own papers to that port, just the same.'

'But if—'

'In each port we find our man and desire him to set out these details – on a regular arrangement as keeps us informed. Then we use this to work up our false papers.'

'It'll never fadge. What if—'

'If we give him, by way of return, details of all the other ports, then our man is in advance of all his competitors. Tell me any merchant cove who doesn't wish this!'

Dillon gave a twisted smile. 'Your idea is a rousing one,

but there's more than a few stumblers I can think of at once.'

'Fire away.'

'Right. The first, how are all these consuls going to talk to each other at the same time to effect the exchange, remembering their facts have to be right up to date?'

'Umm. Any more?'

'Your false papers. Who's going to do the forging? Sir, I dare to say my Prussian scamp has his sources, but you're requiring a motley fleet of hundreds, thousands, perhaps, to have them. And they each have to be perfection in the art.'

'Yes, yes.'

'And, of course, you will need to convey the forged works to the customer on the high seas.'

'Is that all?'

'One last snaffler. Your sainted Admiral Saumarez, known for his upright and god-fearing ways. How do you think he'll entertain the idea that the whole world will know that his Baltic trade protection shall be, at base, deception and trickery, namely sailing under false colours?'

Chapter 46

'Thank you, Sir Thomas. An entirely satisfactory report of your southern cruise,' Admiral Saumarez told Kydd. 'There will be more than a few masters blessing you for ridding the seas of your abominable privateer.' He handed the report to his flag-lieutenant and added formally, 'Is there any other matter you wish to discuss?'

'There is, sir, should you have time to hear me. Of a . . . a confidential nature.'

Saumarez raised an eyebrow, then told the lieutenant, 'Spare us some time together, Flags.' He waited until they were alone, then said, 'If your matter is of a personal nature you can be assured it will go no further than—'

'No, sir, it pertains to our conduct of the war.' He hadn't meant it to come out like that.

The admiral frowned. 'Sir, if you intend to make observation on elements of my dispositions when you cannot possibly be in possession of all the facts then be warned – I will not tolerate them, in private or any other.'

'Sir, merely a suggestion,' Kydd said hastily, 'as occurred to me during my late cruise.'

'A suggestion?'

'A plan as will allow our ships direct access to Bonaparte's ports.'

'I'd be no doubt entertained to hear it.'

'Quantities of our ships have been taken in port, confiscated out of hand, while some individuals have been free to come and go. I wondered much at this, and then my confidential secretary, who is in the first rank of those with languages, volunteered to learn why. He took passage in a Prussian to Königsberg and contrived to discover how it was accomplished.'

Saumarez sat up in sudden interest. 'An intrepid act. My own questioning of successful masters has not been fruitful for reasons of commercial advantage and I'd be most interested to know how.'

'False colours.'

Disappointed, Saumarez sagged back. 'Ah, yes. Deception, trickery. An act more to be seen in vessels of the minor nations lost to honour.'

'Sir. Consider the dire conditions of the Baltic trade at the moment. We convoy hundreds through the Sound and into the Baltic – to what end? With Boney's Continental System starting to clamp in, only some can find a port to discharge. And then—'

'Quite so, you have no need to remind me of such things, Sir Thomas.'

'Then I ask you, sir, what is the method used in general in these days? Naught but a species of smuggling. Landing a cargo in secret, to be taken up by smugglers who convey it away in double-bottomed carts, sugar disguised as sand, hemp as—'

'Yes, yes, I am made aware of these,' Saumarez said wearily, 'but I will have no part in it.'

Kydd remembered that, as naval commander in Guernsey, it was mainly Saumarez who had been responsible for its suppression as a smugglers' haven. 'Sir. The principal problem is the volume of trade we must sustain. Unless we have a method that allows large numbers to dock safely we're in the same situation as if the Sound were closed to us.'

'You have a plan, you said,' Saumarez said heavily, steepling his fingers.

'Sir. It is this.' Kydd paused to recruit his courage. Here, in the great cabin of *Victory*, which had seen the gathering of Nelson's band of brothers in desperate but noble conclave, he was about to suggest prevailing over the enemy by illegal, underhanded means.

'Sir, there is no question that false papers do achieve their object. I simply propose we regularise their use by—'

'Sir Thomas!' Saumarez gasped. 'Am I to understand you wish to persuade me to a course of chicanery in the regulating of the Baltic trade?'

This was the nub of the whole matter but Kydd was prepared. 'No, sir,' he said emphatically. 'The merchant ships will find their own salvation. The choice is theirs. Yours is only not to enquire or condemn.'

'To tolerate—'

'If you do not, your prime duty is made impossible and the Baltic trade fails.'

'And if I do, the world will know that—'

'It will not, sir. That you can be very sure of, as it is in the interest of every master to keep this affair quite secret.'

Saumarez stood up, his face troubled. 'Yet you speak of

regularising. This implies an active role, a measure of direction. I will not have it.'

'Regularising – yes, sir. To bring all to an equal footing, so none by reason of possession of these papers has unfair advantage of those without.'

'I cannot see how this can possibly be achieved, sir.'

Kydd breathed a little easier. His head was still on his shoulders and they were still talking. 'In the line of duty you make use of such intelligence as crosses your desk, sir. There is no dishonour in that. What we do make possible is that intelligence of the soundest kind is made available to the producers of our false papers such that all may voyage in confidence.'

'How?'

'I propose that our retired consuls in each port are given the task of drawing up an exact account of the state of their port with the names and titles of all those in authority and so forth as may assist us. The navy's only part is to send a dispatch cutter up the coast regularly, say once a week, to collect these. The information is consolidated and passed on to those that have the requirement.'

'Hmm. Such would have additional value – market conditions and similar as well as reports of a military nature. Simple, I'll grant, and well thought out.' There was a glimmer of a smile. 'With but one fatal flaw.'

'Sir?'

'Consider. You are asking a merchant-ship master to fly a foreign flag to deliver a cargo directly into a port controlled by the French. If that does not fit any description of the crime of "trading with the enemy" it is difficult to find a better.'

Trading with the enemy. A mortal crime since the outbreak

of war and with the penalty for treason. Kydd hadn't thought of this . . . and there was no answer to it. 'Um, it seems that—'

'Sir Thomas. Allow me to say that this conceit has its merits, which I cannot and will not deny. You were right to bring it to me in confidence for there are many who would misconstrue it. I desire to bring it forward but there are two impediments that bring pause. The one, trading with the enemy. This you will leave with me.

'The other – your consul fellows. How can you be sure we shall receive intelligence that shall be timely and true if there are temptations of a mercantile, a material nature involved? To this end you will select a trading port, find your consul and return to me with a *modus pactum* that demonstrably proves their sincerity.'

'Now, sir?'

'A few days to settle the matter I think not too great a burden. You shall leave immediately. Good day to you, Sir Thomas.'

Chapter 47

'I must object in the strongest possible terms!' Bray said thickly, as Kydd made ready to board his barge. 'Only at the word of a damned foreigner!'

'And my confidential secretary,' Kydd said mildly. Dillon had done his best to persuade Herr Miške to take boat to the frigate but had been unsuccessful. Consequently Kydd must make the journey to him.

Dillon's fishing-boat method had served him well and they headed inshore after dark to the restless whispering of marram-grass-covered dunes where they were quickly hidden from view. Shivering, Kydd waited while Dillon checked his little compass and pointed to the left. Following a path, they headed inland, inhaling a pungent fishy odour in contrast to the purer ocean airs.

The path led to a row of fishermen's huts, sheltered from the sea winds. There was a light in one at the end.

Dillon knocked and, at the peevish enquiry, quietly

answered. The door opened on an old man, shrunken with age but with disconcertingly bright eyes that took the measure of Kydd before gesturing him to enter.

A single lamp guttered on a table, leaving the rest of the room in shadows, and a feeble fire spluttered. They were motioned to take the two wicker chairs facing it.

'Are you sure this is the place?' Kydd murmured. It was a desolate spot, a faint wind moan giving it a sepulchral cast.

'Certain, Sir Thomas. Miške specified strictly when and where he would meet you.'

At the table the old man sat unmoving, his beady eyes glittering, watching.

'Miške's not a man to be flammed, I believe,' Dillon continued, rubbing his hands before the fire. 'A man of presence and sagacity. I'm exercised how you'll persuade him to this course, so against his commercial instincts.'

'Admiral Saumarez will not move until he has proof positive that he will so act. Thus it seems I must be persuasive.'

They sat in silence as the minutes passed.

Kydd grew restless. 'Take a look outside, old fellow, see if he's waiting somewhere else.'

Dillon rose but the old man made irritated gesticulations to remain seated.

'I'll allow the beggar but one bell more, then—'

He broke off and tensed at a scraping sound near the corner. It was an old high-backed chair being turned around by its occupant who'd been out of sight all the time – a diminutive man with the precise air of a watchmaker.

'Mr Miške!' Dillon exclaimed. 'What is the meaning of this?'

With an ingratiating smile, the man pulled the chair closer. 'Why, Mr Dillon, can you not see? It was my little test – to see what tongue you spoke together privily. Your man is English, then. I'm content at that.' A small but serviceable pistol made its appearance on the table in front of him.

'Captain Sir Thomas Kydd.'

'I'm charmed to meet you, sir. And I'm intrigued what brings you here at no little danger to speak only with me.'

'Your service to the Crown as consul before the late occupation of Prussia is well remarked, sir. I'm here to determine if you are able to provide a further boon.'

'Alas, my captain, I'm no longer a consul, being here under an assumed name in the service only of my paltry shipping interests.'

'Which are in marked decline.'

'Just so.'

'Then my proposal will not be without interest to you, sir.'

'Do go on, Captain.'

'It is no secret that the British are suffering a reversal in their Baltic trade. I have a plan that has attracted the attention of my admiral. He states that for it to be adopted he requires the assurance from one such as yourself that it is both possible and practical.'

'You shall tell me more.'

Kydd took a deep breath and detailed his plan.

Miške heard him out politely. At the end he smiled. 'A pretty plan, Captain. And correct in its particulars with but one exception.'

'Oh?'

'You do not give sufficient weight to the venality of the *douaniers*. They are corrupt to a degree that would put an Oriental despot to the blush, and, to my shame and credit, I've been able to take advantage of this on more than one occasion.'

'Then you know who may be approached.'

'I do.'

'And may it be assumed that your brothers in Reval, Wismar and similar should be likewise knowledgeable?'

'They would.'

'Therefore this information held in common would be of use to you?'

'Of incomparable value. Both in the producing of, er, artificial documents and advice to masters on how and with whom they may safely lodge their clearance papers.'

'Then there is only the one concern that the admiral will need allayed.'

'And what is that, sir?' Miške's features took on an unmistakable gleam of cupidity, held within a mask of calmness.

'That any or all of you do render up false information in order to confound your competitors.'

'Ha! The easiest to answer. Should this plan be executed, any who do so will find the information for his port is no longer to be trusted and shipping will no longer come his way. Where are his imports? How then is he to consign his outward goods? For petty commercial gain, this is not to be entertained.'

Kydd gave a broad smile. 'Then we have a course to steer. How soon might we expect your first news?'

'As you will – there are quantities of smugglers in these parts acquainted with the private meeting of ships at sea. Shall we say four days hence?'

Chapter 48

'Splendid work, my dear Kydd. More sherry?'

Saumarez was in the greatest good humour, spreading out Kydd's report as though it told of a win at the races.

'Mr Miške was at pains to point out that all will profit by the probity of each.'

'Quite so, quite so. Well, I've had advice in the question of trading with the enemy. It seems that indeed this is so and only an extraordinary measure can overcome it.'

'Sir?'

'A special licence, to be granted by the Privy Council, which allows free passage, on application by interested parties whose character is known. Apparently this has been a practice for time out of mind.'

'I see, sir.'

'I'm sure you do, Sir Thomas. In one stroke two objects are achieved. Not only is the taint of treason removed – but now we have a means to prevent the enemy imitating us.'

'Imitating?'

'Certainly. If a vessel of a foreign flag is sighted by you, its papers are in the French style and it is bound for an enemy port, what will be your response?'

'To take it as prize?'

'As you should, as it is indistinguishable from an enemy. But in this instance it dares not carry British papers for fear of discovery and incrimination by an enemy privateer. It is safe from arrest from our cruisers, however, for it can furnish a licence which specifies that, irrespective of the documents it carries, the voyage is approved by His Majesty's government.'

'And if it cannot produce a licence, it is an enemy. Why then do they not forge these licences?'

'Ah. Each licence granted is provided with a cypher they cannot know and is separately advised to our contraband cruisers.'

'A masterly solution,' Kydd said, with feeling. 'And the false papers?'

Saumarez winced. 'It were more seemly should you refer to them as "simulated papers", if you please. These are no concern of ours but I'm led to understand that, if our pooled intelligence is conveyed to certain quarters, then these papers will be rapidly produced to order and for a slight fee.'

'A capital success, sir.'

'Due in no small measure to your own good self, Sir Thomas.' There was a trace of embarrassment as he went on, 'Which will be difficult to acknowledge to their lordships, this endeavour being of a nature not to be noticed.'

Kydd gave a wry smile: it wasn't something he particularly wished associated with his name but he knew it to be just as much a contribution to the preserving of the vital Baltic trade as a hard-fought battle. 'I understand, sir.'

Saumarez brightened. 'It is in my gift, however, to show

my appreciation to you in a more direct fashion, Sir Thomas, and I believe I shall in the most handsome manner.'

As *Tyger* shaped course around the Falsterbo reef and into the Sound her captain had every reason for satisfaction. The commander-in-chief had kept his word and now Kydd was working north with orders that released his ship from the daily round of blockade and seaward deterrence in the southern Baltic for quite another place. He was to bring to execution a project of importance, placed in command of a considerable force of men-o'-war that would invade and hold Börnholt, a strategic Danish island.

In effect he was to act as commodore, placed above all other captains, irrespective of seniority, for the period of the occupation. He knew it wasn't a major assault, a heroic thrust against a fortress, carried out in the teeth of an army in the field. The island was no more than half a dozen miles across – although wicked reefs at either end made it three times the size. But its situation gave it menace.

Börnholt was almost perfectly situated in the very centre of the Kattegat, the wider passage between Sweden and Denmark above the Sound. The entire Baltic trade progressed down it, and since the Danes had turned on the British they had made it a deadly weapon: they had extinguished its lighthouse.

There was now no comforting beacon to give warning to foreign mariners of the reefs that stretched east and west of the island for miles, squarely across their path. In the last few months there had been wrecks a-plenty, even some warships catching the reef too late to escape its embrace. Since the ice had retreated, parties had been sent to restore the light but the Danes had seen to it that it remained dark, settling on the island permanently, establishing fortifications and mounting a garrison against any British attempt to return.

Even worse, Börnholt was now a favoured rendezvous of privateers, gathering in their numbers for the rich trade-route pickings. Unusually blessed with fresh water, the island couldn't easily be put under siege. There would have to be a formal descent by a military force of size.

Saumarez had shared all the intelligence he had available and Kydd had the three days' sail to Vinga Sands to plan his operation.

A garrison was housed in small fortifications at the eastern sharp end of the pear-shaped island, gathered about the lighthouse and well dug in. Amounting to some hundreds and including an unknown number of artillery pieces, the forces the Danish governor had at his disposal were more than adequate to defend against any simple boat landing. In addition, at less than a night's sail from the mainland, he could readily call upon reinforcements.

The rest of the island was sparsely inhabited. Not much more than a five-mile-long flat sandy islet patchily covered with low scrub and marram grass, the only heights were lofty sand-hills to the western end and fringing dunes on the north and south shoreline of no more than twenty-five feet or so. The only landing place, and a few fisher cottages, was to the west of the island.

The chart was acceptable, scaled well and with all the usual soundings, current indications and hazards. Almost immediately Kydd saw his first major hurdle. The eastern lighthouse end had a hidden threat. Stretching away like a spear, as long again as the whole island, was a narrow but deadly reef. Off the sandy isle, it consisted of miles of a chain of undersea boulders and what the chart labelled 'cobbles', a fearful trap.

And at the other end of Börnholt a sprawling reef covered the entire sea approaches to the landing for seven miles to seaward, shallow and treacherous. Only small craft could dare approach the landing pier. Anything as big as a frigate could only stand off helplessly out of range as the boats went in.

So how was the capture of Börnholt to be achieved?

There had to be a sufficiently strong force of Royal Marines landed, to assemble and consolidate with field guns, then advance on the fort standing before the lighthouse. This should be fairly straightforward – if the boats heading the miles inshore to the pier were suitably protected from gunboats, which could swarm in from nowhere, scornful of the shallows, able to pull into the wind without trouble and armed with boat-killing cannon. They would be coming out of the west, from Denmark, and Kydd knew they would take a lot of stopping.

But he had full powers from Saumarez to demand what he needed. And this would be a 64- or 74-gun ship-of-the-line that would station itself to westward and, with its over-whelming might, set the vermin to flight.

Kydd reasoned that he could secure the entire operation by positioning a frigate to both the north side and the south, with himself near the objective, the lighthouse, to give close-in gunfire support. One or two smaller sloops or brigs would be all that was needed to deal with attempts to infiltrate reserves or further support.

In view of their vulnerability he would need to go in with double the defender's numbers, so perhaps a thousand marines gathered from the fleet, commanded ashore by a senior officer of rank, although not above a colonel or he would be outranked. He could give full rein to Bray to lead in the boats, which he would relish, retaining Bowden in *Tyger* for when he himself landed at the lighthouse to take possession.

Then he realised he'd committed the sin of forgetting the wind. If it came from the eastern quadrant, it was an easy enough downwind approach to the lighthouse and further vessels were free to choose their track either side and come to at the right place. If from the west, with the inconvenience of a reef, a descent from the east would mean tacking and tacking again into the teeth of the wind, and with every ship being an individual, there was no guarantee they could act together.

It seemed military planning on any scale was no easy matter – and he hadn't even begun to look at the follow-up supply requirements to feed and provide ammunition for his new garrison, or what would happen if the Danes chose to make a stand, the weather turned against him, or an enemy relieving force arrived at an awkward time. Or the question of signals between sea and shore once landed, subsequent defence planning, the need for . . .

So much to consider. Should he have brought in others, asked opinions, delegated?

It was late evening before he had his full plan, but to counter every conceivable eventuality it now required two sail-of-the-line, one at each end on distant guard and three frigates, two on either side and himself on inshore support with one further sloop at the western end.

With a sigh he shuffled the papers and began a respectful demand for the listed military resources. This would go to the station admiral, which for the Kattegat was Admiral Keats and the Great Belt squadron. Kydd gave a tight smile: Keats of *Superb* was a famous fighter and seaman and would quickly see the need for what he was asking. He'd been a little frosty since Kydd's return to sea, following his parading to the public, but Kydd had served under him during the Copenhagen bombardment and found the admiral dour but fair.

Chapter 49

The old *Superb* lay off Vinga, her lines unmistakable even in the sea fret, and Kydd's heart beat faster. His first planned and commanded assault on the enemy. In days it would be launched and his would be the controlling voice.

Keats had returned Kydd's request for an interview with suspicious promptness and now sat four-square behind his well-worn desk in the great cabin, glaring resentfully at Kydd. He picked up a creased paper and waved it angrily. 'I know why you're here, sir, and it's insupportable! Insupportable, I say!'

'Sir?' Kydd asked, in astonishment, knowing he must have received a summary direction from Saumarez by a fast dispatch cutter.

'It's not to be borne, do you understand me? To go over the heads of captains many times senior to you? To approach the commander-in-chief directly to beg an expeditionary command? Disgraceful behaviour, worthy only of a London dandy, I believe.'

Kydd was taken aback at the hostility but guessed what lay behind Keats's attitude. Opportunities for independent enterprise of even this magnitude, with the possibility of a line or two in the *Gazette*, would be a gracious plum to award to a favourite and the admiral had been denied this. For this reason Kydd was prepared to overlook the undeserving jibe about his no doubt well-talked-about Court appearances. That, and his deep respect for the bluff old seaman, loved by his men and a legend in his own time.

'Sir, I was chosen by Sir James for this expedition and I propose to do my duty.'

'Very well.' His ferocious glare did not moderate in the slightest. 'As under my nominal command you'll tell me what this is, and know I'll not feel bound by it.'

It was clear where it was headed: Kydd was inexorably being drawn into a subordinate role under Keats.

'Sir. I have full authority as an independent commander granted me by the commander-in-chief. I appear here as his assignee in the enterprise and out of courtesy to your command – and, as specified in my orders, to seek your assistance in achieving the object.'

Keats glowered. 'You'll be demanding ships of me, men. These you can't have. I've a vital tasking in the Great Belt and they can't be spared.'

'The reducing of Börnholt is ordered by their lordships,' Kydd snapped, 'as being of the utmost importance to the security of the Baltic trade. Do I understand you will deny me the resources?'

'Have a care, sir!' the admiral snarled dangerously. 'For a mere post-captain your manners are lamentably wanting in respect – or do you believe yourself still among your peacocking friends at Court?'

Kydd's voice lowered. 'Sir. We have a great business afoot and cannot afford to quarrel. Do hear my plan, I beg.'

'Carry on, then, if you must.'

Opening his satchel, Kydd drew out his lists. 'A perspective of Börnholt would assist,' he said.

'Flags!' Keats roared. The windows shook. 'A chart. Börnholt and out ten leagues.'

In a few sentences Kydd spelled out the hazards and how he was going to overcome them.

Keats missed nothing. His seaman's eye darted over the chart, taking in the reefs, steady northerly current, distances off the Danish and Swedish coasts, the primary objective. He looked up suddenly. 'So?' he barked.

'I will have the following dispositions when the assault goes in,' Kydd said firmly. 'A sail-o'-the-line to each extremity and . . .'

As he continued Keats said nothing, wearing a grim expression and, by slow degrees, straightening until by the time Kydd had finished he sat bolt upright.

'There, sir. So my requirements are—'

He produced the list but Keats did not take it.

'Sir?'

'Ha!'

'What did you say, sir?'

'I said, ha!'

'If you'd explain to me, sir,' Kydd said stiffly.

'Come.' He rose and went to the stern windows and gestured sharply. 'My anchorage. Tell me how many ships-of-the-line you see?'

The grey, rain-spattered anchorage had more than a dozen ships, but apart from *Pompée*, 64, there were none.

'*Pompée*, sir?'

'Unfit for sea. All others out on station somewhere in the Belt or south o' Denmark. Frigates?'

'Neither. But—'

'You won't find any. They're everywhere on the loose, holding down the villains to the mainland, Jutland. So what does that do to your plan, sir?'

Kydd burned. He was being forced into a corner. 'No change. I wait until the force may be assembled before I move on Börnholt.'

'Not possible,' Keats said, with a grim finality. 'They're relieved on station one b' one, else gunboats and privateers will take the chance to spew forth and cut our lines. There's no sail-o'-the-line available to you. So now?'

'In this case, sir, if you're unable to find me the resources it seems I cannot proceed,' Kydd ground out.

Unexpectedly, Keats smiled. 'In view of the urgency of this operation I don't think that advisable. Shall we take a look at it again, together?'

Uncertain at the change in tone, Kydd agreed.

Taking up the chart and studying it for a moment, Keats looked up pleasantly and said, 'For a dashing young captain, I can only commend you for your mature restraint, your planning for every adverse happenstance. Well done, sir.'

Taken off guard, Kydd mumbled, 'Thank you, sir.'

'Now, this is well and good, but in war we must leave some things to chance. Here, for example, the Danes will certainly come out of the west, therefore a sail-o'-the-line to the east will not be required. And here . . .'

In swift, efficient strokes the old admiral sketched out a plan that in the end reduced the number of ships to four – *Tyger*, another frigate and two sloops.

'There, now. Should your marines show willing it'll be all over in a day.'

'Only a thousand will not—'

'I was thinking more of five, no, two hundred in aggregate. Your ordinary Dane is not to be accounted a fierce warrior at all. Besides, small numbers mean fewer boats, rations and all that tomfoolery.' He was now openly beaming. 'I can find you the frigate – *Riposte* is due here at any hour and I'm sure would be honoured to be included. And I can take a couple of sloops from the southern Norway patrol. There! You can be on your way before the end of the week. How does that suit you, sir?'

It wasn't until he was halfway back to *Tyger* that Kydd realised what had happened.

Very neatly, Keats had avoided being blamed for not assisting but at the same time had blinded Kydd with his authority and reputation into taking on an opposed landing with the absolute minimum of means. And as it was Kydd's plan, with himself in command, there was little doubt as to who would later be condemned if it failed.

In the couple of days it took to summon his fleet he took a long, hard look at the new plan.

They'd come in from the north-east to afford the minimum of warning to the fort by the lighthouse, but the landing would not be made at the western pier over the reef. Instead it would be made halfway along the southern shore where there was deep water much closer, hoping the coastal dune line would give enough cover once in.

He'd made the decision after talking to Clinton, *Tyger*'s captain of marines, whom he'd chosen to take charge of the troops ashore. His grand plan to have a colonel command was now laughable: any would think it wholly beneath contempt to be placed above a mere two hundred men –

who would be volunteers from any ship within reach and he fervently hoped there would be sufficient.

There was little else he could prepare for – landing craft would be standard ship's launches borrowed from ships in harbour and Clinton had suggested boat mortars as their artillery, considering the scrubby sand hard going.

It would be the Royal Marines who would perform the arduous advance over the interior sand hills to the open plain before the fort and a division of seamen in reserve, ready to make landing behind the fortifications when the enemy were engaged to their front.

Chapter 50

Riposte arrived the next evening but Kydd decided to wait for the following morning before he spoke to Mason, the graceless, powder-burned captain he remembered from earlier. And the next day he was granted the welcome vision of the two sloops he'd been promised, *Snipe* and *Forward*. The absurdly young, inexperienced Garland and an unknown commander to take on the Danes on their own ground.

At nine precisely he hung out the signal for all captains. Garland arrived promptly and not far behind came *Forward*'s captain, a lieutenant-in-command, lined and ageing, taking his time coming in over the bulwark. Holding his impatience in check, Kydd discovered this was one Wills, who'd been with his ship for the extraordinary time of seven years, all in the North Sea.

'Where's *Riposte*?' he demanded. It was the custom to refer to a captain by the name of his ship but no one seemed inclined to reply.

In rising anger he paced the quarterdeck for some minutes,

then lost patience. 'Bring the signal to the dip and hoist it again, this time with a gun.'

But there was no response from the frigate.

'Mr Bowden,' Kydd grated, 'go to *Riposte* and desire her captain to attend on me immediately, with an explanation for ignoring my signal.'

It was acutely embarrassing. The two who'd come were trying to maintain a front of interested conversation, which he could not, of course, enter into. He could only continue to pace alone. Mason had better have a good excuse for his behaviour.

Bowden returned with a hard-looking lieutenant, who boarded warily, his manner defensive. 'Lieutenant Byers, who wishes to be heard, sir.'

'Where is Captain Mason?' Kydd demanded.

'Sir. I'm in something of a clinch as it were.'

'I said—'

'He's with Admiral Keats, sir,' he answered, with a stubborn glance.

'Then why the devil didn't you—'

'To complain that he was being signalled to in a derogatory and disrespectful manner by a junior captain. Sir.'

'That I am junior to Captain Mason is neither here nor there. For the period of this expedition I am *his* commander. Is that clear?'

Mason would have received fleet orders the instant he brought to the previous night and would certainly have been told.

'Expedition?' Byers seemed genuinely puzzled.

Kydd's face tightened: Mason was no doubt using the signal to make a point and probably to gain some sort of joint command before he revealed anything to his officers.

Well, he'd find that Kydd's orders came direct from the commander-in-chief and could not be put aside. It would take some time for Mason to return so Kydd apologised to the two captains and told them he would move the meeting to the afternoon.

Clinton took the opportunity to update Kydd and, in calm, imperturbable terms, told of the need for a further fifty thousand rounds of musket ammunition to be embarked, the field sign of a white cross assigned to the first wave, and how his forces would be disposed once landed. It was just the medicine Kydd needed, and he complimented the officer warmly.

'Ours but to put you ashore, then,' he added briskly. 'How's the recruiting? You have your hundreds?'

'I'm promised most,' Clinton said cautiously. 'Should we embark not before tomorrow I'll have my numbers, sir.'

'All captains' was signalled at two.

Mason was the first to board. 'I say, Sir Thomas, my most humble apologies. Some kind of confusion about the orders.' The voice was amiable, but the eyes remained cold and reserved.

'Then there's nothing to stop us continuing our meeting, is there? My first lieutenant, Mr Bray. Do conduct Captain Mason to my great cabin, if you please.'

The other two were not far behind and were escorted below, too.

For some reason Kydd felt the need to delay his appearance and found something to discuss with the officer-of-the-day before turning to follow.

Outside his cabin he hesitated. There were voices at the

table within and one rode above the others. '. . . a mounte-bank, a poseur. I had it from Taylor of *Imperatrix*, saw him as bold as day, prancing about like a macaroni, trying to impress Prinny or some such. Didn't fadge, of course, the man's a dandy and that's that. Why we're given over to such escapes me. Interest at the highest and we all know where, I'd hazard. Well, we'll just have to—'

Kydd thrust forward, the door opening with a bang. He strode past the startled officers and reached his chair at the head of the table as they hastily rose, Mason the last on his feet.

'So now we're all here,' Kydd bit off, 'we'll begin. Börnholt. Be advised this objective is vital and will be taken.'

He paused, letting his eyes challenge Mason's, who held them for a space, then looked down.

'We are not great in numbers, therefore the motions of every ship will be decisive. My orders do reflect this and I desire every captain to give good attention to the single signification signals laid down for this operation. Clear?'

Mason's blank face gave nothing away but the other two were giving them serious study.

Kydd went through the order pack, relating it to the chart and, where necessary, to the large-scale sketch that he'd asked the master to produce.

It wasn't difficult to outline the hazards, particularly the long spit of reef to the east, but Kydd was counting on surprise: their sudden appearing out of the east directly opposite the lighthouse and fortification to occupy them while the boats went in on the southern side, the expected landing at the pier at the western end not eventuating.

Tyger and *Riposte* would arrive together. If the enemy made an appearance, *Riposte* would sail to intercept while *Tyger* would stay with the boats. *Forward* and *Snipe* were to circle the island at three miles off on defensive patrol. If the wind was easterly, they would be in position without beating along the island into it, and if westerly, they were already in position.

There were no questions and Kydd dismissed them with a curt admonishment to prepare to sail forthwith.

Chapter 51

It was time. Kydd had to ignore any unease he felt at their slender numbers, the lack of more naval support. The operation must go ahead. But he was also aware of a swelling feeling – that he had the very best ship and men that ever sailed the seven seas.

In past battles he'd looked aft to the quarterdeck, seen the captain stand a-brace, the picture of contempt for the enemy and the hazards of war – and found strength. How ironic: it was probable that that captain, like himself at this time, would have been imbibing strength and resolution from the sight of his men.

Hull-down from the Börnholt light, Clinton's marines boarded the dozen boats that had been under tow since Vinga, already loaded with their impedimenta. The little flotilla assembled and, with a highly vocal Bray in the lead, they set off with an easy stroke for the several miles it would take them to pass the lighthouse for their beaching point on the southern shore.

Kydd tested the wind, a light and cheerful easterly but one

that had been easing since they left Vinga. Nevertheless this was precisely what he wanted: from their position at the light they could come down on an enemy sailing from the west along either coast.

The sloops departed on their patrols, leaving the two frigates hove to together. They would make their feint towards the lighthouse when the boats were ready for their final dash.

It was going well. The boats were in a disciplined double line and making good progress down the coast. So far there were no signs of alarm or even that the fortification had noticed them.

'Flat the jib out, if you please,' Kydd said to Brice, 'and sail on aft if she needs it. I want to stay this side of the reef.'

The charts gave a steady northerly current for these parts and, hove to, they would slip north unless measures were taken to prevent it.

A mild drift southwards resulted and Kydd was satisfied. The manhandled sail was enough to keep them clear.

He glanced across at *Riposte*. She was now at some distance and seemed not to have noticed *Tyger*'s prudent move. It was not his job to teach seamanship but, on the other hand, he wanted the frigate to be available at rapid notice for response against a sudden threat. A complicated instruction about reefs and weatherliness seemed unnecessary so he turned to the officer-of-the-watch: '*Riposte*'s pennants: "keep better station".'

Then several things happened at once.

At the boats Bray put his tiller down and the line of little vessels began their run-in to the beach. Almost immediately several puffs of white smoke were rising in the dunes in the distance, too far away to make out how many.

And the wind died away to a faint whisper, with a backing that Kydd knew usually preceded a calm, and then opposite wind, foul for their careful plan.

Then came a startled hail from the masthead. '*Deck hoooo!* Coming around the point, I see three – no, five, more gunboats!'

'Get on all sail! To *Riposte* – close with the enemy.' All sails spread and drawing, *Tyger* made for them as well, more gunboats still issuing around the point, but the bulldog-breed vessel was not at her best in light airs.

It could not have been a graver situation.

The gunboats were in a perfect situation to set upon and slaughter the boats, strung out in their haste to make the beach. It was obvious that the expedition had been betrayed. In Vinga there would be those who'd sell information to the Danes if the price was right, and word had reached them in sufficient time to send a force from the mainland three or four hours away.

They'd been hiding out of sight at the other end of the island, quite safe in their reef-strewn waters, waiting for the right moment.

Urgently, Kydd looked behind him for *Riposte* and saw a shambles. The frigate had not complied with his earlier signal to take steps against the northerly current and had found herself beyond the reef to the north. Now required to come down on the enemy, Mason was faced with a lengthy track back against the wind up the reef to its tip and tack about to Kydd's side, or continue on along the northerly shore and intercept the gunboats by going around the other end.

In the lazy airs he'd missed stays and had no option other than to wear about and take the northerly route, but that carried a penalty that made it a near hopeless course. Unlike the south, the north coast possessed a sprawling reef of its own, which would require *Riposte* to round it – a trip of some fifteen, twenty miles to reach the gunboats, which would by then have done their worst.

Forward in her outer patrol was on the same side as *Riposte* and would also face the problem. *Tyger* would meet the threat alone.

Kydd stared ahead, knuckles white on his sword hilt.

Bray was urging on the boats and now they were strung out in a frenzied dash for the beach – and the first gunboat fired a ranging shot. It mercifully passed between them but Kydd knew that time was against them. The warship boats, crammed with men and equipment crowding the rowers, were no match for purpose-built oared galleys manned by professionals, who could quickly close and finish them.

And the worst: the gunboats were within range but he couldn't open fire on them: the boats struggling in for the assault lay across between *Tyger* and the enemy – he'd be firing into his own. The Danes would know it, and could boldly go in for the kill without fear of retaliation.

In just a catastrophic few minutes the entire undertaking had turned to a disaster.

In a cruel haze of inevitability Kydd saw how the gunboats were holding fire as they grouped together for a concerted lunge at the boats; and here he was, in a powerful frigate and completely helpless, *Tyger* closing at half a walking pace in the calms, far too late to make a difference.

He willed his mind to a cold-blooded concentration.

The elements were plain and the foremost was to stop the gunboats. Only if—

And then he had it. 'The gunner and his mate to report to me this instant!' he roared at his startled messenger, who scuttled off to the main magazine at speed. Those on deck, held in fascinated dread by what was unfolding, turned and stared but Kydd didn't care. This was the only hope.

Blinking in the light of day, the laconic gunner Darby and his mate, Stirk, hurried up. In a few short sentences Kydd pointed out the situation. It was quickly appreciated and then he asked a crucial question.

'Well, and I hasn't heard of it done, ever,' Darby answered, stroking his chin.

'It'll go, sir!' Stirk was emphatic, his dark eyes glittering in something approaching amusement. 'Could be y'r cartridge splits in the loadin' but with double wadding it'll serve, I'd wager on it.'

Darby was less sure. 'And if it don't, why, we'll be murtherin' our own.'

'We do it,' Kydd said, with a steely determination.

The gunner departed quickly for the magazine to prepare, leaving Stirk with his captain. 'Make it work, Toby,' Kydd said softly, to his old shipmate. 'I'm depending on you, cuffin.'

There was a brief easing of the hard features and then the weather-beaten seaman loped off to the line of guns.

In a very short time they were ready.

'Eight points to larboard and hold her,' Kydd barked, breaking the stillness.

'Sir?' Bowden looked at him in astonishment. *Tyger* was now apparently thrown off course and heading away into the open sea.

'Carry on.'

Stirk would take the first shot.

The powder monkey brought up the charge in his salt-box. In place of the fat sewn grey serge of an eighteen-pounder full charge, there was one of half the size and bore.

'Load!' Stirk snarled at the gun-captain.

The gun's crew gingerly went through their motions. 'Tomp down main well,' Stirk told the rammer who, taking him at his word, stabbed in viciously, Stirk's thumb over the vent-hole at the breech telling him just when it was seated to his satisfaction. 'Place y'r quoins, then!'

Beneath the breech on each gun was a stout wooden wedge. It rested on the carriage bed and acted as a crude elevating mechanism, being knocked in or eased out to raise or lower the breech. This was the quoin but now it was going to be used in quite another way.

Snatched out of their usual place, together with those belonging to the opposite guns, they were positioned at the ship's side, high end out, in front of each loaded gun.

'Run out!'

With double the usual men on the tackle falls, the gun rumbled out with a will – and when the trunnion wheels met the thin edge of the quoin it reared up, muzzle cocked crazily skyward, thumping into the gunwale ready.

Stirk took his time, motioning the men at the crow to bring the gun more to the left, then gave the firing lanyard a smart tug.

Kydd was ready for it: the gun's unnatural higher-pitched *blam*, the much-reduced recoil but, above all, the flight of the ball.

It had worked!

Lofted high by the added elevation over their own boats, then brought down by the weight of an eighteen-pound ball fired only by a nine-pounder charge, the shot struck the sea well in advance of the leading gunboats, ricocheting on to take all the oars from one side of a hapless craft.

Roars of pent-up frustration burst out up and down the

gun-deck and the men threw themselves at their iron beasts in a fury of action. First one, then another joined until the guns had every one blasted forth. And by the time *Tyger* had gone about to bring her opposite broadside to bear it was clear the enemy wanted no part of it, wheeling in flight, their prey snatched from them. They disappeared beyond the point whence they'd come.

Tyger turned to resume her position off the lighthouse. There was fitful firing from the dunes but already boats were grounding and the red coats of marines flooding up the beach. On the other side no doubt the gunboats would be receiving the unwelcome attentions of *Riposte*.

Again everything had changed. But now there was little doubt that the day was theirs.

Chapter 52

'Two dead, five wounded. It could have been much worse,' Clinton reported to Kydd, as he stepped out of his barge. 'They'd high hopes of the gunboats and, dare I make the point professionally, retreated to their fortifications too precipitately. Our boat mortars persuaded them of their folly and they've yielded.'

They trudged together through the sandy scrub towards the small rectangular fort by the rearing red-banded light-house, its flag at half-mast as though uncertain what should be done.

Capitulation formalities were brisk and to the point.

In short order a sullen mass of Danish prisoners was mustered on the open ground before the fort, their weapons piled in a heap, and Kydd found himself in possession of the little fort.

It was nothing much more than a square stockade with earthen parapets and a two-storey wooden command post.

'Ha. So now I'm governor of Börnholt,' Kydd said, regarding the prim little desk with its neat tray of papers and the dark-stained walls with their uplifting pictures of homeland country life.

Dillon was ransacking the cupboards but managed a grunt.

Kydd settled himself into the comfortable padded swivel chair by the desk and contemplated his next move. The island was inhabited, mainly at the opposite end where fisher-folk had a huddle of dwellings and rack-drying barns. They were keeping to themselves and would be no trouble. The lighthouse was now being restored while stores and a small number of defensive guns were landed for use by the garrison from *Tyger* and *Riposte*.

To all intents and purposes Kydd's task was complete.

There was just a most satisfying duty to perform. As the victorious commander, his was the obligation to write the dispatches of the action.

It was his first such, and he felt the weight of responsibility. Addressed to the commander-in-chief, it would be the account of record, quoted in the London *Gazette*, possibly a paragraph in the *Naval Chronicle* and countless reports in newspapers around the kingdom.

Those noticed in it would be honoured – to be mentioned in dispatches would stay as a feature in an officer's career for life while the naming of a ship's company in action would be recognised by all aboard as notice by the highest of their striving.

It would be difficult to pick out the deserving. Where did extraordinary exertion shade into discharging one's duty? He rather thought Clinton's calm and deliberate deploying ashore, which had rolled back the defenders so briskly, and his early bringing forward of the boat mortars to effect a final surrender bore recounting. But was not that which a soldier should be doing?

On the other hand, there would be nothing in the dispatch concerning the motions of *Riposte* frigate. What amounted to the ignoring of his signal was perilously close to mutiny – at the least a disobedience that imperilled the whole operation. There would be no criticism in the dispatches as this would damn the man's career but, by God, there would be a reckoning later.

'Concerning the Action resulting in the success of His Majesty's Arms in the taking of the Danish island of Börnholt in the Kattegat.'

Over the years he, like every naval officer, had read published dispatches zealously with not a little envy and knew the phrases, which now rolled forth easily. Clinton was named, as was Bray leading the boats in unhesitatingly while the gunboats massed, then the two killed, the three wounded, the rank and names of the Danish principals and, finally, the readying of the lighthouse to resume its duty.

He sealed the packet and sat back. He rather thought young Garland in *Snipe* would have the honour of conveying the victorious dispatch to Saumarez. And it would take both *Riposte* and *Tyger* to lift the prisoners under guard to Keats in Gothenburg, requesting a formal garrison and commandant be sent to relieve them. They should be quite safe for the few days this would take.

Meanwhile prudence dictated that some form of defence be arranged and Clinton was happy to oblige, suggesting an earthworks and guns over to the other side of the lighthouse and that a small division of seamen for general deployment would be a wise precaution.

After that was put in train, Kydd enjoyed dinner and a convivial evening with Dillon and Clinton.

The next day, their small defences were complete, the Union

flag flew high and there was nothing to do but wait for their relief.

As evening drew in, there was a flurry of excitement.

Out of the setting sun sail was sighted, a trim cutter with the typical double-ended hull of the Baltic – bearing a white flag. At first it headed for the landing pier and village but changed its mind on sighting colours near the light and slowly sailed along the coast to it, where it anchored. Under the eyes of the defenders, its boat and white flag made its way inshore with but one passenger in the sternsheets. It was met by a squad of marines in a hollow square while the occupant stepped out and approached. Clinton pushed through and advanced to meet him.

'Premierløjtnant Holstein.' It was a young, intense naval officer who stood rigid and tight-faced. 'Of His Danish Majesty's navy.'

'Captain Clinton of His Britannic Majesty's Royal Marines.'

'I claim cartel under the white flag, sir.'

'For what purpose, er, Lieutenant?'

'To parley concerning the disposition of the island of Börnholt, Captain. Are you the commandant, pray?'

'I am not. That honour belongs to Captain Sir Thomas Kydd. Your English is excellent, sir.'

'Thank you. If you would take me to him . . .?'

A pair of marines discreetly marching behind, they set off across the uneven sandy scrub. 'Not as if this were a rich kingdom that we must contend,' Holstein said, pirouetting curiously on his fine-worked boots and gesticulating grandly out to the side.

'As it must bear the fortunes of war, as do we all,' Clinton said stolidly. They continued on towards the fort, faded plots

of worked land pointed out as being where attempts at vege-
tables for the previous occupants had failed, the land being
so poor.

It was odd behaviour for a clearly well-turned-out officer
but Clinton put that down to the young man's nerves.

Kydd was sitting at his desk, having discreetly seen the
whole through his pocket telescope. He looked up politely
as the envoy was shown in. 'I would know your principals,
Lieutenant,' he said.

'Kapteinløitnant Steen Bille of the Stationen ved Hvaløerne
og Grændsen, Sir Thomas.'

'Who wishes to parley with me. I cannot imagine for what
purpose. As you can see, we have full and complete possession of Börnholt and do not choose to relinquish it.'

'I understand, sir. Yet I come with a proposal that may be
of utility to both sides in this *rencontre*.'

'I'd be happy to hear it, sir, but be aware that I will not
feel bound to accept it.'

'Sir. It is known that the British have taken this island for
the purpose of restoring the light that has for so long guided
mariners through this treacherous passage. My principal now
recognises this as a worthy and humane object and is prepared
to let this conviction stand for all of time. Sir, he proposes
that the lighthouse be internationally regarded as a safeguard
for all ships as pass this way, irrespective of flag. To this end
he offers a treaty of maritime reconciliation. To the cost of
the Danish government and the benefit of all, he will maintain the Börnholt light in perpetuity for all nations, should
you allow him to do so.'

Kydd paused. 'A fine and noble purpose, Lieutenant. And
handsomely received.' He paused pointedly. 'But unhappily
one I cannot accede to.'

The man's face showed little disappointment and Kydd had a fair idea why.

'Sir, do consider—' he tried.

'Sir, the quartering of Danish nationals beyond the natural inhabitants is not to be countenanced by us. This proposition cannot be entertained. Is there anything further you wish to treat, pray?'

Without expression Holstein snapped to attention, his heels clicking. 'Since you choose not to avail yourself of our generosity, I fear there is not, sir.'

'Very well. Escort the lieutenant back to his boat, Captain Clinton. And I bid you good evening, sir,' he said, rising to his feet.

'You did not accept his offer, sir?' Dillon asked. 'In the saving of expenses in the maintaining of our own occupation alone, it would be worth considering.'

'There was no offer to accept,' Kydd said grimly.

'I do not understand, sir.'

'A courageous but entirely unscrupulous act.'

'Sir? It was offered with a generosity of spirit in a foe that I find wholly admirable.'

'He was here in the character of a spy, Edward. Using the sanctity of the white flag to have a good look round, the villain, contrary to the usages of war.'

'Ah.'

'There was never to be an offer. We shall see him again, but with friends, now he knows we are so few. Ask Mr Clinton to step in, if you please.'

Clinton was adamant that any attempt to establish posts down the length of the island would risk having them cut off if there were multiple landings and with only some two hundred at their command it would mean the end for them all.

That left as the only option the concentration of their forces at the lighthouse and fort – but Kydd felt a premonition that this would not see them through a determined attack. He had been forced to send away the frigates: the prisoners had had to be removed and fresh troops and defensive armaments brought in, but he hadn't bargained on this swift reaction. The earliest they could expect relief would be some four or more days ahead and the Danes had every incentive to make their move swiftly. Kydd would have to manage with what he had.

A defensive line was paced out across the width of the island, a joining of the crests of sand hills behind which the defenders might lie, and at two places a rough-hewn platform for their little two-pounders.

The last redoubt would be the fort, which was only a timbered building surrounded by earthworks. It was little enough: how long they could expect to hold out would depend entirely on how many troops the Danes threw into the assault.

Kydd ordered, 'I want to see every man armed – you, the cooks and idlers. And the gun-crews, all of you.' His sweeping gesture included the handful of lowly cooper's mates, carpenter's crew and armourer's sidesmen, who had managed to be left behind when *Tyger* had sailed.

'A cutlass you'd recommend, sir?' Dillon asked brightly.

'If you must, Edward,' Kydd answered, with transparent reservation. His confidential secretary's learning and intelligence were not matched by a warrior's skill at arms. 'There may be a Viking or two who'd yield just at the sight of you,' he added, with a forced laugh.

At the evening meal talk was low and guarded.

'There's always the chance that they'll think this scrap not worth the taking,' Dillon said hopefully, delicately fishing out a stringy chicken leg from the stew pot. He swayed back in his chair as Tysoe leaned over to do the same, elegantly transferring the meat to a dish he bore to Kydd. The big pistol thrust into his belt in no way discommoded this gentleman's gentleman.

'I'd rather believe the Danish to be a more determined crew,' Clinton said soberly. 'As this island is the only piece of Denmark we've ever seized, they'll want it back, if only to restore their honour.'

The wind soughed mournfully in the outer blackness and Kydd shivered. 'Leave us hope that *Tyger* is not delayed in her returning,' he said, with a silent prayer, rubbing his hands before the fire.

A faint cry came out of the night. 'All's well, the fellow says,' Clinton said drily. 'I hope he's in the truth of it.'

Chapter 53

Morning broke with a most unwelcome cast from a Baltic fog, visibility down to fifty yards in a damp, woolly miasma that lay unmoving in every direction.

'At least it'll slow 'em down,' Dillon said, for with fog there were calms and no one was sailing anywhere in the Kattegat in these conditions, but gunboats?

The daybreak patrol left. A single horseman – there were only five mounts on the whole island – and four marines trying to march in the soft and now sticky sand.

With luck the fog would burn off in a few hours but it might linger as it sometimes did in these parts, a dismal pall on the day. In *Tyger* it would be trying, fog droplets forming on every sail surface and ropes hundreds of feet up, keeping up a continuous but irregular bombardment of fat, cold drops that—

A distant flat pop. Another two close together, out in the impenetrable whiteness.

Shots? How . . .?

'To quarters! Stand to! All hands close up to your stations!' Kydd blared.

Men raced to ramparts and outworks to face the distant threat. With their small numbers it took bare minutes.

Kydd stood in the centre, sword drawn; beside him was Clinton.

They waited grimly, then out of the whiteness figures began to form, stumbling towards them.

'Hold your fire!' roared Kydd.

His instinct was right. These were what remained of the patrol.

'S-sir, Danskers are ashore!' panted a corporal. 'We sees 'em come over the hill from th' south. More'n hundreds.' He broke off to take breath. 'They's got gunboats with 'em, too.'

In the fog and darkness the Danes had executed a successful landing in the same place as they had themselves and were now established on land.

Kydd cocked an eye. 'Mr Clinton?'

'Send out patrols to reconnoitre and give 'em pause in their advance,' the marine answered crisply. 'Once we've their dispositions and strength we'll know what to do.'

Parties of marines disappeared into the mist. A blanketing silence descended as Kydd and Clinton strained to catch betraying sounds.

After some time, a sudden flurry of muffled reports to the left, the south, showed that contact with the enemy had been made.

Nothing from the right, the northern shore.

More shots.

Kydd felt for the marines. It must be unnerving out there, shuffling about, senses at a screaming alert for shapes suddenly emerging from behind, in front, anywhere, that could just as well be friend as enemy.

The one priceless advantage they were gaining was that time was on their side. While the fog lingered, no one in their right senses would move forward against a prepared position and an alert defence, so they were safe until it lifted.

The patrols returned as a general lightening above told of the mist thinning, dissipating, but they had only scant information about the dispositions of the Danes.

'Stand to!' All along the ramparts and parapet a pitiful number of redcoats and nondescripts lay beside their weapons, tensely waiting.

The sun burst through in a shaft of brilliant light and in minutes the last of the white blanket had gone. As though in edgy watchfulness the scene held still and silent. Kydd could see nothing of the enemy, but then caught a scurrying off to the left, along the line of the dune top – and more in the scrub to the centre.

Clinton borrowed his pocket glass. 'I see. Hmm. And there.' He traversed the ground slowly, left to right, then pronounced, 'What we have here is the positioning for a general advance. I do believe I will annoy them. Sergeant!'

A body of marines assembled and made off to the left, out of sight to the seaward side of the long dune formation that ran the length of the southern shoreline.

'They'll have to pull back or risk being cut off,' Clinton said. 'As long as we can keep it up we'll be—'

He was interrupted by the most disturbing sound Kydd could conceive of – the heavy, gut-thumping sound of big guns. It could only be the gunboats, so close in they were out of sight below the sand hill's skyline. And bringing doom with them. In a bitterly ironic twist the very thing that the Royal Navy prided itself on, command of the seas, was now with the enemy and, by this one stroke, they had ensured victory for themselves. Whatever manoeuvre Clinton could think of to outflank or drive a wedge by going around the dunes, his men would be under unendurable fire from close range. All that could be done now was to fall back into their flimsy defences and fight off the inevitable frontal attack.

The sergeant and his men straggled back. 'Not good news, I fear, sir.'

Kydd waited for the man to go on.

'All infantry, no guns to speak of in this terrain. Regular troops and—'

'Numbers?'

'Not above a thousand, sir.'

There was an appalled quiet as the news was digested. Outnumbered four, five to one. Only a miracle would see any standing at the end of day.

Unless Kydd treated for terms now.

'This is because there's been landings on the north shore, their forces dug in atop the dunes,' the marine added.

Kydd took it in: at each side of the island the line of dunes converging at the lighthouse was now thick with enemy about to make their move, the relatively flat middle ground, scrubby and featureless giving little cover. He was no soldier but he could see what they'd be up against.

'Strip the centre of men, send 'em to the ends. They'll be coming in off the long dunes,' he ordered.

'Yes, sir,' Clinton said, with just the tiniest trace of impatience. Kydd grinned awkwardly: he should have realised that the seasoned officer knew what to do.

The ramparts were banks thrown up on the only rising ground that was worthy of the name and would make for a cruel uphill slog in the soft going for any wave of attackers. Once they left the shelter of the dunes they had twenty-five yards of open ground, then the steep slope of the ramparts – Kydd felt they had a chance if the marines held steady, kept them at bay in the open ground.

The hoarse braying of a trumpet, startlingly close, was the signal.

On both sides it seemed as if the dunes were suddenly alive with moving forms, rising to advance for the kill, the gleam of blades and forest of muskets a heart-chilling sight.

The marines opened fire: a deliberate, aimed volley that found its mark. Here and there, among the stumbling figures, bodies dropped. Some writhed in agony, others lay as anonymous humps.

The Danes pressed on, the least disciplined wildly throwing off shots at their tormentors but soon it became clear that it was not going to plan. The loose sand was making it impossible to move at more than a shambling stagger and, without waiting for the order for the advance, they broke up and retreated before they'd left the shelter of the dunes.

As the smoke dispersed, Kydd looked along their lines. None of the marines appeared hit and, reassured, he surveyed the field. The advantage was theirs – for now.

'They'll have to take us from the front.' Clinton said. 'Their gunboats can't reach us here and while we're in possession . . .'

Then it would be a very bloody affair.

'How would *you* do it?' Kydd asked Clinton.

'Not sure I'd like to try. He's got the numbers right enough, but that's only of consequence if he can get them here. I don't envy him the decision.'

The uneasy quiet to their front lengthened with an unbearable tension until utterly unexpectedly men poured over the top of the nearest sand hill – more, until the ground was thick with struggling figures heading for the middle ground.

Within minutes muskets were banging up and down the line, but the wave of attackers pressed on and reached the more hard-packed sand between the converging dunes. Then with harsh battle cries they hurled themselves forward into the thinly held British centre.

Clinton had the marines by twos racing inwards, but the dunes had now become firing pits and the enemy's greater numbers told as a storm of bullets hammered into their puny defences, smothering the defensive fire.

'Hold your fire!' Clinton roared.

Kydd glanced at the Royal Marines captain in perplexity, then saw what he was about. In breathless exultation the first wave of the enemy had reached the base of the glacis, the slope at the base of the ramparts leading up to the parapet – and now faced the defenders themselves.

It was a master-stroke. As the fire from the dunes slackened and stopped for fear of hitting their own men, the attackers had to face what must come alone. The glacis was no hard-packed earthen slope to storm up to the final clash: it was that same deadly, slowing sand and it took its toll.

At point-blank range the marines poured in fire and men fell – but others in a paroxysm of despair and courage fought up towards where Kydd and his ragged band of last-ditch defenders waited. At the forefront was the Danish commander – Holstein, his sword a-main, face split by a rictus of screaming as he urged his men on the final yards – behind him others of the same raging desperation, more still behind.

It was madness but of a bravery that tore at Kydd, even as he met the man in a brutal smash at the lip of the glacis, the eyes wild and his blade a swinging bludgeon. Kydd easily parried it and quickly became aware that the man was out of breath and faltering. Another heavy sweep ended in a clash and slither of steel and he knew Holstein was near the end of his strength.

'Yield!' he shouted, against the din of battle around them.

The man looked at him as though he was demented and drew his sword back for a belly lunge but Kydd stepped nimbly aside and, as it whipped by, came down on the wrist but, jostled from behind, it failed. With a snarl, Holstein spun around in a savage lunge to the head. Kydd dropped to his knees to avoid it and the Dane triumphantly lifted up his blade two-handed for the settler.

More in sorrow than anger, Kydd's Toledo steel flashed out and sank into flesh and bone. As the man gasped and fell, Kydd snatched it clear, sparing only an instant for the dying moments of a gallant but reckless foe, then scrabbling to his feet in the whirl of combat.

And before him in an insane charge a bull of a man was ramming a pike towards his stomach. Before he could move there was the ear-splitting crack of a gun by his ear and the man dropped the pike, caught in the stomach. Kydd spun around – there was Tysoe, his empty pistol dangling, a look of comical astonishment on his features. 'Get out of it, you fool!' he yelled hoarsely, and turned back to the fray. There were bodies now on both sides but the attack was thinning. Royal Marines had formed two lines across the top and were crashing out disciplined volleys, which told mercilessly, and the numbers locked in hand-to-hand combat fell away.

Not far distant Kydd saw that one was Dillon, his mechanical thrust and parry against a terrified young soldier who had an insane fit of giggling as he met the blows. At the same time Dillon was trying to end the fight but clearly could not bring himself to kill his assailant.

'Let him go, Mr Dillon!' he bawled. At Dillon's step backwards and lowering of his sword, the panic-stricken youngster ran for his life.

There was now a general retreat, men streaming urgently for the safety of the dunes, and then, quite suddenly, the field of battle was quiet.

It was a stalemate. Kydd could not make an outflanking manoeuvre: the gunboats would slaughter them with grape. The Danes could not go for a frontal assault on the fortification without suffering unacceptable casualties.

It would now be a waiting game. Totally surrounded, the British must rely on what they had. Powder and shot were mustered and found perilously low, but more pressing was the discovery that their water casks had been pierced in the fighting and the contents lost into the sand. The spring to refill them was behind enemy lines. With no water, it was hours rather than days before the torment of thirst did what all the heroics of the day had not.

The Danes could be supplied by sea but sooner or later *Tyger* or another would come on the scene. Right now, though, would the new commander of the Danish forces accept defeat and slink away or would he dig in and send for an overwhelming reinforcement from Denmark, just an overnight sail away?

As the day drew to a close it became evident that the decision had been made. Camp fires sprang into life up and down the sand hills. They were staying.

With two dead and eight wounded, Kydd drew in his lines and did what he could to shore up their pitiful defences but there could be no doubt: at daybreak would come a final reckoning.

There did – but in an unexpected way. A wan morning light stole in and Kydd took in the unreal and wonderful sight of *Tyger* and *Riposte* safely some miles offshore, lying to anchor beyond the reefs where they'd prudently moored during the dark hours.

In a delirium of cheering, Kydd ordered their colours struck, then hoisted again upside-down, the universal signal of distress at sea.

The frigates caught on at once. Sail blossomed, and to one side of the island headed a vengeful *Tyger* and to the other *Riposte*.

Frantic work at the oars took the gunboats clear but there was no reprieve for the soldiers.

'Sir, may I . . .?'

'Certainly, my dear fellow.'

Clinton led his flanking column out to the seaward side of the dunes, another sent to the opposite foreshore, the threat of gunboat cannon fire now banished. The enemy had no alternative other than to retreat to avoid a wedge being driven in but, with the dunes now no hiding place, they were forced into the flat, open middle ground.

When the two-pounders were dragged up and began a fusillade of grape there was nowhere left to go. One by one white flags appeared and the reversal of fortune was complete.

As if in sympathy with the Danish woe, a thin rain began to fall, turning the sandy ground into a sticky sludge and adding to the misery of the defeated, who stood about in sullen groups.

More came down from the dunes, adding to the numbers,

until Kydd realised that the prisoners were beginning to outnumber the captors. If they rose in revolt over the few guards that Kydd could spare, they would be overwhelmed leaving the mass free to occupy the fortifications and turn the situation right around.

That realisation must have sunk in, for an ugly ripple of unrest spread through the throng of prisoners. More came down from the dunes – it was inconceivable that there would not be a mass rising.

The crowd began spreading, moving. Marines with bayonets tried to stop them but what could they do – transfix helpless prisoners?

Then, one by one, several, many, tore themselves from the mass and stumbled hastily away, making for the western end of the island. Soon a sizeable number was heading that way in an incomprehensible dash for . . . what?

There was nothing Kydd could think of to stop the flight and he had to let them go.

Then it penetrated: the reason for the break was to get to the far end of the island and the landing place – and a reef-strewn shoal extensive enough to prevent his frigates entering but not gunboats. If they reached there safely, there would be gunboats a-plenty to pluck them off to freedom.

Climbing to the highest point of the parapet with his pocket spy-glass Kydd watched it all play out. Two, three gunboats curving in for the pick-up, the prisoners piling aboard, then the boats making off into the wind where the frigates could not go.

It was galling but the main object had been achieved: Börnholt was now securely in the hands of the British, who need fear no longer a night-time wrecking on it.

He swung the glass around. There was *Tyger*, a magnificent

sight in the keen breezes and, as he watched, paying off to a broad reach out to sea. What was Bray up to?

It wasn't long before he saw: the gunboats were making good speed into the wind but in the open sea the great driving sails of a frigate would tell. Even though her track was an extended zigzag to either side as she tacked into the wind, she was hauling in a frenzied gunboat in an effortless surge. Aboard, they must have known their fate was sealed but to the last they were stroking away, like demons, towards the distant coast of Denmark.

And all in vain. Her last board placed *Tyger* squarely across their path and the cruelly exhausted seamen collapsed on their oars and accepted defeat. Further off, *Riposte* was doing the same to another.

Victory could not have been more complete.

Chapter 54

At anchor, Matvig

Kydd settled in his chair to let the forenoon routine on deck take care of itself. There was little reason to sweat the ship's company until their orders came, and *Tyger* had suffered little in the Börnholt affair.

Keats had been cool when he'd reported; he'd bristled at the suggestion that Mason be disciplined for his near-fatal disregard of Kydd's signal, and at Kydd's pressing had brusquely wanted to know whether he was demanding a court-martial on the officer's conduct. In the event the operation had worked out well and he'd no real desire to see the man crucified for what amounted to a personal slight so he'd let it go. The day and the field were Kydd's and nothing could spoil that.

Saumarez had been both genial and congratulatory – in his difficult and trying situation there would be few occasions to celebrate but this was one, and he'd been at pains to indicate his satisfaction in the outcome, granting *Tyger* a full week of rest at anchor before rejoining the southern blockade.

Kydd sighed in contentment: nestled in his waistcoat pocket, next to his heart, he felt a warm glow that was meant for him alone. The Fleet Mail Office had delivered into his hands another letter from Persephone – an outreach of her being that had crossed whole seas to tell him of her love and passion.

He took it out reverently to read yet again.

My darling sailor-man!
   Where will my letter find you in Neptune's realm, I wonder and dream? Seeing sights of grandeur and majesty on the ocean's billows without doubt, for which I'm quite filled with envy . . .

Kydd smiled as he read of her new friends.

   It's been such fun! You see, we're all sea-widows here together in Plymouth Dock and we can go to places that we cannot when by ourselves. Each has her special gifts and we entertain accordingly. Oh, and when you're home you're promised to sing for us as you did before – at Saltram, do you remember? Oh dear, and I do hope it won't be long, my sweetling . . .

How could he forget? She had come to his rescue by accompanying him on the piano when he'd hesitated before that noble throng.

Persephone closed with news of the estate, adding,

   Mrs Appleby has been poorly lately but this will be the weather, which has been so spiteful these few weeks. We've been able to manage but . . .

It was still a thing of unreality that someone cared about him above all others. And, wonderingly, he realised he was no longer a rootless being, oblivious to where he'd fetched up among the random gusts of chance and Fate: now he had someone and something to cherish and adore.

A soft knock sounded on the door.

It was Bowden. 'Sir. Probably nothing to worry of, but a Swedish cutter's just entered the anchorage and sought out the commander-in-chief. He's laying alongside now. Seemed in great haste and possibly has news . . .?'

There was no need to report this to Kydd, but if the cutter did bear consequential tidings, the very next thing would be an 'all captains' and a warning of this would be appreciated.

'Thank you, Charles. If it's news it can't be good.'

Within the hour the signal was duly hung out and Kydd's barge was among the first to reach *Victory* and see him mounting the side-steps and into the august portal.

Instantly he became aware of a charged atmosphere, a tense expectancy.

'Something afoot, Puget?' he murmured, to the captain of *Goliath*.

'As you might say,' the officer drawled imperturbably.

'Well?'

'It's happened, is all. What we knew would. The Russians – they're out. Made sortie from Kronstadt in force and are headed this way. God knows what—'

An unsmiling flag-lieutenant ushered them below to *Victory*'s great cabin and Kydd took his seat, pulse racing.

At last – the Imperial Russian Navy had made its move and had come out to fight!

There was now every prospect of a grand fleet battle in

the very near future, the like of which had not been seen since Trafalgar.

If they were overcome by their foe's colossal strength, the Baltic would be Russian and Britain's crucial and only commercial life-line would be severed. Unable to bear the costs of war, a miserable surrender to Bonaparte's will would then be on the cards.

'Gentlemen.' Saumarez looked drawn and old. 'The Swedes have informed me that a Russian fleet of, at present count, nine ships-of-the-line and five frigates has left Kronstadt for the central Baltic under the command of Grand Admiral Khanykov. There is every reason to expect further increase by another route.'

Already this single squadron had numbers equal to their entire Baltic Fleet. All freshly manned, stored and, if rumour was to be believed, of new and deadly construction. And about to fight in their own well-known waters.

'I need hardly state that this could not have occurred at a worse time for us, two of our sail-of-the-line under repair and half of the remainder on station with Admiral Keats.'

Meaningful glances were exchanged. This was close to three to one and even Nelson had not faced such odds.

'Yet I would not have you despair. We have as allies the Swedes, whose naval assets are not inconsiderable.' Catching Kydd's eye, he added, 'And by this I mean their deep-sea fleet, which is not to be confused with their archipelago fleet, lately destroyed at Sveaborg.'

'Sir, I rather fancy that your term "allies" is a mite strong in the circumstances,' Puget intervened smoothly. 'After their somewhat languid showing with the Northern Expedition?'

'There is a Swedish fleet commanded by Admiral Nauckhoff near equal in weight of metal to that of the

Russians assembling at the Gulf of Bothnia. By personal intercession of this officer, our urgent assistance is begged when he sails to confront Khanykov. Naturally I have agreed.'

'May we know who commands the combined fleet in this engagement, sir?' Kydd asked carefully.

'Ah. Therein lies a difficulty but not one to which you allude, sir.'

Saumarez looked pained and Kydd had a stab of apprehension.

'This particular time is doubly difficult for myself, as their lordships have seen fit to lay a special service upon me of a strictly confidential nature that prevents me leaving this station. Any assistance given, therefore, is in the nature of a reinforcement only. Our ships will conform to the Swedish order of battle.'

The captains to a man stared at him in dismay. To face the Russians at last was one thing but to fight under a foreign flag and command was another. And a retaining of forces for this special service implied an even further reduction in those available to send against the enemy.

'Your service, sir. Can it not be—'

'No. The matter is too delicate. I remind you – the Swedes are of a number with the Russians and fight for their very survival.' He looked down at his papers and when he raised his eyes it was with a bleakness that chilled Kydd. 'To this end I am detaching *Centaur* and *Implacable* under Rear Admiral Hood to join the Swedes forthwith.'

Two ships-of-the-line only against the Imperial Russian Navy? This was rank madness!

Graves of *Brunswick* spoke for them all. 'Sir, we've the Russians out in the open at last, our chance to settle with the villains once and for all. If we throw—'

'Be silent, sir!' Saumarez exploded. 'I'll not have my orders questioned!' Pale and quivering, he stared the officer down.

Kydd winced. He'd never seen the fearless admiral in such a state. Only a dire circumstance, stretching his inner resources to their limit, could explain it.

Saumarez recovered himself. 'Not only these will go but frigates and rated vessels in support.'

Into the shocked silence he listed the men-o'-war that would go to face the enemy. Besides the two sail-of-the-line, it would be just two frigates, *Daphne* and *Tyger,* and three sloops.

Chapter 55

Before the sun had set the small detachment sailed into the central Baltic.

Rounding the tip of Sweden, course was set for the maze of islands to seaward of Stockholm where the Swedish fleet lay. Two days of calm sailing under grey, troublous skies, heading for a destiny that was unknowable but the gravest yet confronted by the Baltic Fleet. Towards evening of the second day *Daphne*, ranging ahead and to larboard, signalled the fleet in sight and within hours they were hove to in the midst of a widely spaced mass of ships with no pretence at a formation.

'I counts eleven o' the line,' murmured Bray, surveying the broad spectacle. 'Few enough if the Ivans are out in strength.'

'An unlucky thirteen all told?' said Brice, lightly, his telescope trained on the Swedish flagship.

'It's the fight in 'em that counts, not numbers!' Bray rumbled.

Admiral Hood wasted no time in putting off in his barge and making for the Swedish flagship. He was as quickly back aboard *Centaur* and summoned his captains.

'I'll be very brief, gentlemen. We are as of this moment under the tactical command of Admiral Nauckhoff. We sail at dawn to find the Russians, who are known to have positioned themselves in the Gulf of Finland in support of their invasion troops, and with a view to moving into the central Baltic in direct challenge of our allied control of the sea.'

He paused to look about the half-dozen captains facing him.

Hood was a strong-faced individual and Kydd knew that his audacious service, beginning with the American war, included Toulon with Sidney Smith, Algeciras with Saumarez and the Nile under Nelson. An empty sleeve was evidence of a hard-fought encounter off Rochefort two years before in this same *Centaur* – he was a fighting admiral.

'I won't complicate matters. There will be a lieutenant with the lingo embarked in their flagship to render the admiral's wishes into our signals, to be repeated to us by *Falcon* sloop. Any further signals will be made by me in the usual manner.'

'Sir, do you have knowledge of how the Swedish will conduct the action?' *Implacable*'s grim-visaged Byam Martin wanted to know. Placing their ships in line of battle against the enemy in a pounding match or an advance by column into the enemy's centre, much would depend on the decision and the consequences to the British ships.

An odd lop-sided smile appeared briefly. 'I really cannot say, sir. I rather think that will depend on the result of our reconnaissance of the Russian force, which I have undertaken to conduct.'

This would be done by frigates and there were only two. It would be *Tyger* making first contact with the Russians in this climactic contest.

'Shall we know what force the Swedes will bring to the action, sir?' Martin's long face gave nothing away.

Hood's smile slipped. 'Ah. You should understand that Admiral Nauckhoff and his fleet have been on station at the entrance to the Gulf of Finland since the ice fell back. Some months now.'

This was met by puzzled looks. It was trivial compared to what was endured by those in close blockade of Brest.

'A long time, I'm given to understand.'

'So what you are saying, sir, is—'

'Is that the Swedish Navy is not to be looked upon necessarily as on a level of fitness for battle as our own.'

Blank looks obliged him to continue. 'In fine, they have scurvy in their fleet. Above two thousand cases of which four hundred have proved fatal.'

Scurvy – in this day and age? It was beyond belief!

'The Swedish admiral assures me that most of his ships will sail but he cannot answer to their effectiveness when confronted by the enemy.'

In a cold shock of unreality it sank in. They were being expected to sail against the Russian host among those they could not trust, whose numbers must be counted as nothing. Was it that they were to be sacrificed to buy time?

'I shall be doing my duty, and I'm sure you'll be performing yours, gentlemen. I won't keep you for, as I said, we sail at first light.'

Kydd returned to his ship, his orders for a fleet battle a mere single page. His to be lead scouting frigate and in action to remain within sight of *Centaur*, nominally flag of the admiral of the van but for *Tyger* no duties as repeating frigate.

As he stepped back aboard his ship there was no avoiding the anxious faces that awaited him. They had every right to know what they were facing but would it be merciful to pass on the appalling news of the condition of the Swedish fleet?

'We sail to meet the Russians at dawn,' he muttered. 'On reconnaissance.' He pushed past to the sanctuary of his cabin.

A dreary morning broke with fitful westerlies and a doom-laden leaden sky. The two frigates loosed sail and set out on their mission – alone, the Swedish frigates remaining with their fleet for reasons that Kydd didn't want to know.

As they left, his last sight of the fleet was of a dense mass of ships milling about in no discernible formation, *Centaur* and *Implacable* attempting to establish a van, so noble in their purpose but, pitifully, only the two.

The last known position of the Russians had had them proceeding leisurely down the Gulf of Finland from Kronstadt, heading for the three-way crossroads that to starboard led up into the frozen wastes of the Gulf of Bothnia, to larboard down to the Gulf of Riga and the busy southern Baltic shore, or straight ahead across open sea to Stockholm itself. It didn't need much to see that if there was no interception before the crossing point their search would be impossible.

Daphne gamely followed in *Tyger*'s wake, at twenty-eight guns the smallest class of frigate but in Gower having a captain of the very best kind – thrusting, imaginative and a gifted seaman. She would be tested to the limit as he would be, for in this madness of a confrontation there was every chance that as a last desperate measure they would both be thrown in against ships-of-the-line.

Astern of *Daphne* was *Wrangler* sloop, then *Charger* and finally Bazely in *Fenella*. These three would not face fire – their task was more important. As the frigates made discovery of the enemy, one of them would be sent back to the Swedes with the intelligence. *Tyger* and *Daphne* would stay by the Russians and relay back any developments with the other two until the two fleets came together in the clash of combat.

As they stretched out over an empty sea Kydd wondered what Bazely was feeling at this moment. What was at the root of his bitter talk of Kydd's ambition for a flag and glory? Or was it just the perceived loss of Kydd's friendship as it had been in the past? He would probably never find out now and he put it out of his mind. As long as the man obeyed his orders he must be satisfied with that.

There were lookouts not only in the tops but at the mast-head, their arcs of attention including ahead and astern, for who knew where the enemy might appear?

They were approaching the entrance to the Gulf of Finland where the seas narrowed considerably. Now was the time the search sweep must begin in earnest, with the two frigates abreast placed such that they could keep each other in sight as they progressed; on the outer sides they would be enabled to observe even as far as the shore, the three sloops to keep station with them in the centre ready for their rapid dash back.

When the first Finnish island was sighted, Kydd gave the orders that had them take up their stations for search, and the nerve-racking tracking began.

Extraordinarily, within an hour *Daphne* streamed the heart-stopping signal, 'enemy in sight'.

Tyger put over her helm and closed with the little frigate to starboard, watching the southern shore.

A hail from the masthead confirmed it, and as they neared the distant coast they spotted the Russians. Stark against the far milky-grey of the coastline, two lines of ships abreast – all heavy, powerful, ominous – the enemy, now made real and fateful, stretching out well over a mile.

Kydd's signal went up and was crisply acknowledged. The

sloops to lie to weather of the enemy, the frigates to close in.

There were no orders Kydd could give Gower, for the whole thing was too fluid to predict, but he knew he could rely on the man's nerve and practical good sense. The only direction was for *Tyger* to observe the van, *Daphne* the rear.

Coming from up-wind they could choose their approach, *Daphne* sensibly sailing wide to curve in later and follow in their wake.

Tyger went straight for the oncoming armada, the twin lines coming on inexorably. It was minutes only now but how the devil should he go about it? Heave to and count as they sailed past? Lay off at a distance and rely on telescopes – or do it right and tuck in close enough to make out details?

The decision was taken out of his hands.

From the far side, to weather, first one then several smaller vessels emerged.

In an instant Kydd understood. These were signal repeating frigates doing duty as escort, not one but five – and sheeting in to take *Tyger* together in an inescapable trap.

His thoughts raced: in any other circumstance the obvious course was to retreat immediately, but that was not open to him. He had to get the vital intelligence that would enable a decision to be made by the Swedes – to fight or to withdraw. That they were in a poor condition was not for Kydd to judge: his duty was to bring the information.

Forcing his mind to icy concentration a memory came to him. Years before, the Mediterranean, Corfu – and a jovial Russian commander called Greig.

'Starboard two points,' he ordered.

Tyger's head fell away. The Russian frigates, hard by the wind on the starboard tack, gratefully eased to leeward as they cut across before the bows of the two oncoming lines, the white in their teeth heaping up in their eagerness.

Kydd judged carefully and, at the right point, gave his order. 'Larboard three points. Take us in, Mr Joyce.'

'S-sir?' gasped the startled sailing master, eyeing the grim lines with trepidation.

'Just so. I'm to make inspection of the Russkies, I believe.' Their course was now squarely for the middle of the two lines – it would take them into the heart of the enemy, down between the two lines.

The Russian frigates were fairly caught: laid comfortably over on the wrong tack and, taken by surprise, they could not put about in time to prevent *Tyger*'s apparently suicidal plunge into the line. Apart from the odd report there was no firing at the British frigate as it passed, their men frantic at the rigging. *Tyger* swashed past in style, Kydd oddly reluctant to fire into them.

'Sir – this is lunacy!' Bray hissed urgently, watching the black upperworks of the onrushing ship after ship, the figures now visible crowding on to their foredecks, so alien, intimidating, portentous. 'We can't—'

'We have to.' Kydd gave a tight smile. Since the days of Catherine the Great, lieutenants of the Royal Navy had sought service in the Imperial Russian Navy as a means to advancement. Many had gained it, including Grand Admiral Greig, flag officer of the Ionian Squadron, whom he'd met. And they'd brought with them the traditions and practices of their native service, duly welcomed by the Russians as a royal road to the top table. The Imperial Russian Navy was ironbound in discipline and conformity, each officer personally responsible to the Tsar, and that was what he was counting on.

And it was working. In accordance with the last signal, the two columns were coming on in line ahead, unwavering and true, with a precision that could only have been seen in the Channel Squadron under the eye of the Earl St Vincent – and *Tyger* slipped unerringly between them.

The formation could not change without orders and *Tyger* stolidly kept her course as they swept past first one then the second Russian, close enough to count the men on deck, to see in every detail the double-headed eagle of their colours, the lines of gun-ports, the blocky, squared-off poop and fo'c'sle.

'Get on with it, then!' Kydd chided, as they slashed on, and *Tyger*'s officers, stupefied at the turn of events, hastily pulled out their notebooks and began listing what they'd seen.

Bowden tore his gaze from the sight and, catching Kydd's eye, slowly shook his head in wonderment.

Kydd allowed himself a fleeting moment of satisfaction. It wasn't such a miraculous thing that had them perfectly safe where they were, in all truth. He was relying on the traditions of the Royal Navy being carried over in their entirety and one of these was that, at a fleet-level engagement, frigates were never fired upon unless they fired first. This was how it had been at Trafalgar and every other action Kydd had been in, and this was how it was now.

Perhaps even more importantly was the fact that *Tyger* was inside the two lines – if one or the other line opened up with their great guns it would be at the cost of smashing fire and ruin into the other. For as long as she stayed within the two lines she could not be touched.

And finally: the Russian commander must have known what *Tyger* was about, a full reconnaissance, but it was in his interest to allow news of the precise strength of his majestic force to be taken back to the Swedish admiral to cause consternation and panic among his opponents.

Barrelling along downwind at a closing speed of near a horse's gallop, it wasn't long before *Tyger* emerged from the last of the Russian fleet and lay over to windward to come up with the sloops to pass the intelligence. In a fine show *Wrangler*, under full sail, set off for the Swedish fleet, leaving the remaining British ships to keep watch on the Russians.

It was now a matter of tense waiting until the fleets came in sight of each other and then their job was done. They would lay off while the great spectacle of a bloody clash unfolded before them.

Before midday thrilling news was yelled down from the masthead. The western horizon was filling with topsails – the Swedish fleet was on its way!

The Russians saw it at the same time, for Khanykov began manoeuvring his fleet from the order of sailing into the order of battle – in disciplined progression the columns in line ahead opened up, peeling off one to each side to form a formidable single line of guns to confront the advancing fleet. Just as at Trafalgar, the Swedes would have to endure the concentrated fire of the entire Russian fleet before they could pierce the line and loose their own broadsides.

Kydd stood with his officers on the quarterdeck, silently watching.

Then Bray, intently observing the Swedes, burst out, 'Be damned to it, but they're a lubberly crew if they think to make advance on the enemy like that!'

Instead of the twin divisions of Nelson and Collingwood standing out towards the enemy line there was nothing but a vague mass on the horizon that seemed hardly to be advancing at all. Was this a reluctance to join battle or just disgracefully poor manoeuvring in the face of the enemy?

The Russians shortened sail, barely under way as they patiently awaited the onslaught, a long line of men-o'-war, their guns run out, colours aloft, ready, waiting.

'I see there's some who've fire in their belly,' grunted Bray at last.

From the distant throng of ships, two were becoming more distinct, standing out from the others. And indisputably making for the Russian fleet.

They came on, all plain sail abroad, one in the lead and both relentlessly on course for the precise centre of the Russian line.

Too far off to make out details, Brice picked up on it first. 'We're seeing *Centaur* and *Implacable* showing the way,' he said quietly.

Bray confirmed the British colours, huge war ensigns that proclaimed to all the world that, in accordance with its enduring traditions, the Royal Navy was joining battle whatever the odds.

It was an impossible, glorious sight: Hood was leading his only two battleships into the heart of the foe and nothing would stand in his way.

The mesmerising vision lasted for a short time only – and then in a sudden flurry of activity everything changed.

At Khanykov's main-mast a signal hoist jerked up urgently, emphasised by the thud of a gun.

Mystified, Kydd watched it play out.

As if one, the entire Russian line fell off the wind and wore around, picking up speed to pay off to leeward and away.

Incomprehensibly they were in retreat, headed back the way they'd come.

Dumbfounded, it took Kydd a minute or two before he tumbled to it.

'Ha!' he cried gleefully. 'The Russkies have mistook the Swedish fleet for ours – they think *Implacable* has got off before the others to snatch early glory! Be damned to it – they thought they'd be up against the Swedes alone and now they see it's Nelson's fleet bearing down on 'em instead!'

Whoops erupted up and down *Tyger*'s deck as it became clear what was happening, but Kydd cut it short. 'Our duty is to stay with 'em until they're safely back in Kronstadt,' he said shortly. 'We'll take station to weather, Mr Joyce.'

The two British 74s were not to be cheated of their prey, however, and clapped on more sail in furious pursuit. From *Centaur*'s mizzen peak halliards flew the 'general chase' signal, a brazen impudence, given the odds, but it served to spur on the Russians in their undignified retreat, the smart line-of-battle now a straggling huddle.

It was preposterous but it was happening before their eyes. Their imperishable reputation, won after years of victorious struggle at sea, had now apparently won for them a blood-less victory.

'*Centaur* is not about to lose 'em,' Bray said happily, watching the two sail-of-the-line do their utmost to close with the Russians. Every wrinkle of deep-water seamanship, every trick gained from years at sea, all were deployed in the chase, a show of skills that could not be matched by any without the experiences that service in all the seven seas could bring.

To starboard the low misty blue-grey of a coastline firmed. This must be the entrance to the Gulf of Finland at the end of which were St Petersburg and Kronstadt. They must be not far from Reval, Kydd estimated, a port for valuable Baltic oak and hemp but now in Russian hands.

'We're gaining,' Bray chortled. *Implacable* was now closing with the last of the fleeing Russians, a heavy 74. Straining every rope-yarn she laid her bowsprit level with the ornate stern-gallery and then, by inches, overhauled the unfortunate ship and, in a thunder of guns, the first shots of the battle were fired.

As the ships sped along together firing became general, powder-smoke rising in ragged clouds as the two hammered at each other. For the first time in history a Russian and English battleship fought together on the high seas and the stakes could not have been higher.

Implacable was gaining, and for every foot clawed in, more guns came into play in a furious cannonade. Shamefully, none of the Russian ships next ahead turned to give help and eventually the hapless victim slowed, then stopped, *Implacable* manoeuvring to place it to best advantage under her guns, then pounding away.

It couldn't last: the Russian's guns one by one fell silent, and with *Centaur* now on the scene her colours slowly fell in submission.

Boats put off from the victorious British ship to take possession but Kydd, keeping with the Russian main fleet, sensed a change of mood. The last half-dozen of the fleeing ships were now slowing, hauling their wind and giving every indication that they regretted abandoning the 74.

First one, then several veered about. The Swedish fleet had been left behind, a mass of ships on the horizon, and was not in any position to turn the fighting into a general engagement as the Russians at last took the opportunity to come to the aid of their stricken compatriot.

Centaur signalled *Implacable* to leave her prize and retire and the two hauled off as the Russians came up and resumed command of the 74, now not much better than a wreck.

There would be fuming and cursing on *Centaur*'s quarter-deck, thought Kydd, grimly, for there were hopeless odds now in which to re-start a fight.

Preparations for a tow could be made out but with the Russian fleet regrouping there was no chance to interfere and they were obliged to watch helplessly as the crippled ship got under way.

'The Swedes, sir,' Bowden said quietly, touching Kydd's arm.

Agonisingly slowly, they had brought themselves to some degree of recognisable order – their lateness in joining battle down to their abysmal skills at fleet manoeuvre, which only now were bringing about a two-column advance.

The Russians saw it, too. Once more they turned bows eastward to Kronstadt and shook out sail for the utmost speed in withdrawing.

The 74 was abandoned, the tow cast off and this time *Centaur* came up to slam in her broadsides – but the Russian had been massively reinforced and there was ferocious return fire from fresh gun-crews. It was a heroic contest, the two big ships within thirty yards of each other and locked in combat.

Then Kydd spotted that *Centaur* did not seem to be in control, under topsails slowly but surely drifting into the Russians' quarter. Her bowsprit speared out over the others' main deck and then with a sickening crunch the two came together. Horrified, he saw that in the Russian, crowds of seamen were swarming up on deck – they were massing to board Hood's flagship!

At the last minute *Implacable* reached them and, heaving to off the Russian's bow, began a raking fire into the bowels of the ship. Under the massive assault, resistance wilted. For a second time the colours tumbled down and the ship was theirs.

Kydd watched long enough to see figures leaping into the sea, striking out for the coast two or three miles distant, even as boats began crossing to them.

He tore his eyes away – his duty was to keep with the Russians until they'd quit the field.

By now the Swedes had been making fair progress but not enough to come up with the enemy, even if they made a fearsome sight against the late-afternoon sun. He knew that there was little chance they would be in any position foreseeably to engage but would need to know their location from time to time and therefore *Tyger* must keep her station to weather while the fleet sailed on.

Strangely, the Russians kept close into the land and, in the last of the light, it became clear why. At a striking peninsula of white cliffs, with two offshore islands some miles long, the Imperial Russian Navy put their helm over and, in a stream of ships, disappeared into the bay beyond.

'What's this, Mr Joyce?' Kydd asked quickly.

'It's the port o' Rågervik, where those bound for Reval makes landfall, sir. And in my time 'twas a Swedish Navy dockyard an' secure anchorage.'

'Secure?'

'Forts wi' quantities of heavy guns defending on the island an' the headland. Snug mooring inside as no one gets in 'less they says so. I'd say the Russkies are looking to bide there a while till they knows where they stands.'

Tyger's duty was plain, to keep tight vigilance for two things: that the enemy stayed until a decision could be made, and to watch for reserves slipping in during the night.

The entrance was easy enough, between the peninsula and

the first massive island, but the chart revealed a southern exit beyond the island. At some point the Russians would discover that the fleet that had dogged them was not Nelson's and they might well feel emboldened enough to use this route to make sally behind them.

When he reported to Admiral Hood, Kydd had his plans made: *Tyger* and *Fenella* at the main entrance, *Daphne* and *Wrangler* at the southern exit.

Spies and simple observation would soon tell Khanykov the truth and then he would have every reason to issue out and confront the weakened, demoralised allied fleet. To wrest a victory on such a scale would resound about the world, which of course would never know of or care about the true conditions. And then the Baltic would be Russian.

Hood was courteous enough but Kydd could see the ravages of battle in *Centaur*. If the Russians made a determined attack the brave ship would have little chance of survival. As he left, he tried not to notice the still, sad forms of seamen being sewn into their hammocks and the silent, automaton-like movements of men at the edge of exhaustion as they did all they could to bring their ship back to fighting readiness.

He left with no specific orders for the morrow; he didn't expect any for this was like no other fleet engagement he'd ever been in. As a frigate the fight wasn't his, and without a grand fleet to repeat signals to, there wasn't further purpose, but he knew that this was not what his men would expect. They would despise him for ever if, while the Russians fell on *Centaur* and *Implacable*, like a pack of wolves, he hung back. They would want him to lay *Tyger* alongside the nearest enemy and sell their lives dearly in a final encounter.

The right thing to do was a hard consideration, and he

spent sleepless hours contemplating alternatives. And when a dull grey morning broke, he had no convincing answer.

At first light he went on deck, as was his usual custom, and began a pace about the quarterdeck, seeing the night pale and retreat, the wan grey seascape firm. And there was *Fenella*, criss-crossing their course, as she'd done for countless times during the long dark hours. He knew Bazely would do his duty, in detail and to the letter.

As would he. If a mortally wounded *Centaur* signalled for assistance he would gladly go – but if she ordered *Tyger* to lay off and return to the commander-in-chief that was what he would do.

He watched the brig-sloop fondly, bringing back memories of the bluff, old-fashioned cove, who had once been his friend and step-ashore companion . . .

'S-sir! Am I pixie-led? What do I see at the point?' Bowden gasped, gesturing.

It was a mirage. It had to be: one after another, in grand succession, colours aloft for all to see, it was *Victory*, others – the Baltic Fleet, all of it. Saumarez had shaken off that which had held him and now was here with them!

It was wonderful, glorious, a giddy relief. Up and down the deck heartfelt cheers resounded. What could not happen now?

Chapter 56

J ust as soon as the Baltic Fleet had brought to, Admiral Hood went to *Victory* to report. And before he'd returned to his ship *Tyger*'s captain was summoned.

Saumarez was another man. Sprightly, alert and penetrating, he sat Kydd down and spoke crisply. 'The Russian armament is now in Rågervik. We can't see into it and we need to know its intentions, is it readying to sail against us and so forth.'

'Yes, sir. As the Swedish fleet is not—'

'Quite. Lose not a moment, if you please.'

'Aye aye, sir.'

The two big islands effectively hid the well-sheltered anchorage in the crook of the bay and there was no alternative other than to sail in directly, make examination and leave by the southern exit, braving whatever lay inside – a storm of shot from a dozen battleships or cunningly placed iron-chain booms to rip the bottom out of questing scouts.

Kydd gave the orders that had *Tyger* wheel about southward into the entrance, then noticed *Fenella*, still obeying the last order to patrol the entrance. He'd go in alone, he'd decided: if *Tyger* was disabled or wrecked he didn't want any hopeless attempt at rescue to end costing two ships.

'To *Fenella*, "remain on station",' he threw at his signal crew and, without waiting for acknowledgement, set course round the island for the inner channel.

Almost immediately the top of the cliffs to the left and the round flank of the island erupted into fire: a fierce bombardment converging from both sides and within minutes the sea gouted and pocked with shot-strike.

'Good God,' Bray said, shaken. These were no common field guns but heavy pieces, coastal artillery in place for the purpose of destroying any who dared trespass within.

The storm grew wilder and *Tyger* began taking hits. The guns atop the cliffs to larboard with their increased height of eye could throw their shot far further and they were making the most of it, their massive balls tearing up the sea closer and closer as they ranged in.

Kydd took it in grimly. At this rate it was going to be a desperately run thing. Sooner or later a hit would do serious damage and, dead in the water, *Tyger* would be a sitting target. Yet there was no other course open to him, the task being so decisive.

A harsh crack sounded from forward – it was the foreyard, a shot taking a long gouge out of it towards the mid-line in a shower of splinters. It hung for a moment, then folded inwards and, driven by the wind, hung down, flogging the mast.

Tyger slewed off-course while men fought to control the tons' weight of yard and rigging. No ship could survive in this and there was no point in trying to go further. Some other way had to be found to uncover the secrets of Rågervik.

The frigate wore around, making for the open sea.

'We need to find somewhere to fish the yard,' Kydd muttered. It was more to take time to think, rather than achieve the temporary repair to the foreyard. Without their information a strategic decision by Saumarez would be near impossible and—

'*Fenella*'s leaving station,' grunted Bray in surprise.

The brig-sloop had braced up and, for no clear reason, was making for the tip of the peninsula. She neared, then unaccountably put over her helm sharply to starboard to run down the line of cliffs, so close that her yards seemed to brush the white heights.

'What the devil?' said Kydd, taken aback by the nonsensical move.

'I think I know,' Bowden said sombrely.

'Well?'

'He's going in under the guns.'

Of course! So close in to the cliff face the guns could not depress and could only fire harmlessly over the top of the plucky little ship – but at the risk of *Fenella* taking an uncharted rock or skerry in the shallows beneath. Bazely had nevertheless judged that the lesser draught of his brig would give him this chance and, with outrageous courage, was sweeping on into the inner anchorage.

He was disobeying orders, but who was Kydd to argue?

They couldn't follow in a full-rigged frigate and looked on as the sloop disappeared behind the island. The muffled crump of guns sounded, rolling smoke appearing briefly above the island. It petered out and resumed further in. *Fenella* was getting through!

In a fury of impatience Kydd could only wait. Then he realised it was most likely that *Fenella* would emerge from the other side, the south. He snatched a glance forward – but the boatswain had things well in hand. Capstan bars had been hauled up into the fore-top and preparations were brought along to lash these lengthways around the foreyard at the split – to 'fish' the spar. It would serve in the short term until they could ship a new yard.

He willed *Tyger* on as she rounded the outer island in the opposite direction to position herself at the exit as *Fenella* emerged.

There was another fury of thuds, more roils of smoke snatched away by the wind.

And there she was! Missing her fore-topmast and sails riddled through, she limped into view – and in close chase were at least half a dozen lesser craft: cutters, luggers, yawls, enraged at the brig's audacious penetration of their lair. At *Tyger*'s sudden appearance they turned tail and promptly disappeared.

'She still has to put about, sir.' Brice knew how these small craft handled and had his doubts. *Fenella* had to take up on the other tack in order to make way against the steady westerly, for a short distance ahead the shore of the mainland would force the issue.

The brig cautiously came up into the wind, the yards braced around but at 'let go and haul' disaster struck. With sails full and drawing once more, the mainsail boom gave way and in moments the big fore and aft sail was rent from top to bottom. Unbalanced, with all the headsails and square sails on the fore bearing her off to starboard, in an uncontrollable wallow, the brig was driven back against the island she was rounding.

There was not a thing Kydd could do except watch in dismay.

At first it seemed they had a chance. Immediately clawing into the wind the brig cleared the first point but as the lack of sail on aft told, she fell away, nearer and nearer the wicked bluffs towering up. They tended inwards for a short distance and then, inevitably, sprawled out again in a welter of broken rocks . . . and *Fenella* was carried bodily into the grotesque twist of crags that would be her grave for all of time.

Wrung with pity, Kydd's first impulse was to send his boats to the rescue but stopped. This was a much graver situation than it first appeared. First, the coast was impossibly craggy and sheer. No one was going to get up that near vertical rock-face. Worse, the heaving sea at the base was studded with white-torn black rocks for some distance out – no boat could get in through those.

His mind raced over the common methods of rescue. A keg with a line attached, a raft. Launch them into the seas and float them in. One fatal flaw: the westerly was parallel with the shore and would carry them out of reach down the coast. And the same twist of rock that had taken *Fenella* would ensure they couldn't be set in the water up-wind as they would be carried past well offshore.

It was heartbreaking. Safe and dry on *Tyger*'s deck, he must stand and watch while the gallant little brig was torn to pieces and her company drowned or battered to death as the seas rose. He could see them now, figures clinging to the canted side of their ship, staring out to where men still lived and breathed. After their bold and heroic deed, to meet their end in this way . . . Which one was Edmund Bazely?

He snatched Brice's telescope and focused on the shoreline with a ferocious intensity. There had to be a way!

Not with that cursed twist of rock. It forced out anything to the point where it would drift in always out of reach. It was obvious that no boat could get in, but surely there had to be . . .

Yes. A running jackstay. A line secured somewhere in the rigging of the doomed vessel that would have a travelling block and strop running along it that sailors could grasp and be pulled to safety.

How to get the line to them? The same damnable problem – the line just couldn't be floated in.

He resumed his scrutiny. The tangled rock, a brief patch of sand, a seaweed-covered rock—

Yes! If . . .

'Mr Joyce. Take us in – we anchor in four fathoms, a whisker to weather of the rocky point.' At this depth of water in these two-foot waves their keel would be scending no more than a few feet above that boulder-strewn sea-bed – but not more than a quarter-mile offshore.

While it was done, he worked out the rest.

The launch: under oars it could get to a point just to seaward of the fringing rocks, say a hundred and fifty yards and opposite the wreck of the *Fenella*. It would then throw out an anchor fore and aft and remain as a fixed point – a pierhead, in effect.

Get a line ashore and secured high in the rigging, then range it back to the launch's mast step. That would be the means to bring out the sailors, lofted over the fiendish dark sunken rocks and back to the world of men.

'Mr Bray – here's what we have to do.'

The first lieutenant roared his orders with all the force of his pent-up frustration and men leaped to obey.

The launch was manned and lines, tackle and blocks thrown aboard. Bray boarded.

On impulse, Kydd joined him in the sternsheets. 'Carry

on, Mr Bray,' he said, to his surprised first lieutenant, who made room for him, setting the boat under oars and heading in.

'Bit of a current,' he muttered, working the tiller irritably. It had to be seas swirling around the point, which were meeting their bows and going on to push them off course, but it triggered a prickling apprehension in Kydd.

On the wreck, men saw them approaching and figures raised themselves out of their stupor. Arms waved but some simply stared vacantly.

Fifty yards off, they were nearing the foaming outer crags. They could go no further.

The kedge anchor plunged in at the bows and quickly caught – but the launch immediately slewed about to face into the current and Kydd's presentiment returned in full force. With a sickening certainty he watched the bowman secure a light line to the small keg and cast it into the sea well up against the current flow – then saw it whisked downstream and away before it could make its way inshore to a small group of Fenellas stumbling and reaching.

In an agony of impossibility Kydd took in the second try, the bowman's arm wrenching in pain at the effort. And one more, two.

His mind replayed a scene from another place, another time – the Devon coast, a forlorn wreck with men clinging to it, his doomed attempt to get a line to them, the hours of trying, the cruel and bleak finality, bodies washing in the breakers.

Within a hundred yards, the figures on *Fenella*'s carcass were now unmoving, still. They would know in their hearts that all that could be done had been played through, and now they must face their end while others looked on, utterly helpless.

There – on the crazily canted quarterdeck – a lone figure, struggling upright. It was waving, but not in farewell. A deliberate gesture, repeated. Crossed arms over the breast – the naval distant signal to belay, to secure, to abandon.

It had to be Bazely. In his last hour, telling them it was hopeless and to save themselves.

Hot tears pricked Kydd's eyes. That he must now be witness to his friend's death – it was too much and a ragged lump of misery formed.

Suddenly, like a madman, he flung himself forwards to the bowman, who stood still, stricken. He snatched at the line and brought it in furiously hand over hand until the keg bumped at the gunwale. He slashed at the lashing and when the thin line was free, stripped to his shirt and breeches, fumbling for his belt, tying the rope in a bowline to it, sliding the result around to the small of his back.

'S-sir?' the man said, bewildered.

Kydd could say nothing, still choked by emotion. Ignoring him, in one awkward move he twisted over the side and into the sea.

The water was bitterly cold and took his breath away.

No real swimmer, he struck out for his life, angling high up into the deadly current, aware of vague shouting from the boat. He didn't care, crazily stroking as if pursued by all the demons of Hell.

Salt stung his eyes as waves seethed over him, the cold reaching deep, paralysing. The shore was getting nearer but it was a tiny, precious patch of sand he had to reach or his despairing mission would finish in the victorious, surging sea, eviscerating him among the jagged outcrops.

A glancing blow to his leg shocked him and he saw that he'd been carried down past his landing spot. In a frenzied, all-or-nothing bid he redoubled his thrashing but his limbs were now lead weights and he felt himself tiring, flagging. He struck out wildly in a last desperate flailing – but was knocked askew by his arm nearly being wrenched from its socket. Disoriented, he tried to make sense of it but then the other arm was gripped and he was pulled bodily forwards – a sailor clutched by others had gone into the sea and laid hold of him.

Utterly exhausted he could do nothing as he was manhandled into the shallows and flopped over. And staring down at him, eyes feverish and caring was Bazely. 'You chuckle-headed simkin!' he croaked. 'A gooney juggins who thinks to—' His face suddenly contorted and he looked away.

There was fumbling at the line at his back. 'It's a jack-stay,' Kydd choked. 'Take it to your shrouds . . . travelling block . . . over the rocks.'

Bazely stopped him. 'As if I've never heard o' how to rig such!' he growled, then added, in a low voice, 'Leave it t' me now, Tom. Ye've done your piece.'

He tore off his coat and tenderly wrapped it around Kydd. 'Things t' do, cuffin, will get back.'

Chapter 57

'He's safe, b'gob!' the master breathed.

Brice snatched back his telescope and looked for himself. 'Praise be, an' he is.'

Mr Midshipman Rowan forced himself to a calm. In the drama of the moment, the captain had thrown himself into the sea, a famous and important frigate captain. Why hadn't he called for volunteers or some such? He certainly now had enough salty yarns about service at sea with the legendary Captain Kydd to keep the boys at the naval school in thrall for hours.

He was allowed a peep through the glass. It was confusing at first: the sagging wreck with figures crawling on it, the web of rigging hanging down in a tangle. Then he saw that the tackle was hauled in and being fastened high up in the shrouds, a single impossibly thin line in a catenary curve above the rocks and down to the launch. This was seamanship of the highest order and he watched in awe before Lieutenant Bowden claimed the glass.

Soaring above the rocks, then splashing into the sea, the

first man was hauled in to the launch. *Tyger*'s barge and cutter were on hand to ferry batches of rescued men back from the pierhead to the frigate, but for some reason the first survivor was brought straight aboard *Tyger*.

'Respec's from Commander Bazely an' he's got news f'r the admiral as won't wait,' the man panted.

Bowden stepped forward. 'You have intelligence for the commander-in-chief?'

'The Russkies – they've moored fore 'n' aft, sent down topmasts, unbent canvas. They's going nowhere, he thinks. And f'r numbers, he says—'

'Thank you, we'll get this to Admiral Saumarez this hour. Mr Brice, take away the pinnace and report to flag without delay.'

Brice bellowed for the boat's crew and, seeing Rowan, beckoned to him. 'You have the boat, Mr Rowan.'

A stab of fear and excitement seized him. For the first time he was to act the real sailor in a mission of war!

Heart in his mouth, he swung over to the rope-ladder and down into the pinnace as fast as he could manage, seamen's hands reaching up to steady him as he boarded and took up position in the sternsheets. Feverishly he went over the routines: check the rudder was secure in its pintles, the tiller ropes led fair, the bottom boards in place out of the way.

'Prove the bowman!' he piped, as authoritatively as he could.

The man forward raised his hand. 'Aye aye,' he called.

'Prove stroke!'

The seaman throwing off the lashing of the main-sheet tackle looked up at him in surprise.

Of course – they were going out under sail. 'Very good. Carry on,' he managed.

There were other matters – the mast raised to its step, simple stays rigged, tacks laid along.

Lieutenant Brice clambered in with the *Fenella* seaman.

'Carry on, sir?' Rowan asked breathlessly.

'Do, please.'

'Bear off forrard!' The boat took up with a bang and flap of stout canvas but sheeted in fast and, with a merry chuckle of water under its stem, curved away.

'Sir, around the island to the west'd?' Rowan asked diffidently.

'Which way's the quickest?'

'To the west, sir,' Rowan came back, in a small voice.

Brice said nothing, raising his eyebrows and looking at him quizzically.

Rowan understood. This was the navy: his was the command and therefore his were the decisions.

With the tiller tucked familiarly under his arm he shaped course for the westernmost end of the low, scrubby and oddly green-banded grey cliffs. The sails were drawing well and needed little tending and, with the steady westerly, he could hold a firm heading and listen as Brice questioned the seaman. It would be the lieutenant who would see the admiral, having drawn together all information into a methodical narrative.

The furthest extent of the little headland was coming up, and after rounding it, there would be only a brisk going about, then a quick beat up the island to the open sea beyond – and the Baltic Fleet. To have completed a task of war, however humble – it was a first time for him.

He was close enough to the bleak shore now and yelled importantly, 'Ready about!'

But as he stood to throw over the tiller his world went mad.

From the island came a shout and then he heard a fusillade of musket shots, which whipped and shrieked about him. Gouts of water were thrown up and he heard the slap of balls through canvas followed by the gurgle and cry of a wounded man.

Instinctively he put down the tiller and the boat began to slew about but at the same time Brice stood up to go to the wounded man's aid and as he did so the clew block of the flogging main caught him on the side of the head and he dropped senseless into the bottom of the boat.

His mind frozen with shock, Rowan stood unmoving while the boat completed its turn through the eye of the wind. The sight of the wildly flogging foresail brought him round. 'Tacks 'n' sheets!' he cried, the men's white faces all his way as they scrambled to obey.

It steadied him, the simple naval order, the routine of it all.

The pinnace obediently took up on the new tack and laid out agreeably to seaward.

The air was still alive with the vicious *whaaap* of bullets any one of which could end everything in the blink of an eye. It was a paralysing thought and, for a terror-stricken few seconds, he waited for it to happen, but he thought he'd better get on with things while he was still in this world.

He drew the tiller over and the boat fell off the wind slightly but now they were end on to the muskets ashore, a much smaller target even if he himself was still exposed.

'Trim your sheets, then,' he chided the main-sheets hand, and then to the *Fenella* seaman ordered, 'You, go and see to the lieutenant.' He called down the boat, 'How's that man who was hit?'

'Not good, sir,' one of the seamen forward returned. 'In the guts an' choking.'

In a ludicrous surge of warmth he took in the simple fact that the sailor had called him 'sir', the first time any of them had freely done so. He gulped back the wash of pleasure and, with guilty urgency, called back, 'Find the boat's bag and make him as comfortable as you can.'

The man was apparently severely injured. He should return to *Tyger* and get the doctor to him before it was too late. About to give orders for a gybe about, a contradictory thought slammed in. They were on a mission of importance, of imperatives. Was it right to abandon it for the sake of saving a life?

Everything in him wanted to get the man to care and attention, to be in time to stop the precious mortality ebbing away. He'd never seen a man die and here he was, contemplating being the cause of it. It was unfair – back in Guildford lads his age were still sitting at their desks construing verbs and such without a care in the world beyond the next half-holiday.

But he was an officer. This was what they did. Captain Kydd would want no less than a grown-up and deliberate decision. And it was to go on under a full press of sail and finish the job.

'Bowse in that foresheet,' he threw at the crew forward. Every knot counted now.

It was less than an hour up the dreary coast and then, passing beyond the last point, into view came the Baltic Fleet in all its glory.

He found the flagship and was soon lying off the huge bulk of the fabled *Victory*.

'Boat *ahooy!*' came a hail from the upper deck.

In the pinnace, the bowman didn't hesitate. 'Aye aye!' he bawled back, the indication that there was an officer in the boat that needed due receiving.

Into the massive lee of the first-rate Rowan brought the pinnace around and, as though under eye from Nelson himself, to a faultless alongside at the side-steps and chains.

'How is he?' he hissed urgently, at the man tending Brice.

'Still out to it, sir.'

There was no alternative so Mr Midshipman Rowan swung out of the pinnace and mounted the side-steps, entering the middle gun-deck of the battleship through the ornate boarding port.

'Good God! What's the meaning of this, you rogue?' spluttered the receiving officer, utterly taken off guard by the appearance of a young gentleman at the port instead of a full-rigged officer.

'Intelligence. For the commander-in-chief, sir.'

'You dare to—'

'As ordered by him as not to lose a moment.'

At the man's mingled outrage and confusion, he added, 'We took fire. The lieutenant was knocked senseless and I carry the intelligence myself. Admiral Saumarez will be anxious to hear it, I'm persuaded, sir.'

'If this is your prank, you'll—'

'And I'd be much obliged, sir, if the unconscious officer and the grievously injured seaman in my boat receive the attention they deserve.'

Rowan was conducted through the great ship to the admiral's day cabin.

'Sir, a midshipman of *Tyger*, who insists to lay an intelligence before you,' the officer said doubtfully.

'Well?' Admiral Saumarez frowned.

Before such majesty Rowan's new-found confidence fled. If the captain of a ship was a lord, an admiral a prince, then a commander-in-chief was an emperor, who was glaring down on him, the lowliest of the low.

'M-my lieutenant lies wounded. I r-report in his p-place . . .' Sir Thomas might have phrased it more elegantly but he got it out and was gratified to see the great man ease and perceptibly turn benign.

'A right handsome report, Mr Rowan. You'll want to return to your ship now, I believe.'

Chapter 58

'That's all your people, Edmund,' Kydd said weakly, seeing the last of the Fenellas off on the travelling block.

'Aye,' said Bazely, in an odd voice. 'We've been together a mort o' times, the old girl an' I. Let me stay a space t' say m' goodbyes, there's a good fellow.'

Kydd knew exactly what he was asking and, without another word, swung out on the line and was soon hauled shivering into the launch.

'Commander Bazely will be with us presently,' he said quietly.

Back aboard *Tyger*, Kydd took Bazely down to his cabin. 'You shall be my guest, dear fellow. Doss down in here until we shall know what to do with you.'

'If I can manage sleep in this palace,' Bazely grumbled.

Kydd grinned. He knew how much more splendid his quarters in *Tyger* were compared to those in a little brig-sloop.

'You will, old trout. But first we'll—'

'I needs to know my company are safe and well fettled in this heathen barky. Later.'

Kydd settled back in his comfortable armchair, a whisky magically appearing by his elbow, and closed his eyes.

Some time later he opened them again – he'd heard a garbled account of his third lieutenant being brained, now resting in the sick bay; the pinnace coming under enemy fire, with one casualty, left in the care of the flagship doctor; and a midshipman bracing the commander-in-chief.

He summoned Rowan. Was it his imagination or had the lad changed from a fresh-faced, wide-eyed youngster to a lean, confident youth, who was now telling him why he'd carried on after taking casualties, and in wry good humour describing his encounter with the commander-in-chief himself?

'Mr Rowan, I confess I stand amazed. Do you remember reporting afore me in this cabin just small months ago?' In a surge of feeling he recalled the shy, eager lad, whose countenance had quite unmanned him. And now all that he saw formed before him could only have been brought about by his service in *Tyger*, the ship of which he himself was captain. It was nothing less than a swelling wash of pride that came over him as he regarded the young man.

'Aye, sir.'

'And what did I say?' Kydd said gruffly.

'I shall be acting midshipman only, and if I didn't earn your trust I'd be put out of the ship.'

'Quite so. And this is to say, young fellow, you've well earned that trust and from this hour on you're no longer an acting reefer, you're confirmed in rank and are one with the ship's company of HMS *Tyger*.'

'Th-thank you, sir!' The ardent youngster who lay not so far under the new-found manly confidence flashed through with shining eyes and a huge smile, and Kydd had to turn away for a moment.

'You shall claim a bottle of best claret from my servant to take back to the midshipmen's berth, there for all to drink to your elevation. Carry on, Mr Midshipman Rowan.'

When Bazely returned a little later, he subsided into the other chair and sat unblinking, gazing through the sweep of stern windows at the line of warships anchored in the glittering seas.

Kydd said nothing. He motioned quietly to Tysoe, who nodded and brought another whisky, a large one.

Bazely hesitated, then downed it in one, avoiding Kydd's eye.

'A right hard thing, to lose a ship,' Kydd said softly. 'After all those years and so many miles under your keel.'

There was no response, the bluff seaman he knew so unnaturally twisted by some inner grief.

The man held out his glass. 'I'll need another,' he said hoarsely, 'As I has something t' say.'

'Fill 'n' stand on,' Kydd said gently, invoking the sailor's invitation to lay open a hard thing.

'Aye. Well, it's not *Fenella* – who I'll never forget all m' days.'

He finished the whisky quickly and at last turned to Kydd. 'No, shipmate, it's not – it's you.'

'Me?'

'I'm here t' admit I was adrift in m' bearings when I said . . . the things I did.' He paused, gathering his words. 'If you was a flag-chaser, a glory-hunter, why, you'd never have done what you did today. Nothing in it as would be talked on in y'r clubs an' salons, a fine triumph t' make the ladies gawp. Only a damn fine piece o' seamanship as saved a ship's company from a sailor's grave.'

'Just a jackstay and—'

'And a cove who has the salt t' bring out the line at risk

of his own skin,' Bazely continued, in a charged voice. 'Who did it only . . . f'r a friend.'

'Well, and it's all finished now, Edmund. We'll—'

'Not finished!' Bazely said thickly. 'I did ye wrong, cuffin, and for that I begs pardon. You're no boot-licker o' royalty, no politicking shabbaroon – ye've won all ye have by copper-bottomed seamanship an' a rattling good headpiece. There's not a man I know can stand alongside ye in the article o' bein' a hero and I must have ye know it.'

The hand came out hesitantly but Kydd gripped it hard. 'From you, my friend, I do value it above all things.'

'Then . . . then we'll step ashore t'gether sometime, on the frolic, like – raise a wind as we did afore?'

'Count on it, dear fellow,' Kydd answered, with a deep sincerity. 'I'd wish for nothing more gleesome. To tell it right, I've found this fame and the public eye is something of a poisoned chalice. The pettish misunderstandings, jealousy, the friends I've lost, it doesn't bear the reckoning.'

'Aye, this must be so. But there's square sorts like Keats who'll see you back on the briny where you belong an' will come around to it in the end, while you're always going to clew up with a flotilla o' green-dyed shicers like Mason in the offing, an' these you c'n leave t' stew in their own envy.'

'You're in the right of it, Edmund. But for now what I'd reckon best is to pay my dues to a fine and true sailorman who showed a prime frigate the way in to an enemy anchorage and come out with the news.'

The two friends solemnly raised their glasses and drank – to each other.

Chapter 59

The Great Cabin, HMS Victory

As the dinner progressed, the formality of a command-er-in-chief's entertainment in the great cabin of his flagship eased, then melted away. Flushed faces, happy talk and open laughter filled the hallowed space as was to be expected from those whose destinies had so recently passed from uncertain to assured.

Captain Sir Thomas Kydd was well content with life and sat back to listen to Byam Martin of *Implacable* tell of the last hour of gallant *Vsevolod*, which, he swore, deserved a better fate than to be deserted by her comrades.

Hearing the tale, now in the warmth of the company of his peers, it was ironic to be calmly at anchor and enjoying such fine fellowship and a splendid meal so close to the enemy, now skulking in what could only be fear and trembling of Nelson's heirs.

The cloth drawn, brandy and cigars made their appearance.

Talk died away and faces turned to the centre of the long table: the admiral was getting to his feet.

'Fellow captains. Brothers-in-arms of the Baltic Fleet. I shan't speak for long.' His usual cool-headed, aloof features were lined, strained. 'I entered the Baltic at the beginning of the year with the most grievous burden it has been the lot of any commander to bear – the preservation of the last and only channel for the exports of our industries, which alone pay for this war.'

He looked about him, at the score or more captains, anxious or mature, seasoned mariners or fresh-faced young men, all joined in the one great endeavour, and smiled. 'The Great Belt and Sound are now highways on which our trade is secure, no matter the enduring of gunboats and the worst the weather can bring. Tireless patrols by greater and lesser have near exterminated the privateer vermin and we have finally devised a gateway for our merchant shipping opening directly into the continent of Napoleon Bonaparte.' The smile vanished. 'Yet from the very first there has always been a dire vision, a sceptre that has haunted me since first we passed into these waters. You will probably know to what I refer – the Russians and their fleet.'

There were knowing looks around the table.

'As our forces were divided on their various occasions, I knew too well that all it required was for a determined sortie from Kronstadt to fall upon us in our weakened state, and our bold and noble cause would be finished. Then I received news that finally such had occurred – and with an armament greater than any that has faced our country since Trafalgar.

'In the towns and villages of the kingdom they will not hear of a mighty clash at arms, a desperate confrontation, but you and I know full well what we have achieved together. The Imperial Russian Navy is now locked up within Rågervik and I hold the key. It shall remain there impotent until the ice comes to seize it. Next year when the ice retreats they will find me here waiting, and I will not be moved.

'And I will tell you what it means. In fine – we have won! We have prevailed over the Tsar, over Bonaparte, the elements themselves. In a friendless sea we have established and secured the greatest victory of all.'

Then, beaming triumphantly, he proposed the toast, 'Do raise your glass with me and drink to our prize.

'Gentlemen: the Baltic!'

Author's Note

Rågervik is the second battle of Trafalgar that never was. Long anticipated, it was set fair to be the greatest clash of fleets Britain's navy would face since Nelson's day. That it didn't happen has never been fully explained – why should the might of the Kronstadt imperial battle-fleet flee at the sight of just two ships-of-the-line? Even more so, why did it then skulk in harbour never to exit for the rest of the war? The only conceivable explanation is the extraordinary moral superiority of the Royal Navy at this stage of the war that held its foes in such dread.

At the time Saumarez was blamed for not bringing about a full-scale fleet action but he arrived on the scene just one day later, narrowly missing Khanykov's fleet at sea. The reason for his delay is one of the most remarkable and little known tales of the war.

In the army of Napoleon there were troops from many countries and most of those massing in Denmark for the invasion of Sweden just across the water were those of his ally, Spain. Exploiting unrest caused by rumours of Bonaparte's move to place his brother Joseph on the throne, the shadowy figure of James Robertson, a Scottish Catholic priest, was infiltrated into Denmark to subvert the Spanish field commander, the Marquis de la Romana. He did so, and in a feat of daring and secrecy, the Royal Navy landed parties of seamen in the southern Danish islands and extracted nearly ten thousand front-line troops from under the very noses of the French, thereby making the invasion of Sweden impossible.

Saumarez was torn between sailing to meet the Russians or supporting this absurd-sounding clandestine mission; his decision to do the latter almost certainly cost him a great victory, fame and a peerage, but he knew the greater issue was the Baltic trade and a wounded Tsar would have turned against him.

This victory, however, secured the Baltic for Britain and it marked the beginning of the end for Bonaparte, for it was Tsar Alexander's refusal to enforce Napoleon's Continental System that infuriated the emperor enough to embark on the fatal 1812 invasion of Russia. On Khanykov's return, this Russian admiral faced court-martial in Moscow for cowardice, and in an autocratic and brutal regime was unaccountably able to get away with a sentence of demotion to ordinary seaman for one day. In a tangible reminder of the occasion , the entire stern gallery section of HMS *Implacable* is on display at the National Maritime Museum, Greenwich.

After his escape Sir John Moore, that prickly, stiff-necked military figure, took all his men back to England; he met fame and a hero's death at Corunna later in the year.

The last Danish big-ship fight is still remembered more for the loss of the plucky Willemoes in *Prinds Christian Frederik*, the young man who had stood defiant on a gun raft against

Nelson in Copenhagen. Walking through the remote and sandy hamlet of Havnebyen on Sjællands Odde, you will come across the roads Willemoesvej and Jessensvej, and in the wardroom of the naval artillery school at the tip of the peninsula, with its long-fanged reef, there are further memories.

Johan Krieger, the fiery gunboat leader, has his small share of immortality: a charming portrait in the naval museum in Copenhagen reveals him as a chubby, mischievous soul, who would no doubt have been a fine and jolly messmate at Nyholm, but it is probably fair to say he caused the British more grief than any other Dane during the 'English Wars'.

The attack on Kildin by *Nyaden* frigate, on which I based Kydd's storming ashore, was mentioned in *The Times* as the first ever British incursion on Russian soil and, with other isolated Arctic incidents, would be the last until the failed 1919 intervention against the Bolsheviks. It is a crushingly desolate place and charts of the island are difficult to find: today it is the unhappy graveyard of discarded nuclear submarine engines of the Soviet fleet, but its isolation is a boon for various exotic Arctic fauna.

The Sveaborg fortress still exists and is a popular and interesting attraction in Helsinki under the Finnish name of Suomenlinna, its sudden capitulation fuelling endless speculation and conspiracy theories among Swedish writers. Cronstedt was a genuine hero, leading Sweden to the crushing defeat of Russia at the sea battle of Svenskund some years before. However, after being embayed in Malmö and unable to come to the aid of the Danes fighting Nelson he was publicly humiliated by the Swedish king, Gustav IV Adolf, and rusticated to Sveaborg. His supporters state that there is no evidence from the years after the surrender of a change in lifestyle, indicating bribery or a sell-out, but this in fact would be consistent with the case that he in turn had been cheated by the Russians in the matter of gold buried on the parley island . . .

The capture of Anholt, upon which I've closely based my Börnholt, has its measure of curiosity also. The island was promptly commissioned into the navy as HMS *Anholt* after the success of HMS *Diamond Rock* off Martinique several years before and the Admiralty felt impelled to send for the very same man to take charge, Commander James Maurice, who in that post later victoriously defended it against the vengeful Danes.

For the Swedes this has to be accounted their saddest hour, especially their proud navy, which at this point was riven by factions and defeatism. The Finnish war did not go well for them, at one time an audacious winter crossing by the Russian Army of the ice to the Åland islands threatening Stockholm itself. It couldn't last and the last Vasa, Gustav IV Adolf, was deposed in a scene out of Shakespeare.

In Gripsholm Castle I visited the very room and saw the desk where his abdication was effected. The former monarch was fated to wander Europe, a king without a throne. The weak and faltering king who succeeded him lasted long enough to declare war on England and, finally, the last ally of Britain on the Continent fell. Yet in large part due to the truly exceptional talents of Saumarez the war was conducted without a shot fired, the enemy victualling and supplying their very opponents, with Matvig and other secret bases conveniently overlooked. Above all, the Baltic trade continued without a tremor, even with the British now completely surrounded by hostile nations. Then, because of the state of war against England, the Swedes were obliged to source a new king from closer by, namely Prince Bernadotte, who, once on the throne, felt able to defy Bonaparte and even take up arms against his own countrymen, defeating them roundly.

Yet of all the bizarre oddities of this campaign none can match that of the lengths to which merchant-ship captains went to get their cargoes through. To circumvent the treasonable act of trading with the enemy, application was made for a private licence to do so. At first issued sparingly, by the end of the war these were turned out by the tens of thousands and were accepted on sight by British cruisers, while false papers were carried to get them into an enemy port. The 'simulated papers' were produced by skilled forgers in speciality firms situated in London, the latest information passed on from the Continent, and were so good that before long Lloyds would refuse insurance unless a ship could show a set.

Other scams were introduced: the Danish island of Heligoland, captured by the British, was turned over to the sole industry of cargo laundering where, in an area not much bigger than Hyde Park, colossal amounts of cargo from England were repackaged and re-stowed in a 'neutral' ship before being sent into Europe. Napoleon's officials were helpless to stop this and before long became hopelessly corrupt – Prince Bernadotte considerably helped his offer for the Swedish throne by providing a massive state loan from the proceeds of his involvement. Insurance premiums fell, from 40 per cent when Saumarez first entered the Baltic to the usual two to three per cent when these measures got into their stride.

The French, without command of the sea, found their own ships levied a prohibitive 50 per cent or more and were effectively wiped from the trade routes. Grotesquely they found protection by going as 'neutrals' in Saumarez's convoys and, flourishing genuine papers as simulated ones, they were able to insure their vessels at Lloyds, an English court ruling with impeccable fairness that merely being an enemy did not disqualify them from recovering on a duly accepted policy. It did them little good: under eye they had no chance of loading French export goods and ended taking British goods into the Continent, leading to the established fact that Bonaparte's troops were clothed and booted on their march to Moscow by the factories of the Midlands.

Great Britain owes more than it realises to Admiral Saumarez. The Baltic trade, the only conduit left to it, would have, if severed, brought about the strangulation of the country and the end of the war. As it turned out, the trade swelled and blossomed and by the end of the war had generated a taste on the Continent for British trade goods that spread far and wide and which, after the war, led to an advantage that left Britain in the Victorian era the greatest commercial nation on earth.

I first came across this great sailor and diplomat while researching *Treachery* in Guernsey, where the lieutenant governor, Sir Fabian Malbon, was involved in establishing a fund to replace the Saumarez memorial, dynamited during the war by the German Wehrmacht.

To all those who assisted me in the research for this book I am deeply grateful. Particular thanks are due to two people. Eva Hult, archivist at the Maritime Museum in Stockholm, afforded me the great privilege of handling the actual plans of gunboats created by the gifted af Chapman, whose designs dominated the Baltic at the time this book is set. Ulla Toivanen in Finland, in a warm gesture from a stranger, readily shared insights into her country's culture and history.

I visited many splendid museums in the Baltic region as part of the preparation for this book – but the Estonian Maritime Museum in Fat Margaret Tower, Tallinn, only an hour from Rågervik, stood out, providing a wealth of information.

My appreciation also goes to my agent Isobel Dixon, my editor at Hodder & Stoughton Oliver Johnson, designer Larry Rostant, for his superb cover design, and copy editor Hazel Orme.

And, as always, my heartfelt thanks to my wife and literary partner, Kathy.

Glossary

akvavit	a clear liquor flavoured with caraway seeds much esteemed by Scandinavians
a-low	the opposite of aloft
barkers	slang for firearms
blaggard	'blackguard'
breeches	garment worn by gentlemen before pantaloons and ending at the knee
burgoo	porridge
Carrick bend	a knot to join two hawsers when intended to render around a capstan
chouse	make sport of
coach	that part of the captain's quarters aft used as an office
colours	the distinguishing national ensign flown by a ship
conn	the men and equipment responsible for directing the ship on her course
Continental System	a system of economic warfare, essentially a blockade of Europe against the British by Bonaparte
Cyrillic	alphabet of the Slavic tongues
dame school	basic village school run by a lady of mature years
deal	a length of timber ready planed and finished in use for a building
dirk	a small poignard modelled after the Scottish dirk and worn by midshipmen in place of a full-sized sword
division	the sectioning of a warship's company into a self-sufficient unit for special duties or combat

dog watches	in the Royal Navy a half-watch about sunset to give an uneven number of watches to be served at different times
douanier	French Customs official
double tides	working all day long, i.e. for both tides instead of one
figgy duff	pudding made with suet and raisins
fish-scut	the faeces of fish
flam	to trick
footling	trivial
glacis	a slope extending down from a fortification to slow an assault
griff	how things are done
gunwale	the uppermost strake of a boat
gyre	a swirling vortex; that which causes gyrations
Holger Danske	legendary Danish hero who sleeps in the crypt of Kronborg Castle ready to rise when Denmark is in peril
hove to	result of a manoeuvre to halt a vessel by backing its sails
Johnny Raw	a new-pressed or joined sailor on his first trip to sea
jolly boat	smallest boat aboard used for casual duties
kanonchalup	the larger type of gunboat. Armed with two 24-pound cannons and four four-pound howitzers; seventy men
kanonjolle	the smaller type of gunboat with one 24-pound cannon and two four-pound howitzers; forty men
Kem	mayor of Russian town in imperial times
Kronstadt	main island base of Russian Navy, to seaward of St Petersburg
larbowlines	those men in the larboard watch
League of Armed Neutrality	early attempt of neutrals to combine to resist British searches for contraband on the high seas
lee shore	downwind from the vessel, dangerous in bad weather
lop	small wave with enough curl to cause cresting
mole	a long pier made of masonry to form and protect a harbour
mountebank	a flamboyant charlatan
negus	a hot toddy of wine and lemon
noon sight	the midday reading of the apparent altitude of the sun to derive latitude
pawky	derisively small
perruquier	wig-maker
pinnace	carvel-built boat smaller than a cutter used for communication between ships
Pomor	medieval-origin Russian settlers in the extreme north
powder monkey	seaman, usually a youngster, carrying powder from the magazine to the gun

quoin	wedge-shaped piece of wood to raise or lower the breech of a gun to give elevation or depression
rake	the firing into an enemy down the length of a ship instead of into the side
ratlines	small line strung across the shrouds to form a ladder for climbing into the tops
rencontre	an encounter with lethal intent
rosin	a form of varnish to preserve a ship's side and appear attractive
seigneury	the lordship of an estate granted in fee-simple
shrouds	the ropes each side of a mast in support of it
skerry	semi-submerged rocks off a coast
sough	the soft sound of wind in the rigging
stave	of a cask, the constituent side components; in gunnery, the staff bearing the rammer
stock-jobbing	activity of the middleman in a purchase of securities
supercargo	one charged with the commercial affairs of a merchant ship
tarry breeked	trousers that are smeared with tar betraying the owner as a sailor
tomp	to tamp, to compress from loose
volunteer first class	a child placed aboard ship to gain sea-time before becoming a midshipman
worm	a double corkscrew iron implement on a stave for withdrawing an unfired charge

THE ADVENTURES CONTINUE ONLINE

Visit julianstockwin.com

Find Julian on Facebook

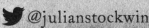 /julian.stockwin

Follow Julian on Twitter

@julianstockwin

Do you wish this wasn't the end?

Join us at www.hodder.co.uk, or follow us on
Twitter @hodderbooks to be a part of our community
of people who love the very best in books and reading.

Whether you want to discover more about a book
or an author, watch trailers and interviews, have the
chance to win early limited editions, or simply browse
our expert readers' selection of the very best books,
we think you'll find what you're looking for.

And if you don't,
that's the place to tell us what's missing.

We love what we do, and we'd love you to be part of it.

www.hodder.co.uk

@hodderbooks

HodderBooks

HodderBooks